# STAN LEE'S THE DEVIL'S QUINTET: THE ARMAGEDDON CODE

# STAN LEE'S
## THE DEVIL'S QUINTET

### THE ARMAGEDDON CODE

## STAN LEE AND JAY BONANSINGA

**TOR**

A TOM DOHERTY ASSOCIATES BOOK
NEW YORK

STAN LEE'S THE DEVIL'S QUINTET: THE ARMAGEDDON CODE

Copyright © 2021 by POW Entertainment, LLC

A Tor Book
Published by Tom Doherty Associates
120 Broadway
New York, NY 10271

www.tor-forge.com

Tor® is a registered trademark of Macmillan Publishing Group, LLC.

Library of Congress Cataloging-in-Publication Data

Names: Lee, Stan, 1922–2018, author. | Bonansinga, Jay R., author.
Title: Stan Lee's The devil's quintet : the armageddon code, a thriller /
Stan Lee and Jay Bonansinga.
Other titles: Devil's quintet: the armageddon code
Description: First edition. | New York : Tor, 2022. |
"A Tom Doherty Associates book" |
Identifiers: LCCN 2021035764 (print) | LCCN 2021035765 (ebook) |
ISBN 9781250776815 (hardcover) | ISBN 9781250776822 (ebook)
Subjects: LCSH: Undercover operations—Fiction. | Devil—Fiction. |
LCGFT: Fantasy fiction. | Thrillers (Fiction)
Classification: LCC PS3562.E3647 S73 2022 (print) |
LCC PS3562.E3647 (ebook) | DDC 813/.54—dc23
LC record available at https://lccn.loc.gov/2021035764
LC ebook record available at https://lccn.loc.gov/2021035765

Our books may be purchased in bulk for promotional,
educational, or business use. Please contact your local bookseller
or the Macmillan Corporate and Premium Sales Department
at 1-800-221-7945, extension 5442, or by email at
MacmillanSpecialMarkets@macmillan.com.

First Edition: 2022

Printed in the United States of America

0 9 8 7 6 5 4 3 2 1

*With love and gratitude to*

STAN LEE
1922–2018

*and*

SULLY BONANSINGA
1937–2020

# PART I

## THE MOST DANGEROUS PLACE IN THE WORLD

The choice between good and evil is made by all who live—with every single heartbeat.

—Stan Lee, 1968

CHAPTER ONE

# Over Yonder at the Edge of Nothing

## 1.

The C-5 Galaxy aircraft pitches and bumps over the jagged air currents above the vast, desolate surface of the Black Sea. The cabin smells of body odor and burning circuits as the leader of a small group of passengers braces himself against the jump seat, checking the luminous dial of his tactical chronograph. It's now pushing 10:00 P.M. Moscow standard time.

*Close enough for government work,* the senior operative thinks as he surveys the dead grey slipstream outside the portholes. As far as the night sky is concerned, he could be anywhere. On a business trip over the Pacific. Approaching Hawaii for a long vacation. Hell, the aircraft could be flying over the little hardscrabble hamlet where he grew up. But his true destination—known only to the other four members of his team, a pair of pilots, and a couple of suits in the Defense Intelligence Agency—is a territory in the Tartarus Mountains between Armenia and Azerbaijan that currently holds the distinction of being the Most Dangerous Place in the World. *Over yonder at the edge of nothing,* the senior operative muses silently. He has a million of these colorful cornpone expressions that he picked up back in his childhood birthplace of Ducktown, Texas. (A QUACKING GOOD PLACE, the man remembers the town sign assuring passersby back in the day.)

A lean and weathered former jock clad in desert camo and body armor, the senior operative is somewhere in his fourth decade, his jarhead buzz cut just starting to streak with grey. Each and every deep line and crease around his icy blue eyes has been earned the hard way. In the field of battle. Under fire. Against the clock. Balancing life and death on a high-tension wire.

Many years earlier, back at Langley, the code name Spur had been conferred upon him during Specialist Training Camp. In those days intelligence operatives didn't have a choice in the selection of their code names. But once in a while the instructors chose handles apropos of a particular subject's skill set. The senior operative had a knack for motivating others, as in "Put the

*Spur* to 'em, Paul!" The truth is, though, over the years the code name became the bane of his existence, an embarrassment, but that's how code names work. They stick to you like a blemish that will never fade.

The man known as Spur feels the center of gravity shifting in the cabin as the aircraft banks over the craggy cliffs of the Balkan coastline. They begin to descend through an invisible chute of Georgian airspace, a sense of levitation tugging at the man's gut. Military transports approach Camp H. S. Sherman near the northern border at a tremendous velocity for planes of this size—much faster than commercial airliners—due to the constant reports of antiaircraft guns along the Gehenna Highway.

Spur gnashes his teeth as the monstrous airship slams through the thickening atmosphere, pitching and yawing in the darkness. The voice next to him sounds all warbly, as though coming through a tissue of water.

"Racking up the air miles—eh, Spur? Got my eye on that Samsonite luggage." The wisecracks emanate from the whip-smart Latina sitting across the cabin, also decked out in camo and battle-rattle, her raven-black mane tucked under her headset. Her code name, Pin-Up, is an old-school reference to her traffic-stopping beauty. The moniker had been given to her when the SEAL team recruited her out of the Second Brigade Combat Team, Fourth Infantry, 358th Police Battalion. She had been a nurse in the 358th, and had gotten hit on more times than a punching bag at Gold's Gym. In civilian life she'd been a working actress in L.A., had shot some national spots, done a few soap operas, but nothing of note.

Now she uses her striking good looks and chameleonlike acting skills to get into places off-limits to the rougher-hewn operatives.

In the intelligence services, code names can be jokey, they can be profane, or they can be cryptic. But on many levels, they are the coin of the realm in this shadowy world of black ops and government wet work, like private passwords for obscure computer applications. In fact, over the years it's been unclear whether the code name grows on the person, or the person grows into the code name. There's no denying the fact that the code names among Spur's team have taken on a certain psychological resonance for each operative.

"Just do me a favor and stay frosty, Pin," Spur says, and then surveys the length of the cabin. "That goes for *all* y'all." He gives a terse nod to the other three agents hunkered along either side of this steel coffin they call a transport plane. Two other men and one other woman. Five operatives in all. All suited up and salty. Ready to rumble. Their HK418 assault rifles on safety, vertical, barrel down between their knees. Each loaded for bear with 5.56-millimeter NATO open-tip rounds. These weapons officially don't exist. Nor do the specialists wielding them. Nor does this mission. "Spur" will file no paperwork, regardless of outcome. Loss-of-life-in-action carries the field acronym LOL, which is highly appropriate since death is merely a cruel joke to these five ghost soldiers.

The architect of today's mission is the section chief of the Special Expeditionary Section of the United States Defense Intelligence Agency. All of which is why the mood in this hollow chamber of steel and nylon strapping has the businesslike feel of an operating room as the aircraft approaches the base. The cabin fills with metallic noises beneath the roar of the engines—snapping, zipping, locking.

Spur unbuckles himself and stands with his rifle slung tight across his chest. "Meter's running, y'all," he announces to the others, his big gnarled hands gripping the rail to steady him against the turbulence as the landing gear deploys with a muffled rumble. "On touchdown, I want eyeballs on the backgrounds. Gunners are stationed in the tower, trackin' us with the escort. We got a lot of real estate to cross to get to that fucking bird. Airstrip's been hairy in recent months. I want lips buttoned." He shoots a look at a wiry African American man adjusting the chin strap on his headgear. "That means you, Ticker. Keep your mouth shut and your safety off."

The agent in question makes a zipping motion across his mouth, knowing full well that the comment from Spur is drenched in good-natured sarcasm.

The operative code-named Ticker is a man of few words. The appellation was given to him by the training staff back at Dam Neck. The word has an esoteric origin. In those days, to "tick" meant to be hyperaware of the passage of time, as in "I still got half the SAT test to go, man, and I'm *ticking* like crazy now with only thirty minutes left on the clock." The code name suited this handsome agent well whether he liked it or not. Mostly due to his razor-sharp intelligence. During his tenure at the training facility, he'd been hyperaware of *everything*—not only the hands of the clock.

Still is today.

In his midthirties with a finely trimmed goatee, Ticker holds the distinction of being the youngest Ph.D. to matriculate from MIT's prestigious Applied Physics Program. He was bound for a tenured position at Oxford when his social-worker wife back in Chicago got herself killed in gang cross fire. Which changed everything for Ticker. In less than a year he was enrolled in the Naval Special Warfare Development Group. Training to be a SEAL. His near genius intellect combined with his relentless drive made him a prime candidate for Spur's elite ghost unit.

The lurch of the landing gear making contact with the tarmac vibrates through the fuselage.

Spur's voice drops an octave, gravely serious now. "It bears repeating!" he yells above the shriek of the engines as the C-5 settles into its rattling taxi across the scabrous runway. "Even though this is smash and stash—fast in, and fast out—we're heading to the asshole of the universe. Always be cognizant of that fact."

Each of the battle-ready agents gives him a nod. The aircraft comes to a jerking halt, electronic pings going off.

Everybody braces for Spur's signal, unaware of the unpleasant surprise awaiting each of them. Spur nods at them. "Let's go to work."

## 2.

At first, everything seems routine. The base is quiet and still in its wee-hour doldrums. Quonset huts, like the frozen spines of dinosaurs, radiate outward from the central terminal. The deserted airstrip stretches past a luminous necklace of xenon landing lights. Planes are lined up along the inner lanes in mothballs. In the far distance, the rugged front range of the Tartarus Mountains scrapes the dark heavens, the snowcapped peaks like ghostly sentinels. The air hangs heavy with ice crystals and petrol fumes.

Following along behind Spur, moving in the Weaver position, his rifle's back sight at eye level just as he was taught years ago in specialist training, the operative code-named Hack wants to let out his nervous energy with his typical barrage of Catskills smart talk. Born in Flatbush, New York, raised in Crown Heights, the only son of a middle-class Jewish couple, the man is matinee-idol handsome with a mop of dark curls, and preternaturally good with anything that has a keyboard, screen, or plug. Over the years he has proven there isn't an embassy, bank, missile silo, or drone he can't break into. But right now, he feels the tightness in his chest that he gets sometimes when things seem too good to be true.

He puts his head down and tries to drive the thoughts from his mind.

Approaching the edge of the tarmac, Spur halts and raises his right hand without even turning around. The others stop in their tracks, muzzles up. Spur's fist clenches. Then an index finger points to the left, signaling to the others that they've reached the bird. Hack sees the dark tail section sticking out from behind a massive storage container. Just for an instant, out of the corner of his eye, Hack sees the smallest member of the unit shifting her gaze like a squirrel startled by a bus.

The diminutive Chinese woman code-named Boo could kill a man twice her size with her bare hands. In fact, her moniker—proffered upon her back at Fort Meade when she was training to be a counterintelligence agent—was a bad joke started by some smart-ass instructor. She was "Boo!" as in all things dark and scary, all things that go bump in the night, all things that get under your skin. Right now, though, something about her body language speaks volumes. She seems to be experiencing the same intuitive dread that has gotten under Hack's skin.

Another silent hand gesture from Spur, and the single-file squad of specialists moves around the storage container and climbs on board the experimental Stealth Black Hawk—an aircraft whose very existence is classified and unknown to all but a small group of aeronautical engineers and functionaries at CIA headquarters back in Langley, Virginia.

### 3.

In the predawn murk along the southern border of Karakistan, only the shepherds and a few scattered groups of copper miners hear the low hum approaching on the wind. It sneaks up on them from the convolutions of glacial moraines and gorges cut like gaping wounds through the mountains. One of the older miners pauses, shining his torch heavenward at the ceiling of black clouds obscuring the stars. A wizened, bearded old sheepherder dressed in the traditional wool cape of the ancient Bedouins, he sees nothing but night sky.

Just for an instant, though, the old man feels a trickle of terror running down his spine, causing gooseflesh to break out along his leathery arms and legs. He has heard that sound before—that deep buzzing noise like an enormous insect scraping along the parched earth. It's a message from God, a portent always followed by bloodshed or upheaval.

The old man shivers as a fountain of dust swirls up behind a dark berm a quarter kilometer away, whirling like a dervish, and then trailing after the specter of death for several moments before dwindling away to nothing.

## 4.

From inside the low-flying Stealth Black Hawk, Spur can see the pilot in front of him, a big man in yellow aviator glasses hunched over the stick, keeping the bird as steady as a chalk line as they hug the ground, skimming along at three hundred kilometers per hour. The onyx-black helo is one of only two prototypes currently in use among U.S. forces—outfitted with extra rotor blades in the tail, a modified Rolls-Royce engine with noise-reduction technology, and exterior sound baffling to keep the craft as silent as a slight stirring of the wind.

Through the windshield Spur can see the shadow-bound landscape rushing under them like a black ocean. He estimates their current altitude at around fifteen meters, well under the radar, low enough to see the cracked pavement of derelict roads and battered directional signs printed in Arabic flashing past them in the predawn gloom.

"Hey, Cap," Spur says to the pilot, raising his voice just slightly above the droning hiss of the blades. According to legend, the bird is so quiet that personnel on the ground can hear voices emanating from the sky as it passes. "Got an ETA yet?"

The broad-shouldered pilot nods at a GPS screen on his panel. A man in his late fifties with the face of a dour bloodhound, Captain Ed Deegan is a legend in Special Forces circles. Originally a field commander in the Seventy-Fifth Ranger Regiment, Airborne, he has kicked ass from Kosovo to the Sudan. "Ten klicks to go," he says. "That's if the intel's to be believed. We'll be there in three minutes. Give or take."

Spur checks his watch. Should be plenty of darkness left

to launch the incursion. Hopefully the warlord Osamir is still residing in his labyrinth of caves. These renegade hideouts are easily breached, porous as hell, with primitive security. Makes a smash-and-grab operation like this one, as Spur might say, *as easy as pecan pie*. As a matter of fact, Spur wants to be back at the base by midmorning with the intel gift-wrapped with some pretty blue paper and a pink ribbon for the brass. "Copy that," Spur says to the pilot, and secures his rucksack for deployment. Inside the field bag are high-def cameras and portable copying gear. "Give us fifteen after dust-off," Spur adds. "We ain't back at the rendezvous point in twenty, send flowers."

Deegan understands.

As the aircraft slows, and a deeper humming vibrates up the fuselage, Spur shoots a glance over his shoulder at his team. They're crouched behind him, headsets and mikes framing their faces, night-vision goggles already on, rifles up high and ready. Best unit Spur's ever commanded in the field. "Let's shake ass out there," he says to them. "No drama. Watch your backgrounds. Wait for the diversionary ordnance, and then get your butts in and out. Shouldn't be more than a handful of guards. Each with a Russian AK. Take them down first, if necessary. Move, shoot, and communicate." He looks at Hack. "Hack, you got the point."

Hack nods, his goggles rattling. Then he says, "Not to belabor the point in any way, but in the likely event we meet up with the target, the rules of engagement are . . . what?"

"Shoot to wound. Get the intel, and get the Sam Hell out of there. Period. You copy?"

"Like a Xerox machine," he says with that New York City twang.

The floor of the Black Hawk vibrates up through their bones, and the g-forces tug at them as the chopper banks around a steep slope in the darkness. Deegan finds a level patch on a ledge and lands the bird. The skids hit hard. Spur feels the impact in his molars as the backwash from rotor blades envelops the aircraft in white noise.

Spur yanks open the jump door, and the agents follow Hack into the night.

## 5.

The cold wind and sheep-shit stench greet Spur as he hops off the ledge and lands on a dusty shelf of rock. He secures his infrareds, switching them on and waiting for the green-tinted world to materialize in front of him. A second later he sees his team like chartreuse apparitions in front of him. Waiting for the signal. He gives it to them.

They hump up a steep slope of scrub without making a sound. Two abreast. The green world of boulder fields and subalpine vegetation swims on either side of Spur, the scrawny alder trees like skeletons. He recognizes the slope from intelligence briefings. The team reaches two thousand meters, and the first cave becomes visible, its dark maw of an entrance unguarded.

"Hold up! Hold your horses!" Spur whispers into his mike. The multiband radio is set to broadcast only to an elite audience of five. A few feet away, Ticker instantly stops digging in his pack for an incendiary device. The plan is to plant three explosive charges around the perimeter. When the commotion draws the guards out of the caves, the unit will then gain entrance and search for evidence of a nuclear weapons program. Human intelligence on the ground in Turkey and Pakistan has suggested that Abu Osamir's terrorist network, known as the Shield of God, has gotten ahold of enriched uranium. But now the look on Spur's face in the darkness makes everybody perk up. "Something ain't smelling right," he says very softly.

"Chief, at the risk of being a nudge," Hack's voice crackles, "can you elaborate on that?" The younger man crouches behind a boulder a few meters uptrail.

"Gimme a second. Keep an eyeball on the perimeter. Be right back."

Spur creeps around a cluster of tangled alders, then scales a rocky buttress. He reaches the mouth of the cave and pauses with his back against the edge of the opening. He raises his rifle. Points the muzzle. And then quickly moves in front of the entrance.

His chest tightens with alarm as he scans the shadowy interior of the cave. He switches on a flashlight. Nothing but strapping tape, empty wrappers, and damp cardboard boxes litter the dirt floor that reaches at least a city block into the depths of the former copper mine. A few discarded blankets and cans of butane suggest it was once inhabited, but apparently that was awhile ago. Spur lets out an agonizing breath.

"Chief?"

Hack and Ticker stand in front of the cave. Guns poised. Ready positions. "I'm no expert, but you might want to come out here." Hack sounds grave all of a sudden. "There's something out here you maybe want to go ahead and take a look at."

Spur emerges from the cave and follows the men across a narrow clearing. They find Pin-Up perched on a petrified limb about three meters above the ground. She holds a pair of binoculars to her eyes, scanning the horizon. She sees something that makes her suck in her cheeks as though she's tasting something sour. Boo stands below her, shaking her head, murmuring something in Mandarin. Dawn is just starting to lighten the edges of the horizon, turning the sky a luminous purple and casting an otherworldly glow on the landscape.

"What is it?" Spur wants to know.

Pin-Up climbs down, and hands over the binoculars. "Make sure you take an antacid before you look."

Spur climbs up, removes his goggles, and takes a peek through the twin lenses.

His throat goes so dry he can hardly swallow. He's barely aware of his own voice as he murmurs, "Well, butter my ass and call me a biscuit."

## CHAPTER TWO
# The Center Collapsing

### 1.

Decades of intel on Abu Osamir paint a picture that could be hung in a gallery of third-world archetypes. Born in abject poverty in Karakistan, the son of a sheepherder, Osamir grew up in the mountain village of Tiblisia. Situated on a craggy shelf of granite, the town had the distinction in the 1960s of being smack-dab in the middle of a burgeoning ground war between the Communists and the Council of Seven Tribes.

For nearly twenty years, the Russians pounded the slender, crescent-shaped nation to no avail. The primitive people of the mountainous borderland along western Azerbaijan banded together with nothing but rusty Israeli rocket launchers, American dollars, and simmering rage to beat back the invasion. And no one profited more from the conflict than the young Abu Osamir. The stocky bulldog of a teenager traded goods with both sides, served as a drug mule between the poppy growers and mercenaries from the West, and began to build a coalition of opportunists with no allegiance to anyone or anything other than their own wallets.

By the time Osamir reached his early thirties, he was the undisputed kingpin of the Karakistani underworld . . . as well as the most brutal of all warlords in the Tartarus region, periodically showing up on the NSA's nuclear arms watch.

Shadowy images from intelligence reports and the rare appearance of Osamir online reveal a squat, thick-necked bison of a man who favors revolutionary garb that would make Che Guevara blush with embarrassment. Berets and bullion fringe and riding boots and silver-plated sidearms are Osamir's trademark fashion statement, and torture the canvas upon which he paints in the blood of his enemies.

In fact, up until today, at this very moment—as Spur peers through the field glasses from his craggy perch—it had seemed that the only things left wanting in Osamir's orbit were secret hideouts in bad need of makeovers. For years, classified satellite photos revealed festering caves, tin-roofed shacks, and rubble-strewn outposts that served as the meager, ever-shifting headquarters of Osamir's operations. Now gaping through the narrow field of vision of the binoculars, Spur has difficulty believing what he's seeing.

Three kilometers away, in a natural amphitheater of stone, a miracle of modern architecture and armament rises up in the magenta predawn glow. Part Gothic fortress, part Mies van der Rohe skyscraper, part Walt Disney house of horror, the building resembles a high-tech spaceship that has landed in the crevices of the ancient mountain range. Soaring steel-framed guard towers flank the curvilinear walls of the structure, each tower equipped with ranks of massive M240 machine guns. Gigantic mortar launchers and immense satellite dishes sprout from the dome-like roof. A cat's cradle of thin red laser beams crisscrosses the ground level, suturing through dust clouds, giving the edifice an impenetrable feeling of "Fort Knox meets the Pentagon."

"Not since I toured Graceland have I seen such a McMansion." Hack's hushed voice crackles in Spur's earpiece, taut with tension. "What do you make of this, Spur?"

Spur swallows hard, and then whispers into his mike, "Looks like old Abu's gone and spent some of his rainy-day money."

## 2.

At this point, Spur reverts to his training, his gaze shifting around the general vicinity of the rocky shelf on which he currently crouches, his skin prickling with adrenaline. *Take your time, cowboy,* the instinctual voice in his head tells him. *Don't run to your death.* He looks through the goggles, glancing over his shoulder. The sun is coming up, turning the green hue of his infrareds as hot as molten lava. He knows whenever an unexpected variable arises to first assess his position, as well as the position of his team.

He sees Hack's skinny ass five meters away, dead ahead, gaping at the fortress like a hound dog on the scent. He sees two other team members—Boo and Pin—up on a ledge to his left, side by side, as still as deer in the dusky light.

"This sure as hell wasn't in the brochure." This new voice belongs to Ticker, his customary witticisms now stretched thin with nerves. "NSA satellite on the fritz again? Anybody ever heard of Google Earth?"

Spur rips off his goggles, and sees the slender African American down on his belly to the immediate right, five meters away on a precipice, squinting through his own binoculars. The first rays of early sunlight glint off the face of his watch—a dead give-away. "Ticker, listen up," Spur whispers into his mike. "Turn your watch around. Watch your metallics. Stand by for a second. Just stand by."

"Boss?" Pin's voice this time, accented slightly with its West Coast Latina spice. "Boss, are you hearing—?"

"I said stand by, Pin!" Spur hisses into the mouthpiece. He hears something. Actually he *feels* it more than hears it: a faint vibration up through his bones, intensifying with each passing second. Is it coming from behind them?

"Boss—?" Boo's voice pipes in through the earpiece.

"Goddamn it, I said stand by. Everybody! Just stand the fuck *by*!"

Ticker's voice chimes in then. "We got company, Spur, three o'clock."

At the same time Spur hears the sizzle of Ticker's warning in his ear, he sees a whirlwind of dust rising behind them, the vibration intensifying, the rumble of engines. Spur's throat tightens. "Everybody, prepare for evasive!"

Almost simultaneously, from three directions, the vehicles and personnel come into view on thunderheads of dust.

It happens so quickly Spur can barely react. From the east a pair of armored Bradleys roar toward them with .50-caliber guns on the ass ends, their tank treads raising a fogbank of thick haze. From the west, snaking down a mountain road, three jeeps filled with gunmen converge. And from behind them, topping the rise, comes a battery of men on ATVs—at least a half dozen of them—aiming machine pistols as they approach.

A silent voice shrieks in Spur's brain: *Ambush . . . it's a fucking ambush!*

He leaps to his feet, and is about to call an audible—sending his people down the slopes in opposite directions in a classic evasive maneuver, tossing diversionary blasts at the perimeter, meeting up later at the safe house—when he sees the magnesium flash out of the corner of his eye and hears the sonic boom one second later. The sound emanates from the rooftop of the fortress. The comet trail of a mortar arcs out over the gorge—

—and then the air erupts and everything—*everything in the playbook*—instantly changes.

## 3.

The massive explosion chews a house-sized crater from the side of the mountain twenty-five meters from the team's position, whiplashing Spur and the rest of them backward on the shock wave.

Spur lands in a shower of gravel, the breath momentarily knocked out of him.

He turns over in the brown wind drift of debris, gasping for air, reaching up to his mike . . . a robotic singsong refrain slamming through his consciousness . . . *save the team, save the team, save them, save them. . . . save them to fight another day.* "Stand down!" he booms into his mouthpiece. "Everybody! W-weapons down! Hands visible where all can see!! Do it! *Do it now!*"

He rolls over. Painfully rising to his knees, he makes a big show out of throwing down his weapons and raising his gloved hands in the international symbol of *unarmed please don't shoot.*

Through the haze he can see the heavy vehicles circling, spiraling closer and closer, countless muzzles staring at him like dead black eyes floating in the dust-fog.

Then he sees a commotion fifteen feet away in the rubble, and his heart sinks.

## 4.

Boo squirms in the dirt while Hack tries to prize something from her mouth, his fingers frantically probing so deep in her throat that she gags and convulses on the ground as though stroking out. In any other context, it might look comical: a big brother trying to rescue the last malted-milk ball from the gullet of his obnoxious little sister.

But Spur knows exactly what's going on and it makes his gut clench: *How the hell does a mission go so far south so quickly?*

Boo grew up in the Hubei Province of China, the daughter of diplomats and politicians. She lived in a beautiful area along the Yangtze River, long regarded as the home of the celebrated ancient Chinese poet and minister Qu Yuan. Legend has it that Qu Yuan, after a distinguished career in public life, took his own life by walking into the Yangtze while holding a rock. The suicide became a deeply ingrained part of Chinese culture, the act itself considered by many as a way to protect one's innocence and life principles.

Was this the reason Boo reached for that white capsule hidden in the lining of her flak vest? Each and every member of the team has one. Each of them knows its purpose. Slip it in your mouth, bite down, and the bitter taste of the botulinum toxin will be the last sensation you will experience on this earth. The body goes into an immediate paralysis—the brain keeping secrets and battle strategies safe in its vegetative state—until you ultimately bleed out all over your enemy's fine parquet floor.

Hack finally gets his thumb and forefinger around the capsule before Boo has a chance to chow down on it. He plucks it from the depths of her craw and throws it across the smoking crater. Then he lays his forehead on hers.

She pushes him away, her face a mask of anger and humiliation.

For just an instant, watching this, Spur's mind swims with contrary emotions and imponderable questions. He wonders if the workplace affair between Hack and Boo has not completely dwindled. He had to step in last year in Libya in order to put the kibosh on it. Romantic entanglements can get team members killed. All of which is why his *own* flirtation, with Pin-Up, is a luxury he can't afford.

In that scintilla of a second, as his mind grapples for a way out of this trap, Spur glances across the ridge and sees Pin-Up on the ground, under the petrified tree, as still as a mannequin. The sight of her in jeopardy makes the secret place in Spur's heart pang with equal parts longing and dread, all of which sets off a series of quick memory flashes . . .

. . . that surreal night in a tent outside Khartoum, Spur alone with Pin-Up . . . the two of them fresh from a successful mission, adrenaline still running high, and liquor flowing freely . . . their faces coming together in strobe-light sparks of heat lightning . . . their drunken kisses awkward and sweaty and desperate . . . their common desire like that of a couple of parched nomads returning from the desert, furiously gulping each other's essence . . . and then . . . then . . . pulling back . . . knowing they are about to commit the Warriors' Cardinal Sin.

The roar of engines drowns his thoughts, the cry of voices in Arabic juicing his adrenaline. The team members have their hands up now. Faces grim. Trapped. Caged animals coiled for a fight.

The first thug to arrive is an older man standing on the passenger side of a rust-pocked Humvee, swarthy like a pirate, his face obscured by the brim-shadow of his camouflaged cap. The morning sun has reached a point of severe angles, blazing in Spur's face, blinding him, making him blink.

"Qaf!—Qaf!—Alan!—Alan!!" the pirate leader bellows at the top of his lungs in Arabic, aiming his Russian assault rifle. "Tawaquf 'aw mitu!—Tawaquf 'aw mitu!!"

Pin-Up comments under her breath: "I believe he's saying, 'Welcome to Karakistan, brave Americans, and thank you for your service.'"

"LA!-TATA!-KALM!—LA!-TATA!-KALM!" the pirate calls out as he hops off the running board and approaches with the muzzle up and ready.

The rest of the ambush closes in on all sides, making a thunderous racket and raising a dust cloud the size of the Hindenburg. More thugs hop out and approach. They're well-armed, apparently as well-funded as their Astrodome of a stronghold. One of these newcomers—a younger man with a dark ponytail hanging out the back of his cap—cries out in heavily Eastern European–accented English, *Hands behind your heads! Now! Now!!*

Not a single member of Spur's ghost unit averts their gaze as they calmly interlace their hands behind their necks. A gangly assistant in a shemagh scarf hops off the back of a Humvee and shackles each member with a zip tie. Throughout the process, each prisoner stares at Ponytail with the stoic patience of a person waiting for a light to change so they can cross the street.

At last, the operative code-named Spur gives Ponytail a cold smile, and then says in his bourbon-soaked drawl, "Your move, hotshot."

# CHAPTER THREE
## The Lord's Prayer

### 1.

The valley adjacent to Osamir's fortress cuts through a vast gorge, bordered on each side by sheer granite rock faces notched out of the land by Neolithic glaciers. Meager forms of vegetation—a few skeletal trees and sporadic whiskers of ironweed clinging to the upper ledges—are all that survive in this harsh, unforgiving ecosystem. The moraine forms a natural wind tunnel, and the sudden gusts swirling down from the Tartarus Mountains make an atonal moaning noise that manages to be both plaintive and psychopathic to the human ear.

On foot, chaperoned by the slow-moving convoy of tanks and armored vehicles, the journey across the valley to the threshold of the fortress takes nearly fifteen minutes. Along the way, the five operatives mostly remain silent, each simmering in their own juices, each plotting their own version of escape, each cursing themselves for walking into such an obvious trap.

Halfway across the valley, his beefy arms cramping behind his neck, Spur starts to suspect that they were set up. He has dealt with traitors in the past. Early in his career, outside a safe house in Damascus, Spur and his people were cornered by a Syrian hit team. Somebody on the inside had tipped off ISIL that the ghost unit was coming. Spur lost three good men that day, and spent the next week and a half hunting down each individual responsible for the ambush.

Now as these dark thoughts pass through his mind like burned leaves tossed by the wind, he notices something out of the corner of his eye. With as much discretion as possible he cautiously glances up at a high precipice to the south. The craggy, windblown summit of the tallest mountain in the area—its peak just a tad over eleven thousand feet in elevation—is still clad in a draping of winter's dirty snow and now practically glowing with the amber brilliance of dawn.

Spur blinks, figuring he must be seeing things. He looks back at his team, surveying each face for any sign that they have noticed what Spur has noticed. He looks back up at the mountain, expecting the creature to be gone, just an errant trick of the light, a meaningless hallucination, but the thing is still there. Goose bumps trace the lines of Spur's arms and back.

At the very top of the mountain, perched on the pinnacle of the summit, as still as a statue in the sixty-mile-an-hour winds, a massive, oily-black wolf stands watching the procession. At this distance, without the aid of some kind of scale, it's impossible to gauge the size of the thing—or even be sure of its genus and species—and for a moment, with the pale sunlight reflecting off its greasy-black fur, something about the way the animal is facing the convoy sends a jolt of icy dread down through Spur's veins. The sight of it makes his scalp crawl. He sniffs and looks away.

He looks back at his colleagues. Not a single one of them has noticed the wolf.

Spur looks back up at the summit, and the creature is gone.

## 2.

They reach the front wall of the fortress and move single file through its massive gates. Half a dozen escorts—armed with assault rifles aimed directly at the backs of the prisoners' heads—keep the group moving with a poke here, a prod there, and a periodic threat snarled in Arabic. The pirate leads the procession across a dusty courtyard, murmuring into his walkie-talkie.

They enter the building through an unmarked iron door. As they descend a series of staircases into the sublevels, Spur memorizes every detail, every flight of stairs, every unmarked door, every trace odor of cumin, cigarette smoke, urine, blood, and stale fear-sweat. Their descent down through the sublevels seems to go on forever, and the deeper they go, the more malodorous and ancient the structure becomes, as though the entire aboveground bastion has been retrofitted over a festering necropolis.

In the lowest sublevel, at the end of an endless hallway, two men stand waiting near a reinforced metal door. The one on the left is a portly, dark-skinned man in camo pants, boots, and flak vest—most likely one of Osamir's middle managers. On the right stands none other than Captain Ed Deegan, the pilot, still sporting his yellow aviator glasses.

Spur knows instantly why Deegan is here, all the puzzle pieces clicking silently together in Spur's brain.

"How much did they pay for your services, Ed?" Spur asks softly as the procession pauses in front of the reinforced door. Deegan lets out a nervous chuckle. The pirate fishes for the key and then fiddles it into the dead bolt.

The tension in the enclosed, claustrophobic space is thick enough to feel against the skin. Spur has trained for tight-quarters hand-to-hand, and could easily launch a surprise fusillade of blows on the nearest gunman, getting the AK-47 away from him within a nanosecond. But there are too many variables, too many weapons in the hallway, too many muzzles pointed directly at his people.

"Tell them what they want to know, Paul," Deegan says under his breath. "And you'll walk out of here with your skin intact."

"You know what I hope?" Spur tells Deegan as the door swings open. "I hope we meet again."

The five operatives are shoved into what appears to be an interrogation room.

The door slams shut behind them, the bolt clanging home with a disturbing finality.

# 3.

Spur half expects Abu Osamir himself to be waiting for them in the room, dressed in full uniform, a ceremonial saber in his hand, a gleam of madness in his eyes. But the empty chamber glares back at them with its roaring silence, incessantly flickering fluorescent light, and scabrous, blood-caked plaster walls.

At first, Spur doesn't notice the crunching noises beneath his boots as he slowly turns and regards the contents of the cavernous cell. He smells the coppery odor of human blood, and he sees his reflection in a massive two-way mirror along one wall, his arms still raised and cuffed behind his neck. In the mirror the others are visible behind him, each still shackled and silent, each with a grim expression, each determined to keep their fear in check.

"Lovely accommodations," Ticker finally comments under his breath, looking around the room.

Pin-Up sniffs back her panic and says, "Wait till they see my Yelp review."

Along the opposite wall, a row of six metal chairs with high backs and restraining straps are bolted to the floor, spattered with old blood as dark as dried tar. Blood-encrusted hacksaws, butcher knives, ice picks, pruning shears, and medical instruments are lined up on death-stained steel tabletops between the chairs. A car battery sits on a pedestal in the far corner, its terminals hooked by alligator clips to tangles of wires and electrodes.

"You've got to be kidding me . . . tell me that's not what I think it is," Boo murmurs, more to herself than the others. She notices the crunching sounds as she steps around the room. Each footstep sounds as though she's walking on potato chips. She kneels and takes a closer look at the tiny flakes on the floor, some as delicate as dragonfly wings, some blackened with dried blood. "Fingernails . . . very stylish, must have used the Marquis de Sade's decorator."

The fluorescent overhead tubes flicker and tick as if insects are caught inside them.

Spur starts to formulate a statement, maybe give them a pep talk, order them to calm the hell down and get their heads in the game, when the dead bolt behind him clangs loudly.

The door bursts open and three beefy thugs in scarves and black berets pour into the room, the man on each flank holding an Uzi machine pistol on the five newcomers. The goon in the middle barks something in a dialect that Spur can't quite understand. Judging by the jerky hand motions, however, and the way the man is pointing at the chairs, Spur gets the general idea.

One by one, at the prodding of Uzis, each of the five operatives gets shoved into a high-backed torture chair against the wall. At gunpoint, their wrists and ankles are shackled to the death chairs. It takes less than a minute and a half to secure each member of the unit to their respective seat.

Less than ninety seconds to seal the fate of these five brave intelligence officers with a final snap of the cold, merciless iron restraints.

The thugs make a hasty exit, slamming the door, throwing the bolt lock, and leaving the prisoners to stew in their predicament.

### 4.

Minutes pass. Seconds. Eternities. No one speaks for the longest time. They just sit there, listening to the muffled voices and the hectic footsteps in the steel corridors outside the torture room.

Spur is not surprised by this waiting period. He's seen it before. It's part of the process, a softening, a prelude to the nasty stuff in store for them. Designed to ratchet up their nervous systems to the point of hysteria, the technique is part of the standard enhanced-interrogation playbook.

The truth is, Spur is more interested in what these people want to know. The questions these jackals ask before dialing up the voltage could turn out to be the best piece of intel the unit could ever hope to retrieve. The only trick will be living long enough to return to the States with the findings.

As if on cue, footsteps return outside the door. The five prisoners straighten in their seats as the door bursts open, and the same three stocky men in shemagh scarves barge into the room. Now one of them carries a long metal contraption that Spur initially misidentifies as a weapon. Another carries a spotlight on a tripod, and a third carries a cheap Japanese video camera that looks as though it might have been state-of-the-art technology about twenty years ago.

In the corner of the room they unfold the metal thing, revealing it to be a portable screen—a sort of makeshift backdrop—with Arabic propaganda scrawled across it in a primitive hand. Spur is in no way fluent but can tell immediately that the words are not exactly "Welcome to Karakistan, Noble American Warriors." He glances across the room at Ticker, who is the team's language expert, and can tell by the revulsion on his tawny handsome features that the words are not good news.

One of the captors comes over to the row of chairs and, for a moment, seems to ponder whom to choose for some unknown honor. His dark eyes land on Spur, and they narrow and glitter like those of a predator in the wild recognizing a natural enemy.

"Let's do it, fellas," Spur says softly, calmly, almost certain that he's about to die . . .

. . . when the thug turns to Pin-Up and unlocks her shackles. The woman gives a shrug, stuffing her terror back down her throat. "I'd love to dance," she says with disgust. The thug yanks her violently across the room as she murmurs, "Does the band know any Cardi B?"

The other two captors have set up the spotlight and camera facing the crude backdrop. They shove Pin-Up to the floor in front of the camera, and hold the muzzle of an AK-47 on her, and yell at her in their native language. On her hands and knees, without looking up, she says, "Ticker, what are they saying?"

On the other side of the room, Ticker shakes his head. "Can't tell, they're speaking too fast."

"Bullshit! What are they saying?"

Ticker sighs. "They're saying, 'On your knees, look at the camera.'"

Spur speaks up. "Don't do it, Pin!"

One of the thugs comes over to Spur and slams the butt end of his assault rifle across Spur's jaw, hard enough to loosen a tooth and break the skin of his lower lip. Spur spits out his tooth, smiles a bloody smile at the assailant, and says, "Take me, asshole. I'm the big fish."

The thug booms something in Karakistani and slams the butt across Spur's temple, making his ears ring, and rattling his skull.

In the meantime, the other two thugs have positioned Pin-Up on her knees, facing the camera, hands shackled now behind her back. She softly begins reciting the Lord's Prayer in Spanish as one thug turns on the camera, and the other selects a rusty machete from an array of edged weapons and knives lying on a nearby stainless-steel caddy. Pin-Up has trained for this moment all her adult life, but now that it's here, all bets are off. The terror contorts her sculpted, lovely face.

The machete holder covers his own face with a pointed black hood.

"*Goddamn fucking savages!*" Spur booms at them, summoning all his rage.

They turn on the spotlight. Horrible harsh light crashes into Pin-Up's face. "*Danos hoy nuestro pan de cada día,*" she softly prays, her gaze unwavering as she stares into the camera. "*Y perdónanos nuestras deudas, ya que también hemos perdonado a nuestras deudoras. . . .*"

Spur howls from his chair, spitting bloody saliva. "*I'm the one you want, you stupid peckerwood cocksuckers—I'M THE GODDAMN HONCHO!!!*"

Rusty Machete Man moves around behind Pin-Up and looks into the camera. He says a few words in his native tongue. Across the room, Ticker translates.

"He's saying, 'We hereby cleanse the world of this unbeliever, this imperialist stooge, this American whore in the name of the Cause.'"

Unconsciously tensing against his shackles, Spur pulls so hard he draws blood from his wrists as he watches the executioner grab Pin-Up's hair, raising his filthy machete and preparing to decapitate her. The thug calls out his litany as though preaching to the camera.

Ticker can barely speak the translation: "He's says that we Americans have awakened a hornets' nest, and we all will perish in the flames of the righteous angry God of the Sacred blah-blah-blah."

Spur bows his head in shame and grief and horror, looking down, the blood from his wrists dripping to the floor, his mouth coppery from biting his lip. Bracing himself for the telltale noise of the blade hitting Pin-Up's neck, he closes his eyes. He prays that God will be merciful and take her quickly. Please. Please. The lights flicker suddenly.

Spur looks up.

The events in the room have slowed down as though seized up in a faulty film projector. Spur sees the thugs looking up at the ceiling, also vexed by the strange flashing of the lights, now flickering so wildly and sporadically it's as though the electrical power has gone haywire.

Spur hears thunder outside the building, which makes no sense whatsoever. The bombast shakes the very core of the sublevel. How is this possible? The last time Spur heard of a lightning storm in the middle of the Karakistani desert was . . . never. Then, without any warning whatsoever, the dynamic in the room changes with the speed of a match tip catching.

## CHAPTER FOUR
## The Illusionist

### 1.

Looking back on it later, trying to recount the sequence of events, Spur will remember a distinct odor permeating the dungeon right at that moment. At first unidentifiable, it conjures odd memories in Spur's midbrain from his childhood—long summer nights back in Texas, the Fourth of July, bottle rockets, firecrackers, and snakes—those unmistakable smells wafting across the room as strong as a punch in the gut. Only later would he realize that he was smelling sulfur. Brimstone. Ancient odors from the center of the earth.

Across the room, at that moment, the three thugs spontaneously combust, the fire igniting first beneath their feet—blinding yellow flames shooting up, magnesium-bright, climbing their legs like luminous centipedes feeding on them, engulfing them, eliciting high-pitched shrieks of shock and pain from each of them. The fire hungrily gobbles each figure as though the thugs are made of wax and accelerant, causing each to stagger and spin in an awkward ballet, macabre pirouettes of sparks and swirls filling the room with the stench of burning flesh and hair, sizzling organs, living creatures cauterized and turned to cinders within seconds.

At last, three separate columns of human-shaped ash collapse and drift to the floor, at which point they are sucked into the substrata of earth below through cracks in the tiles by some inexplicable force, returning the room to its former silence as though the thugs had never existed in the first place.

### 2.

On the floor in front of the propaganda-stained backdrop, still on her knees, Pin-Up looks around, hyperventilating, her heart racing. The stillness that presses down on her at that moment is dizzying, the shrieks still ringing in her ears, and it takes her several minutes to gather her wits enough to even speak. "How did—? What just—? What the hell just h-happened?" she stammers in fits and starts, looking around the flickering room.

The sound of Pin-Up's voice brings the team back to their senses.

"There's an explanation," Spur finally manages to say to no one in particular. "Just gimme a second to figure out what the hell it is."

"I can't wait to hear your thoughts on the matter, Chief." The softly accented voice of Boo comes from one corner of the room, where she's still shackled to her chair, trembling in her seat. Her dark eyes are wide and shiny with dread.

Spur realizes that Pin-Up is still on her knees in front of the camera. "Pin-Up, talk to me. You good? You all right?"

Still on her knees, still looking around the room, trying to get her bearings, she looks a little woozy, soaked in adrenaline and fear. "Fantastic, never better," she lies, wiping a wisp of hair from her eyes. "What just happened, Spur?"

"That's a good question. Maybe let's just start with you getting us out of these shackles."

Taking a deep breath, Pin-Up rises on wobbly legs, sniffing back the trauma, stuffing the shock back down into that dark place where she keeps her foibles, her guilt, her fears and self-loathing. She realizes she has broken her stoic warrior pose by praying like a frightened little girl in front of her colleagues. But there's nothing she can do about that now. Raised Catholic in the barrio, East Los Angeles, she was born Maria Consuelo Caruso, and her Catholicism has clung to her for life, as permanent as a hidden tattoo. She has visible ones as well. She has a singing skull from Dia de Muertos on the back of her neck, and a Mayan arrow wrapped around her left wrist. Ancient symbols of pride, courage, and skill.

She goes over to Spur and inspects his shackles. The steel is sticky from his blood, from all the straining and yanking. She has no key. "Let me find something to pick it open with," she says, focusing on the task at hand in order to steady herself.

She looks across this room full of fingernails and old screams smeared on the walls. She sees the instruments of torture lined up on that rusty steel tray, the knives and pliers and razors gleaming in the flickering, faltering light. She blinks.

Out of nowhere a memory flashes in the silent-movie flicker show of her brain.

*Fifteen years ago. Los Angeles. The back room of a B-level film studio on Melrose. She takes her top off for a disgusting pig of a producer—Jason Peltz, a man who never met a pastry he didn't love, or an actress he didn't want to harass.*

The memory has etched itself in Pin-Up's personal Hall of Shame, and is just as vivid and horrible today as the day it happened. Letting this repulsive warthog of a human nuzzle her breasts, unzip himself, and force her head down into that sickening private place. The musky odors of his cigar and sweat and semen. The neon-purple light from the studio sign behind the window shade. All of it in Technicolor splendor in her memory. And the worst part is, she did it.

She did what he wanted in return for a bit part in a shitty flick.

As if on cue, right then, right at the peak of her self-loathing, the lights in the room go out, plunging the windowless chamber into complete and utter darkness.

## 3.

Blinking, trying to see through the black void, Spur bites down hard on his shock and disorientation. The darkness is so impenetrable, so opaque, so overwhelming that his ears instantly compensate. He can hear the hyperventilated breaths of his team quickening. "Stay frosty, ladies and germs," he advises, his voice sounding thunderous to his own ears. He starts to say, "Take this one step at a—"

He hears another noise he hadn't yet noticed in the room—a rhythmic huffing sound like a fireplace bellows stoking embers, puffing and wheezing mechanically. It seems to be coming from one corner of the dungeon, although in this deep-space darkness it's hard to locate sources of sounds.

Spur glances to his right, and all at once he figures he must be hallucinating from all the excitement. He sees a pair of iridescent yellow eyes floating in the darkness. Definitely animal. Lupine. Fierce. Shimmering. Reminiscent of that moment when a coyote or mountain lion crosses a two-lane at night, and the flash of a headlamp reflects off their eyes like luminous coins.

"Spur?" Hack's voice rings out from Spur's left flank. "At the risk of sounding a bit nebulous, am I the only one seeing this?"

The tone of the man's question raises gooseflesh on the back of Spur's neck as a low, guttural growl reverberates through the darkness. Goose bumps course down his spine and arms. The pair of phosphorescent eyes are levitating now, rising up, four feet above the ground now . . . five feet, six feet, seven, eight . . . as the basso profundo growl intensifies.

The wolf—or whatever the hell it is—seems to be standing up on its hind legs now, and it's *enormous,* its mucus-clogged growl filling the room like the revolving armature of a massive turbine. Spur's whole being is clenched with dread at this unearthly apparition. As a career fixer for the government—a professional warrior—Spur can fight anything on two legs. But *this*—this nightmare—this fetid creature rising in the darkness of the torture chamber—this does not compute in Spur's world.

As if triggered by the terrible eyes floating above him in that vacuum of darkness, he is stricken by a memory—unbidden, unwanted, unexpected—like an old, yellowed, sealed envelope with poison inside it stashed away in one of the forgotten files of his life, buried for decades in the farthest reaches of his mind. He sees himself in a reception area at the Heartland Women's Clinic, downtown Dallas, waiting, hand in hand with his first true love, Lucy Collier—she of the innocent doe eyes and pigtails, barely out of high school—pregnant with Spur's baby.

His name back then was Paul Candell, and his best gal, Lucy, had begged him to let her have the baby. But Paul Candell was about to enlist, and eventually transform himself like a larva becoming a pupa becoming a full-grown imago code-named Spur. Babies had no place in this world. Which is why he proceeded to emotionally strong-arm the woman into terminating the pregnancy against her wishes. The procedure did not go well. Lucy nearly died on the table due to hemorrhaging. After the ordeal, she learned that she would never be able to conceive again.

Spur lost touch with the woman over the years, and rarely even thinks about her other than the occasional 3:00 A.M. bout of insomnia during which he once again wrestles with his pangs of guilt. But today, in this vacuous sinkhole of a room, with those yellow eyes glaring down at him, Spur has a bizarre premonition that he will never fully understand or be able to explain: *The wolflike thing in the room is activating his shame.*

He senses the others having similar unforeseen flashes in the darkness. He can't see them but he can hear their ragged breathing full of anxiety and confusion. He can hear some of them swallowing hard, pushing the dread and guilt back down their throats. Later, Spur will learn of Pin-Up's shameful memory of prostituting herself for the philistine producer, Ticker's disgraceful one-night stand with a lady detective working his wife's murder case, Hack's regretful foray into cybercrime as a young man, and Boo's participation in an honor killing in her village when she was just an impressionable young girl.

Shame and guilt and regret. Waves of it crashing against the stale, putrid darkness. From the general vicinity of those yellow eyes comes a deep, otherworldly voice . . .

. . . and again the dynamic in the dungeon shifts as the creature begins to speak.

## 4.

"It's Aramaic." Ticker's whisper comes from Spur's immediate left, making him jump slightly. "Very old . . . pre-Hebrew. Ancient. Semitic."

Still shackled to his chair, mesmerized by the ghostly voice on the other side of the room, Spur had been trying to identify the language. "Translate it," he whispers.

"I don't know if I can."

"Try."

"All right . . . it's saying . . . the voice I mean . . . it's saying, 'A transaction is what I propose . . . a proposition, if you prefer.'"

The disembodied voice continues droning in a steady stream of raspy syllables, awash in the glottal fricatives of Hebrew and Arabic, but Spur knows enough of those languages to recognize neither in the words drifting through the dark. Aramaic is a language from an era before Christ. The sound of it to modern ears is hypnotic . . . musical.

Ticker's whisper can be heard beneath the voice like a breathy counterpoint. "He's saying . . . 'I can free you, I can imbue you with great powers, I can . . . I can grant you skills . . . which will help you escape this charnel house . . . powers that are unprecedented on earth, abilities far beyond ordinary humans . . . powers that reflect your very natures.'"

"Yeah, sure, check's in the mail," Spur comments ruefully. "Ask him what he wants with us."

"My Aramaic's a little rusty."

"Give it a try."

"All right, here goes." Ticker raises his voice and speaks very slowly and clearly, enunciating the Paleolithic language as best he can, addressing the darkness across the room.

As though a switch has been thrown, the temperature plummets in the room, and the overhead lights flicker on, illuminating the torture chamber.

The creature standing fifteen feet away, facing Spur and his team, takes the breath away.

# 5.

What Spur sees is a lanky figure in nineteenth-century garb—a frayed waistcoat, faded trousers, spats, and a bowler hat—like a forgotten character out of one of the Charles Dickens tales that haunted Spur as a boy. But the Dickensian nature of the thing is belied by its eyes—pure black spheres with no life in them—as well as the bloodless, pasty-white nature of its flesh, as alabaster as bone. Twin ram horns spiral out from under the hat, circling each batlike ear. Its yellow, needlelike teeth become visible when it speaks, the teeth of a deep-sea creature that has never been exposed to light.

Spur looks down at his blood-sticky wrists and sees that the shackles have somehow, spontaneously, over the last few moments, been unlocked. The strange, low rattle of the creature's voice fills the air.

Ticker speaks up then. "He says he only requires an occasional task to be performed by us."

Spur thinks it over for a second, rubbing his injured wrists. His breath shows in the gelid, icy-cold atmosphere. "Ask him if he's the one who burned up those thugs a few minutes ago."

Ticker has started to translate the English into Aramaic when the monster in the waistcoat begins to laugh, finding all of this very funny, the sound of its laughter a hacksaw cutting through metal. Its breath does not show, since it is not technically alive. Finally it says something else in Aramaic.

From across the room, Ticker speaks up. "He's saying, 'Merely an illusion . . . for your benefit.'"

Spur nods. "Okay. I don't know what that means but fair enough."

The low, guttural voice speaking a dead language makes Spur's innards tighten.

Ticker translates. "He says he is an illusionist, first and foremost."

Spur nods.

Ticker goes on: "Now he's saying, 'My medium is malevolent

magic . . . deception . . . elegant lies . . . but I am a businessman at heart.'"

Spur shrugs. "Tell him he's a damn fine magician, I'll give him that."

Ticker translates the English.

The creature lowers its head with feral, insect-like twitches, cocking its bone-white cranium as though it's thinking. Spur watches with morbid fascination, flexing his numb fingers, getting the blood flowing again. He glances at the others, and sees that each and every member of his team has been freed from their bonds, their heavy breathing showing in plumes of vapor swirling from their mouths.

But what Spur *doesn't* see—and won't discover until much later—is that each operative is looking at a different version of the stranger in the room. Boo sees the mogwai, the cadaverous old man with the long beard and empty white eye sockets. Ticker sees the fire-breathing, three-headed djakata of African folklore. Hack sees the skeletal, emaciated dybbuk, the demonic gremlin from his mother's Jewish fairy tales. And Pin-Up—dear Pin-Up, child of cinema, Hollywood survivor—she sees a tattered, scorched, shopworn revenant of a B-movie Lucifer, a carnival barker dressed in an ancient cinnamon-colored silk suit, with serpentine tail, tiny horns, and forked tongue protruding from its blackened maw of a mouth.

All at once the realization strikes Spur like an ice pick thrust between his eyes. This smoky, repulsive apparition before him— this cadaverous thing in the bowler hat—it is very possibly the devil himself. Which is insane. But *there he is* . . . and here are Spur and his team . . . and now the room has become as cold as a meat locker.

At last, Spur says, "Ask him what the deal is with giving us great powers. I have a feeling there are strings attached."

Ticker poses the question in Aramaic.

The thing in black starts reeling off great bursts of the ancient language.

Ticker struggles to keep up. "Okay now he's saying that he has agreements—covenants?—with other members of the human race. These are souls that he has purchased. But they've reneged on their contracts. They are in breach. And he says now he needs a group of killers to hunt them down, to terminate them, so that that he can ultimately claim their souls."

Gooseflesh trickles down Spur's spine. He looks at the others—each team member mesmerized by the monster—and now Spur addresses it directly. "Let's cut to the chase. Are you supposed to be the devil?"

For a moment, the silence in the room unnerves Spur as the thing with the hat cocks its head and drills its empty black gaze into Spur's face. At last, the voice that comes out of the creature is a low, deep, grating rasp, as though someone has recorded the guttural growl of a predatory animal and then slowed it down to a skin-crawling baritone snarl, which has now, almost imperceptibly, switched from Aramaic to English.

"I am Asmodeus . . . ruler of the underworld."

For a moment, Spur stares at the thing in black as it ripples and undulates before his very eyes like a figurine made of volcanic glass dipped in water. Spur gathers himself, gets his bearings back, and says, "The thing of it is, I'm kinda slow. I apologize but I'm confused about something. Why don't you just hunt down these rascals yourself? Deep-six these folks with some of them nasty voodoo tricks you been showing us?"

The creature speaks with an otherworldly accent: "The laws of the universe prevent me from directly killing a soul."

Spur shakes his head. "I don't get it. You can't harm a single human?"

"I must manipulate humans to do such business for me as the need arises."

"You did a pretty tidy job on those three goons about to lop off Pin-Up's head."

The creature waves his cadaverous hand, a slipstream of mold, decay, and rock dust wafting from his every movement, reeking of the grave. "Hallucination, child's play," it explains. "I didn't kill those mongrels. They now lie in comas somewhere, sleeping off the trauma."

"Let me get this straight." Spur is losing his patience. "You're a blue-ribbon liar, a regular con artist, a flimflam man. You make people *think* they're hurt but in order to actually hurt them you gotta hire freelance help. That about the size of it?"

The stranger looks at him again with those black craters in its head. "I have no ability to end a person's life. But I do have the gift of influence . . . possession, if you like . . . and I can cause people to do great mischief if I so choose. Of course, deception is my métier . . . my specialty."

Spur springs to his feet, knocking over the chair and taking a menacing step toward the sinister figure across the room. He stabs his finger at the creature as he says, "Then why in the Sam Hell would we trust you as far as we can spit?"

Taking another step toward the dark figure, scalp crawling with rage, Spur is a coiled spring about to snap. "I don't know how the magic works, how you got in here, how you burned up them boys, and I don't care. All I know is how Abu Osamir plays his game, and this smells like his brand of poker. But now . . . we got our own card we can play and that's *you*. With all due respect, whoever you are—*whatever* you are—you just became a hostage!"

Spur reaches out, grabs ahold of the monster's arm, and visible tendrils of high voltage bullwhip Spur backward. The sheer force of the current lifts him off his feet.

## CHAPTER FIVE
# Twenty-Three Seconds

**1.**

Spur lands hard on the filthy tile floor against the far wall, thrown with such force it feels as though he just tangled with a catapult. Dazed, vision momentarily blurred, breathless, he feels the heat of a thousand furnaces blazing in his face, beams of fiery yellow light shooting up through gaping fissures and cracks opening up in the floor.

He sits up and realizes the world has turned inside out.

He finds himself perched on a jagged atoll of flooring tiles barely three feet wide—a precipice, a narrow crow's nest—precariously overhanging a vast underground chasm of ancient stone, eternal flames, fogbanks of acrid smoke, and figures writhing in perpetual agony. Spur looks up, scans the room, and sees three team members still in their chairs, Pin-Up still kneeling on the floor, unbound yet mesmerized—each of them stricken mute—each isolated on an individual island of flooring, overlooking the hellish, primordial landscape down below.

Just one glance is all that Spur needs to identify the smoldering terrain beneath him, the craggy slopes of volcanic stone plunging down massive crevasses and smoking gullies filled with multitudes of naked, bleeding, suffering figures. Spur saw something like this in a museum long ago in a painting by Hieronymus Bosch, the title of which was *The Harrowing of Hell*. In the painting the underworld is a surreal vision reminiscent of a bombed-out city after a blitzkrieg attack, the gaping ruins of buildings like monstrous mouths hungry for souls, helpless skeletal wraiths hanging upside down, being flayed alive, boiling in tar pits, being sodomized, thrashing and convulsing in flaming pools of brackish black oil.

Then it all vanishes as suddenly as it had appeared, the evaporation of the vision so abrupt it literally takes Spur's breath away.

He topples to his side, and curls into a fetal position on those grimy tiles, the bitter, ashy stench of burned flesh still in his nostrils. Blinking spasmodically, taking deep breaths, he fights the terror kindling in him. Unaccustomed to the inexplicable, Spur is a pragmatist—a man of science, and if science doesn't work, an M16 with a full magazine is the next best thing—but his heart now reacts with raw emotion, hammering in his chest, all his involuntary functions on high alert. Sweat pours down his face.

"Right at this moment," a voice says from across the dungeon, "a battalion of Osamir's minions are rushing to this very room."

The creature in the bowler hat stands in the center of the dungeon, arms defiantly crossed against its chest, eyes glittering scarlet with anger deep in the center of the black holes. "They are heavily armed with orders to make your last hours on earth quite miserable. Trust me, they are quite proficient at this."

Spur rises to his feet, glances at the others, and then looks back at the creature. He braces himself to pose one particular question that he's been contemplating and measuring for a while now but finally speaks it aloud with great trepidation as though dreading the answer. "Who . . . who are you really?"

"I have many names," the dark figure drones in its creaky, corroded, metallic rasp of a voice. "Beelzebub, Mephistopheles . . . Baphomet . . . Mammon. More importantly, you have a decision to make, and time is unfortunately of the essence. If you'd rather stay and be slaughtered that's certainly your prerogative but I need your decision now. Again, all that I ask is that you be available for hire from time to time on a freelance basis."

The creature pauses.

Ticker speaks up. "Basically what you want is for us to be your hit squad."

"Exactly. When the need arises, yes, I will require you to find a rogue signatory of mine and neutralize them. At which point I shall take over and adjudicate their damnation, taking their souls back to where they belong. If you prefer to call that a 'hit,' very well. I call it doing the cosmos a public service.

"You have less than a minute before that door bursts open, so I recommend that that you make your decision forthwith."

## 2.

Five thugs armed with Russian-made assault rifles clamber down a flight of stairs toward the holding pens of the lower level. Choosing the emergency staircases over the leisurely paced freight elevator, they descend with mad purpose and bloodlust in their eyes.

A few minutes ago, their leader—the man who resembles a pirate—got word that the smell of something burning was wafting up from the lowest level. The thugs had been hearing the prisoners' raised voices vibrating up through the floors for nearly half an hour, but the odor of a fire got their attention.

Now the pirate leads the gang of thugs down the last flight of stairs, the men hurtling downward as fast as their legs will carry them on their descent to the lowest level.

## 3.

"Your decision, if you please." The figure in black stands in the center of the room with the nonchalance of a train conductor waiting to punch their tickets.

The five warriors, all out of their chairs now, encircle the creature, standing with hands on their hips, still skeptical, and yet nervously trying to process what is happening. The eerie, otherworldly atmosphere of the torture chamber—the crypt-like claustrophobia, the weird appearance of the devilish creature, the terror and confusion drenched in adrenaline—serves only to heighten the surreal tableau.

The sounds of angry footsteps and bolt mechanisms on rifle stocks clang and click and echo down the hallway outside the door.

Hack speaks up. "Not to be intrusive or judgmental in any way, but may I ask if there's an out clause? In the agreement, I'm talking about."

The being from hell cocks its head inquisitively. "I do not understand the question."

"Well . . . if I may be perfectly candid, what I'm wondering is whether or not this contract between us is . . . *in perpetuity*?"

The creature glowers. "Everything I do is in perpetuity."

## 4.

Charging down the hallway, the pirate fixes his gaze on the last door on the left, the room they call the Pit, hurtling toward it with his AK-47 raised and ready to roll, his gang on his heels, following right behind him, various automatic weapons trained on that same door.

## 5.

In the stillness of the torture chamber, the footsteps drawing closer and closer, the monster in black calmly nods in the general direction of Spur. "I will need your decision now."

Spur stands next to Pin-Up with his arms crossed against his barrel chest, trying to maintain his waning skepticism, trying *not* to believe in this mad magician but failing miserably for reasons that are somewhat inexplicable to Spur. Is there a part of him that still holds on to the old superstitions? Is he secretly willing to make a deal with the devil to be the best at what he does? Isn't he already the best? Is this about ego?

The rumble of footsteps and gunmetal approaches outside the door.

Spur can feel the gazes of his team members on him, waiting for him to make a decision, each and every one of them now giving over to his better judgment. He knows they'll follow him wherever he goes. He knows they'll be loyal to the end. He loves these people with all his heart. They are his one and only true family. He would die for these four humble warriors. But would he forge a Faustian pact for them?

He hears whispers and the dull metallic clicking of cocking levers just outside the door. And in that brief, tense powder keg of a moment, just before the door bursts open, the man once named Paul Candell—the anonymous ghost-assassin known only by the code name Spur—has an epiphany.

These men about to barge in are in league with the savages who only moments ago were about to decapitate Pin-Up. Those barbarians were seconds away from taking her life. They would have chopped her head off with the indifference of slaughterhouse workers carving up a spring lamb. They would have stolen the rest of her life from her in the most vicious, senseless manner. And with that realization the embers of rage building in him begin to smolder. The volatile chemicals of contempt, hatred, enmity, and righteous fury catch fire, and the flames rise up within in.

"Okay, we'll do it," he says finally, without a trace of outward emotion in his voice.

The creature in black vanishes in a dervish of noxious vapor.

## 6.

The skirmish that follows would come to be known as the First Involvement, and would feel to those present like an eternity, but in reality the whole shooting match transpires over the course of a mere twenty-three seconds. The reason for such a precise— albeit brief—amount of elapsed time in the record books is due to the testimony of a single principal participant.

"In order to explain what happened in that dungeon that day," the operative code-named Ticker would later tell intelligence officers, "you have to understand, none of us had any idea what we were capable of yet. All we were told was that we would have powers that supposedly reflected our individual natures, whatever that means. I'll tell you one thing, though. We were all excruciatingly aware that we had no firearms."

Interestingly, Ticker's statement to his superiors also includes the observation that he "felt something snap" inside him the moment his group leader, Spur, uttered the words "Okay, we'll do it."

The man known as "Ticker" was born Samuel Elijah Johnson in Chicago thirty-five years ago. Despite his many academic credentials, he probably did his most important learning in the alleys and side streets of Chicago's Stony Island. He learned to pay attention. He learned to always be aware of who might be walking behind him at night. He learned that love is the greatest antidote to evil but also the biggest risk a person can take in their life. Losing his wife to street violence taught him the precious value of time, and the importance of living every moment to its fullest.

Hence the code name Ticker, and the astonishingly precise blow-by-blow account of what happened that day in that foul-smelling chamber of horrors.

## 7.

At the beginning of it—less than two seconds after the repulsive figure in black has vanished—the massive, leprous iron door bangs open. The sound of it is a broken gong reverberating through the stale air. At this point, the five operatives are still grouped in a semicircle around the center of the room, where the dark figure had stood a moment earlier. Over the course of the next two seconds, the configuration of people in the room shifts.

Spur steps out in front of the others, and the semicircle opens up on either flank.

For just a scintilla of a second the element of surprise distracts the first gunman who lurches through the doorway—the pirate with the camouflage cap—charging into the room with the muzzle of his assault rifle already raised. For a brief instant his eyes bulge. This momentary double take is just long enough for Spur to pounce.

At second number four: Spur clutches the short barrel of the AK in the pirate's arms before the pirate can fire, nudging the muzzle upward toward the ceiling as the first burst of gunfire barks. Bright silver flashes spit out of the weapon as puffs of mortar dust spray down from the joists throughout the fifth and sixth seconds.

By the time the skirmish reaches the seven-second mark, everybody's ears are ringing, and things are developing rapidly at the corners. Pin-Up spins toward the closest stainless-steel tray—scooping up a bloodstained buck knife with the grace of a prima ballerina reaching for the hand of a dance partner—while on the other side of the room Boo grabs a machete off a tray, then tosses it over to Hack.

By second number ten, Spur has shoved the barrel of the AK-47 up against the bottom of the pirate's chin, the thug continuing to obliviously squeeze off rounds, inadvertently blowing the bottom of his own face off. A plume of blood mist hits the ceiling as the pirate goes dark and folds to the floor.

Eleven seconds into the skirmish the remaining four thugs pour into the room, raving mad at the sight of their fallen comrade. The first one of them to squeeze off a round aims it directly at Ticker.

It's a solid, steady bull's-eye of a shot, and Ticker gets a good look at the incandescent spark shooting out the end of the barrel right before a strange, seemingly inexplicable phenomenon occurs—interrupting the flow of the battle right around twelve seconds, a miracle that will be puzzled over for generations. It signals the burgeoning superpower taking root within Ticker (but not yet fully formed or understood).

## 8.

If asked to describe the feeling, Ticker would have to say it is akin to a cough or a sneeze, a sort of involuntary tic over which he has very little control in these early hours of his transformation. On this day, in the heat of battle, it begins with a pop in

Ticker's ears at the exact moment the gun goes off, like a sudden pressure spike. He sees the bullet, the actual full-metal-jacketed .450-caliber cartridge with its hollow tip like the command module of a tiny spacecraft coming toward him in time-lapse slow motion. The round is designed to obliterate a target, a one-shot-kill bullet at 250 yards, perfect for bagging big game or instantly dropping a former U.S. Navy SEAL in a godforsaken underground hellhole.

But on this momentous occasion the cartridge freezes in midair, a metal hummingbird inching through space, a good twelve inches away from the soft tissue of Ticker's face—oozing through the thick, squalid atmosphere of the dungeon, a millimeter per minute—as the passage of time bogs down like a celluloid motion-picture film jamming in a broken projector.

In real time, we are only fifteen seconds into the skirmish, at which point Ticker ducks, and the clock starts back up in earnest. The bullet passes over his head harmlessly and smashes through the cinder block wall behind him.

"Nobody was more surprised by the phenomenon than I was," he explains later in his official statement. "I knew immediately it had something to do with my newly acquired skills, but needless to say, there was very little time at that point to pause and reflect."

By the time sixteen seconds have elapsed Spur has gathered up the dead pirate's assault rifle, racked the cocking lever, and opened fire on the other thugs. The barrage riddles two out of the five remaining goons, sending blood patterns like modern art across the jamb and lintel of the iron door behind them.

Bodies whirl and shudder and throw off gouts of blood as they collapse.

Two seconds later, the surviving goons—three of them left, mortified and shaken—take cover behind the door, each crouching down and returning fire. In all the excitement Pin-Up has already scooped up two of the fallen assault rifles, and now, in an unexpected and spontaneous display of acrobatics, she tumbles into a graceful and mesmerizing roll across the tile floor as she simultaneously fires each AK-47.

The three surviving thugs are turned into pincushions as they are perforated with bullets, convulsing and spouting geysers of blood, and yet still staring in their death throes, gaping with the dazed looks of zombie supplicants beholding the second coming of a messiah . . . as Pin-Up keeps rolling and firing and rolling and firing until each magazine clicks empty, and each thug has buckled to the floor in a mutilated heap.

Twenty-three seconds have elapsed since the dark figure vanished.

## CHAPTER SIX
# The Naked Eye

### 1.

If the exterior of Osamir's fortress resembles Fort Knox on Mars, the five-story-high *interior* of the building—now apparently deserted—reminds Spur of something Kanye West would buy Kim Kardashian. Sweeping circular staircases with gilded banisters and massive cut-glass chandeliers lead from one level to the next, each more ornate and lavish than the last. Enormous portraits of Abu Osamir—in real life an overweight, balding fireplug of a man with a scraggly beard—depict the slovenly warlord as a handsome, broad-shouldered, saintly liberator of the underclasses, friend to all, and lover of children and animals. Side rooms brim with unopened crates of expensive liquor, video games, vintage swords, pornography, and various medieval weapons in display cases. One thing, though, is eminently clear to Spur: Osamir's courage and fortitude as depicted in the portraits does not extend to real life. All signs point to a recent and sudden exodus of the warlord and his minions.

Boo shuffles along behind Spur, one of the goons' assault rifles clutched in her hands, finger on the trigger, chamber loaded, safety off, her eyes scanning the floor as the others follow in formation behind her. Each operative carries one of the weapons acquired in the dungeon skirmish, moving single file now behind their leader in survival mode, hyperalert.

"Watch for trip wires," Spur whispers, "IEDs wired to wall switches, explosives hidden under pillows, sofa cushions, you name it."

Boo feels the thin flesh on the back of her neck prickle as they ascend the last of the staircases to the top floor, which the ghost unit learned only a week ago in their briefing meeting is the command center as well as the residential wing. She feels naked without her headset, which was confiscated during their captivity. But something else is yanking at her attention that she can't quite put her finger on. The feeling has been floating just beyond her consciousness ever since the evil mogwai had intervened down in the dungeon.

When Boo was a little girl—birth name Michelle Lin Chen— she was terrified of the old folktales and ghost stories her grand- father would tell. Growing up in the tiny village of Tingsan along the Yangtze River, she would avoid the annual Hungry Ghost Festival, during which the spirits of the dead would supposedly—according to legend—come out from the under- world and move among the living. Boo would hide in her room for fear they would find her and possess her. Later, when Boo was a teenager, her mother believed that her daughter might very well be a psychic medium, able to communicate with the dead, but this merely served to torment Boo all the more, driving her further into her shell.

Plagued by nightmares and visions of malevolent ghosts, Boo never spent a single night sleeping in the dark until she was well into her twenties. She kept the lights on at all times in her bedroom. She made sure that closet doors were always latched, and the window shades were drawn, and hallways were always well-lighted places. Still, on occasion she would notice, just for an instant, in a mirror, a pale, demonic face behind her, looking over her shoulder. Or she would catch a fleeting glimpse, as she walked past a deserted house, of a figure staring out at her from an attic window. Or she would hear the after-echo of a voice in an empty room resonating in her ear, a cryptic message from the other side that she would most likely never be able to decode.

Becoming a U.S. Navy SEAL exorcised most of those old de- mons for Boo. Older, wiser, and tougher, she had become a lethal weapon by the time she joined Spur's unit, a bringer of death to those whom she judged worthy of it. But every once in a while, in a quiet moment, alone in the dark, she wondered if her targets would one day revisit her, haunt her, latch on to her.

Now climbing the opulent staircase to Abu Osamir's private quarters, she feels a presence looming, hovering over her slender, compact body like an aura, a cold finger tracing the contours of her swan-like neck. She glances up at the baroque, gold-plated woodwork along the ceiling. She sees shapes. Translucent at first, mere smudges against the decorative inlay, the figures resolving slowly into inky black phantoms.

One of them she recognizes. A gaunt face stretched like putty, black sockets for eyes gaping down at her—a ghostly version of the pirate, the leader of Osamir's brigade, whose spirit now writhes in eternal torment within the crevices and convolutions of the fortress ceiling. Other spirits squirm in the fissures and grain like agitated smoke leaching out of the woodwork, seeking deliverance from some kind of hellish limbo. These are the spirits of the thugs, the metaphysical homeless, doomed to suffer and long for salvation for the rest of time.

It remains unclear to Boo how she knows all this, and sees all this, and feels all this—how she is translating these spiritual minutiae, deciphering them, organizing them—but she feels the connection deep within her. It's rooted now in her DNA, complex and interwoven with the afterlife, like fluency in a new language.

Things begin happening then, momentarily pushing the visions from Boo's mind.

## 2.

Bringing up the rear, his assault rifle cradled across his chest, Hack freezes the moment he sees Spur's arm jerk up, palm open, forcing everybody to pause.

The faint, muffled sound of footsteps has broken the stillness of the building. Is it Osamir? A henchman left behind? The noises seem to be coming from somewhere on the top floor, behind a door, down a hallway. Then they cease. The silence is a vise grip squeezing Hack's skull. He feels a strange sensation percolating down through his spine—a hot, tingling vibration in his vertebrae—which somehow, in some innate way, directs his attention to the carpeted step on which he stands.

He kneels, and lays a hand on the fibers of the carpet. His fingertips are now a stethoscope. The heartbeat of the fortress pounds a drumbeat up his ulnar nerve, into his brachial plexus, and from there up his spinal cord to his cerebellum. The rhythm of air conditioners circulating stale, filtered air registers, then the buzz of fluorescent tubes, the hum of computers, the whir of hard drives, the sizzle of surveillance monitors, and the very pulse of electricity coursing through the fortress.

Hack closes his eyes.

An invisible inner world opens up in Hack's head that he barely could have imagined back as an intern at his father's dusty little accounting firm on Mulberry Street, wasting his time in the back office writing code for new stock-trading apps. Back then, before Hack had become Hack, before the grueling years of basic training, before specialist school, before Spur had yanked him out of SEAL Team 3 to be the fifth member of the ghost unit, Hack was known as Aaron Boorstein, just another kid from the neighborhood throwing away the romance and adventure of accounting for a life in the military. But now for the first time since he became a phantom warrior for Spur, an entirely new world flows into him, from the contact point of his fingertips on that carpet.

His brain fills with wire-frame diagrams crisscrossing the bones of the fortress, glistening like liquid metal threads; ultrasonic, infrared, trip wires wending through the air, connecting alarms, booby traps; radiant fibers of light weaving under floors, across doorways, running behind ceilings; ultraviolet, invisible to the naked eye, radio waves armed and waiting to detect any careless trespassers who happen into Osamir's slimy kingdom. Somewhere in the far corners of his overloading mind, he scans for evidence of a nuclear program and sees nothing of the sort.

In the meantime, near the apex of the staircase, Spur has made a series of silent gestures with his hand, urging the team to spread out. Then, with the clench of a fist, he starts up the remaining few steps, the others following him. Hack opens his eyes, sees the team moving, and in a loud stage whisper hisses, "Wait! *Stop!*"

In his mind's eye, Hack sees a luminous crimson filament, ankle high, crossing the threshold of the landing at the top of the stairs.

Spur pauses inches away from it and whispers, "Talk to me, Hack."

"About a foot in front of you," he whispers. "Six inches off the floor. Infrared trip line. If you'll be so kind as to wait for me, I'll flag it."

"Roger that."

Hack hurries up the steps, lifts one foot over the invisible thread of light, and straddles it. "Okay . . . very important, everybody. It's between my legs. Step over it one at a time."

"That's what *she* said," Pin-Up mutters to herself as she and the others do as they're told. One at a time. Each stepping over the trip line. As they do this, Hack hears the muffled footsteps again. Farther away now. Something squeaking in a far-flung room.

"Okay, let's spread out," Spur says.

"Wait." Hack steps over the infrared strand. "If I may . . . hold on a second." He looks up at a small camera mounted at the corner of an archway. He walks over to the wall, touching his fingertips to a light switch. Instantly the shimmering map of the surveillance network inside the fortress materializes in his mind's eye. Hack looks up at Spur and says, "It's your pal and mine, our friendly neighborhood pilot and snitch, Captain Ed Deegan. At the moment he's trying to squeeze his fat ass through an open window. Southeast corner. This level." Spur starts down the hallway when Hack grabs his arm. "He's packing, Spur. An Uzi. Machine pistol. With an extended clip. And if I may be so bold as to make a suggestion?"

Spur tells him he's listening.

# 3.

Seventy-five feet above the scabrous ground, Captain Ed Deegan climbs out the window and steps onto a windswept precipice. The retired fifty-eight-year-old career soldier pauses with one foot on the outer ledge and the other on the windowsill in order to allow the dizziness to pass. His camo pants flap in the wind, his body armor wet under his pits. The air smells of burning tar and mildew. His deeply lined face glistens with sweat. Mountain-climbing rope hangs coiled to his belt, festooned with carabiners. The Uzi dangles off his sore shoulder as he winces at the fiery pangs of agony in his joints—a progressive case of rheumatoid arthritis that's been plaguing him for years—making him wonder who the hell he thinks he is, Spider-Man? Trying to climb down this filthy stone exterior wall at *his* age?

He swallows the panic, and oddly, doesn't even think of getting caught by the SEALs.

Only moments ago he had heard the firefight rattling the sublevel, followed by the purposeful sound of the SEALs coming, their footsteps swift, stealthy, and menacing as they climbed through the levels of the empty fortress. But what Ed Deegan dreads the most right now is not getting captured, humiliated, and probably tortured by his fellow soldiers. Nor is he scared of going to prison, spending the rest of his days in a box at Leavenworth. No, it's none of those things that he dreads the most. What the aging pilot is most afraid of is ending up back in the States, visiting the grave of his late wife, Brenda, after this whole shit show plays out.

Deegan shakes the thought from his mind, and hurriedly anchors the carabiner to a ceiling joist next to the window.

He lowers himself over the ledge and feels the hot wind like a blast furnace on the back of his neck. His joints shrieking in pain, he inches his way downward, letting out a little bit of rope at a time, past the marble gargoyles and antiaircraft turrets, past the gaudy mosaics of Karakistani religious figures embedded in the exterior wall next to complex arrays of surveillance cameras. The toes of his combat boots scuff and scrape all the way down. His knees buckle and grind as though filled with broken glass. He ignores the pain and keeps going, the desert heat scourging him as he descends.

Halfway down, still two stories above ground level, he hears a telltale noise coming from below—a cocking lever on an AK-47, a metallic clunk he recognizes all too well. He tenses. Sucks in a breath. Glances over his shoulder and sees the operative known as Hack directly beneath him, thirty-five feet away, kneeling . . . aiming the blunt muzzle of the AK up at him.

The blast sends a series of five rounds across the wall a centimeter away from the side of Deegan's face, one of the projectiles slicing through the Uzi's strap. The machine pistol slips off his shoulder, plunging to the ground, breaking into two pieces on impact. A voice rings out from the open window above him.

"C'mon, Ed." Spur's Texas twang is unmistakable. His chiseled face appears above Deegan, craning out the window in order to make eye contact with the traitor. "Whattya doing? You're no cat burglar."

With very little forethought, acting mostly on instinct, Deegan pushes himself off the wall with every last shred of strength he can muster. He plummets and lands directly on Hack. The impact drives Hack to the ground, and triggers a wild burst of gunfire from the AK, which strafes the stone wall, sending shards of expensive Pakistani marble in every direction.

Deegan tumbles and rolls, eating a mouthful of dust, but somehow manages to hop back to his feet with a burst of adrenaline and energy that he hasn't exhibited since his days back in the Seventy-Fifth Ranger Regiment.

"For Chrissake, what is he doing?" Spur gripes from his vantage point. "Where the hell is he gonna run to?"

Spur pulls himself back inside the window, and heads toward the nearest staircase.

## CHAPTER SEVEN
# Death Rattle

### 1.

They chase the hobbling arthritic pilot down the rocky slope bordering Osamir's fortress . . . over a footbridge spanning the brackish water of a medieval-style moat . . . across several hundred yards of sun-bleached barrens that could pass for the surface of the moon . . . and into a tiny warren of ramshackle toolsheds, broken-down chicken coops, and decaying horse stables. Apparently, at one time—perhaps decades earlier when the Karakistani royal family was still in power—this tawdry little conglomeration of buildings housed the maintenance crew and grooms that served the wealthy landowners.

Now the ghost unit corners Deegan in a narrow passageway between two buildings, and they drag him into the ruins of a horse barn.

At the end of a row of fetid, rotting stalls—each one featuring the desiccated remains of a dead horse—narrow beams of harsh Karakistani sun cant down through cracks in the barn siding. Dust motes swim in the rays of yellow light. A shopworn wheelbarrow lies on its side, furry with dust. An old wrought-iron chair is shoved against the wall, a pile of ancient leather tack on the seat.

They sit the pilot down on a moldy patch of hay, and let him catch his breath. "S-so much m-money," he stammers, trying to breathe. "Any one of you w-w-w-would have taken it."

"Interesting theory," Spur says, standing over the hyperventilating pilot. "I'll tell you one thing, you're damn spry for an old man. Running all this way without stroking out? Pretty goddamn impressive." The other four members of the team stand on either side of Deegan, regarding him as they would an injured, rabid dog.

"Just . . . get it over with," Deegan says at last with a weary, pained sigh.

Ticker speaks up. "Get *what* over with? You obviously have

a preconceived notion as to what we have planned for you. Why don't you let us in on it so we don't disappoint you."

"You're gonna kill my ass after you torture me and I don't blame you. I'll save you some time. I don't know anything. So go ahead and get it over with."

Spur digs in his pocket, pulls out a handkerchief, and tosses it to the man. "Relax, Captain. We're gonna have a little powwow instead. Have a seat."

Hack and Ticker step in, lift the traitor up, and drag him over to the chair. They shove the tack off the seat and drop him hard, Deegan wincing with pain, his hound-dog eyes filling up with regret, maybe even a little fear. "Real sorry it ended up this way, folks."

"You can make it up to us," Spur says.

"How do I do that?"

"By passing along some information."

Deegan shrugs. "I just fly the bird, I'm not in the inner circle of anything."

"You've been working counterintelligence out of the Sixty-Sixth Support Brigade. First Battalion, right?"

Deegan looks up, blood still smeared on his lip. "How did you—?"

"Never mind how I knew. I was in the Sixty-Sixth for three years—Delta Force—so don't piss on me and tell me it's raining."

"Like I said, brother, I just . . . I shuttle folks to and fro. Once in a while, an opportunity presents itself for me to make a few bucks on the side."

Spur feels anger smoldering in his belly. He can feel the same tension building among the other members of the unit, all of them looking on, watching through the dust motes and mildew, burning their gazes into the weathered old pilot slumped in the chair, his dreams of finally buying his yacht and living the high life shattered. "I'm not your brother," Spur says to him now. "I'm not your buddy, I'm not your bro, or your dude, or your pal, or your friend. I'm the guy that's gonna get information from you. Do you read me? *Brother?*"

Deegan just nods a weary nod.

Spur glowers at him. "Does Osamir have nukes?"

"How the hell would I know?"

"Where is he?"

Deegan shrugs. "I have no earthly idea."

"One more time." Spur's unwavering gaze holds Deegan like an insect pinned to a board. "Where did Abu Osamir go?"

"I told you, I have no clue."

"Let's try something else. Have you seen or heard, or are you aware of, any past, present, or future evidence of a nuclear program being developed by Osamir?"

Again Deegan shrugs. "Anything's possible."

"That's not an answer."

"I'm just saying I can't give you any specifics because I'm just—"

"I know, I get it." Spur grinds his teeth. "You're just a simple country pilot."

Deegan stares up at him. "Whattya want me to say?"

Spur ignores the question, the rage beginning to burn in his guts, beginning to spread through him with the insatiable force of a wildfire. In fact, at the moment, Spur doesn't even notice that the anger building in him is unlike anything he's ever felt in his life. It's a living, breathing thing inside him, visceral, malignant. He begins to lose track of what he's doing. He sees Deegan's face changing subtly into a garish, painted visage of a carnival clown leering and laughing at him. Through clenched teeth, Spur practically snarls at Deegan, "So you're saying there's no talk of underground labs . . . or . . . mobile reactor facilities on train cars . . . or . . . or rumors of acquiring yellow cake, or uranium-235, or plutonium-238, or . . . or . . . neutron-tube production . . . or . . . evidence of long-range missile research . . . or any fucking thing that could remotely be construed as evidence that this dickweed wants to fuck with the rest of the goddamn world!"

The clown face just shakes its head back and forth with very little emotion.

*"Where the fuck is Osamir?!"*

Deegan gives another shrug, and the parasitic wrath growing within Spur erupts, and he is lurching toward the pilot, making a fist with one hand, grabbing the man by the neck with the other, and drawing back his muscular arm for a single death punch that will surely kill the man instantly, when all at once Spur hears a familiar voice call out.

*"Spur no!"*

A feminine hand clutching at Spur's shoulder slams the breaks on the runaway locomotive of Spur's anger, and he pulls the punch.

Whirling around, he sees Pin-Up standing behind him with an urgent expression tightening her dark, exquisite features.

## 2.

Pin-Up locks gazes with Spur, his stare so intense it feels as though he's staring through the back of her skull. The others sense it as well, the silence pressing down among them as oppressive and thick as a fog. Something horrifying and inexplicable is happening to each and every one of them, and Pin-Up can feel it fomenting inside her at this very moment—a transformation she doesn't understand, didn't ask for, doesn't want, and is finding repulsive, like the onslaught of a horrible neurological disease.

It started a few minutes ago as she watched the interrogation of Captain Ed Deegan. With each frustrating nonanswer, each arrogant shrug, Pin-Up found herself hating the man more and more. She felt herself fantasizing about hurting him, poking a weak spot, wounding him permanently. And that's when the shift came.

The sensation is like being dipped in a noxious chemical bath, the invisible substance starting at her feet, rising up her ankles, climbing her legs, and enveloping her upper body in its oily, resinous, catalytic fumes. Finally, as it washes up across her face she realizes the feeling is coming from *Deegan*. It's almost as though a broadcast signal has begun to emanate from the traitorous pilot, and Pin-Up, somehow, miraculously, maddeningly, is absorbing it with her satellite dish of a brain. She feels a shift within her then, two seismic plates sliding over each other, driven by the signal from Deegan's head, cloaking Pin-Up in a new persona.

When she absently glances down at her hands she jerks back with a start. Her natural hands had once been creamy specimens, perfectly shaped, with tapered fingertips and flawless skin, an asset that had landed her more than a few hand-modeling gigs early in her screen career. But now, her hands have transformed into the wrinkled, reddened, dishwater-rough hands of a worn-out pilot's wife, the late Brenda Deegan.

"As much as I'd love to see you deck this disgusting prick," Pin-Up says now in the voice of a haggard wife, "I think I can get him to talk." Smoky, bourbon-cured, the voice is that of a woman scorned, a woman beaten, a woman cheated upon.

The sudden awe in Spur's eyes tells Pin-Up everything she needs to know about what's happening. She needs no mirror to see that her perfect café au lait complexion has paled and gone ashen. She requires no reflection to understand that her high cheekbones have fallen, her eyes fading from a deep chocolate brown to a colorless grey, like the sky right before the rain comes. Her features have sunken into deep creases, crow's-feet and worry lines.

Meet Brenda Allison Deegan, born 1959, died 2013. The woman's ghost walks over to her former husband, and looks down at him.

From his chair, Deegan seems to be looking up at her but not exactly seeing her yet. His face has gone blank, perhaps because it's taking awhile for his brain to process what his optic nerve is sending to it. His mouth moves but no words come out.

"Oh, Ed," Pin-Up says to him. Brenda Deegan's distinctive, husky voice is filled with remorse and sadness. Her face is drawn and beleaguered. But her eyes—her rainwater-grey eyes—grip Ed Deegan with the righteous, unwavering gaze of an ancient Hebrew judge. "What have you gone and gotten yourself mixed up in now?"

The change in the pilot's face begins with a welling up of those hound-dog eyes, the tears brimming over and tracking down his grizzled features. His mouth is still moving, but not a single word has come out since Pin-Up transformed.

Then the man's face collapses. All the years of cheating on his wife, manhandling her, blaming her for all his shortcomings, treating her like garbage even as she succumbed to breast cancer . . . all of it destroys his face until he's sobbing as he looks up at her. "I'm so s-s-sorry, honey," he murmurs.

"You might as well tell them what they need to know, Ed," she says. "Tell them where Osamir is. It'll be good for your soul."

"He's . . . He's . . . He's . . . ." The man begins to speak but something clamps down on his voice. His hands reach up to his neck, something invisible strangling his voice, cutting off his air, suffocating him.

Right then the shrill voice of Boo rings out from across the stable. "He's having a coronary," she warns. "He's dying."

Ticker reaches down to the pilot, feeling his pulse. "Hack, gimme a hand with this." The two operatives gently lower Deegan to the moldy carpet of hay, and loosen the collar under his Kevlar vest. The man is gasping now, his watery gaze still locked on to Pin-Up, who hovers wraithlike over him. "He's . . . he's—"

Defaulting to her instincts as a nurse, Pin-Up kneels and tries

CPR. The others look on. Deegan has gone limp. Pin-Up palpates, breathes into the pilot's mouth, palpates again. Deegan shudders, lets out a halting breath. His mouth moves again.

Pin-Up leans down, her ear to the man's lips. Faint words come out of Deegan . . .

. . . and then, a moment later, a death rattle, and the pilot is gone.

## 3.

The heliport platform sits high above the grounds of the fortress, baking in the brutal Karakistani sun, heat waves radiating off the deck like phantom gauze in the blazing winds. They find the Black Hawk where Deegan left it, sitting between a small, single-seat reconnaissance chopper and a larger Apache Long-bow equipped with .50-caliber outboard machine guns. The Apache looks like it just came from the showroom floor, which once again makes Spur marvel at the magnitude and extent of Osamir's private army . . . an army financed by . . . whom? Satan? Spur still finds himself ruminating on the implications of the day's events, questioning whether any of it is real.

The five operatives pile into the Black Hawk, and Ticker climbs behind the stick. With hundreds of flight hours in both fixed-wing and rotary-wing aircraft, as well as a year and half as a naval aviator hauling SEALs off aircraft carriers in the Persian Gulf, Ticker, the Renaissance man of special ops, can pilot just about anything with a wing or a blade.

Spur takes his place in the shotgun seat and uses Deegan's cell phone to plot a course to Osamir's hideout. The last word uttered by Ed Deegan in his death throes sounded at first like *Pah-tha-la*. Or perhaps *Pachala*. Spur hastily scrawled the word on the dusty ground of the stable, and then, minutes later, with a ballpoint pen from Deegan's pocket, wrote it on a scrap of paper. But now a quick online search shows that the only logical place on the map is a tiny hamlet called Patala in the Tartarus mountain range a hundred kilometers (or about sixty miles) to the north.

Hack, Pin-Up, and Boo strap themselves into the jump seats in the main cabin.

They've brought along three large road cases packed with arms and equipment taken from Osamir's arsenal—enough ord-nance and provisions to launch an incursion on a small country. They have ten assault rifles, twenty cartons of 7.62-millimeter subsonic ammo, a dozen high-capacity magazines, five PBS-1 silencers, two .50-caliber machine guns, three Glock 19 side-arms with laser sighting devices, a Mossberg 500 pump-action shotgun with extra shells, two dozen M67 grenades, an RPG mini-cannon, night-vision goggles, MRE field rations, headset radios, and kit bags for each member of the unit. The mission parameters are now unknown. The duration of the mission is unknown. The environment of the target area is unknown. The fortifications and number of hostiles guarding Osamir are all unknowns.

But Spur realizes—as he secures his shoulder straps and switches on his headset—that the greatest unknowns are the implications of what transpired earlier that day in that subterranean prison cell. The further Spur retreats in time and space from those events, the more unreal, illusory, and dreamlike they become. Had the bizarre developments in the torture chamber all been a series of collective hallucinations? Had he and his fellow operatives been gassed or poisoned down there?

All his life Spur has heard urban folktales of petite little moms emerging from a car crash to lift two tons of wreckage off their kids. Or how about the old axiom that we use only ten percent of our brains? But still . . . those well-trod adages don't begin to explain how Hack would be able to see invisible trip lines. Or how Pin-Up could manage to shape-shift into the ghost of a woman she has never met, a woman so powerful and terrifying to Ed Deegan that she literally scared him to death.

*And yet:* Underneath all this speculation is a feeling far more vexing and disturbing than mere skepticism over the burgeoning superpowers revealing themselves among his colleagues. Raised in the Baptist traditions of the South, a churchgoer to this day, Spur has always believed in the Christian concept of God and Satan. He has always accepted the idea that the devil is a fallen angel, a supernatural being expelled from heaven for being unclean. From early childhood, Spur went along with the old myths that the devil is the serpent in the Garden of Eden, the dragon in the book of Revelation, the accuser of Job, the tempter of the gospels, the Prince of Darkness. And now . . . somehow . . . for reasons so opaque and complex they're making his head spin, he has come face-to-face with the real thing and has made a deal with it. And now, like Faust, he is, to put it bluntly, royally fucked. If he refuses to believe it, he's lost . . . adrift . . . vulnerable. If he believes it, he has to face the fact that he works for the devil now. There are no good options here.

He flips on his headset mike, and is about to say something to his people when he abruptly stops. Becomes very still. Blinks.

The idea strikes him out of nowhere. It hits him down the center of the bridge of his nose with the force of a sledgehammer. So simple. So elegant. So perfect. He presses the SEND button and says, "Buckle up, folks . . . when we're airborne I'm coming back to have a little visit with y'all."

Ticker fires up the engines, and the bird lifts off the hot concrete, lurching upward into a blast furnace of wind that would not be out of place in the burning pits of hell.

# PART II

# PART II

## DARK MATTER

Light thinks it travels faster than anything but it is wrong. No matter how fast light travels it finds the darkness has always got there first, and is waiting for it.

—Terry Pratchett

## CHAPTER EIGHT

# Act as If Ye Have Faith

## 1.

"It's like we're infected, like we've all caught this horrible fucking virus."

Pin-Up sits on one of Black Hawk's jump seats—midcabin—as the chopper climbs into the upper altitudes, bumping over turbulent air. She has to practically yell to be heard over the roar of the wind and the howling of the rotors.

"Pin, look—" Spur starts to say from the other side of the cabin, strapped into an opposing jump seat, wanting to offer an alternative way of looking at the situation, when he notices the dread burning in Pin-Up's gaze like a smoldering ember.

"I want out," she says. "It's disgusting, and I don't want to have anything to do with it. These aren't fucking superpowers, they're a disease, and this . . . this *thing* in the dungeon, this mass hallucination, magician, con man, whatever it is . . . *it isn't Satan*. This isn't the fucking Middle Ages. There's no such thing as a Faustian pact. All that Old Testament crap is just a fable, it's just mythology, invented by humans, written by . . . I don't know . . . Babylonian storytellers, Hebrew scholars, whatever . . . I don't care. I know I prayed to God down there in that dungeon when I thought I was a goner, I'm not ashamed of it. I was tormented by Catholicism when I was little, okay. But now, I don't need this shit."

An awkward pause ensues.

Visible through the aft windscreen is a narrow slice of landscape rushing under them. Primordial. Desolate. Ancient granite crevasses and jagged gullies cleaving the barrens like open wounds. Dry riverbeds branching in all directions with the haphazard serpentines of desiccated capillaries. This is ancient land, harsh, lawless, and hellish.

After a long moment, Boo speaks up from an adjacent seat. "Did it hurt?"

Pin-Up looks at her. "Did *what* hurt?"

"You know . . . when we were sweating Deegan . . . and you . . . you *changed*."

Pin-Up shrugs. "It was fucking creepy, I can tell you that much. I wanted to take a shower afterward. Plus I had no control over it. It was like a spell coming over me . . . or . . . or a seizure . . . or *whatever*. I sort of knew what I had to do but it was fucking sick."

After another pause, Spur says, "Can we at least run down all the points of consensus?" He restlessly taps the steel toe of his field boot against the Black Hawk's metal floor grid while the others think it over, choking down their field rations, grudgingly chewing mouthfuls of Navy-issue Spam and papery dried peaches. Veteran Special Forces operatives know to eat whenever they can because they rarely get the chance. They bivouac and sleep whenever the opportunity arises, which is rarely. In the field, Spur has gone a week with only a few hours of shut-eye and nothing but water and wormy crab apples . . . and maybe even a few of those worms for good measure.

"Good idea," Hack says then. "Can we all agree that something weird has happened to all of us? Call it 'paranormal' for lack of a better term?"

Nobody objects.

"So if we all accept that part, then you have to accept that these powers . . . or whatever you want to call them . . . they're real. They're not a trick. They're not just in our imagination."

"Okay, wait a second—"

"Pin-Up, with all due respect, let me finish." He takes a deep breath, and parses his words. "Look. I'm no expert in the metaphysical. Okay? I know bupkes about Christianity, and God, and the devil." He looks at Spur. "I'm with Pin-Up when it comes to being agnostic." Then he looks at Pin-Up. "But I know what I saw back there, Pin. I know what I felt. I felt my brain link up with an entire electrical system just by brushing my fingers across the carpet in that McMansion of Osamir's. What I'm saying is, being agnostic doesn't mean you don't believe in anything . . . it just means you don't know for sure."

Pin-Up lets out a sigh, and then says to Spur, "What about you? Have you felt anything like a superpower brewing in you?—If I'm not being too personal?"

Spur takes a deep breath. "I'll be honest with ya. I'm guessing here. But when I was a kid, I could break and saddle and ride any horse on my uncle's ranch. That ain't the reason I got the code name Spur though. I got it 'cause I could get folks to fight their asses off in the field of battle. Not through fear, not through intimidation. I just figure out what drives a person, and I reflect it back at them. That's how I spur them on. Now, down in that dungeon, when I turned that pirate fella's AK back onto him, it came to me like it was almost involuntary. I turned that dickwad's anger—his viciousness—literally back in his face. I guess the key here is what we do with these powers. In other words, how do we poke the devil in the eye with them?"

From the far end of the cabin, Boo speaks up. "Is that the priority now? Fighting the devil?"

"Yes, ma'am, I think it is. Maybe it always was, you know what I mean?"

Boo looks at the floor. The little Asian woman gives off an air of fragility, as though her pale skin and tiny features are made of porcelain, but her looks are deceiving. She can slip through the tightest cordons. She can shadow the most dangerous targets. She has seventeen modes of assassination, and they're each silent, sudden, and lethal. "Let's say we all agree that this . . . this thing that appeared to us down there . . . let's say it's actually supernatural. You can call it Satan. Or as my father would call it, the mogwai." She looks up at Spur. "In China there's really no Prince of Darkness ruling the underworld, no horns, no tail, not like in your culture. There's only this vengeful demon, looks like an old man who crawled out of the grave. Long beard, grey skin and bones, eyes gone, just bone-white holes where his eyes should be. But I digress. Let's say this thing is real supernatural evil. And we've made a deal with it. Let's add that to the pot."

Spur nods. "Okay . . . I'm with ya, go on."

She smirks. "I've dealt with a lot of different enemies over the years. So many targets, I can't even count them. I get sent a dossier, and I go wherever I have to go to find the target and take them out. Some of them I live with in my dreams. There was that doctor in Iran. That family in Lebanon, the lady scientist in Moscow. Did these people deserve to die? Maybe. Or maybe I'm going to be on an express elevator to hell when I die. Maybe all this is a foregone conclusion. Maybe I've already made a deal with the devil years ago and wasn't even aware of it. But while I'm still drawing a breath I cannot see how we can win. If this is true supernatural evil, how can a bunch of dog soldiers fight back? Superpowers or no superpowers. You see what I'm saying? You cannot fight City Hall."

Her words seem to hang in the droning noise of the cabin as the Black Hawk climbs farther up the craggy wilderness of the Tartarus range. Spur keeps noticing out of the corner of his eye, through the aft window, the jagged terrain passing under them like images from a dream. Prehistoric glaciers slicing into deep gorges of ashy granite, patches of subalpine meadows burned clean of vegetation from the unremitting wind and sun—all of it bringing to mind the hallucinations of that terrible hellscape conjured in the pits of the torture chamber. It seems those events in the dungeon happened years ago, despite the fact that they transpired only that morning. Spur feels as though the memory of the way things were before the bargain is fading with each passing minute. He realizes that no matter what happens, they can never go back. They can never be like they were before the events in the torture chamber.

He feels the implacable gaze of Boo on the side of his face like a laser, and he glances over at the diminutive assassin. "When we were on the stairs back at the fortress," he says, "you saw something. You got something going on in that big brain of yours."

She nods and looks at the floor. "If you're wondering what my superpower is, your guess is as good as mine." She looks up at him. "I saw ghosts. In the ceiling. In the woodwork. Not exactly a superpower but if I were to venture a guess I would say my new skill is not exactly making balloon animals and baking cookies for my Girl Scout troop. I'm sure it's like everything else in my life—on intimate terms with the Grim Reaper." She shrugs. "But hey, that's show business, right?"

"There's an old saying from my Baptist upbringing." Spur speaks now to the group as a whole. "I don't remember if it's in the Bible or on some bumper sticker I saw on the back of some goddamn pickup. But anyway, it resonates, and it's what I think might save us. 'Act as if ye have faith and faith shall be given to you.' What I'm saying is, if we choose to believe in these superpowers, we can use them against the devil. The trick is owning them, believing in them."

Boo looks at him. "Using them for good is what you're saying?"

"Precisely."

"But if we do that, it seems to me the devil will just take the powers away."

Across the cabin, Hack is nodding, staring off into the imaginary distance, murmuring, "In perpetuity."

"What's that?"

Hack looks up. "The contract, the deal we have with this *schmendrick*."

"Yeah go on."

"He said it was in perpetuity."

Spur gets it now. "Sweet Jesus on buttered toast, you're right."

Pin-Up furrows her brow. "I'm sorry, you lost me with there's an old Baptist saying."

Boo is slowly nodding, her eyes blazing with recognition. "He said everything he does is *in perpetuity*."

Spur reaches for his headset, puts it on, and taps the mike. "Ticker, you getting all this? You hearing this up there?"

## 2.

From the cockpit, the grey mountainous landscape pouring under the Black Hawk's metal belly, Ticker swings his headset mike up to his lips. "Every word," he says, raising his voice over the metallic drone of the rotors. "Hack, I think you cracked something wide open here. I'm no lawyer but I believe 'in perpetuity' means 'permanently.'"

"Damn straight it does," Spur's voice crackles in Ticker's ear. "The legal definition if I'm not mistaken is something like 'unending and perpetual.'"

Ticker keeps nodding. "By his own admission he can't take them away. These powers—whatever they are—they're locked. Forever. For all time."

Spur's voice says, "Therefore we can use them against him."

"Do good with them."

"Hell yes."

Ticker starts to say something else when the bird lurches suddenly. He grips the stick and pulls back, the nose refusing to rise, the engines howling, the entire helicopter pitching forward as though a massive weight has begun to tug on the fore section.

Flipping switches, toggling the throttle, Ticker can hear the others tumbling to the floor in the rear of the cabin.

"Ticker!" Spur's voice sizzles, taut with alarm. "What's going on?! Talk to me!"

"I don't know! Hold on!" Ticker hollers into the mike over the shrieking of the engines as the massive bird struggles to raise its nose back up. "Trying to avoid going into a dive!"

The voice in his headset booms: "*What in the flying fuck is going on?!*"

"Not sure, it's feels like—"

Ticker freezes in his seat, the words sticking in his throat, as he sees huge, needlelike claws the color of hot tar appearing from beneath the Black Hawk's nose. "It's a . . . it looks like a . . . it's a . . ."

His voice is drowned by the grinding, keening, metal-on-metal shriek of the engines as the ice-pick claws reveal themselves to be connected to huge ursine paws, with articulated fingers that lift the rest of its massive girth up and over the top edge of the fore section. Then, three distinct and terrible heads come into view in the violent winds.

On the left, the head of a massive cobra opens its enormous jaws, its scaly yellow-striped head bobbing menacingly, its poisonous fangs the size of tusks. On the right, the deformed cranium of a mangy rabid dog snarls furiously, its yellow eyes rolling back with obscene hunger, its drool flagging in the gusts. The Black Hawk goes into a dive.

Somewhere in the depths of Ticker's memory, an image of the African demon djakata lies partially formed from his childhood imagination, fueled by fairy tales that his Nigerian grandfather used to tell him . . . and now the third and most horrific head from those fairy tales rises up from the middle of this mutant demon: a humanoid nightmare in three dimensions, cadaverous and black as mold, with a huge repulsive mouth full of piranha-like teeth and eyes the size of ostrich eggs.

It's as real as the metal rivets outside the Black Hawk's curvilinear windshield, and now it locks its mesmerizing gaze on to Ticker. The three demonic heads begin to laugh and chortle and guffaw in unison as Ticker wrestles the stick. "*La yumkinuk hazimatay,*" the human-shaped head snarls at Ticker, and somewhere in the back of his panic-stricken mind the translation of the words registers as "You cannot defeat me." And in that single spark of a synapse in his brain, Ticker hears a voice answering the monster. "*Try us, motherfucker . . . we'll send you back to the center of the earth where you fucking belong.*"

The aircraft careens and rolls through the fierce alpine winds. The ground is coming up fast. Ticker can see it in high definition below the edge of the windshield. Five hundred feet and closing. His ass levitating out of his seat now. Three hundred feet . . . two hundred and fifty feet. The altimeter spinning wildly. Two hundred feet . . . the laughter melding with the yowling winds and ululating engines . . . one hundred and fifty feet . . . one hundred feet . . . seventy-five feet . . .

. . . and the creature vanishes.

## 3.

Ticker yanks the stick as hard as he can, his breath knocked out of his lungs from the demon's shocking disappearance. The aircraft groans and bucks as it soars upward at the last possible moment, the g-forces pressing Ticker deeper into his seat cushion.

"Everybody in one piece back there?" he inquires after getting his bearings and leveling the aircraft.

Through the earpiece comes Spur's country patois: "We're about as shaken up as farts in a fan factory but we'll live. What in tarnation happened?"

Ticker's voice goes somber. "He was listening to every word we said."

After a pause, Spur's voice says, "Gonna have to do something about that."

## 4.

They land on a high plateau in a remote area of the Tartarus Mountains, the rotor kicking up a sirocco of dust. One by one they hop out. Heavily armed, covered in camo and body armor, headsets on, helmets secured, Oakley aviator shades across their eyes, they take no chances and keep the safeties off. They can't afford to infiltrate the area in the guise of regular folks, posing as tourists in street clothes as they have in the past. Not this time. Too many nooks and crannies for a sniper to position himself in. Plus, the higher elevations surrounding the area make the team members vulnerable to ambush. Their cover story today is that they are private contractors charged with policing and building infrastructure in the northern provinces of the country.

The village of Patala is visible in the distance, maybe half a kilometer away, hugging the side of a mountain like a cluster of barnacles clinging to an ancient ship. Mud shacks the color of tobacco sit on terraced levels all the way up a steep slope of subalpine scrub and emaciated trees. Terra-cotta rooftops line the main dirt road that snakes haphazardly through the middle of the village as though it were laid by drunks with vertigo. Spur estimates a population of a couple of hundred sturdy, clannish mountain people.

But the unknowns are burning a hole in Spur's gut as the team sets out on foot toward the hamlet: What percentage of those two hundred salt-of-the-earth hill people are hostiles? What portion of them are sheltering and protecting the warlord Osamir? The land is tribal, rough, and unforgiving, and it also makes for an arduous hike.

By the time they reach the outer rungs of the village, the sun has vanished behind a wall of storm clouds obscuring the craggy peaks of the Tartarus range. In the grey half-light of dusk, they come upon an old man in a filthy white robe and a New York Yankees baseball cap. Ticker politely questions the man in the local dialect, and the man answers with a barrage of glottal syllables that sound mostly like gibberish to Spur.

"He says something's going on at the schoolhouse." Ticker whispers this to Spur, which causes the team to exchange a series of glances. These are not exactly looks of concern or worry. During a mission the ghost unit does not have the luxury of getting worried about anything. They simply focus deeper at the first sign of trouble, affecting a Zen-like calm. All of which is happening right now as Ticker asks the old man to elaborate.

"He says somebody's pulled a school bus up to the building."

Spur purses his lips thoughtfully. "Ask him if this is unusual."

Ticker poses the question, and the old man answers with another salvo of words. Ticker frowns. "He says the bus is from somewhere else, none of the children in Patala need such a thing . . . they all live within a stone's throw of the place."

"Thank the man," Spur says, and then turns to the others. "Hack, go boost us a vehicle, biggest and fastest you can find. Pin-Up, you approach the school from the east side of the village, stay in close contact. Boo, you head up there from the west. Watch your backgrounds. Ticker and I will go up through the center of town, and try to find out whatever we can. I don't want a bloodbath so ask questions first, shoot later."

They spread out, and start up the slope toward the one-room schoolhouse.

## 5.

Spur and Ticker find a couple of young boys playing backgammon on an old barrel outside a humble little café. The tin-roofed shack has sun-faded photos of Persian movie stars on the fly-specked windows, and signs for different brands of Turkish coffee, and for local tobaccos that are dried and sold loose on the premises.

Each of these two boys chews on a plug of chaw as they listen to Ticker question them in his formal Karakistani dialect, asking about Abu Osamir, and if the boys would have any idea where the warlord might stay when he's visiting. Spur studies the tawny, windburned faces as they chew and listen. When Ticker finishes, neither boy answers—probably out of fear of retribution—but one of them points.

Spur follows the direction of the young man's stained index finger and sees a large barnlike building about thirty meters down the road with boarded windows and a pitched roof with a phalanx of satellite dishes and antennae.

"Call me crazy," Spur mutters to Ticker. "But that looks suspiciously like a safe house."

Circling around behind the property, they discover the back door is unlocked.

Inside the building, the rooms are in disarray, floors littered with packing straps and ribbons of duct tape, clothing strewn willy-nilly, beds unmade, closets hastily plundered, and dresser drawers rifled and left open. In the front room, frayed cables stick out of the walls where computers and hard drives have been yanked from their moorings. The air smells of cumin, smoke, and stale body odors.

Spur looks around the front room. "Sure looks like somebody left in a hurry."

"Hold on," Ticker says. "Over there." He points to a ratty, shopworn sofa on the far side of the room, so old it slumps in the middle like a worn-out footbridge. "See it?"

"No I don't. What am I looking at?"

Ticker goes over and kneels in front of the couch where the corner of something metallic sticks out from under the runner. He pulls out a laptop. "Correct me if I'm wrong but this could be a treasure trove."

"Merry Christmas to us."

## 6.

"Shit-shit-shit-shit-*shit*," Pin-Up murmurs to herself, peering through the scope of her Remington 700 rifle, on her belly behind a grove of skeletal alder trees. Darkness is closing in, and the sky is hectic with lightning and roiling black clouds.

In the scope's narrow field of view she can see the ramshackle one-room schoolhouse maybe a hundred meters away, nestled in a modest little olive grove overlooking the weather-beaten tile rooftops of the village. With the bronze bell on its roof, its faded red paint, and its white picket fence, the building looks displaced in time, as though someone plucked it from the American West from about two centuries ago and flew it over here.

A battered, rust-pocked school bus sits in front of the building.

And what Pin-Up sees then through the scope makes her breath catch in her throat, her midsection clench, and her trigger finger tingle.

The situation is far worse than she imagined.

## CHAPTER NINE
# The Caesura

### 1.

"Hack, it's Pin-Up," she whispers into her mouthpiece. "You copy?"

"You don't have to yell," the voice with the Brooklyn edge crackles in her ear.

"I hope you got some wheels for us because we got a major situation developing here, and it's developing rapidly."

"I'm working on it, give me a chance already."

"Spur, you copying this?"

Spur's voice pops in her ear. "We can see the schoolhouse and the bus. What the hell are these jackals up to, Pin?"

"They're using little ones as human shields. I don't have a good shot. Repeat: I do not have a shot at the present time."

Through her scope she can see Abu Osamir in the waning light of dusk—a stout little man with a long beard dressed in khaki military garb, red beret, and riding boots—being ushered around the rear of the school bus by two of his thugs. Five middle-school-aged children surround the warlord, their tiny hands interlocked, their faces ashen and drawn, shuffling along with Osamir as he climbs onto the bus.

There are already a gaggle of children sitting mute and terrified inside the school bus, which idles softly, its driver also one of Osamir's bodyguards, preparing to depart any second.

A pearl of sweat drops into Pin-Up's eyes against the scope's cup. "Spur, please advise."

Spur's voice in all the earpieces: "Hack, what's the status with the wheels?"

The static on the other end buzzes with the grating roar of a truck engine, practically drowning Hack's voice: "On my way!"

"What's your ETA?"

"Like any second!—I got a visual on the schoolhouse!—Stop with the nudging!"

Pin-Up wipes the sweat from her face. Her eye pressed to the scope's cup, she has the back of the driver's skull in her crosshairs.

"I now have a clean shot on the driver," she says into the mouth-piece. "Spur, please advise now."

The bus door closes behind Osamir and his retinue, the air filling with the noise of gears grinding. The engine revving. Black exhaust belching from the tailpipe. The headlights flaring on as the behemoth begins to pull away from the school.

"Hold your fire." Spur's voice pops and sizzles in Pin-Up's ear-piece. "Everybody, fingers off the triggers, too many friendlies on the bus, too tight in there."

Pin-Up sees a run-down, rust-pocked old Willys Jeep Truck the color of mud careering around a corner a block east of the departing bus.

The Jeep's headlamps are off, the night rolling in, thunder rumbling overhead. Hack is behind the Jeep's wheel, his eyes blazing with laser-like concentration. The truck looks decades old and has tufts of hay and goat shit petrified on its quarter panels.

Pin-Up springs to her feet just as the Jeep skids to a halt on the hardpan.

Keeping low, staying behind the olive trees, Pin-Up descends the hill with her rifle cradled in the ready position as lightning creates a surreal flicker show out of her plunge down through foliage. Keeping tabs on the fleeing bus in her peripheral vision, she reaches the Jeep at the same moment Boo bursts out of a grove of lemon trees to the west.

Each woman climbs into the cab, taking a seat on the rear bench. Meanwhile, the bus has cleared the far crossroads, and has vanished around the corner in a thunderhead of dust, exhaust, and the flashing strobe light of the imminent downpour.

Spur climbs into the cab's shotgun seat, and straps himself in. *"Go, Hack, now!"*

Hack puts the pedal to the floor, and the Jeep howls as it lurches after the bus.

The Jeep fishtails around the crossroads—Pin-Up and Boo holding on for dear life—as Spur points out the yellow blur of the bus taking a sharp turn at the bottom of a hill about a hundred meters away. "I got him," Hack mutters, yanking the lever on the steering column, shifting the standard transmission into low as he plummets down the hill. "May I be so bold as to ask where the hell Ticker is?"

Before Spur gets a chance to answer, the first blast flashes out of the indigo shadows of the bus's rear window, the round strafing the corner of the Jeep's windshield, causing a spiderwebbing of cracks to spread across their line of vision.

## 2.

Ticker races toward the Black Hawk as fast as his legs will carry him, despite the handicaps of extra weight on his back, treacherous footing, encroaching darkness, and the storm starting to spit rain in his face. His body armor alone weighs over twenty pounds. Add to that his field garb, his weapons, his kit bag, his climbing gear, and he's carrying the equivalent of a full-grown teenager with an eating disorder on his back.

He can see the silhouette of the aircraft in the middle distance behind the veils of rain like a sleeping dinosaur. It sits maybe three hundred yards away, its main rotor reminiscent of the wings of a great beast frozen in time. In fact, as Ticker draws nearer and nearer to the Black Hawk, that notion of freezing time sparks in the folds of his brain.

He feels the infinitely complex clockwork of his budding superpower spreading within him, the invisible circuitry like an upgrade installing itself in the operating system of his body and soul. Even as he runs—pumping his arms with each powerful stride, his russet face beaded with rain and sweat—he can feel the tendrils of rewiring branching down through his central nervous system, connecting up with the space-time continuum as an application might link up with the digital cloud.

The truth is, Ticker does not yet possess the vocabulary to articulate what is happening to him and his colleagues in the unit. Ticker is a thinker, an intellectual, a scientist warrior, but he also believes in the empirical—those things that are verifiable by observation or experience rather than theory or pure logic. Newton saw the behavior of the apple, and built a theory with which to explain it. Ticker has already begun to do the same with the dark magic proffered upon them by the devil.

He reaches the aircraft.

It takes him around ninety seconds to board, strap himself behind the stick, get the engines humming, and start the rotors spinning. By the time the Black Hawk begins levitating off the ground, the rain has gone from light to heavy, from a vertical sprinkle to a horizontal, wind-driven, icy torrent that assaults the fuselage and bathes the windshield as Ticker throttles up and urges the chopper into the fray.

Almost immediately, visibility dwindles to less than three hundred meters. Full darkness has closed in, and Ticker can feel the headwind dragging on the bird's massive nose as he soars through the rain. The mountainous landscape has turned into a cathedral of black silhouettes, the great swaths of gorges and dry riverbeds turning to grey arteries snaking up the southern edge of the Tartarus range. The winding dirt roads now appear as delicate veins in a vast network of sheer cliffs and overgrown wilderness. The occasional smattering of lights reveals a remote village, streetlamps or fire pits burning in the storm. Ticker can smell the musty odors of carbon monoxide and woodsmoke wafting through the cockpit's corner vent.

A minute later he spots the Jeep and the school bus hurtling up a narrow asphalt highway into the higher elevations, each vehicle skidding dangerously around tight corners. The road looks perilous, the gravel shoulder on each side alternately skirting sheer cliffs and thousand-foot drops. Intermittent gunfire flashes from the rear of the bus, causing Hack to swerve and wrestle the Jeep around tight turns. Even from a height of three hundred meters, Ticker can see that nobody is returning fire from the Jeep, obviously concerned about collateral issues with the kids.

"Spur, you copy?" Ticker says into his mouthpiece, hearing nothing but static. "Spur, this is Uniform Hotel Lima . . . do you copy?"

Spur's voice is inaudible in the gusting static and rain. The storm has picked up. Great heaving squalls crash against the bird's windshield, threatening to throw the Black Hawk off course. Lightning strobes across the dark heavens like luminous electric eels slithering through the void.

Resisting the urge to ignite the massive tungsten searchlight mounted to the belly of the Black Hawk, Ticker descends to two hundred meters, and then down to a hundred and fifty, so close now he can see the heads of children bobbing and ducking down beneath the windows of the school bus, flinching at each blast of gunfire issuing out of the rear. The road is leading them into an ever more hazardous route across a treacherous divide.

"Spur! Anybody home?" Ticker wrestles with the stick, the wind gusting rain against the canopy. "Copy please!" Static hisses from the earpiece. "We got a problem! Spur, can you copy this already?"

Down on the ground, directly ahead of the fleeing bus, through the billowing rain, about five hundred meters away, the two-lane blacktop makes a sharp hairpin turn. About a hundred feet above the hairpin, not yet visible to the driver, a bridge has collapsed, the road washed out. The obstacle sits precariously between two deadly precipices, each giving way to a thousand-foot plunge into a craggy ravine and certain death.

Ticker can see that the bus will reach the death trap in less than thirty seconds.

Maybe it's the children in peril below him, or the burgeoning power within him, or simply the shock of seeing that washout in the flicker of lightning like a ghost, but right at that moment a random memory streaks across Ticker's mind as the Black Hawk slams through the storm a hundred meters above the doomed school bus.

## 3.

*"Sit up, Boy! Pay attention!" The stern, cranky, Italian piano teacher with her cat's-eye glasses and Sambuca breath slaps a ruler down on the boy's hand. "Read the music, and show me where is the pause! DO IT NOW!"*

*The ruler comes down again, hard, snapping across the boy's knuckles. Ticker remembers vividly wanting to cry but not being willing to give Old Lady Sabitini the satisfaction. He looks at the sheet music. It's a cantata by J. S. Bach—Jesu Joy of Man's Desiring—the little black notes swimming in the boy's watering eyes.*

*"Where is it, the caesura?!"*

*The boy points to a symbol at the far end of the staff—two parallel diagonal lines, commonly known among musicians as "railroad tracks"—and the ruler freezes above the boy's hand as though caught in a tableau, a snapshot, a moment in which time loses all meaning.*

*"Correct!" the old woman squawks with the brusqueness of an angry crow. "And what does it mean this symbol of the caesura?—explain to me!"*

*The boy mumbles.*

*The ruler. Poised. The piano teacher breathing out her horrible licorice breath. "I did not hear what you say! Again what does the caesura mean?!"*

*"Railroad tracks mean stop," the boy murmurs. "And then start again."*

Nearly three decades later, flying a multimillion-dollar Black Hawk helicopter through a biblical storm over a primordial highway, Ticker flinches at the memory. Syncopated with the strobelight flash of lightning, the fragments of the jigsaw puzzle in his brain click into place: The moment in the dungeon when the feeling coursed through him that he could literally stop a bullet by slowing down the passage of time. Click! The sheet music propped up on the facing of a spinet piano, the musical notes of the staff paper flowing into the symbol of the caesura. Click! The sight of a .450-caliber round with its copper jacket and nose cone like a tiny cork hanging in space, moving so slowly it seems to freeze in midair. Click! A little boy's slender brown fingers playing the notes of *Jesu Joy of Man's Desiring* on the keyboard of a battered spinet piano back in Chicago, the same instrument for which his mother scrimped and saved before purchasing it from a pawnshop . . .

. . . the fingers abruptly lifting up.

Click!

The silence invades the cockpit like a poisonous gas. Ticker can't hear a thing but his own heartbeat, thumping in 4/4 time—a metronome set to accompany the Bach cantata *Jesu Joy of Man's Desiring*. Through the Black Hawk's nose window he can see the two vehicles wending their way toward the fateful hairpin turn.

He rams the stick forward, and the Black Hawk leans into a steep descent . . . closer, closer. Ticker can see the school bus take the turn at a dangerously high speed, the tires going into a skid on the wet asphalt, the vehicle listing sideways, threatening to tip over. The bird swoops down on the washed-out section of highway . . . fifty meters below the skids . . . forty . . . thirty . . . twenty.

In the explosive magnesium-bright lightning Ticker sees the bus driver make a futile attempt to slam on the brakes the moment the washout materializes in the veils of mist and wind. The vehicle fishtails sideways. The Black Hawk looms so closely now—fifteen meters above the bus—that the main rotor wash envelops the vehicle in waves of cyclonic haze as the vehicle goes into a wild spin across the gravel shoulder.

Ticker sees the bus career off the precipice and plunge.

Somewhere deep in the folds of his brain he sees the caesura symbol on an old yellowed page of sheet music, at the end of a phrase, at the top of the staff . . .

. . . the long, tawny fingers of a little boy lifting off the keys . . .

. . . the silence ringing.

## 4.

Ticker feels a bump, as though the skids have touched down on an invisible hard surface in the middle of the sky. At the same time the rain freezes in midair. Later, doing his own research on atmospheric science and the space-time continuum, he will learn that raindrops fall at different speeds according to their size, but no raindrop—or school bus, or human body for that matter—can fall faster than its terminal velocity, which is the speed at which gravitational forces are exactly the same as the upward air resistance.

All of which is why Ticker literally gasps when he peers out the Black Hawk's side window and looks down at the environment below.

It appears as though the Milky Way galaxy has fallen to earth. The night air is spangled with an infinite number of glistening raindrops frozen in time like glassine beads. Some of the bigger drops have been stretched by the wind and now hang in midair with tadpole-shaped tails like tiny shimmering weather vanes.

Ticker swallows hard, gaping at the dreamlike landscape, trying to take it all in. Even the ambient light—what little there is of it—has taken on a frozen quality like fireflies in amber. Ticker looks down at his own hand in its fingerless driving glove as though in disbelief, flexing it compulsively as if checking to make sure he's still awake, and breathing, and sees what he thinks he sees.

The Black Hawk sits as still as a cantilever in midair above the gorge.

# CHAPTER TEN
## Extraction

### 1.

Ten meters below the aircraft, the school bus—which also hangs in midair, canted slightly at an angle in midplummet—is as immobile and rock steady as if it were supported by invisible granite pillars sunken into the earth. In the faint, frozen light, Ticker can see hallucinatory detail such as dirty rainwater beaded on the roof of the bus, a little girl behind the rear window as motionless as a mannequin with her terrified face pressed against the glass, the barrel of a sidearm sticking out a jagged hole in the driver's window—midblast—the flare from the muzzle now congealed into a radiant plume of static yellow flame like a flower midblossom.

Ticker takes a deep breath and sits back against his contour seat. Even the upholstery of the pilot's chair has a crackly, petrified quality to it. He looks up, gazing through the canopy portal, and sees the rusty Jeep and his four colleagues less than a hundred meters back down the road, unmoving, immobilized on their approach. Ahead of them, directly above the Black Hawk, the collapsed bridge has taken on a decorative quality, like a fake disaster in a department-store window, the violent rushing floodwaters as lifeless and artificial as wads of cotton and Saran Wrap. Ticker forces himself to look away, breathe, think, get his bearings, and figure out his next step.

A strange and unexpected feeling of loneliness washes over him. Is the entire universe at a standstill? Are cars frozen in midcrossing on the Golden Gate Bridge? Are people inert and motionless at Tiananmen Square? Is there a member of Parliament standing at a podium, arm raised, facial expression seized up in mid-diatribe? Ticker feels the weight of being alone in the world, and sadly it feels familiar. It feels as though he has time-traveled back to his childhood, and he's that same little boy trying to please his piano teacher, playing by himself on the practice keyboard in his room, getting bullied on the way to school, dreaming of getting out of his neighborhood and becoming a scientist, or maybe a soldier fighting for his country.

He climbs into the rear cabin, noticing his movement is slightly more lethargic and labored than usual, as if he just stepped onto the surface of a planet with a more intense gravitational field. He shrugs off his body armor and field gear. Inside a metal cabinet he finds the rescue basket. He pulls it out and unfolds the five-foot-high netting of nylon rope, the solid fiberglass seat, and the polyethylene flotation cylinders wrapped around the middle and the top. From another cabinet he pulls out a massive coil of tow cable.

It takes him awhile to figure out how to attach the cable to the hoist outside the midcabin door. In all his years of flying A-6 Intruders off the decks of aircraft carriers, he was never called upon to rescue anybody at sea.

The basket traditionally requires at least two, if not three, people to operate. It takes several minutes for Ticker to devise a way to trigger the winch, and change the direction remotely from the basket. By the time he rigs a separate cable for the switch housing, it feels as though an hour has passed. But he's not sure about that. Elapsed time is deceptive in this immobilized universe.

Besides, he had noticed early on that his watch had stopped.

At last, he's ready to extract the children from the suspended, plunging bus. As he climbs into the basket, and thumbs the DOWN button—slowly lowering the apparatus through layers of shimmering opalescent raindrops—it occurs to him that he should take his time, take it nice and easy, and be very careful.

After all, it's dawning on him that he has all the time in the world.

## 2.

In the early moments of the rescue, Ticker learns many things about the process of stopping time. Upon first entering the bus, squeezing his way through the rear emergency exit door, letting the basket hang just outside the hatch, he learns that the little girl who became motionless while pressing her face against the rear window had wet herself. The damp spot is apparent across the front of her little OshKosh corduroy overalls. As part of this still-life tableau, the wet spot is more heartbreaking than ever.

He also learns that prying a little girl's fingers off a door handle and wresting her cheek from a window—amid an episode he is coming to think of as the caesura, the hole in time, the rest stop—are delicate procedures. Apparently the human body in stasis is stiff but pliable, as though in the early stages of rigor mortis. He takes the girl in the overalls up first, lifting her out the rear exit, and holding her in his lap in the basket as he thumbs the UP button.

Another thing Ticker learns is that not only does a school bus full of children—thirteen in all—take a lot longer to clear than he originally predicted but the bodies that he extracts fill up the narrow cabin of the Black Hawk a lot faster than he would have guessed. After the eighth or ninth child, he has to start wedging them into every square foot of available space. He stashes one little boy behind the navigator's seat, one little girl in a storage cabinet, another pair of them underneath the rear jump seat. When he gets them all situated, he returns to the bus for one last extraction.

Abu Osamir sits in the front of the bus, in the bench seat directly behind the driver, his eyes pinned open, teeth exposed, his bogus uniform soaked in sweat, looking like a gargoyle on the side of a building. Of indeterminate age, the warlord has a reptilian air about him, his thick neck wattle the color of cowhide, his cunning eyes buried in crow's-feet. He wears a profusion of jewelry, and a bedazzled gun belt with a gold-plated .45 in the holster, and he smells of smoke.

Reaching down to him, lifting him from his seat, Ticker notices that Osamir's beached whale of a body weighs less than he would have guessed. Is this an effect of the time pause? A fleeting thought courses through Ticker's brain: How easy it would be to toss the chubby tyrant out the back hatch, and watch him float there for a second before Ticker removed the time spell. How satisfying it would be to watch the evil warlord plummet a thousand feet to his death in the icy gorge. But that's not how it works. Even now—with the unit supposedly in league with the devil, enjoying the fruits of their new powers—that's not how the team operates. Whatever the cost, as far as Ticker is concerned, Spur's ghost unit works toward justice, Faustian pact or no Faustian pact.

But as he carries the warlord to the rear exit and loads him onto the chair, Ticker wonders if he would be as cavalier about leaving the bodyguards on the bus to perish in a fiery death plunge had the djakata not made its appearance. He has no problem leaving the thugs to die. In fact, he craves seeing them fall to their deaths. This is the new Ticker . . . Ticker Two-Point-Oh.

Moments later he's back in the frozen Black Hawk, climbing behind the stick after securing plastic zip ties around the wrists of the warlord, when it occurs to him that there's one last issue to address.

He looks over his shoulder at the crumbling two-lane above him, the ruins of the bridge, and the glistening, frozen water of the washout. Through the canopy portal he can just make out the headlights and grille of the Jeep frozen on its approach, obscured behind the hanging beads of static rain. Behind the Jeep's rain-stippled windshield he can see the faint outline of Hack's face—eyes bugging in midsurprise as the Jeep rounds the hairpin and he gets his first glimpse of the bus going over the edge.

Ticker lowers the side window, squeezes his slender body through the aperture, and climbs up the side of the aircraft to the main gearbox. From there he vaults across a five-foot chasm, catching himself on an outcropping of stone.

From there, it's a short ascent up a rocky slope to the surface of the road.

The Jeep sits in its icy stasis like a still-life titled *The Moment Before Impact*. Each member of the unit gapes straight ahead, registering the terrifying implications of the ruined bridge and the bus careening off the precipice. Ticker cracks open the driver's-side door. The hinge creaks like an ice tray. He leans in and shifts the Jeep's transmission into neutral, and then yanks the hand brake.

Just in case.

### 3.

Back in the Black Hawk, in the pilot's seat, Ticker grabs the stick, closes his eyes, imagines the caesura symbol on that antique page of sheet music, at the far end of the staff, those two tiny railroad tracks . . .

. . . and the slender brown fingers of a little boy striking the keys . . .

. . . the music starting back up.

### 4.

"*Whoa!*"

Hack feels the engine lurch without warning, the transmission revving impotently, the hand brake suddenly locking up the front end. The chassis shudders, sending the Jeep into a skid. This all happens spontaneously, as if the Jeep has *willed itself* to suddenly grind to a sideways stop ten meters from the collapsed bridge.

The four operatives sit there in the silence of the stalled Jeep, stricken speechless for a moment. The bus has vanished. The Black Hawk has vanished. The team sits mute, clutching their seats, gaping at the windshield as the storm rages and bullwhips across the glass.

Spur starts to say, "What in the name of all that is holy just—?"

The explosion rocks the mountainside, rattling the Jeep and sending a ball of flame the intensity of the sun up through the storm and into the black churning sky. For one terrible moment the maelstrom turns night into day, the shock wave shaking the Jeep, sending hairline fractures through the windshield.

In the rear, Pin-Up stares at the floor, shaking her head sadly. "Those poor kids . . . in the bus . . . those poor poor kids."

"May I ask what the hell just happened?" Hack still has his hands welded to the steering wheel. "Something just happened, Spur, but I'll be damned if I know what the hell it was."

Spur hears static crackling in his earpiece, the startled screams of children, and Ticker's voice raised, yelling something. "Say again, Uniform Hotel . . . didn't copy that."

The drone of the Black Hawk's engines rise above the raging winds.

"There!" Boo points. "Twelve o'clock!—See him?"

A moment later they all see the dark silhouette of the bird swooping down through the rain directly in front of them, the backwash of the main rotor swirling black smoke from the explosion across the highway. The Black Hawk descends to about thirty meters, close enough for Spur and the others to read the registration number stenciled on the bird's tail boom. They can barely see Ticker behind the windshield, piloting the aircraft, yelling over the noises of engines and terrified children.

"Ain't copying shit in this pea soup!" Spur yells, addressing both the Black Hawk and the team members in the car. He thumbs the SEND switch. "Repeat that, Ticker. Please repeat."

In between the bursts of static, portions of Ticker's transmission crackle in Spur's earpiece: ". . . got the . . . and . . . [garbled noise]."

Spur says into his mike, "Copied part of that, give it to me again."

". . . [static] . . . got the kids . . ."

Spur looks at Hack, and then shoots a glance at the two women in the rear. "Copy! Copy that! You got the kids on board the bird?"

Static . . . then: ". . . Affirmative . . . all thirteen of them . . . and . . ."

"Well slap my head and call me stupid!" Spur glances at the others. "You got all them kids safely off the bus?" The other team members look at one another incredulously. Spur swallows hard. Part of him knows that Ticker's newly acquired powers of time management are likely involved. "How the hell did you pull that off, Houdini?"

". . . long story . . . and I got . . . [static] . . . in the . . . [more static]."

Spur leans in. "Did not copy that last bit.—Say again."

After another burst of interference, Ticker's voice returns to the earpiece, enunciating loudly and clearly. "I got Osamir."

Spur stares at the rain, wondering if he heard what he thought he just heard.

# 5.

Back in Patala, they find a local—an elderly lady, a former schoolteacher—to help return each and every hostage, unharmed, to their parents. It turns out the townspeople lived under the brutal yoke of the warlord, were bullied by him, some even murdered and disappeared by the little self-proclaimed crime boss.

The town's constable provides Spur and his team a place to serve as a holding cell—as well as a twenty-four-hour guard—to keep Osamir on ice while arrangements are made to return the warlord to America for trial. Spur contacts Central Command at Alan Baker Airfield just outside Naraka, the largest city in Karakistan. He gives the man in charge a heads-up that the unit will be arriving the next day with a prisoner and a laptop that very well may yield actionable intelligence.

A well-to-do local family in Patala makes available a large vacant hunting lodge five kilometers to the west—fully furnished, two floors, situated on a lovely mountain lake—in which the unit can rest up that night. Spur and his team gratefully accept the hospitality. Not a single member of the unit has gotten a minute of sleep in forty-eight hours.

By the time they make it to the lodge, completely spent from all the adrenaline-charged action, they are more than ready for a good night's sleep. The storm has passed, and now only a light rain drums against the terra-cotta roof tiles.

Boo, Pin-Up, and Hack retire to their guest quarters before Spur even has a chance to say good night to them and thank them for a job well done. Everybody wants to get to the bottom of what has happened to the team over the last few days, but for now, exhaustion has set in, and at the moment, what most of them need is simply a little relief.

## 6.

For Boo, relief comes that night in the form of a knock at her door.

She's in the bathroom when she hears it, still dripping wet from a hot shower, still completely nude, her raven-black hair clipped into a swirl on top of her head. "What now," she groans as she fumbles for the sateen robe hanging next to the shower that appears to be one-size-fits-very-few. She quickly slips it on, and heads across the small studio apartment toward the front door.

The guest quarters at this venerable old lodge all feature vintage Eastern European decor—deer antlers on the walls, tarnished sconces, worn-out Persian rugs, and ancient canopy beds that appear to have last been slept in by Vlad the Impaler. The air has a stale pine-scented quality to it, like that of an old taxi. Boo answers the door on the second chorus of knocks.

"Not to be forward or presumptuous in any way but I found this in my room," Hack announces, standing outside her door in his own lodge-issued, ill-fitting robe, holding a bottle of something ruby-colored in one hand and two plastic cups in the other. "It occurred to me what a shame it would be to drink this alone, especially since the establishment provides not one but two lovely plastic cups with each complimentary bottle."

"This is not what I would call a good idea," she says, standing her ground, holding the door open only a few inches. She notices that Hack's chest is partially exposed, the barbed-wire tattoo tracing along his collarbone. She looks away for fear of wanting to see the rest of that muscular torso.

"I know, I get it," he says, "we're not supposed to fraternize. Bad for group cohesion, dangerous in the field, takes our eyes off the ball, blah-blah-blah-blah-blah—"

"Get in here before somebody sees you."

She yanks him into the room and carefully shuts the door behind him.

He can't take his eyes off her. "I give you my solemn word, on my mother's grave, this is a purely platonic visit."

"Your mother's still alive."

"What I mean is, in the *event* of her death . . . God forbid."

With a sly smile she loosens the belt on her robe, allowing him a glimpse of her lithe, creamy white midsection. "Strictly innocent, huh?"

"My hand to God, I will be a gentleman at all times." Ogling her body, he absently drops the bottle and the cups on the faded rug, and shrugs off his own robe. He's now fully aroused. "Ma'am, I assure you there will be no monkey business."

"Thank God for that," she says, dropping her robe to the floor. "I will hold you to that."

He reaches out, lifts her tiny naked body off the floor, and carries her over to the bed. "I will keep my hands to myself, and I will be a good listener." He lowers her to the bed, and he enters her.

And sure enough, relief soon comes for both of them that night . . . again and again.

# 7.

Ticker finds a bottle of brandy in a cabinet in the main room, and Spur joins him for a nightcap before turning in.

"You trust these folks to keep that son of a bitch Osamir safe and sound over there in that porous little jailhouse?" Ticker poses the question as he settles back into an armchair next to the fireplace, which now pops and crackles with a congenial fire built by Spur with a few of the dry alder logs piled next to the hearth. The rain murmurs outside the tall windows.

"I do," Spur says, sinking into an adjacent armchair, taking a sip of the brandy. "These people have seen so many hardships over the years, endless war, every goddamn country on the map invading on a regular basis, and they're still a strong, decent lot, folks that just want to be left alone. They'll guard that motherfucker real well, trust me on that."

Ticker nods. Sips his drink. Stares pensively into the fire.

Spur looks at him. "How the hell did you get them kids out of that bus?"

Ticker smiles. "I'm getting better at it." He looks up. "I'm starting to think of it as the manipulation of time."

"That's what we're calling it now, huh? Okay. Fair enough." After another thoughtful sip, Spur says, "Tell me how it works."

Ticker looks back at the fire. "I don't know yet. That's the thing. It's all intuitive at this point." He sips and thinks about it. "I'll tell you one thing, though." He looks at Spur. "Whatever we agreed to down in that chamber of horrors . . . with whatever that thing is . . . it's real, Spur. I'm telling you. It's as real as this brandy."

Spur thinks about it, still trying to process it. He takes another sip. Raising his glass. "Then it's pretty goddamned real. This is fine and dandy stuff, ain't it?"

Ticker nods. "Yessir. I believe it's older than you are."

Spur laughs. He toasts. "Here's to old men and older liquor." They drink.

Spur stares at the fire and finds himself wondering if he is indeed getting too old for . . . what? Being an intelligence operative? Making deals with the devil? Whenever he starts ruminating about such things, he always thinks of Peyton Manning winning the Super Bowl with the Broncos at age thirty-nine . . . but at Spur's age? Forty-three? Such thoughts always lead to his longing to be with Pin-Up, and his embarrassment to even think he has a chance with her. It killed him to see her terrorized in that dungeon. He wanted so badly to hold her afterward, to assure her that he would always be there for her, but that's not how it works for fellow professionals in this crazy racket. And now that the stakes have been raised in such a surreal fashion, it's more ridiculous than ever to pine for her.

Ticker shoots a glance at Spur. "You do realize he's listening."

"Who is?"

"The devil, our benefactor . . . whatever you want to call him . . . he hears everything we say. I guarantee he's listening right now. As we speak. I can feel it, Spur. He's keeping tabs on his new toys."

Spur thinks it over as the rain rings off the window wells, and the fire sizzles and snaps. He takes another sip. "Okay . . . let's say he is. I got nothing to hide. Let him listen. Besides, I'm not sure there's a fucking thing we can do about it."

Ticker stares at Spur for a long moment, and then says, "Maybe there is." He licks his lips pensively. "I have an idea." He pauses.

"It might help us deal with this . . . this little *situation* in which we find ourselves."

Spur looks at him, and can tell by the expression on the man's face he's very serious.

## CHAPTER ELEVEN
## Jump Cut

**1.**

Ticker puts his brandy down, gets up, and paces as he talks. "Full disclosure . . . I never believed in the bogeyman. I was a science nerd as a kid. It helped me deal with those terrible years we call childhood. Having an explanation for everything helped me get through it. But over the years I learned the truth."

Spur watches him carefully. "Which is?"

"There are things out there for which there *is* no explanation. Ask any physicist. Does the universe add up? Does it make sense? *Hell, no.* Not even gravity behaves the way you learned in grade school."

Spur shakes his head. "You're losing me, old hoss. Put it in the King's English."

"Okay. How about this? Newton's law. We all learned it in third grade. Right? All together now: Every object in the universe attracts other objects with a force determined by its size and mass? The earth is a lot bigger than an apple . . . hence the apple falls to the earth?"

"Sounds familiar."

"Well, back in the eighteenth century, the theory made sense. The world was in three dimensions back then. But Einstein blew all that out of the water. He added a *fourth* dimension. Time. This changed everything. It began this new era of theories about space-time continuums, and objects that can pass through other objects without even changing their—"

"Hold your horses, hoss," Spur interrupts, cocking his head dubiously. "Where's all this going? What are you getting at?"

"Think about it. We now know that eighty-five percent of the universe is made up of a special kind of matter . . . matter that does not behave the way it's supposed to behave . . . matter that doesn't absorb *or* emit light . . . matter that cannot be seen directly or be detected by any conventional means. But they know it's there. Screwing with us. Fucking with time and space."

"That's all fine and dandy but what if it's just a theory. How do you even know for sure it's there?"

"They know it's there by the way it affects visible matter, the way it causes things to happen that have no other explanation. They call it dark matter." Ticker stops pacing. "That's our guy, Spur . . . that's Satan . . . or djakata . . . or the mogwai . . . or whatever you want to call him. That's who he is. That's what came at us in that underground torture room. Dark matter. Or at least the personification of it."

"Okay . . . so . . . what in the holy hell do we do with all this?"

Ticker thinks for a moment. "My papa used to say, 'Sometimes, son, when the shit comes down, you just gotta go back to the woodshed, get your bearings, educate yourself.' There's a lot of truth to that, Spur. Like those brainiacs at MIT and NASA, constantly learning, persistently curious, always questioning . . . we need to study this monster. Figure out the effects *he* has had on visible matter over the eons. On people. On societies. There's a body of evidence out there, Spur. Religious texts, eyewitness testimonials, volumes and volumes written over the centuries, some of it bullshit, sure, some of it folklore, but some of it is actual empirical evidence that could give us nuggets of wisdom and insights into our new . . . what would you call him? Our client?"

Spur shrugs. "It's as good a word as any, I guess." He grins then. "Tell me what this idea is that you've been cooking up in that big ol' brain of yours?"

Ticker smiles almost wistfully as he goes over to his snifter, which sits where he left it on the end table, the last few fingers of brandy in the goblet. He swallows all of it. Then he sets the empty glass down and wipes his mouth. "I'm going to try something," he says now to Spur, speaking in a grave, low tone as though he's about to do something imponderable and insane like stand on his head and recite the entire Old Testament in Hebrew. "Bear with me. I'm new at this."

"What the hell are you . . . ?" Spur abruptly falls silent when he realizes that the slender, handsome man before him has put his head down, extending his hands, and moving his fingers as though mimicking the act of playing a piano. It's a completely random gesture—a silent non sequitur—that makes absolutely no sense to Spur, but it does have an air of deep introspection or meditative prayer.

Ticker's head lolls from side to side for a moment, his eyes rolling back in his skull.

"Ticker, are you . . . ?" Spur starts to inquire if the man is okay, or if he has maybe suffered some kind of seizure, but again, Spur's words get stuck in his throat when he sees the change.

## 2.

Spur springs to his feet, dropping his brandy on the beautiful Persian rug. He can't believe what he has just witnessed with his very own eyes, the transformation sparking across the room like an awkward jump cut in a motion picture.

Blinking, letting out a silent gasp as though he has just been slapped, he sees that the parlor has instantaneously transformed. The walls are now festooned with the trappings of a makeshift shrine or place of worship. Paper crosses and Stars of David and other cryptic religious symbols hang in what is seemingly every square foot of available space. Incense smolders in jury-rigged braziers made from coffee cans and ashtrays. The air smells of cloves and candle wax. Bowls and jars—presumably found in the hunting lodge's kitchen—now sit at every corner, each receptacle filled with a clear liquid that for some reason Spur assumes is holy water. He wants to say something, comment, react in some way, but his eyes are drawn to Ticker.

The handsome warrior stands across the room in the exact spot that he had stood one second ago, before the change occurred. He now wears different clothing, a large leather portfolio under his arm. His olive-drab T-shirt has, through some dark magic, instantly changed into a colorful linen tunic, the casual kind favored by Karakistani men. His camo pants have been replaced by linen parachute sweats. His tightly cropped onyx hair appears to have grown at least a half an inch, or has been brushed differently perhaps. He still wears his combat boots, but now they have a crust of amber-colored dirt on them, the insteps caked with dried clay from a long, arduous hike.

"What in the wide world of sports . . . ?" Spur looks around the room at the improvised sanctuary. The parlor now looks as though it has been decorated for a home communion or a do-it-yourself bar mitzvah. For a moment, Spur keeps his distance as though his colleague has instantaneously become radioactive.

Ticker looks around the room, and then down at the tunic he's wearing as though embarrassed suddenly, as if his zipper is open. "Oh yeah . . . right . . . sorry . . . I promise it will all make some kind of crazy sense in a minute," he says, trying to remain sanguine and calm about whatever miracle he has just visited upon the firelit chamber. He sets the portfolio down on the armchair next to him. "I tried to remember what I was wearing when I left," he says sheepishly. "My T-shirt was soaked through with sweat, completely drenched by the time I got to the city."

Spur rubs his eyes, trying to process it. He shakes his head. "You went to the city? When? Just now? What city are we talking about? You got my brain rattling around like a BB in a boxcar."

Ticker lets out an exhausted sigh. "I'm sorry, Chief," he says. "Still getting used to this power, this . . . this time-manipulation trick. Trying to master it." He motions to the chair. "Sit down. I'll explain everything. I promise it'll all make some kind of sense if you just . . . let me explain."

## 3.

It is a lot to swallow, but so was the rescuing of thirteen children from a bus that had already slipped off a precipice and had begun to plunge to its certain obliteration at the bottom of a thousand-foot gorge. To a mesmerized Spur, Ticker calmly explains that he had stopped time in that cozy little parlor one week ago. Seven days would pass for Ticker, but only an instant, a heartbeat, a *blink* elapsing for Spur. One entire week—during which the sun would never rise—afforded Ticker the freedom to walk out the door, head south, find a small garage, and procure a bicycle. (Ticker had learned in his previous encounter with his new power that motors and engines are paralyzed during the caesura; and that's when he realized that he had much yet to learn about his new power.)

From Patala he rode the two-wheeler west toward the capital. Moving through the unchanging predawn shadows, he passed the frozen scenes of village life as still as dioramas—farmers and fishermen out early, children as motionless as statues on their own bicycles, hunters aiming their rifles midblast as they attempted to bag their first wild boar of the morning.

From his mission briefing back in the States, Ticker knew that the largest university in Karakistan was located in the capital city of Erebus, which a road sign informed him was thirty-five kilometers away (or twenty-one miles), which was a lot of territory to traverse on a vintage single-speed two-wheeler with bald tires and bad brakes.

It took him nearly twenty-four hours to get to the city, due to treacherous mountain roads and road signs that he could barely translate. Ticker is fairly fluent in Karakistani—as well as the various dialects and splinter languages, such as Karsi and Lashto—but he has a better understanding of the spoken languages than he does of the written versions, most likely due to all the umlauts, accents, and circumflexes peppering the text. At two separate junctures he had to stop, rest, have a few berries, drink a few handfuls of stillborn creek water, and climb to high ground in order to get his bearings.

He found the Karakistan University of Natural Science and World Cultures at exactly the same moment he had stopped time in Patala: predawn, just after the rainstorm, the darkness misty and redolent with pine musk from the alpine forests, the sky just beginning to turn from the black of night to the luminous blue of first light. That magic-hour indigo glow persisted the entire time he was gone, as though it were a vast backdrop in a cosmic movie.

Upon his arrival he squeezed through the library's first-floor window, and wandered the deserted building for a few hours, getting the lay of the land, passing the empty departments and endless warrens of ancient first editions in their crumbling original book jackets, most of them translations from English or French or Italian into Karakistani. On the third floor, at the end of a main aisle, an archway led into the Azali Mohamed Falijah Memorial Religious Center. It was there, in that airless, claustrophobic stillness, that Ticker discovered one of the world's most extensive collections on demonology, witchcraft, and Satanism.

For the next five days, he perused, studied, and made notes on every last shred of information he could find on the devil. The meaningless hours turned into meaningless days as he read chapter after chapter, abstract after abstract, citation after citation on the theology, psychiatry, mythology, and various world traditions revolving around the Prince of Darkness. He studied Satan's origin story. He sketched all the various incarnations from all the art and literature on the devil down through the ages. He pored over eyewitness accounts of exorcisms. He read and notated Dante's *Divine Comedy,* H. R. Wiggim's *Enciclopedia de Diaboli,* Marlowe's *The Tragical History of the Life and Death of Doctor Faustus,* and Daniel Mussolino's *A Brief History of the Devil,* pausing only for periodic trips to the men's room or to the nearest vending machine, which he broke into mostly for the endless supply of peanuts.

During this time, Ticker learned that he could hold the caesura even while asleep. He catnapped several times during his stay at the university, sleeping on a couch in the teachers' lounge, fully expecting to awaken to a world restored to its normal time flow. But much to his amazement, the power was apparently so deeply rooted in his subconscious, it held during his dream-haunted naps.

Later, on the fifth day of his self-imposed course of study, Ticker took a break and found the night watchman's office. The old man in the grey uniform sat stone-still at his cluttered desk with his Styrofoam cup of coffee poised an inch from his lips. Ticker stole his .38-caliber snub-nose pistol, his ammo belt, a change of clothes from a small trunk under his desk, a few tools from a drawer, and a candy bar sitting next to his pack of Sherman cigarettes.

By the end of that five-day crash course on Satan, Ticker had filled a leather attaché case with sketches, illustrations, pages torn from books, historical pamphlets, archival copies of liturgies, transcripts of exorcisms, and nearly five hundred pages of personal notes. On his way out of the library, he happened upon the campus interdenominational chapel. He made a quick side trip inside it, and took some liturgical supplies, such as incense, a few vials of holy water, a small bronze crucifix, and various shawls and scarves emblazoned with different symbols from different religions.

On the trip back to Patala, he passed the same frozen, unchanging scenes of village life that he had passed on his way to the city. The farmers and fishermen had not budged from their early-morning vigils. The same children remained as immobile as statues on their bicycles. The same hunter crouched in the same cover of foliage, his rifle still at midblast as he attempted to kill the same wild boar that hung motionless in midair a hundred yards away as it leaped over a hedgerow, struggling to flee its human predator. By the time he returned to the hunting lodge, he was exhausted and yet exhilarated to find the firelit parlor exactly as he had left it.

Spur still sat in the corner of the parlor by the fireplace, the flames of which stood as stationary as luminous blooms.

He was on the edge of his seat, his face frozen in an expression of alarm, his jaw set in the tense moment right before he uttered the words, "Ticker, what's going on . . . ?"

# 4.

After hearing the whole story, Spur finally comments: "I love the redecorating." The man from Texas leans back in his chair and looks around the room. "I'm presuming this has something to do with what you learned down there in Erebus about Old Scratch?"

Ticker nods. He levers himself out of his armchair and paces the room some more. "Turns out I was right about the devil being ubiquitous . . . a real snoop, always listening in. But there's a way we can short-circuit it."

"By making paper crucifixes?"

Ticker gestures at the walls. "It's the next best thing to finding a mosque, a church, a synagogue . . . a place of worship. He can't touch us inside these places, can't hear us."

"Cone of silence, huh?"

"You don't believe any of this, do you? You don't believe one whit of it."

Spur sighs and looks around the room. "Not true, Tick. Not true at all." He measures his words. "I was a believer from the moment I got thrown across that dungeon and got a look-see at what was below us." He swallows hard. "The thing of it is, the devil and his dirty deeds were hammered into me since I was knee-high to a grasshopper. East Texas Baptists are crazy mothers. That shit does not go away. I can see with my own eyes we're in the middle of something and it ain't natural. I may be dumb but I ain't stupid. I believe we can turn it around, though, turn these powers against the son of a bitch."

"Then what's wrong? Something's wrong. I can see it in your eyes."

"Hell, I don't know. I don't know whether to check my ass or scratch my watch."

"What is it, what's the matter?"

"You're a much smarter man than I, that's for damn sure." He looks deep into Ticker's eyes. "I appreciate what you did. Makes all kinds of sense. Hell, maybe that's my problem. The crucifix. The trappings of the church. It's getting a little *too* real for my taste."

Ticker smiles. "Know thy enemy."

"I'm with you."

"It all starts with who this bastard really is . . . where he came from."

Spur nods and thinks about it for a moment. "Fallen angel, right?"

"Sort of. Yeah. But it's more than that. The devil's somebody we recognize, somebody we've seen on battlefields. See, at one point, according to the Christians, he was an angel but he got a little cocky and attempted a coup in heaven against God. Staged a rebellion. Got one-third of the other angels to join him."

Spur nods. "Got his ass kicked by God, though, right? Got sent to the lake of fire?"

"You bet he did. And the fallen angel set himself up down there. Became a tyrant. Spreading anti-creation propaganda for all time. Spreading hate for God's children. Maybe he was the first real terrorist. In the truest meaning of the word, you know what I mean?"

"I sure as hell do."

Ticker paces some more. "It feels familiar to me for some reason," he says after a beat. "The spreading of lies, the wreaking of havoc in the world. Promoting chaos, disorder, fear, despair. You see what I'm saying?"

"You're on to something. Sounds a lot like those radical terrorist groups we've come up against over the years. The nasty ones, the ones with no ideology other than genocide and world domination."

"Exactly!" Ticker snaps his fingers and points at him. "It's beyond politics. Always has been. It's either side of the spectrum, the worse ones are all the same—the Nazis, al-Qaeda, the Klan, the Mongol hordes, the Khmer Rouge, Unit 731—they use the same playbook. We know it well."

"Are you saying they're on the payroll? They're working for him?"

"Yes. Absolutely. No doubt in my mind. It's there in the literature, if you know what lines to read between." Ticker stops pacing and looks at him. "That's my point, Spur. We know how to infiltrate these kinds of groups. That's what we do. It's pure counterintelligence, man, that's our *thing*. And there's no reason why—"

Without warning a muffled voice whimpers from the end of the hall, a strangled, feral moan of pain and shock, which interrupts Ticker's flow and gets Spur up and wide-eyed. "That sounds like Hack," he says.

## CHAPTER TWELVE

# A Hole in the Universe

## 1.

The dream comes out of nowhere, penetrating the tranquility of his deep sleep, spanning a single instant but seeming to last an eternity.

In the beginning he finds himself sitting alone on the grounds of a lovely, serene Japanese garden. Mosaics of stone, delicate bonsai trees, and exotic patchworks of moss in beautiful quilt-like patterns stretch as far as the eye can see. The colors are vivid—emeralds and teals and opals—the earthen floor beneath him as soft as a kitten's fur. He's drawn to a small array of tiny stones about ten feet away.

The dreamer crawls over to them. They are charcoal-colored, and smoothed by eons of rain- and stream water, embedded in the moss and configured in a rectangular arrangement that seems familiar to him. But in the dream he can't quite put his finger on the reason he finds the grouping so significant. He touches one of the stones. He discovers they're loose, and they can slide along threads of vines that are stitched between them. He can calculate mathematical problems with such a cluster of objects.

An abacus!

Memories flood the dream, memories of the dreamer's father teaching him as a little boy to use the ancient Asian invention, grooming the lad to be a number cruncher. The father is a mere disembodied voice in the dream, less a human than a monolithic presence, a shadow looming over him: "Aaron, six times seven is . . . what? Remember to move seven beads on six wires. Do you see?"

The abacus shifts before the dreamer's eyes. The grey stones change to pale yellow teeth—*human teeth*—aligned in neat little rows, six down, ten across, sunken into the ground, but loose like timeworn pebbles. Some of the teeth feature tarnished gold fillings, the tooth enamel cracked with age, radiating sickness and tragedy.

The spaces between the teeth begin to crumble like sand in a sieve, and the dreamer sees light leaking up through the seams. Narrow beams of yellow light . . . flickering . . . crackling. The teeth become keys on a laptop, and the keyboard is porous, leaking the incandescent glow of flames within its circuitry, a horrible fire, a firestorm ten times the heat of burning magnesium.

The sounds of human misery and anguish emanate up from between the keys, an entire apocalyptic world visible through the seams of the keyboard, a shock wave bending trees, razing buildings, and vaporizing bystanders. The dreamer opens his mouth to scream but cannot make a sound. He hears the collective wailing of agony down in the inscrutable guts of that keyboard. Between the seams he sees the telltale effects of a nuclear holocaust. Hundreds of thousands of innocent souls turned to ash, the shadows of human figures scorched like tattoos into the ruins of the cityscape.

## 2.

Hack awakens with a start. Two figures stand over his bed. The morning light seeps through the window shades, making him flinch. He sits up, heart racing, eyes blindly searching the room, trying to fix on his surroundings and make sense of things. He doesn't remember returning to his room the previous night after his tryst with Boo. He doesn't even remember his room all that well.

"Hack, you okay?" Spur says, putting a hand on the man's shoulder. "You were moaning like a gut-shot dog there for a second."

"I was . . ." Hack's voice is garbled and weak. He swallows. "I was . . . I was having one lollapalooza of a dream."

Ticker nods. "No shit."

"Vivid as all get-out, and disturbing as hell, if you want to know the truth." Hack takes a deep breath, swings his legs over the side of the bed, and sits on the edge running fingers through his unruly hair. His chiseled face is creased with angst, imprinted with the wrinkled pattern of the bedding beneath him. "I was . . . I was in a garden, and I saw this . . . I don't know what else to call it but a *vision*." His expression abruptly changes. "Wait a minute. Wait."

He sees Abu Osamir's laptop across the room. It sits on a table under the window, the lid closed. Dust motes drift through a beam of sunlight glinting off the metallic surface of the computer as though a celestial finger is ordaining it. Hack spent the wee hours the previous night using back doors and remote-access tricks in a futile attempt to get past Osamir's security firewalls. He tried going through a URL in order to grab the server list. No luck. He tried keylogging, data capturing, back entry through email, and half a dozen different malware programs, all to no avail.

Now he realizes, as he sits on the bed, the tentacles of the dream still clinging to him, that he didn't try the obvious approach, the technique that never would have occurred to him before this mission to Karakistan. He pushes himself off the bed and pads barefoot over to the window.

"Bear with me," he says to the two men looking on with concern. "I've been banging my head against the wall all night with this *fakakta* Walmart computer, but maybe I missed the obvious back door. Time to try Occam's razor on this puppy."

He pulls a wooden chair in front of the table, takes a seat, opens the laptop, takes a deep breath, and touches his fingertips to the space bar as though he were a charismatic preacher practicing the ancient sacrament of the laying on of hands.

A spark jumps up in his face—brilliant and hallucinatory, an optical flare in his field of vision—as he feels himself drop through a hole in the universe.

## 3.

At first he can't breathe, and can see only a blur of color rushing past him on either side, as well as above him and below him. Every color in the universe streaks past him, brilliant, luminous, blindingly bright, a kaleidoscope of fire. He feels a sense of hurtling through space, or perhaps a tunnel; it's hard to tell which, he's moving so fast.

He gasps as he careens around a corner, the centripetal force tugging on his face, his stomach, his testicles, making him feel like a pinball that's been launched into play by a heavy hand. Before he can get his bearings he plunges down a steep, winding trough, and then crashes through a radiant barrier of liquid magenta light crisscrossing his path.

He bursts into a vast phosphorescent grid that could easily be either a landing strip for an advanced alien race or a grandiose hallucination in the mind of a schizophrenic on psychoactive pharmaceuticals. Cryptic, iridescent pathways form an impossibly complex network that stretches endlessly in every direction. Nodes and switches and junctures reminiscent of an insane railway system form linkages, binding the countless pathways.

All at once he's floating, not unlike an astronaut walking in space, drifting over this gargantuan circuit panel.

He sees images like brilliant little tide pools reflecting back up at him in the eddies and vortices of this immense electronic cerebellum. He sees mathematical equations, posed photographs, wire-frame diagrams, pornography, coded messages, shopping lists of luxury items purchased over the years, and awkward photos taken by Osamir of nameless dignitaries standing stiffly on the grounds of the fortress.

At last, Hack's attention is drawn to a blueprint visible directly beneath him—an underground manufacturing facility labeled as follows:

> **27KW Miniature Neutron Source Reactor**
> **Azazel, Karakistan**
> **34.94° N 64.14° E**

### 4.

Spur and Ticker gape at the ghostly doppelgänger sitting with its back turned to them, hunched over the keyboard, seated on the very same ladder-back wooden chair on which Hack had plopped down less than a minute ago. The ghost—or the avatar, or the digital phantom, or *whatever* it is—has layered over Hack's physical form like a sparkling second skin. Now Spur and Ticker stand there agog, staring with awe at a human figure enveloped in pixels, which swim and glitter and roil for a moment before the starry Hack-shaped figure—with its mind-boggling infrastructure of glowing benday dots—turns toward its two colleagues.

Re-forming back into an ordinary-looking intelligence operative with dark curly hair mussed from a restless, dream-riddled night, Hack rises to his full height, looks at his friends, and says, "How fast could a person call in an air strike, do you think?"

### 5.

The C-130 Hercules departs later that day on the outermost tarmac of Carcosa Air Force Base in Karakistan's Annwan Province.

The sky is low and overcast, the brooding clouds the color of lung disease, as the gigantic aircraft lifts off and roars toward the western horizon.

From the ground, the massive four-engine prop plane appears to literally vanish into a pipeline of dirty grey clouds.

A few minutes later, the tower at Carcosa gives the C-130 the go-ahead to climb to ten thousand feet and proceed on its flight plan, which will take the aircraft across the Caspian Sea, and then north across Eastern Europe, and finally straight west over the Atlantic to the United States. Four separate refueling stops are scheduled along the way. Officially the trip is a cargo haul; a couple of Abrams tanks and an armored Bradley vehicle are being returned to Fort Bragg in South Carolina for service and cannibalization.

The books show that the plane has a minimal crew—a pilot, a copilot, a loadmaster, and an Eighty-Second Airborne liaison—and that's it. There's no record of the other six passengers on the C-130 that day.

"Delta Tango, this is Sierra one-one-four-five, J-TAC, please affirm," Spur says in his patented drawl into the secure radio hand mike in the rear of the massive metal cavern that passes for the C-130's cabin. He has called in a dozen air strikes over the course of his long career, but for some reason *this* one is making him nervous. He keeps thinking of Osamir's pathetic gambit of using innocent schoolchildren as human shields.

"Delta Tango, eleven-forty-five, affirmative, go ahead, Sierra." The voice from CENTCOM crackles in Spur's ears as the plane hits a stretch of bumpy air. The cabin creaks and shudders for a moment.

"Target number Echo-one-four, need independent verification on the ground," Spur says into the mike, a plug of Red Man chewing tobacco bulging in his cheek. It's pure superstition. He chews the stuff whenever he gives notice of a successful mission, gets pinned down by enemy fire, or calls in for air support. "Bravo Foxtrot, coordinates three-four niner-four, Delta November, six-four one-four, Delta Echo . . . standing by for that India Victor."

Spur sits on a nylon contraption that serves as a jump seat in the aft compartment of the aircraft. Ticker sits on one side of him, Hack on the other, both of them intently listening in.

Through an open hatch, Spur can see the central cargo bay with the hulking tarp-covered tanks lined up like dominoes. On the other side of the vehicles a second hatch—at the moment, closed up tight—leads into the middle cabin, where paratroopers traditionally sit on long bench lines, sweating out the wait, attached to their jump lines like babies to their mother's umbilical. Pin-Up and Boo are currently on watch in this middle cabin, the warlord Osamir shackled and cross-legged on the floor. Before departing, Spur checked on him. The plump little tyrant was softly praying to his own private god. Spur found this last-minute entreaty to a higher power highly ironic.

After a blast of static, the dispatch replies, "Affirmative on that India Victor . . . we're go for redline at eighteen hundred hours . . . Golf Michael Tango. Repeat we're on for redline at eighteen hundred hours."

"Copy that," Spur says, looking at his watch, and sliding the hand mike back onto its cradle on the box at his feet.

He chews his Red Man furiously, going over all the contingencies banging around his head, all the things that could go wrong. From the moment he got the location of Osamir's underground factory from Hack, he's been making every effort to ensure that there's no collateral damage, no villages nearby, no friendlies in harm's way. Since the factory is still under construction, and the crew is on their weekend break, the facility should be empty. But who knows? A security guard or two could be skulking around the place.

Spur doesn't like unknowns . . . but in this case there's no alternative.

## CHAPTER THIRTEEN

# The Damnation Dance

**1.**

An hour into the flight, Pin-Up gets restless. Clad in her body armor, her hand instinctively clutching the grip of the M9 pistol on her hip as she leans against the bulwark, she can't take her eyes off the little fat warlord on the other side of the midcabin.

Still dressed in his ostentatious military regalia, the tyrant sits in the lotus position on the iron floor, his wrists shackled against his lap, his dark grey eyes downturned as he softly prays, his words—in whatever language they're being spoken—too soft and low to register to Pin-Up's ears over the churning drone of the plane's props.

Curiosity gets the better of her. She walks over to the barrier of nylon netting that separates the warlord from his captors.

Pin-Up asks the chubby little man if he speaks English, and he gives her a nod.

"What are you doing?" Pin-Up asks. "Dealing with buyer's remorse?"

He cocks his head, vexed by her question. "I do not know what you are meaning."

"You're praying, right?"

"Yes."

"So I'm just wondering if you're having buyer's remorse about your deal."

Confusion tightens his expression. "I am not understanding."

"Yeah, I bet you're not." She smirks. "I bet you're weighing the pros and cons between Leavenworth and eternal damnation."

"I am praying to Allah."

"Little too late for that, isn't it?"

"Why do you say such things?"

"Leave the poor man alone," a voice jokes from across the cabin. Leaning against the starboard wall, perched on a jump seat, still clad in her field camo, Boo looks restless, jittery, her gaze compulsively flitting around the cavernous steel confines of the cabin as though she's seeing phantoms in the ironwork. But right now she manages to give Pin-Up a good-natured wink. "The man's just trying to adjust to his retirement."

Pin-Up chuckles, and then walks across the cabin and takes a seat next to her. "You okay?"

"Yeah, I'm good."

"You don't look so good."

Boo stares at her. "Thank you, that's so sweet." Her voice is bathed in sarcasm. "I've been working on my look. I'm glad you like it."

"I'm not throwing shade, Boo, I'm just saying you seem edgy."

"What are you talking about? I feel fine."

"Why don't you take a break? Go get some chow up front with the boys."

"No thanks," Boo says tersely. "I'm good. I appreciate the thought though."

They sit in silence for a moment, each staring at the lattice of steel and complex webbing of cargo rails that comprise the aircraft's floor. The fuselage rattles over another stretch of turbulent air. They should be approaching the Caspian Sea any minute now, the point at which the aircraft will climb to fifteen thousand feet, which is protocol for spy planes and military escorts. Pin-Up clutches the grip of her M9 even tighter, and tries to swallow a creeping sense of vertigo.

The monotonous murmuring of Osamir's voice starts to get to her. She takes a deep breath and tries to drive it from her mind. She throws a glance over at her colleague. "What do you make of all this, Boo?"

Boo looks up. "What do you mean?"

"I know we've already talked it to death but what do you *really* think is going on? You know . . . with the so-called devil? With these new—whatever you call them—these powers we're supposed to be getting used to? These skills we're supposed to be mastering?"

Osamir abruptly stops praying.

Another figure—as yet unseen, unnoticed—now occupies the cabin.

"What do I really think?" Boo frowns as though trying to solve a complicated mathematical equation. "The truth is, I don't think we understand it yet. But at the same time . . . it's clear that it's real. It's as real as anything. You know what I mean?"

"I know exactly what you mean." Pin-Up thinks about it for a moment. It doesn't occur to her that Osamir is practically fluent in English, and now is listening closely to the conversation. Pin-Up measures her words. "Can I ask you a personal question?"

"Do I have a choice?"

Pin-Up's smile fades quickly. "What do you think your part of the deal is? Your power? What is it?"

Boo just shakes her head. "I don't know . . . like I said before, it has something to do with . . . death maybe?"

"Death?"

Boo shrugs. "I don't know . . . death and dying, spirits. Ghosts."

"With a handle like Boo?" Pin-Up says after a pause. "I would expect nothing less."

"Very funny." Boo gives her a sidelong glance. "With a name like Pin-Up . . . you should talk."

Pin-Up smiles to herself. "Touché."

Neither woman notices the dark humanoid creature clinging to the ceiling behind them. In the dim, diffuse light, the spider-like thing could easily be mistaken for an animatronic prop from a horror film. The slimy, segmented body bristles with dark, thick hair and pulsates with hideous, inexplicable life. But it's the face—with its cadaverous features, luminous crimson pupils, flesh like black mold, and lascivious smirk—that bears the distinct impression of one who is about to meddle in the lives of these three people.

## 2.

Over the years, a grudging friendship has blossomed between Boo and Pin-Up, a sisterhood of scars, evolving and deepening over time despite their differences, like an ironweed poking up through the paving stones of their journey. Early on, they dealt with the awkward fact that they both had a thing for Hack—a competition from which Boo had emerged victorious, but only for a few weeks until Spur caught wind of it. But the greater irony was that Pin-Up had been too busy dealing with her own issues to even notice such things.

Despite this disconnect, though, the two women have always seemed destined to be friends as well as comrades in arms. Never mind the fact that each had saved the other's life more than once in the field of battle. They had begun to appreciate each other as human beings. Pin-Up discovered Boo's Zen-like stoicism, and began to admire it. Conversely, Boo respected Pin-Up's self-deprecating wit. Also, for a woman with such stunning good looks, Pin-Up was extraordinarily humble—maybe even to a fault—completely clueless of her power over certain types of men. Little did Boo know, however, how much grief Pin-Up had to endure due to this otherwise admirable trait. Especially in that desolate wilderness full of predators known as Hollywood.

In fact, at this very moment, all at once, out of the blue, one of these very same predators, otherwise known as Jason Norbert Peltz, now appears—miraculously, impossibly—on the floor where the warlord sat only a moment ago as the aircraft now climbs to fifteen thousand feet and starts its water crossing over the Caspian.

Pin-Up slowly rises out of her chair, her gaze locked with horror-stricken wonder on the little balding film producer sitting cross-legged behind the nylon netting where Osamir had been praying one instant earlier. Now Peltz looks up at Pin-Up with the same disgusting smirk he had proffered upon her that fateful night she had entered his back office, and found herself alone with the man.

"It's okay, sweetheart . . . I won't bite . . . why don't you come a little closer," he murmurs just as he had purred to her that night, his voice husky and smoky, with a trace of Hoboken in it, an atonal dog whistle that only Pin-Up can hear.

She pulls the ten-inch tactical knife from its sheath on her thigh.

Across the cabin, Boo frantically unbuckles herself and leaps out of her jump seat. "Hold on . . . Pin . . . what the hell are you doing?"

Pin-Up barely registers the sound of Boo's voice. She raises the knife and slashes the nylon netting open as though unwrapping a side of beef for slaughter. Jason Peltz, the two-bit movie producer and serial rapist, looks up at her with a lewd sort of anticipation on his jowly face, his pouchy eyes twinkling with lust. "That's better," he purrs. "All nice and cozy-like, you and me."

She leans down and slashes the shackles apart, while across the cabin, the sound of the jump-bay hatch spontaneously un-latching pierces the droning chorus of the plane's props.

# 3.

Boo whirls and gapes at the hatch as it slides open under its own power.

The wind and light explode in her face, shoving her back against one of the cabin's structural pillars. She holds on to the girder as the slipstream slams through the cabin, tugging at her, sucking documents and loose items such as pens, tools, packing straps, and candy wrappers out the swirling vacuum of the hatch.

Alarm buzzers sound. Boo tries to get to the hatch, but the wind is smashing through the cabin. The tinny squawk of a radio voice echoes from somewhere else in the aircraft, but Boo can't tell who it is. The pilot? Spur? Out of the corner of her eye, she sees movement, bodies grappling, and then the inevitable horror unfolding.

Pin-Up has the knife pressed against Osamir's throat, and is dragging him toward the open hatchway, as though it were her doing all along, to will the door open, to be judge, jury, and executioner, the blazing hatred in her eyes—one degree away from madness—causing Boo to suspect that she might be under the influence of the mogwai.

"*Stop, Pin-Up, stop goddamn it don't do this!*"

Ignoring Boo's entreaties, Pin-Up drags the warlord closer and closer to the raging winds. Osamir is shrieking now, his voice wailing in the upper registers of the castrati, suggesting an animal being skinned. He digs the heels of his riding boots into the metal flooring in a futile bid to stop the attacker's forward momentum, but Pin-Up is a freight train of righteous rage, dragging him closer and closer to oblivion.

With one powerful heave, she shoves the little fat man out of the plane.

## 4.

Drawn by Boo's angry cries, Hack is the first to arrive in the mid-cabin section. He charges in with his hand on the grip of his .45, Ticker and Hack several paces behind him. He stumbles to a halt when he sees the open hatchway, the light and the noise of the props drumming in his ears, an inhuman scream echoing out on the winds.

Then everything slows down for him when he sees Pin-Up on the floor, curled into a fetal position, zombielike, and Boo, near the open hatch, madly grabbing for a parachute harness mounted on the wall. She yanks the whole bail-out pack off its moorings, and then, hugging it to her chest, she spins toward the gaping doorway . . .

. . . and like a figure in a nightmare that can't be stopped no matter how fast Hack lunges, no matter how loudly he booms a warning cry, no matter how desperately he reaches out for her . . .

. . . she leaps off the ledge, plummeting into the unsparing void.

Hack trips on a cargo rail reaching for her, nearly falling out of the hatch himself. He catches himself on the doorjamb. Then he leans out of the opening, the wind scourging his face as he gets a horrifying glimpse of the two figures in free fall below him, each of them plunging toward the choppy grey waters of the Caspian.

The closest figure—Boo—tumbles and thrashes as she tries to simultaneously stabilize herself and steer her fall toward the other figure a few hundred feet below her—Osamir—who spins wildly, arms and legs akimbo, his robe flagging violently in the unforgiving wind.

Hack is practically paralyzed with panic, mesmerized by the sight of Boo managing to get her arms through the straps of the chute pack as she free-falls. Hack has had enough experience with airdrops to know that fifteen thousand feet allows for about a minute of free fall before the chute must be opened.

Thirty seconds left . . .

. . . and the two figures are getting smaller and smaller above the vast churning sea as the plane continues on its flight path. Spur and Ticker reach the aftcabin and crowd the windswept gangway, not believing what they're seeing. Hack madly digs his binoculars from his belt pack. He peers through them, his fingers numb from the cold wind. In the narrow field of vision he can see Boo soaring closer and closer to the flailing figure below her. She reaches out . . .

. . . fifteen seconds left . . .

. . . and it looks as though she almost has her hand on the warlord's arm. She makes one desperate grab. Her fingers just miss the edge of his robe. He thrashes and spins . . .

. . . ten seconds left . . .

. . . and Boo makes one last lurching grab, a sort of Hail Mary move to save Osamir, when all at once a flash of light erupts from below, making Hack flinch, jerking his eyes away from the blinding white-hot supernova exploding in the binocular's visual field . . .

. . . five seconds . . .

. . . four . . .

. . . three . . .

. . . and with his naked eyes Hack sees the ocean open up and swallow Osamir in a maw of fire. The little man flails and shudders as the flames of hell swirl around him, enveloping him, encasing him in agony, his shriek so piercing as to be heard fifteen thousand feet above the spectacle, over the noise of the C-130 engines, and for miles in every direction, a keening howl of the damned . . .

. . . two . . .

. . . one . . .

Frantically raising the eyecups of the binoculars back to his eyes, Hack searches for Boo on the edges of the blazing inferno. All he sees now is the hellfire closing around the warlord like a great mouth, chewing, swallowing, and digesting him for all eternity.

The warlord vanishes within the vortex of the Caspian, the flames contracting inward like an immense iris closing down.

"Oh God no," Hack mutters under his breath as he glimpses a bat-winged object floating on the surface of the ocean. Spur and Ticker stand behind him, speechless, gazing out the hatch at the orange fabric of Boo's parachute sinking into the sea.

It will be recorded in classified transcripts as the first official casualty of the ghost unit.

## 5.

For the rest of that day, the four surviving members of the unit go about their business in a state of shock. Spur calls in air support to help search for Boo's remains, making sure that his superiors back home receive a coded message containing the bad news. Spur also requests that they keep a lid on the details surrounding the deaths of Osamir and Boo, as well any specifics relating to the classified operation in Karakistan.

It takes them quite awhile to find Boo's remains due to the fact that the chute—which had opened too late—had drifted a half a mile from the original point of contact. Late that afternoon, a rescue boat out of Hakim Naval Base in Azerbaijan locates her through the use of sonar. Divers recover her body from the ledge of a reef on which it had gotten tangled in the residue of a shipwreck from the nineteenth century.

A perfunctory effort is made to find Osamir's remains, despite the fact that everybody in the unit knows all too well that no one will ever find a trace of the infamous warlord. The details of his death will be left vague in the official records of the mission, but it's obvious to Spur and the rest of his team that Osamir now resides elsewhere, pursuant to the stipulations of his contract.

Pin-Up has very little memory of how it all went down. She recalls seeing and hearing the hallucination that was most certainly conjured by the devil—the warlord cloaked in the form of an abusive film producer—but this does not mitigate in any way her guilt and sorrow over her part in her friend's death.

That evening, at 5:30 P.M. Greenwich mean time, an A-10 Thunderbolt II attack aircraft drops fifty thousand leaflets across the northern tip of Karakistan, just outside the city of Azazel, warning any indigenous people in the area to evacuate. Six and half hours later, at midnight, a B-2 stealth bomber drops satellite-guided bombs on Osamir's nuclear factories, drug labs, and construction projects with zero damage to the surrounding areas and civilians. The shock waves can be felt as far away as Erebus, and the black haze of smoke will hang over the mountains for nearly a week afterward.

It is, to be blunt, the end of one era, and the beginning of another.

## CHAPTER FOURTEEN
# The Lowering

**1.**

"You'll have my resignation on your desk first thing tomorrow morning," Pin-Up murmurs, not even looking up. She sits on the floor of the aircraft's midcabin next to the flag-draped coffin, her face puffy from sobbing, as the C-130 begins its bumpy descent into Canadian airspace over Prince Edward Island.

They'll be on the ground in Delaware in less than an hour and a half.

"Not a chance, girlie-girl," Spur comments as he paces the width of the cabin. "You're making about as much sense as tits on a bull. I don't want to hear any more of this crapola, and that's a goddamn order."

She looks up at him, her almond-shaped eyes rimmed in red from her losing battle with the tears. Normally a stoic, battle-hardened woman who would rather have open-heart surgery than reveal her emotions, she has been awash in guilt and grief for practically the entire Atlantic crossing. She has her arm around the head of the coffin as though she were comforting a child, bracing it for whatever heavy weather might be in store for them. "This is all on me," she utters. "I lost it. You've said it a million times, Spur. That's one thing our job doesn't allow. We lose it and people die. Jesus, Spur, I used to be a field nurse, for Chrissake. I used to *save* lives."

Spur stops pacing and tries to put a lid on his anger. "I'm gonna need you to stop this right now. Seriously, Pin. We need to stay frosty as a unit . . . or we're *all* gonna be up Shit Creek without a paddle. You follow me? Each and every one of us needs to stay cool. You understand what I'm saying? Now I don't know exactly what Mr. Mephisto pulled on y'all back here, but I'm telling you, it ain't your fault."

Pin-Up visibly cringes at this kindness directed at her. The waves of grief come again. She leans forward, shuddering at another onslaught of emotion. Her tears drip on the hard, cold metal flooring. The plane thuds over another stretch of rough air.

She clutches the coffin tighter as if it were a life raft.

Spur softens when he sees this, and he goes over to her. He kneels and touches her shoulder. "It ain't your fault, missy. You read me?" he whispers in her ear. "It ain't your fault."

The other two men in the midcabin keep their distance, holding on to the jump line, steadying themselves against the intermittent turbulence. To Spur's left, Ticker keeps staring at the floor, sheepish and at a loss for words. Hack has also remained silent for the last several hundred miles, compulsively wiping his eyes, trying to come up with something funny to say, to make Pin-Up smile, but he keeps losing the words.

The unit customarily braces for the death of a member. The training and the psych profiles given periodically get at the heart of working in the field of black ops, the rules of the game, and the various methods of minimizing the emotional toll—all of it, every last piece of it, a pile of horseshit. Spur knows this sad fact backward and forward. Every member of the ghost unit is all too aware of it. The ugly truth is, each mission—every single operation no matter how clean, no matter how successful—destroys a piece of the operative. Every death of a fellow combatant steals a little bit of the soul. The only way to deal with it is for the survivor to take whatever they need to get through the night, and the next day get back on the goddamn horse.

Swallow, rinse, and repeat.

But now Spur realizes a new variable is working insidiously on his team like a virus. They are untethered to reality, disengaged with the norms and mores of intelligence work. They are operating on a new level, inchoate, mysterious, innate, inexorable—most of which they are just beginning to unravel. Have they sold their souls as part of the pact? Spur feels absolutely zero regret about Abu Osamir not being allowed to enjoy his day in court. In fact, if he is being honest with himself, Spur would be forced to admit that watching the filthy depths of the Caspian devour the little warlord felt good on a very shallow, fleeting, empty-calorie level, as though it were a form of pornography.

Even now, very faintly, very subtly, Spur feels the need growing within him to see the next evil bastard bite the dust. Is this part of the bargain? How can he possibly parlay something as disturbing as this new calling—a calling filled with bloodlust and vengeance—into action that benefits the common good?

But isn't the unit already serving the common good by hunting down the Abu Osamirs of the world? Isn't the planet a better place without Abu Osamir on it? Maybe losing Boo is part of the bargain. Spur glances down at the coffin.

The burnished midnight-blue vessel has stainless-steel handles and ornate details in the finish. The interior is lined with soft, pale-blue velvet, and was originally designed to hold the remains of dignitaries and high-ranking officers. Pin-Up chose the coffin at Hakim Naval Base, and supervised the placement of Boo's pale remains into the folds of the container.

The petite body had been in pristine condition just before the lid was closed, devoid of any postmortem cosmetics or mortician's tricks. Her death had been ruled as "an accidental drowning in the line of duty," from which she exhibited very few outwardly visible wounds. Spur had gotten a glimpse of her dressed in her Navy dress blues right before the lid came down during the chaplain's reading of the sailor's prayer:

> *My family's prayers are with me*
> *No matter where I roam.*
> *Please listen when I'm lonely*
> *And return me safely home.*

## 2.

The C-130 touches down at Dover Air Force base at around 3:00 P.M. eastern standard time that afternoon. The weather is blustery and brisk for late spring, the sky low and scudded with clouds the color of cold pewter. The wind assaults the team as they descend the aft ramp in pairs, two abreast, their expressions somber, their strides mired in fatigue. Hack and Pin-Up are the last to deplane, the two of them walking on either side of the flag-draped casket like ragged, camo-clad pallbearers.

The crew at the airfield has been briefed on their arrival and has prepared a van to transport Boo's remains to their final resting place. Although word of the fallen operative has trickled down the chain of command, the 436th Air Wing has blacked out all media and kept a tight lid on any personal information or background on the deceased leaking into the general population.

Now at the base of the ramp, a unit of four transport specialists greets the team with dour faces and stiff-armed salutes. They gather around the coffin. Hack reluctantly steps back, his handsome features demolished by sorrow, his eyes welling up again. A piece of him has broken off, a piece he never expects to regain, but he's good at stuffing back his emotions, and he does it now.

Pin-Up refuses to let go of the brass handle. She lingers there, downcast, eyes wet.

"Ma'am?" The group leader's voice is respectful and yet raised slightly against the raw salt breezes coming off Delaware Bay.

"In a second!"

The volume and sharpness of Pin-Up's voice causes all those in attendance—including Spur—to lower their awkward gazes to the tarmac. Pin-Up mutters a prayer under her breath—so faint as to be almost inaudible—as she strokes the coffin.

At last, Spur very calmly steps forward, gently takes her arm, and says very softly, "Let's let her go now."

Tears track down Pin-Up's face as she relinquishes her hold on the container.

## 3.

"C'mere," Spur says to Pin-Up after taking her into an adjacent hangar and borrowing a private office from the Air National Guard. The room is two hundred square feet of dusty parquet tile, an empty desk, a swivel chair, and not much else. Spur angrily pulls the venetian blinds shut with a single yank.

Pin-Up comes over and stands in front of him, wiping her eyes.

Spur grabs her by the shoulders and gently shakes her. "Stop it!"

"What . . . ?" She looks up at him as though she's half asleep. "What the fuck are you referring to?"

Spur loosens his grip on her shoulders, but keeps his hands on her arms. "I know you're hurting. We all are. But I'm warning you, you've got to stow this shit before it eats you alive."

She swallows hard. "Please let go of me."

"Not until you promise you'll get this shit under control."

"Fuck you."

He stares at her. She stares back at him for a long moment. Spur feels the very air around them crackling with tension. Without warning, the compulsion returns, rising in him, making his skin tingle.

He pulls her into a furious embrace, their lips finding one another, an onslaught of kisses ensuing. The sensation of free fall makes his head spin. He feels his body awakening, the spark flooding his loins, fueling his erection, and before he knows what's happening he's unbuttoning her top. Pin-Up tears her shirt the rest of the way open, popping the remaining buttons, their lips remaining locked together throughout. She unclasps her bra, her full breasts dropping into his hands. He slams her against the wall behind the door, pushing between her legs, making her moan with pleasure . . .

. . . when the sound of footsteps and a radio voice crackling outside the office pierce the moment. Spur freezes, and puts his hand over her mouth to silence her moaning. The noises in the corridor fade away as the guard moves on. The moment collapses. Their ardor instantly cools.

"Not now," he says.

She pulls her bra back over her breasts. "I know . . . but it begs the question. When?"

"I don't know," he says. "It's killing me. I think about you constantly."

More voices outside the door interrupt. Pin-Up pulls her top back on, quickly buttoning the buttons that have survived the moment. She straightens her hair, and Spur gives her a sad little nod before opening the door and leading her out.

## 4.

Echoes. Muffled vibrations. Subtle shifts in gravity penetrate the strata of steel and fabric, reverberating faintly up through the bones and tendons and viscera of the deceased. The coffin is being transported in a vehicle. Perhaps it's being shuttled to its final resting place, the sense of movement apparent now in the centripetal push and pull.

Sometime later, the coffin is placed onto a bier or a platform or some kind of pedestal. The faint sounds of drumming and myriad voices whispering respectfully register somewhere in the sleeping synapses of the deceased. In some deep chasm of her medulla oblongata she hears wind rattling leaves, branches swaying, intermittent creaking sounds—all of it registering somewhere deep in her awareness—*a military funeral!* They are laying her to rest at Arlington. It is the premier honor for a service member, and in her persistent sleep state she smiles.

Seven rifle blasts—three repetitions, twenty-one rounds—shake the deceased awake, erupting with the force of twenty-one nuclear warheads in her sleeping brain. Her eyes flutter open.

## CHAPTER SEVENTEEN
### Rotten Valentino

#### 1.

The Honorable Senator Margaret Elizabeth Winthrop awakens that morning in her private sleeping quarters at the Dirksen Building, a silent scream caught in her throat. She gapes at the ceiling of the renovated back office, the ornate copper medallions swimming in her bleary vision. Her spindly fingers fumble at a bedside pedestal cluttered with her countless pill bottles, moisturizers, emollients, and night creams as she chokes back the shriek lodged in her throat.

Only the faintest sound of a moan comes out of her as she levers her scrawny body into a sitting position, swallows a Valium, and tries to shake off the diabolical images of her nightmare. A stick-thin woman in her late sixties, her sharp angles currently cocooned in a three-thousand-dollar Oscar de la Renta silk robe, Margaret Winthrop has the look of an aging duchess draped in the accouterments of women half her age. From her bleached-blond, six-o'clock-news-anchor hairstyle to her elaborate lacquered nails, she radiates money and power. But just under the glossy surface is an embittered, lonely soul—thrice divorced, estranged from her children and grandchildren alike—armored with a layer of hate and xenophobia like an invisible carapace. But on *this* morning, she is at a disadvantage due to the half-life of the horrendous nightmare that refuses to let go.

The dream began—as so many of her nightmares have in recent months—innocently, in a museum.

Margaret is alone, walking from alcove to alcove, perusing oil paintings of scenes from her life. At first, the artwork features benign tableaux—her three weddings, her children posed in Norman Rockwell holiday scenes, her swearing-in on the Senate floor. But then, very gradually, as she dives deeper into the warrens and nooks of the museum, the paintings darken in both hue and subject matter.

She sees herself captured midcoitus in a squalid Motel 6 during a brief affair with an intern back in her state senate days in Ken-

Strange. Complete paralysis. As numb as an ice sculpture in her blue uniform, she can see only darkness, but the darkness has a texture to it—a waffle pattern of deeper black against a field of black. She realizes she's staring at the lining of her coffin's lid. Panic as sharp as an electric current bolts down her sinews. Her eyeballs toggle in their sockets wildly, the primal fear of claustrophobia and being buried alive catching fire within her. How did this happen? She remembers tales of premature burial—Edgar Allan Poe, Ambrose Bierce, *The Twilight Zone,* it all comes flooding back to her like a movie projector running too rapidly, the film slipping off the sprockets: free-falling, hitting the surface of the grey Caspian Sea, all her wind and life knocked out of her . . . then sinking . . . sinking . . . sinking like an anvil, sinking into the dirty depths and swirling, icy currents.

Her eyes well up with emotion. She may be dead but she can still cry, thinking back to her father's funeral along the Yangtze River, Hubei Province, seven days of mourning, her family dressed in their colorful funeral garb, cherry blossoms falling along the banks of the river, the sun peeking through clouds as though the heavens were welcoming her dear father. She feels something coming undone beneath the coffin . . . a loosening, a creaky heaving of wood and heavy rope.

The lowering follows, even as the echoes of the Remington rifles linger on the breeze. She feels the hoist lowering her into the earth. She feels the thud as the coffin hits bottom. She hears the thump of dirt hitting the top of the box. She wants to scream, to cry out that she's not dead—not exactly—but the state she is in will not allow it. Handfuls of earth continue to hit the top of the receptacle every few seconds, and it sends her into a fugue state of raw terror.

What happens next is almost beyond her powers of comprehension.

She feels something shift within her. At first it disorients her, makes her dizzy, and causes her mind to reel like a gear that has slipped its cog. She feels buoyant, galvanized, a snake that has shed its skin. The heavy feeling of doom begins to lift, replaced by something more powerful, more primordial—a sense of purpose. She flexes her fingers for the first time since she died. She can feel the surface of her skin tingling. Her paralysis fades. She can feel her legs now. Considering the impact of her fall into the Caspian, her body and her soul have weathered her demise quite well.

## 5.

Over the course of her transformation she has heard the rumble of a backhoe filling in her grave. Then silence for a long stretch. Then an unnerving sound rising up from beneath the muffled wailing of the wind. At first she thinks it might be an engine— another grave being filled in—after all, it *is* Arlington National Cemetery, and lately the place has been busy. But the noise begins to sound like many engines whirring busily.

Now she realizes that what she's hearing are the voices of the dead.

They come in waves, in snippets of different accents from different eras in different voices, each melding into the next, a Greek chorus of fallen warriors:

". . . my dear beloved Florence, I rue the day that I left Cincinnati . . ."

". . . inexpressible joy and pride to know I did my share at Anzio against the Nazis . . ."

". . . as a member of the Forty-Second Ohio Volunteers I have seen . . ."

". . . the winds at Tannenberg were of such terrific velocity that . . ."

". . . on the tail end of Operation Arc Light we dropped hundreds of them five-hundred-pound bunker busters . . ."

". . . at the second battle of Fallujah I get turned around and like a dumbass I accidentally step on a land mine and that's curtains for me . . ."

On and on it goes, an endless mosaic of memories, over four hundred thousand buried since 1864, each timeworn voice a casualty of war, some of the deceased known and loved by others, some anonymous, all victims of battles both historic and overlooked, jumping across the centuries and back again, the tone of each testimonial neither sad nor joyous, neither angry nor resolved; they are simply providing witness down through time of somebody somewhere who fought and died for the United States of America.

## 6.

At length, in the velvet folds of her coffin, Boo has to cover her ears. She can't take one more moment of the voices. They have become overwhelming to her, unbearable in their tragedy, their impassive stoicism, their existential loneliness. She removes her hands from her ears and discovers that the voices have stopped. Did she will them to cease?

She quickly realizes that she must try to escape her interment. She can tell by the low buzz of crickets and the lack of ambient traffic noises that it's the middle of the night. She also knows that her best chance of digging herself out of the ground is while the grave is fresh, and the soil has not yet hardened over. Tonight is indeed the night.

She takes a deep breath and realizes all at once with great consternation that her lungs are no longer drawing air, which is how she has already spent so much time underground bereft of oxygen.

*Of course!* How could she be so clueless? When one's dead one doesn't need to breathe, but she's not really dead, is she? She has all her faculties, her flesh seems warm, and she even appears to be swallowing, blinking, and moving her chest as though she were a normal living, breathing person. Are these involuntary physical tics merely habitual? Or is she caught in some sort of limbo between life and death?

Driving the interminable questions from her mind, she feels around the inner walls of the coffin for something she might use as a tool. All she can feel are the layers of tufted velvet lining. She discovers a seam between the two portions of the lid—one portion designed to swing open for viewing, and the other permanently shut—but she has no way of wedging the headpiece open.

Her shoes!

She realizes that she's been buried in her dress blues, a uniform she rarely has the gall to parade around in, but *the shoes*! They are blocky, stiff, onyx-black wing tips—straight out of the box, never worn—and now she wriggles one off one foot with the other toe, shimmies her hand downward, and grabs it. She slams the hard edge of the sole up into the seam of the coffin lid. It makes a dull thud but the headpiece doesn't budge.

It takes several tries. Utilizing her martial-arts training and ability to break two-by-fours with the heel of her palm, she finally shoves the shoe far enough upward into the seam to nudge an inch-and-a-half gap between the coffin's headpiece and tailpiece. A few cubic inches of dirt sift down onto her lap. The lid gives a little. She keeps at it. The lid opens wider. More loose soil rains down on her.

For the next hour or so she is relentless, using the shoe to scrape at the dirt, loosening it, letting it fall into the coffin, piling it at her sides, scraping some more, shoveling and piling, shoveling and piling, until finally the lid opens wide enough to allow a small avalanche of dirt to pour into the coffin.

The rich Virginia loam completely covers her, reeking of decay and mold and ancient humus, but oddly she doesn't gag. She doesn't choke on it, or even hesitate.

She begins to tunnel her way out, mole-like, using her delicate little bare hands—hands that have wrought righteous vengeance upon evildoers over the years—to dig her way back to the world.

## 7.

Halfway to the surface, she feels something leathery to her left. Like an old coat or a hat made of cowhide. She digs and claws at the dirt around it, clearing it away from the object, until finally she sees that it's a face—a pale, bloodless face—archived in the dark, incessant, indelible memories of her childhood.

"Greetings, my dear," the face of the mogwai says to her in its original Mandarin tongue from its earthen nest four feet below ground level. "Welcome to the underworld." Its voice is something from another planet—a deep, buzzing, sepulchral drone. "You have crossed over to the in-between."

Paralyzed with contrary emotions—terror, confusion, hate—she says nothing, just stares at the talking face encased in earth.

"Cat got your tongue?"

"What do you want from me? What do you want from any of us?"

The mogwai's eyes are all white, like antique ivory cue balls, slightly yellowed with age, buried in a face so wrinkled and ancient it looks mummified. Its jagged teeth are the color of old brass, its long beard a tangle of brittle spiderwebs. "You must understand the concept of reciprocity, no?"

"Reciprocity? You're talking about the deal we've made with you?"

"I assume you're an educated woman, are you not?"

"What has happened to me?"

"You are empowered with the agency of death, you are one with the Diyu."

"What does that mean?"

The egg-white eyes fix themselves onto her. "You are now

kindred with the realm of the dead. You may pass among the living but you are hewn from the fabric of the dead, and can commune with the spirits, move from life to death and back again with impunity."

"And what good does that do me?"

*"Silence!"* The face in the ground puckers like a seedpod shriveling in time-lapse, cobweb eyebrows narrowing with rage, blackened lips peeling back from sickening serrated teeth. "I'm warning you . . . your ego will destroy you if you're not careful."

"I have no ego," she informs the desiccated face. "I'm dead, remember?"

"Your insolence will be your demise," the mogwai tells her. "Down through the ages others have struck the same bargain as you, other warriors from other times, and they, too, allowed their egos to destroy them."

"Wait . . . others have made this same deal? Others have been given these powers?"

"Heed my warning, woman." The face dissolves into the black grains of earth like a tide pool evaporating. "You are all my property now."

"Wait! What are you saying exactly? What do you mean by property?!"

The face has almost completely vanished, leaching back into the ground like a slurry, the droning voice fading, an insect in her ears. "You are doomed to one day return to the fires of the netherworld from which your powers originate."

## 8.

Arlington National Cemetery lies dark and quiet in the middle of the night, as calm as the still surface of a lake. The rolling hills of white marble tombstones—dotted with the occasional oak or maple standing silent sentry—seem to softly glow on nights like this, when there's a full moon. But on this particular night, if one were to look more closely at around 3:30 A.M. eastern standard time—perhaps from the vantage point of Patton Drive along the southern edge of the cemetery, maybe with binoculars or field glasses—one would see a ghastly phenomenon occurring at the northwest corner of Section 60.

In the shadows of the old magnolia tree, where the woman from Special Forces was buried earlier that day, a diminutive figure pushes her way out of the freshly turned dirt. Silhouetted in the moonlight, the figure pauses in front of the tombstone recently carved with the following commemorative words:

SPECIALIST MICHELLE LIN CHEN
US NAVY
SPECIAL FORCES
USS GEORGE WASHINGTON

The individual lingers there for a moment, appearing to process what is engraved on that stone. Then the figure turns and walks away into the night . . .

. . . unaware that a second figure has materialized in the shadows behind her, oozing from the darkness as though made of smoke.

Unseen, unidentified, this second figure follows the tiny woman out of the cemetery and down a lonely, deserted stretch of Washington Street, each individual passing in and out of pools of sodium-vapor light like an escapee from a dream.

# PART III

## THE SERPENT'S GAMBIT

Put on the whole armor of God, that you may be able to stand against the schemes of the devil. For we do not wrestle against flesh and blood, but against the rulers, against the authorities, against the cosmic powers over this present darkness, against the spiritual forces of evil in the heavenly places.

—Ephesians 6:11–12

## CHAPTER FIFTEEN
# Speak of the Devil

### 1.

In a leafy suburb of Washington, D.C., along the Potomac River, sprawls the thousand-acre government complex known as Naval Support Facility Anacosta. On the southwest corner of the base sits a nondescript office building that houses the headquarters for the Defense Intelligence Agency. The Special Expeditionary Section of the DIA—the group responsible for everything from the extraction of kidnapped dignitaries to the assassination of rogue dictators—is relegated to the sublevel of the headquarters building, as though the entire division were a randy teenager best kept under wraps in the basement for fear of embarrassing the family. Over the years, rumors have plagued the agency that the SES has been mixed up in a whole host of dirty tricks and mind-bogglingly classified programs, from Area 54 UFO research to the study of soldiers under the influence of LSD.

Right now, in that very sublevel, in that very department, a phone is ringing in the outer offices of the section chief.

"Bull pen," the skinny man in thick glasses says into his phone at the reception desk. Dressed in nerd-casual khakis and a Neil deGrasse Tyson T-shirt, Hanley is a typical worker bee in the SES division—antisocial, multiple degrees, on the spectrum of Asperger's somewhere, and annoyingly intelligent.

"Code name, please."

The voice on the other end is terse, male, recognizable as the dispatcher for the Special Operations Unit. Hanley knows the drill.

"Cthulhu," the receptionist replies. Hanley loves the cloak-and-dagger routine. It appeals to his perpetual feelings of alienation and estrangement from the ordinary world.

"PIN number, please."

"238855."

(The distance in miles to the moon.)

Hanley hears a series of clicks, and then the dispatcher's voice returning. "Get this down, Ca-thul-who. Bravo-niner plus three will rendezvous with Silverback at nineteen hundred hours at the following coordinates." Hanley scrambles for his secure laptop. "38.8048 Delta November, 77.0469 Delta Whiskey. Read them back to me, please."

After hurriedly typing them into his laptop, Hanley reads them back.

The other end of the line clicks, and the connection goes dead without ceremony or sign-off.

## 2.

Colonel Sean McDermott is Silverback—a nod to the huge, imposing, striped male gorilla—the code name a not-so-subtle allusion to both McDermott's status and stature. At six foot four and two hundred and seventy-some pounds, McDermott tends to intimidate despite his sweet, gentle nature. A former linebacker for the Michigan State University Spartans, as well as a veteran bouncer at several East Lansing nightspots, McDermott towers over his peers at the agency, most of whom look like white-collar refugees from a *Dilbert* comic strip. Plus McDermott's ruddy complexion, big muttonchop sideburns, constellations of freckles, and flaming red hair give off the air of an ancient Celt, as though he is perpetually about to reach for his longsword and shield, and lop off somebody's head. His taste for tartan plaid vests and Meerschaum pipes doesn't help matters. Only his large, soulful, hazel eyes reveal a window into his tender heart.

In fact, at this very moment, those same hazel eyes are wet from the grieving process, which began at the funeral he attended the previous day. Boo had been a gem in the crown of the Special Expeditionary Section, an operative whom McDermott had personally selected from the crème de la crème of the SEALs. And now she's gone. Just like that. It's the vagary of asymmetrical cold warfare—the best and the brightest are considered not only expendable but in the event of their death are automatically banished from their fold, disavowed by the intelligence community as though they never existed in the first place. All of which is why McDermott lobbied for an unorthodox public funeral at Arlington for Boo, and also why he suddenly perks up when he sees the direct message flash on his screen from Hanley's station:

```
BRAVO-NINER PLUS THREE TO RENDEZVOUS WITH
SILVERBACK—1900 HOURS AT THE FARM.
```

The man code-named Silverback hurriedly gathers his things. He has not yet had a chance to commiserate with Spur and the rest of the team. For security reasons, they were not allowed to attend Boo's funeral. Instead, upon their arrival at Bolling Air Force Base, they were rushed into a sort of quarantine, housed in the adjacent residential facility, separated and questioned and briefed and examined like astronauts returning from space.

## 3.

The protocols go back to the Cold War era, and the rampant paranoia and suspicions that operatives might bring back something on their shoes or a tracker on their tail or perhaps a brain in their skull that's been washed and programmed to assassinate an American intelligence officer or politician. Of course, nothing of the sort has ever happened. No record of any Manchurian candidate or chemical Trojan horse exists. But there is one thing that Silverback and just about everybody else in the intelligence community believes deep down in their marrow: *You can't be too careful in this crazy business.*

"The turn's up here, on the left," Silverback says to the driver. "By the big willow. See it? Up there on the left."

They are en route to the place that has come to be known as the farm.

The journey has taken them over an hour, following the winding two-lanes and gravel roads that snake through the Virginia rural backwaters, the sun drooping low in the sky as dusk sets in. Silverback sits alone in the rear of the SUV, the driver an airman from Bolling still in his camo and cap. The thick leafy countryside streams past the tinted windows of the black Escalade as Silverback thinks back to that last time he saw the man code-named Spur.

It was in the briefing meeting with the boys from the Pentagon, quarreling about whether or not Osamir had acquired nuclear capabilities—and there was Spur sitting back, chewing his tobacco. "Anything's possible in this old world," he said finally. "We'll go over there and get to the bottom of it, and if he's got 'em, he ain't gonna have 'em for long."

They make the turn, and the moment Silverback sees his spread in the waning light of the sunset, he immediately feels better.

Fifty-four acres of rolling hills, wooded meadows, fenced-off pastureland, and a grand homestead high on a tree-lined berm, the estate was bequeathed to Silverback by his father, a railroad man who had struck it rich in the 1970s when Amtrak boomed during the oil embargo. After the senior McDermott passed away, in the late 1990s, his only son, Sean Junior, was just beginning to climb the bureaucratic ladder in the intelligence community. Inheriting the farm was, at first, an irritant to Silverback—just another item on the to-do list for the overworked perpetual bachelor—but as the years passed, he found it a refuge. It became a place to get away from the insanity of D.C., a place to recharge, a place to think.

The driver pauses at the front gate to punch in a code, then wends his way up a series of switchbacks and hairpin turns to the main house.

By the time they arrive it's a quarter to seven, and the magic-hour light has blanketed the lavish two-story, ten-room Victorian in a golden radiance. The air smells of clover and hay. Silverback thanks the driver, and then carries his overnight bag up the cobblestone walk to the front porch. He is just inserting the key into the dead bolt when he hears a familiar voice.

"Look at you," the voice says from behind him. "The master of the manor!"

Silverback turns and wipes his eyes. "God, it's good to see all of you."

## 4.

They had been strolling along the adjacent pasture, inspecting the beautiful strawberry roan and her foal, when the Escalade had pulled up the winding access road. Spur saw it first and suggested they head up to the house. Now they have all gathered at the foot of the front porch, taking turns getting bear-hugged by the weepy section chief. Silverback can barely hold it together. He cries softly into Spur's shoulder as he hugs the man, and murmurs condolences, and then repeatedly sniffs back tears as he gives Ticker, Hack, and Pin-Up each a warm embrace.

Spur can see that Silverback is genuinely heartbroken by the loss of Boo, and even after inviting the team inside, pouring each of them a drink, and sitting down with them in the living room, the big man can't quite let go of the sorrow. He seems to be having a difficult time even speaking clearly.

"She was . . . she was special . . . wasn't she?" Silverback takes another belt of scotch. "She deserved better than this."

Spur nods, and remains silent, noticing the others staring at the floor, also nodding.

Hack speaks up at last, his voice stretched thin with grief and regret, his eyes moist. "I still can't wrap my head around it. She was . . . my best friend . . . my compass. She was true north, man."

"It was my fault," Pin-Up finally confesses.

Spur shoots her a look. "Pin, come on."

"I didn't say anything in the debriefing. I told them Osamir jumped."

Spur lets out a sigh, wondering if they should just tell the section chief everything. Get it all on the table. "Is this the right time to do this, Pin?"

She shrugs. "I don't know if it will *ever* be the right time."

Now Silverback has fixed his gaze on her, setting down his drink, his big, chiseled Irish face an open door, empathetic, concerned, a benevolent parent. In the congenial atmosphere of that living room, with the soft glow of kerosene lanterns and antique Tiffany lamps driving away the vastness of night, Spur realizes that Silverback is the only human being on earth outside of the unit that he trusts completely. But how does one tell the story of what happened in Karakistan without sounding like a lunatic? Where does one start?

"I told them how Boo tried to save him, and her chute opened too late," Pin-Up goes on. "That part's true. But the warlord didn't jump."

Silverback has gotten his tears under control and now studies the beautiful Latina sitting on the end of his sofa with a furrowed brow. "You can speak openly here, Pin," he says. He looks at Spur. "The place gets swept twice a week. It's clean, bug-free. Well . . . if you don't count the roach problem in the basement."

Pin-Up continues: "The thing is, I was under the influence of—"

—and right then she stops abruptly, her eyes narrowing with confusion. At first she looks as though her mind has suddenly gone blank. Then she appears to be trying to swallow something stuck in her throat. "I was under the influence of . . . of . . ."

She glances at Spur. Disoriented and baffled, she opens her

mouth but no words will come out. For a moment she leans forward, straining to speak, looking as though she's about to vomit.

"Pin-Up? You okay?" Silverback rises from his armchair, starting toward her.

She waves him off. "Fine . . . I'm fine . . . totally fine." She takes in a breath. "Just a little tired, I guess."

"Do you want to turn in?" Silverback sits back down, looks at the others. "You folks must be bushed. All of you. There's a private bedroom for each of you, beds all turned down. Private bathrooms."

"No, no . . . I'm good," Pin-Up says. "It's just . . . it's been a long couple of days."

From across the room, Hack speaks up. "Sean, may I ask, if I'm not being too pushy, have you seen the debriefing transcripts?"

Silverback nods, pouring himself another splash of scotch. "I have indeed. And to be honest with you, they seem . . . incomplete."

Spur nods. "Incomplete."

"I don't mean you falsified anything. Nothing like that. What I mean is . . . it seems like you were each holding something back."

Spur takes a deep breath and looks around the room at each member of the unit. "I think maybe it's time for full disclosure. Is that okay with everybody?"

They all nod.

Spur looks at Silverback. "The ambush went down as reported. We were set up. It was that son of a bitch Deegan—the Black Hawk pilot—but that's not the weird part." He shakes his head, letting out an incredulous little chuckle. "I guess 'weird' is an understatement. At gunpoint they led us down to this . . . it was a torture-chamber-type situation. Anyway. We were ridden hard and put away wet. Hadn't even gotten a chance to eat our oats when they came back in with a video camera. They did a number on Pin-Up . . . nearly lopped her head off . . . but then . . . then. Then."

Silverback looks at him. ". . . And then what? What happened?"

Spur swallows. Blinks. It's like he had just been driving along on a straightaway, all the memories spreading out in front of him as he recounted what happened, when all at once he drives off a cliff. A shade is pulled down on the imagery. He plunges into an abyss where his mouth won't work anymore. The words won't come.

He knows what he wants to say . . . but it sticks in his throat like a chicken bone. It's as though invisible fingers are strangling his vocal cords, paralyzing his voice.

Then he realizes the same thing had just happened to Pin-Up. She was about to describe the devil's intervention in the aircraft when the invisible choke hold had clamped down on her words. Moments later, in the same fashion, Spur was about to relate the devil's handiwork in the dungeon—the fire-and-brimstone illusion that had appeared to have sucked the thugs through cracks in the floor—when his own voice had failed *him*.

They were each about to speak of the devil when they each hit that same black vacuum in their streams of consciousness . . .

. . . a spell cast by the master spellcaster.

## CHAPTER SIXTEEN
# Patron Saint of Dead Meat

### 1.

Boo walks for hours, up and down the deserted thoroughfares of Arlington, Virginia, getting her thoughts together, gathering her bearings, becoming accustomed to her new . . . condition? Is it a condition? Or is it a power to be harnessed? Or is it madness to think she can go on like before, caught in this half-life limbo, this state of conscious death, this realm of the in-between?

At one point she manages to ask a passing paperboy out on his predawn route if he could give her directions to West Alexandria. The paperboy tells her it's about five miles to the south, and describes in great detail the best route to take on foot. During the brief conversation, the freckle-faced young cherub does give her a few strange glances, but apparently her dress blue uniform crusted with grave dirt doesn't completely unnerve him. This is, after all, the D.C. federal corridor, where all manner of fringe government elements prowl the night.

Later, passing a store window, Boo sees her reflection, and discovers that she has indeed changed. Her flesh is now so pale it looks almost translucent, as though her tendons, nerves, bones, and even the blood in her veins—albeit stagnant—are all visible within her chiffon-like epidermis. She has no sense of thirst or hunger anymore. She breathes only by habit. No oxygen fills her frozen, inert lungs.

And yet: She keeps walking through the night with the unflagging gait of an automaton. She knows about Silverback's farm west of Alexandria. Spur has characterized it more than once as a default rendezvous point if the unit is somehow separated and scattered to the winds. Boo remembers visiting it a couple of times in recent years for briefings, but can't recall its address. She has no money on her, no cell phone, no identification, no means with which to contact Spur—evidently morticians find wallets of little use to the dead—but what would Boo say to him if she *could* reach him? *"Hi there, Spur, this is a voice from the Great Beyond speaking."*

Halfway to West Alexandria, she realizes she's being followed.

Every few moments, out of the corner of her eye, she detects the fleeting evidence of a figure tailing her, keeping a constant distance of maybe a half a block to a block behind her. In the murky predawn shadows, she can't even be sure it's human, the way it seems to wax and wane as though passing behind panes of frosted glass. Each time Boo makes a turn, she catches a momentary glimpse of an elongated, human-shaped shadow spilling across the intersection. Then it vanishes as abruptly as it appeared. Finally, Boo passes the massive display window of a hardware store, and pauses.

She gazes in at a model bathroom display with decorative fixtures, marble sinks, and a great oval mirror gilded in bronze. She studies her reflection in the mirror. She notices that her dark eyes have faint cataracts filming them. The corners of her mouth have deepened, creased with wrinkles she had never noticed before. She looks older than her thirty-eight years.

To make matters worse, there's a corpse standing behind her in the mirror.

## 2.

She whirls around with a start.

The ghost steps back, hands going up in surrender. "Lady, I mean you no harm, I swear to God." The spirit speaks in a deep, gravelly voice cured with equal parts bourbon, cheap cigars, and the Bronx. Apparently, in life, he was a soldier—a medic by the looks of his tarnished, battered helmet with its single red cross like a faded pink marquee over his abomination of a face. Judging from his tattered, worm-eaten uniform—complete with a row of entry wounds apparently caused by high-caliber bullets—he had put in his service many years ago.

"Who . . . who are you?" Boo demands, her back pressed against the store window. "And why the hell are you following me?"

"I'm a friend, trust me," he says. His leathery face is skin and bone, the mummified flesh stretched across a knobby skull, the whites of his eyes the color of old buffalo nickels. His teeth are rotted little stumps that reveal the decomposed, maggot-ridden maw of his throat as he talks. "Name's Eiger . . . Corporal Jeff Eiger . . . but you can call me Charon. Everybody else does."

Boo gapes at the phantom. "You were a medic."

The ghost nods. "Bingo! Dog Company, Second Battalion, Seventy-Fifth Ranger Regiment. Seen a lot of boys end up deep-sixed over there . . . Omaha Beach, Hürtgen Forest, Hill 400 . . . but when I saw you checking into that boneyard yesterday I knew you was special."

Boo stares. "Wait . . . Omaha Beach? That's World War II. That's D-Day."

"Code name Operation Neptune," the specter says with a trace of pride in his wood-chipper voice. The streetlight behind him shines through his spindly form like the faint beams of an X-ray, tiny shafts of light shooting out the front of each bullet hole. "Lost almost three thousand GIs that day . . . I was a busy little beaver, I tell ya, pretty near fourteen thousand wounded. But that's not where I got the nickname Charon. I don't suppose you know the reference by any chance? Charon the ferryman?"

"Yeah, actually, I do. It's from Greek mythology, right? Charon was the boatman, carried souls of the recently deceased across the River Styx?"

"The girl wins the stuffed poodle! Right you are, little lady."

She thinks for a moment. "Why don't you go ahead and call me Boo."

"Boo, huh? I like that." The ghost gives her a wink, the brittle eyelid threatening to crumble off his face. He glances over his shoulder as though he's forgotten something. "You mind if we find a little cover somewhere . . . someplace not so . . . public? I want to tell a little story about a certain individual." He looks at her. "This is an individual you're probably already familiar with, if my instincts haven't dried up with the rest of me. There's something you should know about . . . something important." His expression sinks into itself, and sadness tugs at his putrefied eye sockets. "The fact is you're in an awful fix . . . you and your friends . . . you're in danger. I'll explain everything once we get off the street."

With a shrug, Boo says, "Lead on, Macduff."

The ghost looks at her. "Who's this McDuff?—I told you my name's Jeff Eiger."

## 3.

They find a boarded building on University Avenue, and Boo climbs the fire escape to the roof. The ghost is waiting for her.

"It ain't the Ritz, but it'll do," he says, leading her across the leprous tar-paper roof to a dry spot next to a massive iron chimney.

The sun is just beginning to lighten the horizon to the east, driving away the night. Boo can see the chain of lights leading to Alexandria in the distance. To the west, the dark rural hinterlands stretch like a great black ocean. Somewhere in that vast blackness is Silverback's farm, and Boo's only hope of finding refuge. "Let me take a wild guess," she says. "This so-called individual? He wouldn't by any chance be the Antichrist, would he? El Diablo? Old Nick? Mephisto?"

The ghost looks down in shame, shaking his head. "I call him Lou."

"Short for Lucifer?"

He looks up. "Cute, huh? It was his idea. He has this thing about being called Lucifer. Long story . . . not worth the telling."

"One of my associates believes that he's somewhat . . . ubiquitous. In other words, he listens in, and can hear us most of the time." She gives the medic a sidelong glance. "You sure you want to delve into this right now?"

Charon smiles. He points to the cross on his helmet, tapping it with his cadaverous finger. "No worries. As long as I'm under this . . . we can delve all we want, he ain't gonna get a good connection."

"Did you make a deal with him?"

The ghost swallows hard. "Let's just say, I backed out of a deal . . . and I got myself cursed." He glances over his shoulder again. "Tell you what. Let me start at the beginning, and I'll tell ya why I noticed you and why I know you and your pals are about to be in a world of shit."

## 4.

His story starts after his basic training. February 1942. He had volunteered earlier that year for specialist training as a combat medic, and by the time he had learned how to stanch bleeding, apply dressings, sprinkle sulfa powder on wounds, and pump as much morphine as he could get his hands on into the poor GIs, he was shipped out. In the South of France, the ambulance driver for the Second Battalion had perished under heavy bombing, and now they needed a new driver as soon as possible.

Business was brisk for Corporal Jeff Eiger, and he hit the ground running, taking over the ambulance unit, shuttling back and forth from one battlefront to another, burning hundreds of gallons of gas a day, saving the lives of thousands of wounded young boys, and spending his spare time fraternizing with the local *belles femmes*. But it wasn't long before the Nazi scourge spread across the glorious hills of Provence from Marseille to Toulouse. It was as though an epidemic—a fever of evil—had infected the villages and wineries and cafés. Rape, theft, beatings, and all manner of plundering went on twenty-four hours a day.

The ambulance unit was effectively shut down, forced out of business, pushed back toward the sea, where they hunkered down in the coastal hills, withstanding nightly shelling from Luftwaffe bombers. But Eiger refused to take the occupation lying down. He surreptitiously went on midnight runs, conveying wounded members of the resistance to hospitals in the south. He saw things on those runs that would live in his nightmares the rest of his life (and beyond).

One particular Nazi officer—Lieutenant Hans Schliegel—was fond of black magic. He would hold nightly rituals and Satanic balls in a burned-out church near Avignon, and enjoyed staging blood orgies and sacrificing virginal girls whom he had plucked from unsuspecting farm families. One night, as Corporal Eiger was busily transporting Schliegel's victims to and fro—most of whom would eventually die—he ran into a roadblock on a lonely two-lane the likes of which he would not be able to conjure in a thousand nightmares.

"It was a pile of human bones," the ghost murmurs in his sandpaper voice on that windy precipice as the sun rises on another Virginia day. "I'll never forget it. I slammed on the brakes and I sat there in the darkness in that ambulance, staring at the blasted sculpture for God knows how long."

"What was the point of it?" Boo asks. She has been pacing the length of the rooftop for most of the story but now she pauses.

"It was a gate to hell, I guess," Charon tells her with a shrug.

The beams of early-morning sun slant down from the east, shining through Charon's body as though it were made of gauze, the tiny rays shooting out the bullet holes almost festively, like a Christmas display. The yeasty scent of a local bakery opening for its morning rush drifts on the breeze, a strange counterpoint to the horrors being related by the ghost. "It was a doorway made of human remains," he elaborates. "It had like an archway at the top made of skulls, some of them still bloody. The opening in the middle was empty but somehow I knew it wouldn't be empty for long." He pauses, slowly shaking his decomposed head.

"Go on, Charon."

The ghost shivers. "Sure enough, here he comes, materializing out of thin air in that doorway, the son of a bitch, appearing there like some kind of damn maître d'. 'I've been waiting for you,' he says. 'Call me Lou,' he says. Well, I don't need no guidebook to tell me who I'm talking to. Know what I mean?"

Boo looks off into the distance. "The mogwai," she utters to herself.

"What was that?" the ghost asks.

She looks at him. "Nothing. Forget it. Tell me what he looked like."

Charon scratches his chin. "I don't know . . . he sure didn't look like some devil outta the funny pages, I'll tell ya that. He didn't have no horns or tail or nothing. He was small, and . . . and . . . he had a look to him like a rabid dog, you know, with yellow eyes and sharp little teeth. He wore this black three-piece suit like a mortician would wear with the boutonniere and all, and his hair was slicked back, and his skin . . . his skin was . . . was . . . kinda of slimy like a snake."

Another pause.

And then this: "He says to me, 'Have I got a deal for you, ferryman.' He says, 'I need somebody to hunt down folks that have defaulted on contracts, and then carry them across the Great Divide for me. Just like Charon.' Then he says to me, 'You seem perfectly suited for such a position, my good man.'"

The ghost pauses for a moment, as though the telling itself has drained him. Boo waits. She knows that this is the difficult part of the story.

"I told him to piss up a rope, and then I slam the ambulance into reverse, and I tear outta there." He pauses and swallows back the sorrow. "That night I got killed on a ridge overlooking the vineyards; I didn't see the machine gun nest until it was too late. I didn't know what hit me." Another anguished pause. "I woke up in Arlington, and he was waiting for me. Perched on my tombstone like a buzzard. He says to me, 'How's it feel?' I say to him, 'What . . . being dead? It ain't nothing special.' He laughs and says, 'You're not just dead . . . you're cursed . . . cursed to wander in limbo for the rest of eternity for defying me.' Then he vanishes in a whiff of hell smoke. And that, as they say, is all she wrote."

Boo has been nodding for the last part of the story, almost as though she could see it coming. She looks up at him. "You said we were in danger—my friends and I. How do you know this?"

"Buddy of mine from the cemetery, young kid, got killed in Desert Storm when he was just nineteen, poor bastard. I try to help out some of the other spirits when I can. Some of them, they get stuck here. They ain't cursed or nothing. They're just angry."

"I understand."

"So this kid, he decides he wants to haunt the sons of bitches that sent him over there, the chicken hawks, the fat-cat senators who never met a draft they didn't want to dodge. For years now this kid has been going bump in the night over at the Dirksen Building where some of them senators work and sleep and have their little peccadilloes. So this kid tells me just yesterday, right after you show up, there's this senator over on Capitol Hill, a real piece of work, name of Margaret Winthrop. You familiar with the name?"

Boo knows all about Winthrop. A former businesswoman from Kentucky, Margaret Winthrop rode a meteoric rise to success a few years ago, becoming the first woman to be elected to the U.S. Senate from that state. She was an overnight sensation on the talk-show circuit, famous for her "straight talk" and her bestselling screed *The Soul of an Enlightened Woman: Seeking Common Sense Solutions for the Children and Our Future.* Notorious for the cold, calculating, callous behavior that earned her the nickname the Louisville Slugger, she seemed to have the Midas touch, and nowadays is hated by both the Right *and* the Left. She also regularly testifies before the Armed Services Committee in favor of closing down the Special Expeditionary Section of the DIA, as well as putting out to pasture entities such as Spur's ghost unit. There is very little love lost between Boo and the honorable senator from Kentucky. "Yeah, I've heard of her," Boo says flatly.

"Well, according to the kid, the senator's entered into a little business proposition with our friendly neighborhood Antichrist." The ghost pauses, gazing out at the dawn. His dead face is pallid and wrinkled in the light, like bread dough that's been left out too long. He turns and trains his milky eyes on Boo, his expression darkening. "Old Lou's been busy. And the truth is, he's fixated on you and your people right now."

With a sigh and a nod Boo says, "I understand, believe me."

"Long story short, he can't quite figure out what to do with ya. But I'm telling you, little lady, as a fellow limbo-walker and patron saint of dead meat . . . the devil is cooking something up for you guys, and it ain't pretty. And it ain't gonna be easy to untangle."

Boo slowly nods and gazes to the east, feeling the tug of her destiny somewhere out in the granite facades and marble statuary of the capital city.

tucky. She inspects a rendering of herself beating her eldest son—only nine years old at the time—with a fireplace poker, breaking the boy's nose and necessitating a hundred and eleven stitches. She discovers a triptych of her arrest in Lexington during Christmas recess five years ago when she killed a jogger while driving under the influence. She had managed to slither out of the subsequent arraignment by bribing a judge, and saw that the record was expunged by New Year's Day.

At last she comes upon the final alcove, a shadowy chamber of horrors with interpretations of hell down through the ages. On the walls are Jan van Eyck's fifteenth-century depiction of the damned being eaten by monstrous, fanged demons . . . the Italian painter Giotto's terrifying fresco of a fat, wormy, gluttonous Satan devouring and shitting out the remains of sinners . . . and the last one, the one in front of which Winthrop has paused for what seems an eternity in the unhinged space-time continuum of her dream: Hieronymus Bosch's *Garden of Earthly Delights*. In the painting the netherworld is portrayed as a surreal coastline along a filthy, oily, brackish body of water, populated by naked souls being tortured and consumed by birdlike monsters participating in cannibalistic orgies of vomit, ejaculate, and blood.

At length, the painting itself seems to open up like an enormous Venus flytrap . . . drawing Margaret Winthrop into its expressionistic hellscape . . . until she is swallowed by the grey and sepia abominations of Bosch's fevered imagination . . . an enormous feathered demon with dead eyes like black cannonballs pouncing on her and devouring her . . . until she's drowning in her own juices and choking on her silent scream that no one but she will ever hear.

All of which has rattled her to her core in her private quarters on the sixth floor of the Dirksen Building.

She draws in a deep breath, moves to the edge of the bed, and shoves her painted toenails into her slippers. She rises on shaky legs and moves across the room to the armoire. She shivers in her robe, gooseflesh prickling down her arms and legs. At some point during the night the temperature has dropped in the room. She wonders if the heat has gone on the fritz again. She has zero confidence in the idiots that maintain the building. She pulls a long knit cardigan from the armoire and has just put it on when she catches a glimpse out of the corner of her eye of a figure floating outside the window.

"I am not crazy," she mutters under her breath as she continues to button the sweater. "I am not manufacturing all this . . . it's as real as this sweater," she assures herself as her quickening breaths begin to show in the morning light.

She turns and faces the window.

The figure is gone.

"Margaret," a voice corroded with phlegm and smoke says from across the room. The accent is unmistakable. The words are not the speaker's native language. "My dear malevolent Margaret. Pardon the intrusion but we have work to do."

She turns and sees the monstrous corruption of a man now sitting on an armchair by a ficus plant.

## 2.

The thing in the armchair has visited Senator Margaret Winthrop on more than one occasion, but upon each appearance she must summon great willpower in order to hide her repulsion and terror. Like a capo in some metaphysical crime syndicate, she has to play the part of the good soldier and not stare or show her disgust in front of the boss.

"First order of business," the creature announces in its unidentifiable accent, its pasty white face practically glowing in the morning gloom. Senator Winthrop has come to think of this putrid specimen as the Rotten Valentino, due to its nominal resemblance to the silent movie star of the late teens and early twenties, although *this* version stands nearly seven feet tall in its funereal tuxedo with its swallow-tailed coat and piss-yellow cummerbund. The thing's gaunt, cadaverous features are stretched like a veneer of clown white over its elongated skull. Its eye sockets are empty and bottomless, topped off by shoe-polish-black hair, neatly parted and greased back over a prominent cranium. "I must initiate the disposition of another team of ingrates, for which I need your assistance."

The woman sighs and glances at her reflection in the full-length mirror across the room, primping the sides of her hair. "Namely?"

The thing in the tuxedo seems annoyed by her curiosity. "Namely Paul Candell—a.k.a. Spur—and his four insolent playmates. I have given them every advantage, and they are plotting against me, squandering their supremacy and betraying me. Can you imagine?"

"How are they betraying you?"

"In simple terms, they have decided to be in breach of contract."

"I don't understand—don't you have tremendous power over people, power to possess them, to get people to do whatever strikes your fancy?"

The creature expels the weary sigh of a father trying to teach a recalcitrant child. "Only a handful of human beings walking the earth have the intestinal fortitude to fight back. Ironically, this is the very reason I entered into an agreement with these five renegades in the first place—it was due to their innate backbone, their strength of will." The creature makes a sour face. "Destiny can be a slippery slope, Margaret. I operate in a cat's cradle of prophecies and portents. There are those who believe that just such a group as these five agitators will either bring about the destruction of mankind . . . or the end of my reign . . . whichever comes first. Hence they must be dealt with straightaway."

Senator Winthrop thinks about it for a moment. "May I ask what you plan to do about all this?"

"I suppose I will have to find a more malleable group to intervene."

"And who would that be?"

"Never mind that. You are going to assist me. Yours is not to question why. Yours is but to do or . . . oh, you know the rest."

## 3.

The sun rises across a cornflower-blue sky over Silverback's farm, the day as bright and clear as a jewel. Behind the main house, the freshly mowed lawn warming in the morning sun fills the air with the sweet grassy perfume of summer. A hundred yards from the back door sits a large red barn hewn from native longleaf pine, used for the storage of equipment, feed, and seed.

Ticker rises early today, before dawn, in order to prepare said barn for a serious talk with the rest of the team.

In real time it would take Ticker almost eight hours to dress the building in interdenominational religious garnishments. But in the caesura the task encompasses less than the blink of an eye. In that miraculous pause, which he is now mastering with frightening aplomb, he builds a five-foot cross from timbers he procures from the storage loft. He also paints the Seal of Solomon over the entrance, and the Star of David over the north windows, and the Wheel of Dharma above the stalls, and the Khanda of Sikh-ism over the gas tanks. Finally he makes votive candles out of cit-ronella smudge pots, and carefully places them in a huge circle . . .

. . . in the center of which the team now gathers to address their situation while the section chief has gone to run his morn-ing errands in Alexandria. They have at least an hour before he gets back.

"What happens when our fearless leader discovers that you've turned his barn into a do-it-yourself chapel?" Pin-Up muses, sip-ping her morning coffee in the soft ambient glow of candlelight.

"After we're done talking, I'll do another time pause," Ticker says. "Trust me, it'll all disappear in a snap—like magic."

Clad in his customary casual garb—an olive-drab T-shirt, camo pants, and work boots that he pulled out of his locker at Bolling Air Force Base—he is still damp under the armpits from all the work. His caramel skin has a sheen of sweat on it, and other than the mysterious infinity symbol tattooed over his left biceps he would not look out of place bellied up to a bar, having a beer, or passing the time at some PX playing pinball.

No one would guess just by looking at the man that his IQ is north of 200.

"Speaking of magic," Spur says, gazing at the candles, won-dering if all these counterspells and superstitious gestures are really worth their effort, "I'm getting the feeling that the cat's gonna have our tongues no matter how we try and explain to Silver what really happened in Karakistan. Seems like old Lucifer likes to stay incognito." Dressed in his chambray denim shirt and jeans, his shit-kicker cowboy boots as pointy as tiny torpedoes, he fits right in at Silverback's farm. All he needs now to complete the picture is a pitchfork and a dour farmwife by his side. "And without the Satanic element coming into our story, none of this crazy shit will make any sense."

"A blessing in disguise, if you ask me," Hack chimes in from the other side of the luminous circle.

Spur looks at him. "What are you thinking? We're all ears."

Their gazes turn toward the boyishly handsome tech-head in the leather jacket. Hack paces, thinking. "All I'm saying is maybe there are other ways to explain the acquisition of such powers. I know it's a ridiculous question but aren't there any other plausible causes for such a meshuga thing to happen?"

Pin-Up lets out a nervous chuckle. "Uh . . . let's see . . . how about we tell him we won first prize in the Karakistani State Lottery, which was a frozen turkey and a new set of superpowers for all of us?" She sighs. The striking quality of her face has not been diminished one iota by her lack of makeup, or her baggy sweater, or her scuffed Doc Martens.

"Now wait a minute," Spur says. "Maybe Hack's on to something."

Hack looks at Spur. "What I'm saying is, if we demonstrate these powers to Silverback, and then give him an explanation that's even remotely plausible . . . he'll accept it. He won't have a choice, is what I'm saying. He'll see the skills with his own eyes."

Spur snaps his fingers. "And if you think about it, even if we *did* tell him about the deal with the devil, he's never gonna buy that."

"Very good, boychick," Hack says. "Silverback is a believer in the natural more than the supernatural. His world revolves around hard evidence, and logic, and science, and the rule of law. Which is why we need to give him something that he can sink his teeth into. Something he won't feel the need to question too much."

Spur stares at one of the votive candles, thinking it over, mesmerized by the flickering light. "So there was uranium-235 in that underground facility of Osamir's, wasn't there?"

Nods all around.

Hack smiles. "I think I see where you're going with this—yes, absolutely, radiation would be a good starting point, a good culprit."

Spur shrugs. "What do they say in the movies? It's so crazy it just might work?"

Ticker speaks up. "There's something else I've been thinking about. Maybe it's just as crazy, I don't know."

This gets everybody's attention. Spur gives him an encouraging nod.

"Something occurred to me while I was draping this place in religious artifacts." Ticker looks around at the icons and adornments scattered around the barn. "I don't know . . . maybe I'm losing my mind." He looks at his friends. "You're all going to have to promise, if I get into this . . . you won't have me committed."

"That's quite a preface you got going there," Pin-Up says

with a smirk. "Ticker, please. We're all on intimate terms with crazy. There's nothing you could say that would move the crazy needle—it's already pinned."

Ticker looks at her, and then says very softly in a low, conspiratorial voice, "I think we have an opportunity here."

He walks over to the big double doors that serve as the barn's main entrance. He gazes up at the six-pointed star he painted in white Rust-Oleum across a stray piece of drywall. "It's called the Seal of Solomon." He points to the other six-pointed star hanging on the other side of the barn. "The other version, the one over there, you'll all invariably recognize it as the Star of David. They're both powerful symbols."

He turns and ponders the white, interlaced, equilateral triangles that make up the star symbol emblazoned across the wallboard above the lintel, now partially obscured behind a veil of dust motes. Each point of the star has a little crown of three arrows, and there are capital letters scrawled above and below the star: A . . . G . . . C . . . A. The Latin word "expus" is handwritten in the center of the symbol.

The word "expus" means "spit out."

"Solomon's Seal is commonly used in witchcraft," Ticker goes on. "It's used to bind unwilling spirits, and also, allegedly, to ward off evil acts of the devil."

Hack speaks up. "So what's this opportunity you're talking about?"

Ticker turns and locks gazes with him. "The opportunity to destroy the devil. Permanently."

The sentence itself sounds almost incantatory, dangerous, heretical, the words hanging in the musty atmosphere of the barn like a noxious fog. For the longest time no one speaks.

At last Pin-Up breaks the tension. "Destroy Satan? Works for me. I checked my calendar, I got nothing going on all next week."

"Here's the thing." Ticker pauses for dramatic effect. "When I was brushing up on the mythology of the devil back in Erebus, I kept running across this repeating motif in almost all the literature. There's this aspect to Satan that appears everywhere, again and again, in scripture, in the gnostic gospels, in scholarly tomes—this sense of emptiness. It's what Professor Mussolino of the Consiglio su Demonologia calls 'the moral void—the vacuum of soullessness.' It's so unnerving, so overwhelming for a normal person to encounter this kind of evil. It's beyond psychopathic behavior, beyond the demented acts of serial killers. It's like a black hole. All of which makes the devil so powerful. He's the archetypal bogeyman—a cosmic bully—and it's extremely terrifying for an ordinary human being to interact with that."

Ticker pauses again, and Pin-Up speaks up. "So what's the takeaway here?"

"The takeaway is that the devil is the ultimate bully, and all bullies are alike—even the supernatural ones—in one respect."

Spur finishes the thought in a soft, revelatory voice, barely a whisper. "They fold under pressure."

"Precisely!" Ticker claps his hands together. "Think about it. The devil is a fallen angel, and angels are immortal, sure, but they're also vulnerable to counterspells, to the forces of heaven, to holy relics, and maybe, just maybe, we can use these things against him. It's all there, right in front of us. He cannot directly destroy any of us, and contractually, according to our verbal agreement, he cannot remove our powers." Ticker once again pauses, looking from face to face, searching for consensus. "I truly believe that we can use these powers to destroy him."

Another stretch of silence grips the room until Pin-Up finally responds. "Honestly, that's the opposite of what I think we should do."

Spur looks at her. "We're listening."

"The best way I can explain it is this. You want to do good? You want to make a difference? These scumbags that have sold their souls for a buck . . . for fame, for power . . . for the freedom to hurt others . . . they're the ones we should be destroying."

Ticker looks at the floor. "I get it. Believe me. I get what you're saying."

Pin-Up looks at Spur. "I say we just do the bounties he's hired us to do, and be thankful we only sold him our services and not our souls."

"We *did* sell him our souls though," Ticker says. "Don't kid yourself."

"Why do you say that?"

"Because we made a deal with the devil. We're bought and paid for."

They all stare at Ticker, each and every one of them, silently ruminating now, trying to ignore the feeling that they've crossed some kind of Rubicon, and something game-changing is about to happen.

## 4.

The situation room in sublevel B of the Pentagon is a windowless, oblong chamber of acoustic tiles, burnished wood, and recycled air. It's a room for serious contemplation of serious issues, a highly charged, symbolic choice of venues at which to hold an emergency meeting of the Senate Select Committee on Intelligence.

"Ladies and gentlemen, we have a developing crisis on our hands," Senator Winthrop announces, launching into the heart of the matter after the half dozen committee members who happen to currently be in D.C. and available for such an important meeting have taken their seats: four men and two women, each one a senior senator from their state, each one opening their briefing book with a grim, purposeful expression on their face.

Margaret Winthrop has always been a preening, self-absorbed peacock of a woman, and now, once again, she is onstage, on the *world stage* as a matter of fact, albeit out of public view, and as always she wears her go-to power outfit for the occasion—her double-breasted, navy-blue Ralph Lauren blazer dress accentuating the serious tone with its peak lapels, gold-plated buttons, and streamlined silhouette.

"This is a crisis that must be addressed immediately," she tells her committee members, fixing her frosty blue eyes on each senator, one at a time, as she promises, "I refuse to sugarcoat the situation we find ourselves in. This is an emergency of the highest order. You can follow along in your books with my verbal read-though of today's classified memorandum."

She clears her throat with great drama, a woman who has learned well the manipulative ways of politicians, and has enjoyed enhanced powers of persuasion and influence pursuant to her agreement with the one known to some as the Father of Lies.

Senator Winthrop then proceeds to read the memo without pause as the others follow along.

"It has come to my attention through anonymous sources in the U.S. embassy in Karakistan—confirmed by independent sources on the ground in both the U.S. and that country—that a team of operatives working under the supervision of the Special Expeditionary Section of the Defense Intelligence Agency, while working under deep cover in the northern democratic region of Karakistan between the twenty-first of May and twenty-third of May of this year, have committed war atrocities in the name of human intelligence gathering, including torture, wrongful deaths, and violent acts visited upon the citizens of Karakistan without due process or due cause.

"In addition to the aforementioned crimes, the same team of operatives has caused the wrongful deaths of informants, members of their own unit, and innocent citizens of Karakistan. Also, due to an ill-advised air strike called in by the leader of the team in question—code name Spur, full name Paul Elliot Candell— innocent locals were killed and/or injured as a result of collateral damage caused by the bombings.

"It is the opinion of this chair that immediate action should be taken to apprehend, charge, and prosecute Candell and his three surviving operatives. A copy of this memorandum has been sent to the attorney general's office, the U.S. Marshals Service, the director of the Defense Intelligence Agency, and the chief officer of the Special Expeditionary Section. The world is watching. May the Lord have mercy on their souls . . . and God bless America."

## CHAPTER EIGHTEEN

# Hard Targets

## 1.

That afternoon Silverback returns with an SUV full of groceries, liquor, building materials, mulch for the garden, and a replacement ink cartridge for his printer. Spur meets him at the top of the driveway. "Good Lawdy Miss Clawdy. You got a full load there," he says. "Let me give you a hand with that."

They carry the bags inside. In the kitchen, after Silverback has put away all the items, Spur says, "I wonder if we might have a little powwow, you and me and the team? Maybe out back, maybe on the porch. It's such a honey of a day."

Silverback thinks that sounds fine, and he even makes a pitcher of lemonade for the occasion. They all sit down around the fire pit, the afternoon sun warm on their backs. Silverback lights a pipe, and they all sip their lemonades as Spur eases into their revelation.

"Wanted to fill you on something," Spur begins. "Something that happened in Karakistan."

"Okay."

"What we're about you tell you, we haven't told a soul. And we'd like to keep it that way."

"Okay, fair enough." The big man thoughtfully puffs his pipe. In the brilliant sunlight, his big thatch of red hair looks redder than ever, his hazel eyes blazing with interest as he looks at all the earnest faces. "You got me intrigued, that's for sure."

Spur turns to Hack. "Hack, you want to go ahead and demonstrate?"

Hack nods. "Silver, can I possibly take a look at your cell phone for a second."

Silverback shrugs. "Knock yourself out." He pulls it from his pocket, sets it down on a side table hewn from a gorgeous slab of Virginia live oak. "Battery's low but it should pull the plow well enough."

Hack puts his thumb and forefinger on the phone and closes his eyes.

Silverback abruptly straightens in his chair—over the years he has developed a sort of perpetual slouch as an unconscious antidote for towering over everybody, but now he sits bolt upright and gawks, wide-eyed, at the transformation.

Hack seems to ripple in and out of focus, his skin sparkling in waves that shoot out from the phone. His head lolls slightly as he mutters, "Your first stop was Whole Foods, where you spent two hundred and eleven dollars and fifty-three cents on groceries, including three live lobsters and six prime fillets you're planning on turning into a lovely surf-and-turf feast for the gang tonight. Should I go on?"

"Um . . . by all means. Please do." Silverback stares at the luminescent coating of light enveloping Hack.

Hack continues: "You also made stops at Beldon's Liquor World, Home Depot, Chayton's Lawn and Garden Center, and U-Spray-It Self Service Car Wash on Three Pines Road. Between stops you checked the weather app once, your secure email server three times, and your blood pressure app twice, which seems a tad excessive, if we're being honest with each other. By the way, I notice from your healthcare provider's portal that you've been concerned enough about your health lately to be having an ongoing conversation with your cardiologist, and you have three separate tests on your calendar over the next six weeks—an EKG on the twelfth, an MRI on the twenty-third, and an angiogram next month on the eighth, which I applaud. One can't be too careful nowadays. By the way, since midnight last night you received sixteen emails. Eleven of them you deleted without opening. Five you opened and read before deleting, one of them—I believe it was from Cthulhu—had the subject line 'Something's Up at the Marshals Service,' the gist of which was that Cthulhu had no idea what was going on with the Marshals Service but he had received two separate messages on his secure line from two separate friends at the DIA regarding weird chatter among folks in Operations, and you—Silverback—should be aware of the fact that something's going down, and you should probably look into it. I believe you replied with a single-sentence response, which was: 'Thanks, kid, I'll look into it.' Which, if I may add a personal note here, your reply doesn't sound like you're super worried about it."

With a sort of gobsmacked paralysis Silverback has grown very still, and now watches the shimmering envelope of energy fade from Hack's epidermis as Hack pulls back from the phone, breaking the ghostly connectivity between his fingertips and the device. At last, Silverback finds his voice. "What's going on?"

Spur rises to his feet as though he's about to deliver a speech to congress. "I don't know where to start," he says, beginning to pace back and forth across the front of the fire pit, his hands in his pockets.

"How about we just start with *what the fuck*? What is going on?"

Spur sighs. "The thing of it is, I wasn't sure you'd swallow it if we didn't begin with a demonstration."

"Swallow *what*?" Silverback has a sour expression on his face, not exactly anger, but uncomfortable. "Spur, just cut to it."

Spur stops pacing and looks at him. "Something else happened in Karakistan." He looks at Ticker. "In the sublevel of Osamir's fortress, down in that dungeon." He looks at Silverback. "We got exposed to something. It did a number on us . . . something we're just beginning to deal with and understand."

"Exposed to what? Something chemical? Like a weaponized virus? Something of that nature?"

Spur shakes his head. "We don't know for sure. We believe it has something to do with radiation. Somehow the exposure has managed to rearrange our genetic makeup, reshuffle our DNA . . . or something like that." He locks gazes with Silverback. "It's given us these new . . . skills? Powers?"

"Radiation?" Silverback swallows hard. He looks nauseous, like he's having a bout of reflux. "Did you have the med team get readings when you debriefed? When you got examined did you mention this?"

"Absolutely. We would never endanger anybody. We said we wanted to be checked on any possible levels of radiation. Just to be sure. We told them that we believed that Osamir had uranium-235 on the premises, hidden, and was either storing it down there or had stored it there in the past. But we all tested negative, Sean. No sign of radiation on the surface of our skin, in our blood or urine or stool. Totally negative."

Silverback looks as though he's going to vomit. His words come on a labored series of breaths. "I'm still not . . . I'm not clear about what you mean by . . . 'skills' . . . or 'powers.' Like are we talking . . . physical skills?" He looks at Hack. "How did you discover all that about my day just by touching my phone?"

Hack shrugs. "Put it this way: What I used to do with code and hardwired devices, and the little tricks of my trade . . . it now comes naturally, literally through my fingertips." He thinks for a moment. "It sounds like crazy talk, I admit, but it's like I've become the binary code *myself*. I've become the zeroes and ones."

Silverback looks at the others. "Did you all get this same power?"

Spur looks at Ticker. "Show him."

Ticker takes a deep breath, looking around the property. "Okay . . . let me try something." He indicates a row of shaggy dogwood hedges across the yard, lining the driveway. "Those dogwoods over there. Keep your eyes on them."

Silverback furrows his brow with confusion. "What am I looking for?"

Spur interjects: "Simply put, we each have a different power. Ticker's has to do with time . . . the manipulation of time. He can put the physical world on pause. Go ahead, Tick, show the man."

Silverback blinks, and realizes that the hedgerow has magically, impossibly, instantly been *trimmed,* and Ticker is no longer standing on the other side of the fire pit.

"Judas Priest!"

Silverback jerks with a start when he realizes that Ticker stands inches away now, his shirt damp down the front from sweat, a pair of hedge clippers in his hands. "I borrowed these from the garage," he says. "You'll get my bill for the landscaping."

"I . . . I don't . . . I'm trying to . . . it's just . . . I'm trying to . . ." Silverback clutches his chest, slipping off the chair. He hits the ground hard, and writhes in pain.

Pin-Up springs to her feet. "Spur, I think he's having a heart attack."

Spur rushes over to the man, kneeling and unbuttoning Silverback's collar. He speaks with great calm. "Take it easy, old hoss . . . gonna be just fine . . . fine as a possum eatin' a sweet tatcr, just breathe . . . breathe."

Pin-Up is already dialing 911 on Silverback's cell phone.

On the ground, convulsing, Silverback struggles to breathe.

## 2.

"ETA in ten minutes," the pilot announces into his headset mike, raising his voice over the roaring drone of the rotors, nudging the stick to the left as the Comanche chopper banks over the silver anaconda of the Rappahannock River gleaming in the afternoon sun.

The other seven occupants of the aircraft—three on each side of the cabin, one in the forecabin, each man heavy with body armor, assault webbing, helmet, and harness—fidget in their seats. There is an air of tension in the aircraft that's anomalous among this group of U.S. marshals. Normally they would conduct a search-and-apprehend mission such as this with the collective calm of a cadre of Buddhist monks. But the cognitive dissonance stirred up the previous morning when they were given their orders has gotten under their skin.

The Special Operations Group of the United States Marshals Service is the tactical wing tasked with the most dangerous duties. This group of seven men currently strapped into this aircraft make up SOG's A-team, a group of marshals that has cleared more than 125,000 felony warrants over the last decade. On the majority of their missions they have avoided discharging their weapons, and the few firefights in which they have been engaged have ended quickly with zero collateral damage. They are consummate professionals. But today feels different to the deputies in the Comanche. Something smells rotten about this whole mission.

"Boss, can I ask you something?" the youngest officer present, Special Deputy Marshal Gerry Simms, says into his mouthpiece, addressing the leader, U.S. Marshal Frank Moon, who sits up front, directly behind the cockpit, chewing his Juicy Fruit furiously, his AR-15 under his burly arm as though it were an extension of his body.

"Go ahead, Simms," the leader says into his mike, his deep, resonant voice crackling in the younger man's earpiece.

"May I speak freely, sir?" Simms swallows his nerves. He is well aware that each and every marshal on the aircraft can listen in now, but it doesn't matter, the stakes are too high not to say anything.

"You're not in the infantry, son, you're a goddamn federal marshal, so go ahead and say whatever it is you want to say."

"Well . . . the truth is . . . this one just doesn't feel right."

"What do you mean?"

The younger man takes a deep breath as the chopper banks, the center of gravity shifting. "C'mon, Skip, you know what I'm talking about. These are our own guys we're talking about here. Navy SEALs, right? Most of them? These people are military."

A long pause ensues. Simms can feel the others hanging on every word as they fly north toward Silverback's farm. He knows they feel the same way he does.

Below the Comanche's iron belly the Potomac River valley passes in a blur—verdant, teeming, fecund—the vegetation like the spines of deep green behemoths sleeping in the hazy rays of the sun, the crisscrossing vineyards and orchards looking almost cryptic, like crop circles, messages from ancient astronauts.

Simms glances at the back of Moon's head, the thick neck, the body like a steamer trunk, the buzz cut visible in the stubbly folds of skin beneath the man's helmet. Moon is a legend. But legends fall. It happens all the time. There's something wrong with the man. Ever since he came out of that locked-door meeting with Senator Winthrop the previous day. His eyes had changed. There was a whiff of something in that room that trailed after Moon as he exited with his orders—something like a match head that had recently been struck and blown out—an old acrid kind of smell, bitter and sulfurous.

Moon's voice crackles in Simms's ear. "So you don't think it's possible for a soldier to go bad?" Moon chuckles. The sound of it reminds Simms of the scraping of flint on a lighter. "I got news for you, Simms, the military supplies the majority of the criminal element in this great country of ours."

Simms lets out a frustrated sigh. "But, sir . . ."

"Spit it out, Simms."

Simms measures his words. "The shoot-to-kill order."

"What about it?"

"I mean . . . is it really appropriate here? I mean . . . I know these folks have been accused of terrible shit but a no-knock warrant? Hard targets?"

"What can I tell you, Simms?" Moon's voice sizzles and pops in the earpiece. "They're a danger to society. Like rabid dogs. Gotta put them down."

Simms shakes his head. "All I'm saying is that it seems a little . . . extreme? I mean . . . it's not normal protocol, right? It's not usually what we do . . . or at least . . . it's not what we strive to do. To me it seems like, in a way, it's committing the same crime *these* folks are being accused of. Right? Killing the warlord without due process?"

Moon twists around suddenly, glowering at the deputy marshal. The older marshal's eyes have changed over the last twenty-four hours. His dark pupils have grown until they've practically taken over his eyes. "We follow orders, Simms. That's *our* due process."

"Sir, these are American intelligence operatives. Don't they deserve the same consideration as a warlord taken into custody?"

Moon's lips curl back away from his teeth, forming an ugly, sneering smile. "C'mere, Simms. Lean forward for a second."

"What?"

All the eyes of the other passengers are now on this exchange.

"Don't be shy," Moon says. "C'mere . . . lean forward . . . a little closer."

The senior marshal reaches up and with his forefinger traces a symbol on the younger marshal's forehead—a single long line down the middle, and then a shorter, perpendicular line near the bottom—an upside-down cross, a corrupted version of the crucifix.

Simms goes cold.

He sits back in his seat and exhales, an icy trickle seeping down his spinal column like centipedes crawling down his vertebrae, spreading through his body, obliterating his thought process, baptizing him in hate. It rises up his gorge—pure unadulterated contempt for Spur and the other criminals of his unit—and then Simms smiles the same lascivious, demented smile as the one that had stretched its way across Moon's craggy features a moment ago. "Thank you, sir," Simms says. "I understand now."

Moon's smiling lips part ever so slightly, revealing just the tip of a forked tongue poking out, tasting the air. "Pass it on to your fellow marshals." His voice resonates in the earpiece.

Simms unbuckles himself, climbs out of his seat, and then moves from deputy to deputy, performing the sacred black rite of initiation.

Spreading the hate.

Girding for the massacre.

## 3.

That day, by midday, moving like a shadow behind the tree line along the highway, Boo has hiked all the way out to the corner of Highway 236 and Three Pines Road, about five miles west of Alexandria, a heavily forested area interrupted only by the occasional farm, rest stop, or gas station. She was told by a young cashier about a mile back down the main road that a farm that matches her description is located just off of Three Pines, rumors around town suggesting that it's owned by some bachelor government man who keeps a low profile in the area. "A nice enough guy," the kid added. "Comes in for a six-pack of Mickey's big mouths or some Red Man every week or so, a big guy, Irish looking."

Now she hears a siren piercing the stillness of the woods on either side of Three Pines Road, echoing over the trees, approaching from the direction of the farm. She hides in the sticks, peering through the foliage as a small armada—a police car, an ambulance, and a dark blue Chevy Tahoe SUV—races past her, revealing familiar figures in the vehicle bringing up the rear. Just for an instant Boo catches a glimpse of Pin-Up sitting in the front passenger seat of the SUV, nervously chewing her fingernails while Spur drives. Somebody's been injured or has taken sick, and now Boo pauses in the clouds of gnats and dapples of sun filtering down through the branches as the armada vanishes into the distant heat rays.

She considers hitchhiking back to town, finding the nearest hospital . . . but then thinks better of the idea, and decides it might be wiser to wait at the farm for the others to return.

## 4.

Tactical leader Frank Moon and his marshals arrive at Silverback's farm just before 1500 hours that day in a Humvee supplied by the Alexandria National Guard station.

The vehicle booms down Three Pines Road and skids to a stop at mile marker number eleven, a hundred yards from the foot of Silverback's drive. Marshal Simms kills the engine. Moon climbs out the passenger side, and softly shuts the door, the latch making a muffled click. The other six marshals climb out, careful not to make any excess noise, laden with weapons. Their faces within their helmets show little emotion.

The men move as one organism now, silent, composed, almost robotic as they secure their harnesses and chin straps. Frank Moon is poker-faced, cold and dispassionate, as he gestures with his hand to three of the younger marshals. A forefinger points at each of them—

(*YOU, YOU, and YOU*)

—followed by a jerk of the thumb and a sweeping motion toward the farmhouse—

(*MOVE IN FROM THE WOODS*)

—and then he holds his arm straight up and makes a gun gesture.

(*RIFLES AT THE READY*)

At this point, three of the six men give nods and peel off to
the right, plunging single file into the grove of white pines and
birch adjacent to the property. They vanish into the sun-spangled
motes of particulate floating through the undergrowth, barely
making a sound, their safeties off, their eyes scanning. Their pupils are so huge now they look artificial, like a doll's eyes.

The team leader then turns to the other three, and delivers a final quick succession of hand gestures ordering the men to make
their approach in pairs from either flank of the front of the property. The final gesture is Moon pointing to the barrels of their
assault rifles, followed by a wiping motion—

(*SHOOT TO KILL*)

—culminating with a fist moving up and down.

(*GO NOW!*)

## CHAPTER NINETEEN
## Cutting Ties

### 1.

Watching from behind the barn, Boo can see the heavily armed team of federal marshals in their Kevlar and helmets closing in on the farmhouse. She sees the leader coming up the drive with his AR-15 to his eye, twitching at every sound, swinging the barrel toward the slightest rustle of leaves or rattle of branches in the wind. He makes his way toward the front porch, crouching behind an old live oak and giving his team hand signals.

Boo knows they will find nothing of interest inside the house, no Silverback, no ghost unit, no clues to where they've all gone off to. But then it occurs to Boo how she might be able to insinuate herself into this developing situation. She sees the team of marshals converging on the front of the house. She sees one of the men raising a battering ram. She sees the signal given, and the battering ram being slammed into the great oak door—once, twice—the third time being the charm.

The door breaks off its hinges with a crack that echoes over the treetops.

There's something odd about the way the marshals are moving—something off that Boo can't quite decipher as they all pour into the house with guns raised and ready—their body language, posture, and movements slightly stiff and jerky, as though they're attached to puppet strings. The leader, a big brawny bull of a man in black body armor and with a Viking bearing, twitches every few moments as though suffering from some sort of neurological disorder. Boo shivers in the sunlight, Charon's warning reverberating in her brain: *The devil is cooking something up for you guys, and it ain't pretty.* Right then she realizes the lead marshal is exhibiting all the telltale traits of demonic possession.

If she were technically alive, her heart would begin to beat faster as she waits for the team of marshals to do a sweep of the house. Moments later, she hears monotone voices from inside the farmhouse calling out—*"Clear!"*—and the crackle of a radio voice echoing. She realizes that word will soon reach the marshals in one way or another that Silverback, Spur, and the rest of the unit have departed for a hospital. In fact, the marshals will likely learn the exact hospital, department, and room into which Silverback has been admitted.

Boo realizes what she has to do. She gets very still. She waits.

When the first figure appears in the front doorway, Boo steps out from behind the barn. The figure in the doorway—one of the younger marshals, his eyes like onyx marbles—notices her immediately, and he raises the muzzle at her, and he lines up the shot. "Freeze," he says in a peculiar tone of voice, almost mechanical sounding, as though in a trance.

She keeps walking.

"I said freeze, bitch!"

She keeps walking until she's standing in the middle of the driveway, less than thirty yards from the man currently aiming an M16 at her. She stands there for a moment in her soiled burial uniform as other marshals emerge from the house, aiming their assault rifles at her. One of the marshals raises a collar mike to his lips, whispering, "That's not one of them, is it? Is she one of them?"

Boo raises her hand and gives them the middle-finger salute.

Half a dozen high-velocity rounds go into her midsection. The impact of all those bullets passing through her causes her petite body to remain upright for a moment, shuddering in a death dance of blood mist and cordite smoke . . . until she finally drops.

## 2.

The Asian woman does not match the description of any of the four operatives. Nor do the marshals have time to wait for a medical examiner to show up. So they put her in a body bag, and load her in the rear of the Humvee. They roar out of there at just past 1530 hours.

By the time they get back on the highway and head east, Marshal Frank Moon has already radioed in to the Marshals Service dispatcher, and has asked for a quick search of any suspicious activity involving one Colonel Sean M. McDermott, Jr., within a ten-mile radius of the farm over the last twelve hours. "Have there been any police calls or emergencies or any mention whatsoever on the squawk box of this gentleman?" Moon taciturnly inquires in his baritone drone. "Also, do a search for any incidents or active calls involving the following individuals: Paul Candell, Maria Consuelo Caruso, Aaron Boorstein, and Samuel Elijah Johnson."

A moment later, the radio voice crackles, "Hotel Lima, we have a 911 call placed by a cell phone owned by a Sean McDermott at twelve hundred thirty-five hours . . . and one other thing."

"What is it, Bravo Delta?"

"Paramedic call-in to Kenmore Alexandria Medical Center with a patient of the same name, McDermott, in apparent cardiac arrest, en route at twelve hundred forty-five hours."

Moon thumbs the radio mike off as soon as he has the information. No sign-off, no thank-you, not another word to the dispatcher.

Simms, behind the wheel, does not have to be told to floor it.

## 3.

Less than five minutes later, the Humvee rattles to a stop at a crossroads, an indicator light blinking—CHECK TIRE PRESSURE—and the ping of a caution alarm causing Simms to put the vehicle into park.

Marshal Frank Moon asks the younger marshal what the fuck he thinks he's doing, and Simms explains that they have a flat tire.

"Sir—?" a voice says from the rear seats.

Moon twists around, fixing his black gaze on the young tactical officer with the goatee. "What is it, son?"

"We got a . . . problem." The young man indicates the rear cargo bay. Craning his neck, Frank Moon can see what the officer is talking about. The body bag has been torn open from the inside, and now lies crumpled and empty on the floor of the cargo area. The rear door has swung open a few inches.

Lead marshal Moon has no reaction other than a slight twitch at the corners of his mouth. "Simms, Nalls . . . fix the tire."

## 4.

Silverback sits on the edge of a paper-covered examination table in a private room at Kenmore Alexandria, listening to the staff cardiologist drone on about stress and heart health.

"I'm putting you on a low-fat, plant-based diet to get those numbers back to where they should be," the doctor explains. "But the good news is, your heart is strong, and the digoxin has managed to ease your vitals back to where we want them."

Silverback rubs his neck. Shirtless, hooked to an IV line, his freckled skin pale in the halogen light of the examination room, he looks and feels a lot older than his fifty-nine years. His chest hair is iron grey, and his huge, sagging pectorals lie on his belly like beached jellyfish. "I just find it hard to believe it was a panic attack," he marvels, mostly to himself. "I've never had a panic attack in my life."

The doctor, a well-groomed, middle-aged man with aviator glasses, holds his clipboard to his chest as he gives Silverback a quizzical glance. "Tell me again what you were doing when you had the attack. Were you involved in something stressful? Strenuous? Something . . . out of the ordinary?"

Silverback lets out a nervous chuckle, and then shoots a loaded glance across the room at the four members of the ghost unit standing along the wall, each of them intently looking on with the relieved expression of someone who has just been told the growth is benign. Silverback locks eyes with Spur and says, "Oh, you know, nothing that stressful . . . just a few dark miracles in my backyard."

The doctor wrinkles his brow with bemusement. "Excuse me?"

"Never mind, bad joke," Silverback says with a crooked grin. "I just never knew how much a panic attack can imitate a heart attack."

The doctor nods. "It can be frightening . . . the tightness in the chest, the shortness of breath, the sweating and dizziness."

"I thought I was a goner for a second there—I couldn't breathe. Couldn't move. It really felt like I was dying."

"It can be terrifying," the doctor commiserates. "Even the temporary paralysis."

Silverback sighs. "Well, I promise I'm going to try my hardest to give up the scotch and T-bones."

"That's the spirit," the doctor says, tearing off a form and handing it to Silverback with a smile. "Here's a prescription for low-dose oral digoxin . . . if you feel any further symptoms. And if you have any more arrhythmia or chest pain, get yourself to the ER stat. You understand?" He unhooks the IV. "That's about it. You can get dressed and go home." Then he gives him a wink. "And good luck with the T-bones."

The doctor walks out.

"We need to talk," Silverback says to Spur and the others. "While we were waiting for the test results a text came in on the secure line." He gives them a grave look. "You're not going to like it."

## 5.

The carbon-black Humvee roars eastward along the blasted asphalt two-lane toward Alexandria with a new tire on the right rear—the old one stowed underneath in the rear cargo area (along with the sharp-edged crowbar from the Humvee's tool pouch that the "dead" woman must have used to tear a hole in the tire). All of which has baffled Marshal Frank Moon. From the window of the farmhouse he had seen a half dozen 7.62-millimeter rounds penetrate the woman's tiny chest, a strike that would kill a rhinoceros. But somehow the little bitch managed to slither away. Now Moon rides up front in the passenger seat, stone silent, the bloodlust stewing in him.

They are approaching Alexandria, the highway widening into a four-lane thoroughfare known as the Little River Turnpike.

The afternoon rush has begun, more and more cars crowding the interstate. At the wheel, Marshal Simms pushes the Humvee—keeping it at a steady seventy miles per hour—weaving in and out of clusters of slower-moving vehicles. In the rear seats, the sounds of high-capacity magazines being loaded and inserted, and rounds being injected into breeches, fills the silence with hectic metallic clicking like the scuttling of insects following the impulses of an invisible, pervasive, inexorable hive mind.

## 6.

The Kenmore Alexandria Medical Center has a chapel on the lower level, just past the cafeteria, at the end of the main corridor. It's very subtly marked, with a single plaque that says INTER-DENOMINATIONAL PLACE OF WORSHIP and a simple sun symbol carved into an otherwise unmarked oaken door; the sanctuary on the other side of the door is far larger than one would expect. Above the fifty rows of pews, the ceiling vaults upward two stories above the carpeted floor. The atmosphere—redolent of candle wax, incense, and the musty pages of old well-thumbed Bibles—has a stillness to it that contrasts greatly with the bustle of the other floors.

"This is so ridiculous," Silverback murmurs under his breath, pacing across the front of the room near the all-purpose altar, which features a three-foot-tall crucifix on a small stand, a floral Star of David, and the Islamic crescent carved from hardwood, mounted on a pedestal. "This is not how it's supposed to work," he grumbles, pacing and shaking his huge head. "I should have known Margaret Winthrop would pull something like this—it's right up her alley."

Pin-Up shushes him. "Calm down, Silver. You're going to bust another gasket." She sits in the first pew, her hands in her lap, cradling a Bible. The feel of it comforts her, despite the fact that she's been having pangs of dread jolting through her all day. Is it woman's intuition? "Besides," she says, jerking her thumb toward the rear of the chapel, "there are other people in here trying to pray in peace."

For the last few minutes, since the five of them hunkered down near the altar for their little chat, at least a dozen people have slipped in and out of the chapel. Most of them were nurses or orderlies, and most spent only a few minutes in the back of the room, genuflecting or silently praying, probably asking their personal Gods to intervene in some medical drama unfolding at this moment in this very institution.

Then they would quickly slip back out the door like the waitstaff at a busy restaurant.

"Let's everybody just calm down," Spur says from the end of the pew, where he sits chewing tobacco and thinking over their dilemma.

The troubling text message had been sent by Cthulhu that day, who had heard from a gossipy pal at the Pentagon that Senator Winthrop had called an emergency meeting with her committee, and was leveling serious charges against Spur and his operatives, and now has involved the SOG unit of the U.S. Marshals Service, who, most likely, at this very moment, are scouring the D.C. corridor with an arrest warrant with Spur's birth name on it.

"Just take a deep breath, old hoss," Spur says. "It'll be okay. We'll figure something out." Spur gives it some more thought.

"Hell, sometimes there's only one way to skin a cat. I say we go back to D.C. and face the music. Fight it out in court." He looks at the others. "Why not shine some light on these lies. It's the best disinfectant, right? Expose these rotten apples to the public. What do y'all say?"

"Wait a minute . . . hold on a second," Silverback says. He glances at the door in the rear of the church. The other worshippers have finished and departed. Silverback lowers his voice and says, "Maybe we ought to consider going in the opposite direction—underground I'm talking about."

Ticker speaks up. "Define 'underground.'"

"Okay. Look at it this way. Unless I'm missing something here, you've got these unprecedented new powers now. For whatever reason. Each of you. *Superpowers*. Right? Is that fair?"

Ticker frowns. "What are saying? You think this is a comic book were dealing with here?"

Silverback shrugs. "No. Absolutely not. That's exactly my point. This is the real world. And believe me, it's lot more deadly than the pages of a comic book. You think those supervillains in comic books are a pain in the ass? You ought to see my roster of bad actors around the world, hostile regimes, neo-Nazis, jihadists that want to eradicate the West, American terror groups that want to obliterate all brown people . . . drug cartels, organized-crime syndicates, street gangs that will shoot your mother in the head for the twenty bucks in her purse . . . and maybe the worst of all, people like Margaret Winthrop, smug little fascists in sheep's clothing, hypocrites who are more interested in consolidating their power than defending the Constitution. *Those* are the real supervillains."

After a long pause, Hack says, "All due respect, it would be great to get some details. What do you mean by underground?"

Silverback rubs his two enormous hands together. "Okay, I'm just spitballing here but let's say the four of you officially cut ties with the ordinary world. To me, this is how you'd be able to best serve your country from this moment forward . . . by vanishing into legend . . . into myth."

Ticker chimes in again: "How exactly does one do that in this day and age?"

Silverback looks at him. "I'm glad you asked. You do it by dying."

Spur cocks his head incredulously. "You want to run that by me again?"

Silverback paces some more. "Think about it. I can help facilitate this. I can officially declare all of you deceased. Cause of death? How about radiation poisoning? Makes perfect sense, right?"

Spur glances at the others, a pang of longing stabbing at his heart. He knows the toll this would take on each member of the team—never being able to see their civilian friends and loved ones again. But on a deeper level, for Spur, there's no getting around the melancholy feeling that he has no one who would miss him that much.

"The point is, you'd be off the books forever," Silverback goes on. "Working under deep, deep cover. Your code names would become your handles, and nobody would ever know your true identities. You would be the ghosts in the machine. And from that point on, for anybody out there considering wreaking havoc in the world, you would be, in the back of their mind, that scary thing that goes bump in the night."

"A superteam," Spur says softly, as though trying the concept on for size.

"Precisely."

Spur rises to his feet, taking in a deep breath and pondering the religious icons adorning the altar. Is this his destiny? To reflect back at his enemies their darkness in the name of light? To use the tools of the devil to do God's work? He remembers when he was a kid watching the Baptist preacher down the road, a whirling dervish of a man who preached in front of a four-piece rock band—drum kit, organ, electric bass, and a Stratocaster guitar—vamping and riffing behind the holy scripture, the so-called devil's music put to Good Use.

Processing it all, Spur finally says, "I ain't saying I'm on board with this yet but if I were, and if one were to name a team such as this . . . this superteam . . . these ghosts in the machine . . . I think I got a contender for a possible code name."

Silverback shrugs. "Lay it on us."

"The Devil's Quartet."

Before Silverback has a chance to react, a voice from the back of the chapel chimes in, reverberating up in the rafters: "Excuse me!"

All gazes turn toward the rear of the chapel near the door.

The voice belongs to a woman who must have slipped into the room only moments ago, a small Chinese woman dressed in a formal blue military uniform, the front of it marred by six bloodless holes. "You got the name wrong, Spur . . . it should be the Devil's *Quintet*."

## CHAPTER TWENTY

# Black Orbs

## 1.

It takes less than a second for the realization to register—the conflict between what their eyes are taking in and what their brains are telling them is impossible—paralyzing them for what seems a thousand eternities as the word "Quintet" echoes in their ears. For that brief scintilla of an instant, Spur and the others stand stone-still at the front of the room, gawking at the specter of their dead friend and fellow operative.

From the back of the room, Boo breaks the tension by saying, "Would it be too much to ask to maybe get a hug from somebody?"

"Oh my God," Hack finally cries out, and then charges down the center aisle. He practically knocks the little woman off her feet with a desperate embrace and a voice crumbling with emotion. "Oh my God . . . how did you? Oh my God . . . is this part of your . . . ? How did you . . . ?"

Pin-Up moves in and strokes her arm and struggles to keep her voice steady. "Sweet Boo, how in God's name did you pull this off?"

"Trust me, it wasn't easy." Boo lets out a flinty sort of laugh, as the others gather around her, taking turns hugging her and stroking her hair and touching her face. It's as though they need to feel her flesh to be sure she is real, that she's not some hallucinatory wish fulfillment or some cruel prank being played on them by the devil.

The last one to embrace her is Silverback. By this point, he is sobbing, his tears soaking both the front of his tartan plaid flannel shirt and Boo's uniform. "God, I've never been so happy to see somebody in my life," he murmurs, hugging her so tightly her feet leave the ground for a moment.

"It's good to be back," she says with her trademark understatement after Silverback sets her back down on the floor with great care and tenderness, as though setting down a figurine made of

Baccarat crystal. "Dying's not all it's cracked up to be," she reports with a crooked smile.

"I saw them . . . I saw them put you in the ground with my own eyes," Silverback stammers.

She nods. "You should try climbing out of a grave sometime. It's not as simple as it sounds."

Hack can't take his eyes off her. He sees the crust of grave dirt on her patent-leather shoes, the translucent quality of her skin. "Not to be overanalytical or didactic in any way but this is all a lot to process," he mutters more to himself than anyone else. "But thank God, you know? Thank God . . . thank *God*."

"I missed you, too, kiddo." Her eyes meet Hack's and waves of emotion are silently exchanged.

Ticker is mesmerized by the bullet holes in her uniform. "Back in Karakistan," he says very softly, as though Boo is a bird that could fly away at any moment, "you saw ghosts, right? You saw the souls of the dead back there?"

Boo nods. "I did indeed, and now, alas, I'm one of them."

"But you're not a ghost, per se."

"Nope. I'm still solid matter." She taps on her arm. "Last time I checked, at least."

Hack puts his arm around her again and squeezes, and he speaks through his tsunami of emotions. "I'm no expert but you feel pretty damn solid to me."

"We should get you upstairs immediately," Spur says, examining with alarm those scorched holes running diagonally across her slender chest. "Get the doc to do a once-over on you."

She smiles wistfully. "I don't think that's such a terrific idea."

"Why not?"

She looks at him. "Because . . . here. Give me your hand."

Spur steps forward and lets her lay his fingers on her neck just above her carotid artery. He frowns. "I'm not getting a—"

"Yeah, exactly."

Spur steps back, rubbing his fingertips together incredulously. "Well, if that ain't nuttier than a soup sandwich." He looks at her. "You look a little peaked but I reckon you're doing pretty damn well for being dead."

"Fit as a fiddle," she says. "As superpowers go, it comes in handy."

"What's with the ventilation?"

She looks at her chest. "The results of a little run-in with the U.S. Marshals at the farm." She looks at Spur. "You do know they're dogging you as we speak, right?"

Spur nods. "We got the news—Winthrop's up to her old tricks."

"I managed to slow them down but they're gonna be showing up any minute. You got any weapons on you, by any chance? We may need to fight back. These guys are under the influence of more than just D.C. corruption . . . if you get my meaning."

Spur and the others exchange loaded glances. Everyone but Silverback gets her meaning.

## 2.

The medical center's ground-floor reception area is a spacious, glass-encased, parquet-tiled vestibule off Kenmore Avenue. It is run, managed, and ruled over by a Rottweiler of an old woman named Mary McCarty. Spindly limbed in her powder-blue pinafore, her hair an otherworldly shade of peroxide silver, her deeply lined face as dour as a cigar-store Indian's, the receptionist gazes out the massive glass entranceway and sees the commotion coming down the sidewalk in the front of the building.

Seven heavily armed federal marshals—marching two abreast, one in front, leading the squad, faces twitching, eyes like black stones under the brims of their helmets—slam through the double doors and pour into the crowded foyer like a black Kevlar flood. All gazes of those in the waiting area, those sitting on contour benches, those reading magazines, suddenly jerk upward and fix themselves on the battalion of grim-faced Spartans passing the reception desk and heading for the nearest bank of elevators.

"Excuse me!" Mary McCarty calls after them with the same sharp bark of a schoolteacher admonishing students roughhousing in the hallway during school hours. "Gentlemen! You're going to need passes to enter that wing!"

The stocky, bearlike leader pauses and turns toward the old woman. His eyes are polished black orbs. Lifeless. Sharklike. "Government business," he drones in a toneless, corroded voice. "Can you tell me where I can find a patient by the name of Sean McDermott?"

Mary McCarty loses her nerve the instant she sees those eyes. Her sinewy, liver-spotted hands—the same hands that have slapped at unruly teenagers disturbing the peace of her foyer—

now tremble convulsively as she pecks at her keyboard. "He's been treated in the ICU, and . . . and . . . he's been officially released but he's probably . . . you know . . . still up there gathering his personal items."

"Up where?"

"S-second floor," she says.

Without a word the invaders turn and march toward the elevators, leaving the people in the foyer in stunned silence.

# 3.

"We've got sidearms and extra mags in the Tahoe," Spur says to Boo.

"Where is it?"

"In the parking garage—somewhere on this level, I believe. It's what's left of the armory at the farm. It ain't gonna win any world wars but it'll get somebody's attention . . . slow them down a little bit."

Silverback cannot stop gaping at Boo, as though she might evaporate at any moment. "Is this power of yours . . . this condition . . . is it . . . was it the radiation that did this?"

Boo looks at Spur. "Radiation? Um . . . I'm not quite sure I—"

"It's okay, Boo," Spur jumps in, tap-dancing a little. "We told Silverback about the radiation in the sublevels of Osamir's fortress—how we got exposed to it, maybe got mutated by it—and how we ended up on the other side with these powers."

Boo nods. "Right . . . right. That's exactly what happened. It was the radiation. Had to be. I mean, what else *could* it be?"

"Silverback's the only one we've told about these skills, Boo, he's the only one that knows anything about them."

Silverback looks around the chapel, his voice barely a whisper. "'The Devil's Quintet.'" He looks at Boo and then looks at Spur. "It does have a ring to it." He ponders it for a moment. "Why the *devil*, though?"

Spur shrugs. "Scares the bad guys? I don't know. It just popped into my head but it seems to fit."

Silverback is nodding. "You know . . . the more I think about it, the more I like it. The fear factor could definitely be an asset, part of the team's mythology." He gives it some more thought. "Maybe going dark *is* the best way to go. The type of person who's afraid of such a moniker is most likely the type we want to thin from the herd."

"Maybe that's true," Spur says. "But you'd have to thin half the state of Texas if you're going to remove anybody who's afraid of the devil."

"Or any old-school Catholic who's seen *The Exorcist*," Pin-Up adds. "Like my folks, all my cousins, and every one of my aunts and uncles in East L.A."

Silverback starts pacing again, contemplating the possibilities.

Spur is getting nervous, the walls of the chapel pressing in on him.

## 4.

On the second floor, in the ICU department, the crowded nurses' station comes to a complete standstill. The head nurse, a greying, middle-aged mother of four and grandmother of eleven named Evelyn Rockway, stands up from behind her computer screen and starts to object but stops herself when she sees the strange behavior of the heavily armed marshals pushing their way past befuddled orderlies and moving down the aisle of ICU examination cubbies as though it were enemy territory in a foreign war zone.

For a moment Nurse Rockway just stands there, staring, paralyzed, as the marshals violently yank curtains open, sweeping the muzzles of their assault rifles into the examination spaces, within which each startled patient is caught unaware, recoiling in horror. At last, Nurse Rockway manages to reach down to her keyboard and send a text to the hospital's head of security:

OMG Jim are you aware of what's going on up here in ICU?

The horde of heavily armed marshals reaches the end of the ICU aisle, and the younger officers pause for further orders from their broad-shouldered leader like worker bees turning to their queen. The leader whirls around and storms back toward the nurses' station.

"Do you know if a patient by the name of Sean McDermott has left the premises?" he asks Nurse Rockway in his otherworldly voice. The man has black ball bearings for eyes, and the corners of his mouth twitch with irregular tics as though jerked by invisible strings. "We have a warrant for his arrest."

Evelyn Rockway moves her lips but at first can barely get the words out.

# 5.

"Of course these kinds of things have been tried before," Silverback is saying, pacing the length of the front pews. "Some of them successful. Some . . . not so much. The whole idea of an underground team of vigilantes—hell, it goes back to the 1800s and Dodge City. But it's a lot harder to pull off nowadays. Remember Hastings and his unit?"

Spur remembers them well. They were just kids back in 'Nam—three of them, each former Delta Force, very talented, deadly accurate snipers, led by a legendary lieutenant from the Thirty-Eighth Cavalry Regiment named Benjamin Hastings. After the war, they vanished into the woodwork, becoming a hit squad for the highest bidder. Throughout the eighties and early nineties, the richest client was always America . . . until it wasn't. In 1997, the Beaucoup Morte, as they came to be known, took a job for Khalid Sheikh Mohammed, who would go on to become the operational commander for the 9/11 attacks. After that, Interpol gave the three members of the Morte the top three slots on the International Ten Most Wanted List, but it was an empty gesture. Their bloated corpses were found in '99 floating in the Ganges River in India. Later their remains vanished from a Calcutta pathology lab.

"Yeah, I remember those fellas, Hastings and them," Spur says. "They crashed and burned because of greed . . . hubris . . . I don't know what all."

Spur looks at Boo.

She has an odd expression on her face, which makes Spur wonder what she's learned from the dead, or if she knows something about the fate of the Beaucoup Morte, which she would rather not talk about right now. Is there a connection to the devil in all this? Maybe every bad thing that happens in this world has some thread running through it that leads to Satan. And maybe not. Maybe people can do a bang-up job at being evil all by their lonesomes.

"I'm thinking we should bring Cthulhu into this," Silverback is saying now.

Ticker interjects. "You think that's a good idea though?"

"What do you mean?"

"The less people who know about something the easier it is to keep it a secret. Right?"

"Of course," Silverback says. "But we're going to need somebody at ground level like Cthulhu, somebody on the outside who knows everybody. That kid is an amazing resource because he's such a nerd, a gadfly, whatever you want to call him."

Spur realizes he doesn't even know the young man's birth name. "Does the kid have security clearance?"

"You bet," Silverback says. "He's got DOD collateral clearance, and he's—"

A crash at the front of the chapel abruptly cuts off Silverback's words.

The doors have burst open, and now three of the seven federal marshals lurch into the chapel, their AR-15s raised and ready, their front sights finding the targets gathered at the altar.

# CHAPTER TWENTY-ONE
## Engagement

### 1.

In that fraction of an instant before the guns roar, Silverback and the Quintet drop to the floor. The behavior is purely instinctual. Basic training never leaves a soldier's DNA. If measured on a stopwatch, their bellies meet the deck in less than two-thirds of a second, which is one-third of a second before the bullets begin to fill the air.

Plaster erupts. Candles burst. Stained glass shatters. Pieces of flooring chip off and go flying. Shards of woodwork explode in sequential puffs of dust that almost instantly bind the air in a fog of particulate as thick as gauze. Which is a blessing in disguise. It gives Spur and the others a cover of haze behind which to move out of the line of fire.

The marshals press in. The gunfire lifts momentarily as the clang of cocking levers and the metallic rattling of shells hitting the floor ring off the walls. By this point, Spur and his people have managed to quickly crab on their bellies around the altar, taking cover behind the columns flanking the shrine.

Spur hears a noise behind him—a hissing sound like steam escaping—but there's too much going on for him to look into it.

Ticker crouches, his back against the pilaster. He tries to stop time—visualizing the keyboard, his fingertips, the caesura—but another salvo of gunfire rings out, distracting him, making him flinch against the pillar. Plaster dust puffs above him. Bullets puncture the back wall. The noise deafens, piercing Ticker's eardrums, making his ears ring.

Out of the corner of his eye he sees something unfolding that squeezes his chest. "Boo! What are you doing?!"

The little woman has crawled out of hiding, bullets tracing through the haze like lightning bolts mere inches over her head, turning the back wall to Swiss cheese, sparking and puffing in successive gouts. Ticker can't believe his eyes as Boo scoots along the floor toward the end of the pews.

Meanwhile, on the other side of the sanctuary, Pin-Up has crawled over to a jagged portion of the hardwood cross, and she hurls it across the chapel. The fragment slams hard into the far wall with a loud crack, shattering into slivers.

The marshals twitch toward the noise, firing off a booming fusillade like a fireworks display in the direction of the sound, unaware that it's a diversion, unaware that they're firing at nothing, unaware that Boo is scuttling quickly toward them from the opposite side of the chapel. She springs to her feet and leaps at them—gazelle-like—her delicate, tiny hands splayed open in the attack posture of an ancient martial art known as Kumanah.

The youngest marshal—his peach-fuzz goatee belying the glow of ancient evil in his eyes—whirls around just in time to take a direct hit in his Adam's apple, the heel of Boo's splayed hand like a cudgel, snapping his trachea with the sharp crack of a celery stalk breaking. His gun discharges a burst into the ceiling.

The other two shooters spin and see nothing but their comrade—Goatee Boy—staggering backward, holding his throat, gasping for breath with no gun in his hand. They don't see Boo leaping up against the parapet behind them, wall-walking, practically weightless, the AR-15 in her hands now.

She takes a half a dozen steps, her body practically horizontal, and by the time she lands behind the confused gunmen they have lost track of what's going on. Boo spins and scissor-kicks one of the assault rifles out of the hands of one of the marshals. The other one fires at her—point-blank—the round penetrating her belly and exiting out her back, having little effect on her, puffing debris from the wall behind her. The shooter gapes at her, stunned. Boo counters with another spinning kick, driving the man back on his heels. He tries to get his bearings but Boo slams the butt of the rifle across the bridge of his nose.

The marshal staggers. Boo shoots his right foot. The marshal goes down.

More tactical officers pour into the chapel—two older men—their black eyeballs scanning wildly. Boo sees Pin-Up about twenty-five feet away, on the other side of the aisle, rising to her feet. Before the newcomers have a chance to pull their triggers, Boo tosses one of the assault rifles to Pin-Up, who catches it and dives to the floor.

She empties an entire clip at the officers, who also dive to the floor, taking cover behind the back pew. All of which allows Boo enough time to charge back to the altar with an assault rifle in each hand . . .

. . . plunging behind one of the pillars like a baseball player sliding into home.

## 2.

"With all due respect, that was what I would call foolhardy," Hack says to her, taking one of the guns from her, checking the clip. He ducks down when another salvo of gunfire flashes and thunders at them from behind the rear pew a hundred feet away.

Boo returns their fire, yelling above the din, "I got their guns away from them, didn't I?"

"Yeah and you got a hole in your tummy I could drive a truck through."

"It's just a scratch."

"Right."

"Hack, you've gotta face the fact I got no blood to lose, no organs to fail."

Another barrage erupts mere centimeters above them, driving them to the floor, raining debris down upon them. Hack returns the gunfire. He shoots one, two, three rounds . . . when the assault rifle clicks empty. "Fuck!—*Fuck!*" he hollers.

On the other side of the altar, Spur hears the noise behind them again, a hissing sound, maybe an unfamiliar human voice, it's hard to tell in all the tumult. Spur has been hearing it ever since the first cadre of marshals attacked.

"Psssssst!"

"Do hear that?" he asks Ticker.

"Pssssssssssssssssst!"

He twists around and sees an elderly gentleman sticking his head out of a trapdoor no bigger than a dumbwaiter next to the front parapet.

"Sir!" the old man whispers loudly, and then ducks down again when another surge of gunfire booms, sparking and chewing divots in the parapet wall, sifting plaster dust down upon the trapdoor.

"What in the name of jumpin' Jehoshaphat?" Spur says.

"This way!"

The old man is waving Spur over to the three-foot egress concealed in the floor.

## 3.

A stooped, balding little man, the priest wears small, round, rimless eyeglasses that lend an air of an Old World scholar; but Father Manny is anything but Old World. He was removed from his Baltimore parish years ago for condoning the use of contraception among his parishioners, allowing divorced people to receive communion, and marching in gay pride and pro-choice parades. But today, reaching out to these fugitives is perhaps the most modern, controversial, and, in a way, *intuitive* act Father Emmanuel Lawson has ever committed as a member of the clergy.

"This way," he says, as though he were a host at a fancy restaurant showing a group of customers to their table, his voice as soft as a lullaby as Spur and the others follow him down iron steps embedded in the wall. The roar of gunfire still echoes above them. "And if I may ask the last one in to do me an enormous favor and make sure that the trapdoor is latched behind you."

The priest leads the team down to the bottom of the steps, a platform that opens out upon a dusty cement vestibule reeking of mold and must.

"Welcome to the sub-sublevel," he says as he waddles across the landing, the hem of his robe so dirty it looks scorched. The members of the team reach the bottom of the ladder one at a time, breathing hard, scanning the unfinished walls and bare lightbulbs hanging on frayed cords. The priest pauses. "Is everyone in good working order? Nobody hurt?"

They tell him that they are, believe it or not, all okay.

"I don't mean to be rude but we need to hurry," the priest says then, turning on his heels, and leading them around a corner and down a narrow passageway lined with exposed plumbing, ancient conduits, and crumbling brick bulwark. "This way to the garage," he says, walking as briskly as his vestments will allow. "It's at the far end of LL2, as the custodians refer to this floor . . . home of our modest little rectory, the pathology lab, and a large contingent of rodents who appear to have been here since the ground was broken a hundred years ago."

"Sure appreciate the helping hand, Father," Spur says as he hurries along beside the priest, carrying the assault rifle at his side.

"Call me Manny," he says. "My full name is Emmanuel Lawson

but most of the worshippers who find their way to the hospital's chapel come to know me as Manny . . . or Father Manny, if you're in a more liturgical mood."

Spur glances over his shoulder to make sure everyone is alert, uninjured, and moving quickly.

### 4.

Federal Marshal Frank Moon hears voices as he crouches behind the black Humvee, peering through his binoculars at Silverback's navy-blue SUV parked on the other side of the underground garage. It sits about fifty yards away, between a battered Honda Civic and a windowless panel van. The air in the lot is chalky and stuffy, and the fluorescent lights embedded in the low ceiling buzz and gleam off the rooftops of scores of other cars—the vehicles of family members in the throes of all manner of medical issues.

But at the moment Moon and Simms are the only living, breathing humans in the lot.

"They vanished from the sanctuary," Simms announces in his druggy monotone, listening through his earpiece to the tense voice of one of the marshals still in the chapel one floor up.

Frank Moon winces at the eerie chorus in his head, the legions of voices chanting in Latin—*INTERFICERE! ILLOS! OCCIDERE! EOS! OMNES! OCCIDIT! EOS!*—which causes him to bite down on his back molars so hard he cracks a tooth. "They'll be here," he says. "Any second now. I can feel it."

"Yes."

"Start the engine up."

Simms circles around the front of the Humvee, climbs into the driver's seat, and fires the massive diesel engine. The low rumble of 250 horses vibrates the still air of the parking garage.

Simms waits with his hands glued to the steering wheel like a mannequin in a Humvee showroom, his onyx eyes aimed straight forward, waiting for the next order of business.

### 5.

"Hold it," Spur whispers to the others as they reach the metal door at the end of the passageway marked PARKING GARAGE. He carefully cracks the door open just a few inches, peering out at the silent fluorescent-drenched garage. He sees zero people. He hears sirens from up on the street level, police on their way, most likely answering a flood of 911 calls about World War III break-ing out in the chapel. Then Spur sees Silverback's Tahoe SUV sit-ting about twenty yards away, under the lighted sign that says ELEVATORS.

He gently closes the door, turns to the group squeezed together in the passageway behind him, and says very quickly and quietly, "We need to skedaddle before the entire Twenty-Third Precinct shows up, and we need to do it on the down-low. I want every-body to keep an eye on the peripheries, be aware of any friend-lies sticking their noses in the line of fire. We only got about a half dozen rounds left in these fifteens until we get to the vehicle and can crack open our ordnance. Okay? Everybody got it? On my signal, all right?"

Nods from everybody except the priest.

"Father Manny, we owe you one." Spur extends a hand for a shake. "You saved our asses, and I can't thank you enough."

The priest looks at him. "Take me with you."

"Say what?"

"Please take me with you," the little old man says, wringing his palsied hands. He shoots a glance behind him, and then looks back at Spur. Behind the thick lenses of the priest's spectacles his droopy eyes are moist, filled with emotion. "I'm about to be fired from this place just like the last place I was assigned. I can't seem to hold down a regular position at a place of worship."

"Father, this is about to get extremely hairy—we don't have time for this. I can't take on another person. I'm sorry but that's just the way it is, and it is what it is."

Spur turns away but the priest tugs on his arm, pulling him back. "I can help you," he says.

"Father—"

"No, you don't understand. I know all about you . . . God showed me."

Spur gives him a sidelong glance. "God showed you?"

"I know how it sounds but it's true. He showed me in a dream. Your name is Paul Candell but you go by Spur because that's your code name and you work for the intelligence services so you can't be throwing your real name around like a drunken sailor."

Spur stares, a cold finger of dread touching the base of his spine.

"I knew you would one day come to this hospital," the old man says. "That's why I applied for the job here, all of which raised eyebrows at the archdiocese. I think they wrote me off as a heretic."

Spur's voice is so low now it's barely a whisper: "Holy shit on a shingle."

"I can help you," the priest persists. "Please. Please take me with you."

Spur exhales. "Okay. Fine. Fine. But you stay down, and you stay in the background, and you stay safe and quiet and out of the way, all right?"

The priest says that's all right with him, and the others just shrug and shake their heads.

## 6.

Moving quickly, staying low, guns at the ready, eyes wide open and scanning every shadow behind every parked car, Spur and his team hasten across the dusty cement deck toward the Tahoe.

"Wait!" Hack whispers as Spur is reaching for the driver's-side door handle.

Everybody freezes behind Hack, a single-file line, with hackles raised, nervous gazes on the periphery. Spur crouches down. "What is it? What's wrong?"

"Not sure, give me a second," Hack says, his skin tingling, the back of his neck bristling. He brushes his fingertips across the rear quarter panel. The snap of a spark crackles off his skin. He lowers himself and crawls under the SUV.

The greasy undercarriage looms above him, an impenetrable labyrinth of pipes and cables and nodes. He sees old wires and new wires. He notices out of the corner of his eye his skin beginning to glitter, his epidermis becoming reflective, luminous, stippled with microscopic particles, tiny ones and zeros.

He feels current running through him, his center of gravity being sucked up into the ironworks of the chassis, his consciousness wending its way through cables, around joints and phalanxes of circuitry, faster and faster and faster . . . until he slams to a halt inside a shiny new explosive device. Hack recognizes it from his time spent in the Explosive Ordnance Disposal team in Baghdad in the early aughts.

Hack yanks the green wire off the terminal, rips the device from the chassis, and crawls back out from under the vehicle. "It was set to go off the moment somebody decides to shift into drive," he says, handing the disabled car bomb to Spur. "Now we can go. You're welcome."

Before Spur can say a word, a barrage of gunfire erupts from across the lot.

## CHAPTER TWENTY-TWO
## Hot Pursuit

### 1.

They all dive for cover. The driver's side of the Tahoe sparks and clangs and dimples with bullet holes as the team collectively crawls around the front of the vehicle to the opposite side. Boo, Pin-Up, and Spur have the rifles, and they return fire around the corners of the SUV, emptying the remaining rounds until each weapon is clicking impotently.

Meantime, Hack has crawled into the front seats, keeping as low as he can in order to squeeze behind the wheel. He frantically fishes in his pocket for the keys as another fireworks display lights up the air outside the SUV, shattering windows and sending glass particles swirling down on top of everybody.

The others crawl into the vehicle through the rear passenger side door. Ticker reaches into the way-back for the road case with all their weapons while Silverback helps Father Manny into the rear seats. Ticker starts pulling out machine pistols, assault rifles, and extended-capacity magazines.

Hack gets the Tahoe started and revving as the last members of the team pile in.

Ticker sticks the snub-nose barrel of a TEC-9 out the jagged maw of a shattered window. Hack floors it. The SUV plunges ahead, pressing everybody into the seats, sideswiping the panel van as Ticker fires. The machine pistol roars. The barrage of sparks ricochets off the tops of cars, driving the marshals down under their Humvee.

In the side mirror, as the SUV booms up the ramp toward ground level, Hack can see the two marshals climbing into their vehicle, a plume of carbon monoxide visible belching out the back . . .

. . . as the Humvee charges after the SUV.

### 2.

By this point, Alexandria, Virginia, is gripped in its customary rush hour. Thousands and thousands of white-collar government workers up and down the D.C. corridor have shut down their computers, drawn their shades, turned off their lights, and knocked off for the day. Parking lots have begun to bustle and eventually clear out at the Department of Justice, the U.S. Postal Service complex, the Veteran Affairs Building, the Department of Defense, the U.S. Treasury, Homeland Security, the General Dynamics campus, Northrop Grumman, and myriad smaller employers up and down the Potomac.

By the time Frank Moon's Humvee has taken up its hot pursuit of Silverback's navy-blue Chevy Tahoe—in which rides the newly christened Devil's Quintet—a steady stream of commuters, buses, delivery trucks, semis, and car poolers have clogged the major thoroughfares. Add to this the retinue of Alexandria police cruisers—who are now only minutes behind the chase, and are currently sending out calls for backup and roadblocks—and you have the makings of major gridlock and pandemonium on the main interstate, 495, which ultimately leads commuters out of town.

"I would take the shoulder," Spur says from the front passenger seat, the SUV screaming along. He sees the tie-up ahead of them, the brake lights of cars winking on in every lane. He glances over his shoulder, and sees the midnight-black Humvee about a half a dozen car lengths behind them and closing fast. He can see the big, burly lead marshal leaning out the passenger window with an AR-15 in his arms, his eye fixing on the rifle's front sight. "And I would do it pretty quickly if possible," Spur adds, trying not to alarm anybody.

The boom of a single blast echoes over the top of the slowing traffic.

The Tahoe's rear window shatters, causing the priest to gasp, and everybody else to duck. Pin-Up climbs into the rear cargo bay and returns fire—her assault rifle now loaded to the gills with a high-capacity magazine holding thirty rounds—the muzzle of her weapon spitting fire out the jagged opening. She places a half a dozen rounds across the Humvee's grille, aiming for the radiator or any other critical component she might disable with the strafe. She jacks the lever again, and tries for the front tires. Sparks bounce off the macadam as the Humvee weaves in and out of the slower-moving traffic now in a classic evasive maneuver.

They are about to slam into the rear end of a stopped car when Hack yanks the wheel.

The Tahoe veers onto the shoulder and rumbles past the hundreds and hundreds of vehicles at a standstill. In the opposite side mirror Spur sees the black Humvee gaining on them, coming up hard and fast on the shoulder. The brawny lead marshal fires off more shots, bullets sparking off the Tahoe's rear quarter panels.

From the rear cargo bay Pin-Up fires back at him, one of her rounds grazing the marshal's right shoulder. But oddly, he barely seems to register the puff of blood and tissue flinging off into the wind. He keeps firing, and Hack picks up the speed. The SUV hits eighty miles per hour. Pin-Up ejects the empty mag, slams another clip into the stock, jacks the lever, and then gets an idea.

She puts the gun down and focuses on the driver, the baby-faced young marshal, whom she can clearly see through the glare of the Humvee's windshield.

## 3.

Pin-Up's new skills have been developing within her like those photographic negatives dunked into that chemical bath, slowly resolving from blurry images to those of crystalline clarity. It is dawning on her that she may very well be the superhuman version of those chemicals, a living, breathing rendering apparatus that can embody the most intimate secrets of others. She can now, perhaps under the right circumstances, scare a person to death by turning their angst—their lifelong trauma, fears, and narcissistic desires—into solid form. Like a dark version of the pinup queen of yore—the voluptuous calendar woman on the walls of filling stations and body shops—she reflects back at the ogling gazers the dirty little secrets of those who gaze.

She is Cassandra . . . the Valkyrie . . . the Siren. She is the fever dream personified.

All of which is how she locks on to that baby-faced marshal behind the wheel of the Humvee. Her eyes become satellite dishes, capturing and recording and rendering the transmissions oozing off the face of the young marshal in the driver's seat. She sees his younger incarnation, all peach fuzz and zits and freckles. She sees memories of his absent father, a cop on the beat who was never home, never offering any love or affection.

But most importantly, at that very moment—as an assault rifle blazes out the Humvee's passenger window, and an atonal chorus of sirens echoes across the sky—Pin-Up sees in her mind's eye the abusive, alcoholic, bitter woman who was left behind in the squalid row house with the son whom she never wanted in the first place.

Closing her eyes, Pin-Up brings to life this cruel sociopath of a mother.

## 4.

Closer . . . closer . . . Marshal Gerald T. Simms gains on the Tahoe, so close now he can read McDermott's bumper sticker: DON'T TOUCH ME I'M NOT THAT KIND OF CAR. Which kindles zero amusement in the young man with the black-marble eyes. He pushes the Humvee as fast as it will go . . . when something catches his attention out of the corner of those onyx eyes. He shoots a glance out the driver's-side window, and he blinks, and blinks . . . and blinks.

In the opposite lanes, the oncoming traffic has jammed, the slower-moving drivers gawking at the chase. As Simms zooms past the congested vehicles, he makes eye contact with one of the drivers. The woman behind the wheel staring back at him with the dour expression is in her late forties, with pale skin, ashen blond hair, sunken eyes, and the deep lines and wrinkles of a heavy drinker. Of course he recognizes her instantly.

The last time he saw his mother was eleven years ago back in Baltimore. She had been on a weeklong bender, and had nearly burned down their row house one night when she fell asleep on the living room sofa while her cigarette was going. The next morning, Simms—then only nineteen—had reached his limit. He packed up and told his mother he was leaving for good, and he would probably never see her again. On his way out the door, he paused and looked back at her. Still slumped on that same shopworn couch that she nearly immolated the night before, Celia Simms said nothing, just glowered at her son with the same dark expression that this driver—at this very moment, in the eastbound lanes of Interstate 495—is exhibiting as she stares zombielike at the young marshal in the passing Humvee.

Simms blinks some more. He sees that gloomy, haggard face staring out from every vehicle, from behind every window. His mother is driving every car. She's every passenger, every child, every parent, *everyone*. Staring. Silent. Grim. A scream begins to slither up Simms's gorge, threatening to explode as his mother's face passes in a flickering blur like a horrible magic lantern. He starts to cry out when he realizes he's about to slam into Silverback's SUV.

In that terrifying instant before the Humvee collides with the SUV's rear bumper, Simms sees a figure behind the shattered glass of the rear window, crouched in the rear cargo area, staring at him: *Celia Simms, his silent, hateful mother.*

*"Stop it!—Stop it!!"*

His scream pierces the roar of engines, shatters the demonic hold over him, and reduces him to a lonely, mixed-up teenage boy . . . right as the Humvee's front grille smashes into the SUV.

The collision shoves Simms into the dashboard and sends Frank Moon—who is leaning out the window, firing controlled bursts—lurching forward, nearly falling out of the vehicle. His rifle flies out of his grasp. The weapon tumbles to the pavement, and Frank catches himself on the side mirror, and with great effort pulls himself back into his seat.

By this point, the younger marshal is crying, his face a mask of agony. His eyes have returned to their normal size and color. "I . . . I . . . I . . . don't know what's happening," he sobs.

Marshal Frank Moon reaches down, pulls the Glock 19 pistol from Simms's holster, thumbs the hammer back, presses the muzzle to Simms's head, and fires. The blast jerks the younger man sideways as the exit wound sprays blood and brain matter across the driver's window. The Humvee swerves, drifting dangerously close to the median. Frank Moon grabs the steering wheel. With a complete lack of emotion, he kicks at the driver's-side door handle until the latch breaks.

## 5.

In the Tahoe's side mirror, Hack can see the Humvee swerving and fishtailing, the driver slumped, his head lolling, blood on the window, and the driver's-side door banging open in the wind.

Hack sees the older marshal kick the younger man's remains out the opening. The body flops to the pavement and rolls wildly into the path of one of the oncoming police cruisers. The shriek of brakes comes too late. The cop car runs over the body of the younger marshal.

"At the risk of stating the obvious," Spur says from the front passenger seat, reloading his assault rifle and gazing over his shoulder at the carnage receding into the distance behind them, "we gotta give these yahoos the slip A-SAP before there's a hell of a lot more collateral damage. You know what I mean?"

Hack knows exactly what he means. In the back seat, Ticker and Silverback also know what Spur is talking about. They sit silently reloading their weapons on either side of Father Manny, who looks surprisingly sanguine, his hands folded in his lap, his gaze downcast. Is he praying? Hack hopes that he is, and hopes it's a good one. Boo and Pin-Up are in the rear cargo area. A faint, translucent coating covers Pin-Up like a caul, the faded outline of an avatar fizzing away like spindrift as she reconstitutes back into her original self. Hack's not sure what she just conjured and launched at the marshals, but it sure seemed to spook the driver.

Glancing out at the side mirror, Hack sees the Humvee gaining on them. The older marshal has managed to climb behind the wheel, and has gotten the Humvee under control and now has it floored. As the black behemoth closes in, the muzzle of a handgun flashes outside the driver's-side window, another ten rounds booming in the wind, strafing the SUV's roof.

*He's going for a head shot,* Hack thinks as he notices the three police cruisers behind the Humvee, looming closer and closer, sirens wailing, chaser lights flashing. Hack turns back to the road ahead.

An exit ramp appears as they round a bend in the interstate, about a quarter mile ahead of them. It banks off to the south, hooking into a two-lane asphalt road snaking through the verdant Virginia farmland. Hack sees high-tension wires . . . patchwork fields . . . trestles and endless train tracks . . . and inspiration strikes. "I don't mean to be bossy or imperious in any way," he announces to his passengers without fanfare. "But if I were you guys, I would buckle up and hold on."

He pins the accelerator to the floor, the SUV thundering at nearly a hundred miles per hour now. In order to fool the vehicles on his tail, Hack stays in the far left lane as they approach the exit . . . and then, at the very last possible moment, he yanks the wheel.

The tires screech, and the centripetal force shoves the others against the left side of the interior as the SUV turns so sharply it nearly goes into a roll. The vehicle hits the ramp at ninety-five miles an hour. Wrestling the wheel, struggling to keep the machine from spinning out, Hack reaches the bottom of the ramp and abruptly makes a sharp turn to the south.

The g-forces cause the rear end of the Tahoe to momentarily slide sideways. Hack gets it under control and roars southward on the narrow two-lane. He shoots a glance over his shoulder and sees pandemonium on the interstate near the ramp. Two of the three police cruisers have been reduced to tangled wreckage in the center median, the third stopping to assist.

But the Humvee has managed to make a U-turn, and now rumbles down the ramp less than a couple of minutes behind the SUV.

Hack says to Spur, "Be a mensch and do me a favor, will you?"

"Of course."

"We need to trade places."

"How in God's green earth are we gonna do that?"

"Full disclosure: I'm going to stop."

"You're gonna what?!"

From the back seat, Ticker says, "You think that's a good idea with this guy breathing down our necks?"

"I got an idea, is the thing," Hack tells them. "I need this schmuck to catch up with us, and I need to have my hands free."

Spur takes a deep breath. "If you say so."

Hack lifts up on the accelerator and brakes them to a stop under a massive live oak. He throws the door open and hops out, hollering at Spur. "C'mon, Skipper! On the double!"

Spur gets out and hustles around the front of the SUV, passing Hack coming the other way. They climb in their respective sides, and slam their doors. Spur can see the Humvee raising a cloud of dust as it approaches, maybe a minute away now.

He stomps on the pedal, and the Chevy Tahoe rockets away.

Hack starts fiddling with the radio, trying to tune it between stations.

"Now what in the name of Sam Hill's horny toad are you doing?"

"Trying to find a pathway to the high-tension wires."

"The what?"

He fiddles with the tuning knob until a low hum buzzes out

of the speakers. "Trust me, I got this," he says very softly, very lightly pressing his hand down on the radio's faceplate . . .

. . . as his flesh begins to softly glow with luminous microscopic mosaics of ones and zeros.

## CHAPTER TWENTY-THREE

# A Clap of Thunder in a Metallic Sky

## 1.

Their powers are evolving. With each passing day, each passing hour, they push the limits and learn more and more about the extent of their skills. The variations and iterations are mind-boggling. It's not that they have become gods—all-powerful, immortal, indestructible, omniscient—but rather that they have become what scientists might call transhuman. *Neo-human*. Is this all the work of the devil? Perhaps. But something about the way Father Manny is observing them, watching the chase—the knowing look in the old man's eyes, the slight curl at the corner of his lips into a very subtle and yet gratified smile like that of a parent beholding a child riding their bike for the first time without training wheels—speaks of things such as Fate, Providence, and Destiny. They will soon learn the magnitude of Father Manny's prophecy, but at the moment they are immersed in the struggle to evade the demonic marshal behind the wheel of the coal-black Humvee, which Spur now sees in the side mirror approaching them on the twisting two-lane.

The rural highway cuts through the rolling tobacco fields and pasturelands of western Virginia, lined with endless high-tension wires looping from pole to pole, connecting landlines and microwave stations, teeming with current. The afternoon sun hangs low in the sky, elongating the shadows across the road, flickering against the windows and chilling the air as it blows in through jagged holes in the glass.

Spur pushes the Tahoe past ninety-five miles per hour, then past a hundred, then past a hundred and ten. He feels his gut levitate. The SUV careers around a turn, and then screams up and over a hilly section of the highway, all of which reminds Spur of the roller coaster rides at the Texas State Fair when he was a kid. In the rearview mirror he can see the Humvee closing in, roaring over the hills so fast its tires seem to momentarily leave the ground.

All at once, Spur sees the demonic visage of the lead marshal behind the wheel, bearing down on them, his black eyes blazing with hate, and Spur recalls something the devil casually revealed back in Karakistan: *I do have the gift of influence, and I can cause people to do great mischief if I so choose.* Spur wonders if he misheard this boastful declaration. Did the devil mean he could corrupt "all" people or "most" people? Logic would dictate that someone as powerful as Satan could easily infect the souls of the Quintet, and get them to do all manner of tricks against their wills like doomed circus animals. But for reasons Spur may never understand, he has a sense of being relatively impervious to demonic possession. If he were forced to articulate the feeling, the closest analogy Spur would be able to make is that he and his team are a bad fit for an evil spirit—like a light socket the wrong shape for a standard bulb. He has no science to back this up, but like everything else in his life lately, instinct and intuition are driving his every move.

In fact, right at this moment, Spur can feel the bloodlust radiating off the marshal in the Humvee, and it stirs something in him, something terrifying that he can't quite define. Is this a reverberation of his own superpower? He has not fully grasped the nature of his new skill, and yet he knows it has something to do with reflecting an enemy's powers back at them. He knows that he has not been truly tested, the skill remaining somewhat mysterious and inchoate, but there will be plenty of time for exploring such things. At the moment there are far more pressing matters . . .

. . . such as listening to Hack's halting yet urgent directions as he hunches forward in his seat, his hand hovering over the faceplate of the radio, tendrils of brilliant white current streaking into his palm as though his hand were a divining rod.

"Half a mile . . . an intersection . . . a train crossing," he murmurs, "take a right . . . and if you would be so kind as to go west along the tracks . . . and then it would be great if you could wait for my signal."

Spur does a double take. It registers all at once, what he is finally seeing in those high-tension wires stretching along the edge of the highway, looping from pole to pole, so ubiquitous, so common along every rural route in America that they become invisible. Spur stares, for a moment almost mesmerized by the evidence of Hack's astral body pulsing along the wires at a hundred miles an hour, a giant fuse burning in fast motion, pure energy following the progress of the Tahoe, heading south toward the train crossing.

## 2.

Freed of his corporeal body, unleashed from the physical world, weightless, Hack has become pure current. Streaking through the wires. Searching. Seeking. Hunting for the next tributary node. Straight ahead he can see the intersection and the train crossing, the cables and transformers like an enormous cloverleaf. He targets the red tunnel of light designated RICHMOND, FREDER-ICKSBURG, AND POTOMAC RAILROAD.

He plunges into the narrow channel of luminous crimson diodes and circuits, and now he is running parallel to the tracks along an access road. The pipeline comes alive suddenly, and Hack feels as though he's a pinball bouncing from terminal to terminal in a storm of brilliant flashing red light as the train draws near.

He forces the words out of his physical mouth down in the SUV. "Spur, it would be fantastic if you could tell me when you see a train coming. Behind us, on the parallel tracks."

He hears Spur's voice as though it's coming from a great distance. "I see it! A big mother of a freight train coming!"

"Is the Humvee close?"

"So close he's about to tickle my ass!"

"Good . . . so . . . now . . . if you could be so good as to stand by. On my signal, I want you to pull off the road as fast as you can!"

For a moment, the scarlet radiance and ear-piercing noise engulf Hack. He streams along with the train, his gaze fixed on the route ahead, enveloped in the sequential flashes of signal lights and transformers and current converters and warning signs. He can see the wire-frame map of the rail line unfurling ahead of him, and in half a mile the road climbing a hill while the train plunges into a stone tunnel that cuts through a vast hillock of old-growth oaks and gnarled foliage.

"Get ready, Spur . . . in about thirty seconds I'm going to ask you to pull off the road at the bottom of the hill!"

It takes fifteen seconds for the train to reach the tunnel and plunge into the darkness.

Meanwhile, the two vehicles climb the steep hill that runs along the wooded berm crowning the tunnel. More gunfire blazes out the Humvee's driver's-side window as the two vehicles crest the hill and plummet down the other side. Spur is flashing back to the Texas State Fair again, and the floating sensation as the roller coaster slams down the big slope.

In the cyberspace tunnel of flashing warning lights and tangles of circuitry, Hack reaches out for the signal wires with his virtual hands and yanks them free of their moorings, a portion of the channel flickering into darkness, disabling the signal crossing.

At second number twenty-five, the two vehicles reach the bottom of the hill and follow the road as it abruptly curves toward the crossing apparatus just west of the mouth of the tunnel.

"Now, Spur, *now*!! Pull off the road as fast as you can!"

## 3.

The railroad crossing at the bottom of the hill is a notorious blind spot for both drivers *and* train engineers. Which is why the crossing signals at that juncture are exceedingly important to avoid catastrophe. Thirty seconds before a train emerges from the tunnel, the red lights are supposed to begin flashing, and a bell is supposed to begin ringing, and the gigantic twin wooden masts are supposed to automatically lower to a horizontal position across each side of the tracks.

But since Hack has manually disabled the crossing signal from inside the system, the apparatus remains still and silent.

When the Tahoe abruptly pulls off the road—midcurve, without warning, thudding across the weeds before skidding to a halt—the Humvee is going too fast for the marshal to correct its forward momentum. With the signal dark and nonfunctioning, neither Frank Moon nor the engineer operating the train is alerted to the impending disaster.

The Humvee skids across the tracks at the precise moment the massive freight train bursts out of the darkness of the tunnel.

The collision makes a spectacular sound like a clap of thunder in a metallic sky as eighteen thousand tons of iron and cargo smash into the Humvee. The vehicle folds in half, glass and steel erupting in all directions, air brakes shrieking, the train's forward momentum carrying the crushed Humvee for at least a half mile before the vehicle's gas tank ruptures.

The explosion lights up the sky and shakes the very ground on which the Tahoe sits, an enormous fireball roiling and levitating into the heavens.

## 4.

By this point a keening shriek of metal on metal pierces the wind, the train's air brakes slowing the cars enough for the engineers and loadmasters to stick their heads out open windows in shock and apprehension. Livestock fidgets and scrapes within cattle cars. Iron pinions shudder as the train finally grinds to a stop.

Inside the Tahoe, Hack's bodily shell returns to its natural state as he pulls away from the radio, his flesh faintly glittering and then fading back to normal. He turns and looks at Spur. "Not to be a pessimist but if we weren't fugitives before this, we have definitely gotten ourselves on that list now."

"Yeah," Spur agrees. "That little old ship has definitely sailed."

Ticker speaks up from the rear seats. "Then maybe we ought to get our fugitive asses in gear, and get the hell out of here."

## 5.

For quite a while they drive in stony silence, the Tahoe wobbly from all the gunfire and stunt driving, the engine ticking and rattling, with alarming vapors pouring out from under the hood. In order to avoid the armada of police cars, Spur travels the backwater two-lanes and farm-access roads, zigzagging in a southerly direction across Virginia as the sun sets on the rolling hills. He knows he's going to have to find alternative transportation soon. In these parts, state police and county mounties don't take kindly to passing vehicles riddled with bullet holes.

Every few moments, Spur glances into the rearview and studies their faces—each of them downcast and gloomy in the waning daylight. He knows exactly what they're thinking. They just killed at least three federal marshals, maybe more. They have crossed a dark Rubicon now, and it doesn't matter that most likely it was the devil's influence that made those marshals attack with such viciousness. Actions have consequences for the sane. But it's too late to reverse the course of events. They will vanish into the underground now. It's a fait accompli.

By the time full darkness rolls in, they are approaching the outskirts of Roanoke. Spur has no idea why he's chosen a south-by-southwest route out of harm's way. Maybe it's just a random direction, a flip of the coin. Or perhaps he's secretly heading back to Texas like a homing pigeon. At the moment, in fact, all he knows for sure is that he is in for a penny and in for a pound now, and he also needs to acquire a new vehicle or he and the team will spend the night in some backwoods jail.

At length they come upon a truck stop blazing with sodium-vapor light and garish billboards for everything from cheap burritos to a local strip joint.

The place is fairly deserted, and there's a rust-pocked Dodge Caravan parked in the side lot that looks road-worn yet sturdy. Hack and Spur go inside the mini-mart and see a few people playing video games in the back. One older woman with a big grey bouffant stands at the cash register, reading a horoscope paperback. Spur gives Hack a nod, and Hack slips out a side door while Spur distracts the cashier by buying up half the store's supply of beef jerky, candy bars, and bottled water.

When Spur comes back outside, he sees the Tahoe sitting empty at the pumps. Hack has already managed to trigger the Caravan's keyless entry system, transfer the ordnance, get the team on board, fire the engine by brushing a fingertip across the ignition, and climb behind the wheel. "Bless your pea-pickin' heart," Spur says to him as he climbs into the shotgun seat.

"Just doing my job," Hack says as he pulls out of the lot in the freshly stolen minivan.

"Chalk up another crime for the Devil's Quintet," Pin-Up wisecracks from the third row.

Nobody thinks it's very funny as Hack drives away in the southbound lane.

Moments later, they pass a sign that says KNOXVILLE TENNESSEE 173 MI.

## 6.

"Tell me about this dream," Spur says to the priest as they cross the Tennessee border.

They've been on the road now for over two hours. They've made two stops since acquiring the Caravan—one to fill up the tank, and one for a restroom break—learning once again the hard way that possessing ill-gotten superpowers does not alleviate a person's need to relieve themselves.

Along the way, they've discussed the blowback from the afternoon's debacle with the federal marshals. Silverback predicts a coordinated nationwide manhunt. He also suggests that they initiate a "wipe" with the assistance of Cthulhu and his trusted operatives. In the parlance of deep-cover counterintelligence, a "wipe" is when an operative is officially removed from society—and in this case the ranks of the Defense Intelligence Agency—through the staging and manufacture of their death. Cover stories, certificates, autopsies, and police records are forged. In some cases, the unidentified remains of John and Jane Does are procured from cooperative pathology labs and medical schools for burial in closed-casket ceremonies.

It's a nasty kind of nuclear option for any decent intelligence operative who dreams of having a normal life, and the more people who know about the very existence of the phenomenon make the ruse more likely to be leaked, and the process more dangerous than ever. All of which is why both Silverback and Spur have each individually agonized—in their silent ruminations, over the last hundred miles—about discussing such a classified procedure in front of Father Emmanuel Lawson.

But ultimately they each came to the same conclusion: Father Manny is trustworthy and should be brought into the fold.

"Well . . . first of all, ever since I was a young missionary in the Sudan I haven't had many dreams—at least ones that I remember—so this one was a doozy, one which I shall never forget." The priest sits between Ticker and Silverback on the second-row bench seat like the tiniest antique nesting doll, wiping his spectacles with a handkerchief and speaking so softly the others have to lean in to hear him above the road noise. He pauses to put his glasses on. In the darkness of the interior, in the occasional flash of a traffic signal or vapor light, his ancient face looks even more ancient, like old parchment that's been wadded and scorched in places. He turns to Silverback. "You were in the dream, by the way. McDermott? Is that your surname?"

The big Irishman looks a little taken aback for a moment. "It is indeed," he says. "And I can't wait to hear how I ended up in the dream of a padre I've never met, never even laid eyes on."

Father Manny makes a sound that's half chuckle, half sigh. "That's just one of the mysteries of a dream full of them."

Ticker pipes in. "The Lord works in mysterious ways, right? At least that's what I've heard."

"You are spot on, my son. Spot on. It's one of the eternal truths."

From the front seat, Spur says, "I'm guessing that's how you found us? You tracked down a Sean McDermott, and then you saw that he was admitted to the hospital that you were assigned to?"

"Not exactly . . . there were other clues in the dream, and I searched for years for this hospital by the name of Kenmore. Remember this was before we had the internet. When I finally found the medical center in Alexandria, I lobbied to be assigned to that hospital because I knew one day you would come there."

"You say this is before the internet? You mind my asking when you had this whackadoodle dream of yours?"

The priest looks at him. "It'll be twenty-three years ago this August."

The drone of the engine and the burr of the wheels on the road are the only sounds that can be heard in that dark interior for a long moment as the passengers process what the priest has just revealed. Through the windshield Spur can see the white lines of Tennessee State Road 126 clocking under the van with hypnotic rhythm, the occasional rural mailbox or reflector blurring past them. Beyond the reach of the headlights, on either side of the road, stretches a black ocean of undeveloped forests and soybean fields, all of it so dark it might as well be the mountainous wilderness of Karakistan.

At last, without tearing his gaze from that impenetrable landscape, Spur says, "I'm thinking that maybe you oughtta go ahead and tell us about this dream."

## CHAPTER TWENTY-FOUR
## Eblis

### 1.

*In the dream the priest found himself wandering a desolate wasteland in some far-flung, unfamiliar nation, the hot wind whipping his robe, his sandals worn and his feet blistered from traveling a great distance on foot. He had no provisions, no water, no idea of what he was seeking, or why he was trudging through this sandblasted landscape. All that he knew was that he was searching for something or someone, and it was urgent, and he would find them or he would die trying.*

*Throughout these early parts of the dream, the priest felt a strange, disturbing anxiety that he was being watched. And followed. He would see dark shapes—humanoid figures—out of the corner of his eye. But when he would pause and gaze up at the crest of a sand dune or the edge of a rocky plateau, he would see nothing.*

*Finally, he stopped and glanced up at a high precipice to his left.*

*It was a craggy, windblown, sun-bleached hillock, and at its apex, standing there as still as a dark sculpture in the gales of furnace-hot winds, was a massive, oily-grey, impossibly huge wolf. It stood on its hind legs as a man would stand, its eyes glowing like burning embers as it glowered down at the priest. It radiated a malignant sort of hate, and it spoke to the holy man through telepathic means.*

You will never be able to vanquish me, *the creature announced, its baritone snarl reverberating only in the priest's mind.* I am immortal.

"I don't believe I've had the pleasure; I have no disagreement with you," *the priest replied with his normal speaking voice.* "Why would I want to vanquish someone with whom I have no dispute?"

Because . . . I am Eblis, *the voice of the wolf creature buzzed between his ears.*

*The priest felt a wave of dread wash over him. "Eblis? You are the fallen angel?"*

*The wolf creature vanished then as suddenly as it had appeared.*

*"Are you there?"*

*Only the barren, noxious wind answered the priest. "Where have you—?"*

*The priest felt a tap on his shoulder. He whirled around with a start, and found that the monster was standing directly behind him.*

*It towered over him, standing at least eight feet tall, and at this proximity its eyes burned like lanterns, its fur knotted and moldering as though petrified. Its blackened lips peeled away from its razor-sharp fangs, forming an obscene abomination of a grin, its incisors dripping with drool.*

*In the priest's head a distorted noise like laughter rang out, followed by the words, ET COMEDENT ANIMAM TUAM VIR SANCTUS!!*

## 2.

"The words are Church Latin, archaic," Father Manny softly explains in the darkness of the minivan's interior as the vehicle rumbles through the murky shadows of a Tennessee night. The priest has been talking now for at least ten minutes without taking a breath, and Spur and the others have been hanging on every word, waiting for their appearance in the dream.

"Can you translate it for us?" Spur asks from the shotgun seat.

The little old man reaches inside his robe and pulls an object from the breast pocket of his shirt. It's a dog-eared, well-thumbed, spiral-bound notebook that looks as though it was purchased sometime during the Clinton administration. He asks if Spur would mind turning on the dome light.

Spur obliges, and the priest pages through the little notebook until he finds the appropriate faded notes scrawled in his tight, obsessive handwriting many years ago. "I'm sorry to say my Latin has never been what it should be. What the creature said to me was 'I will eat your soul, holy man.'"

"That definitely sounds like our guy," Pin-Up ventures from the third-row bench, her sculpted cheekbones illuminated for a fleeting instant as the minivan passes a streetlamp.

"Keep going, Padre," Spur says.

"I should probably mention here that this dream was unlike any other dream I had ever had. It lasted almost twelve hours. I'm not a late sleeper, you see—more of an early bird, I guess—and the older I get the less sleep I need. Five hours is pure sloth for me. But this night, this fateful night, I slept as though I were hibernating. Looking back on it, I often wonder if I was trapped in the dream.

"Anyway, at this point in the dream I began to back away from this creature—this terrible angel, this wolflike demon—and as I did so, it laughed at me, and tossed its head back, its tongue waggling out of its snout. The tongue elongated then, and it lashed out at me almost like a bullwhip.

"It was . . . this tongue was forked and . . . and serpentine and . . . and . . . and it stung me in the center of my neck, in my Adam's apple, and I couldn't breathe. In the dream, I couldn't breathe. I remember that distinctly, I remember it to this day. I remember making notes about it the next morning. The other priests in my rectory that night, they mentioned hearing horrible gasping and coughing coming from my room."

Spur asks if any of the other priests came to his room to check on him.

"They did indeed, and I'm told I called out to them . . . something like 'I'm fine!' . . . 'It's just a dream!' . . . 'Go back to bed, Father O'Neil!' . . . but the strangest thing is, I have no memory of that. None whatsoever. I do remember in my dream getting stung by that terrible tongue, and staggering backward on the burning sands of that desolate place. I staggered and staggered . . . gasping for breath . . . when the very ground beneath my feet gave way. And I fell. I fell through the earth into hell."

The old man pauses here, and seems to be summoning courage to merely continue relating the horrifying events of the prophetic dream.

## 3.

In the darkness of the front seat, staring at the hypnotic thrum of the highway, Spur keeps the fact to himself that he has seen this very same fallen angel that the priest has been describing. Spur saw this creature on a hilltop in Karakistan. And Spur has gotten to know this monster a hell of a lot better than he ever would have thought possible.

The priest continues: "I knew I was in hell the moment I sank through that sand and landed on a table in a dark room lit by torches and crowded with the pathetic, ragged, demonic souls of the damned. There were all manner of the deformed and mutated. There were dogs with human faces, cows and goats with human heads, pitiable beings stunted by sin and degradation. I could barely move as they capered and danced around me—gargoyle-like, some nude, some barely dressed in tattered undergarments, their faces so distorted and corrupted by their iniquities that they appeared to have reverted to primitive, primordial beings." He thumbs through his notebook. "The next morning, I described them in my notes as having . . . 'rotten teeth too big for their heads, and brow ridges, and canine ears that crawled with maggots.'" He shivers slightly before going on. "I truly believed that they were about to feast on me, and I would die in the dream . . . and I would most likely also expire in my bed in real life.

"But then something miraculous happened. Across the chamber a figure appeared in a doorway. The demons saw it, too, and they scattered like insects exposed to light. In their hasty departure they knocked over a torch, which rolled across the stone floor to the doorway, illuminating my rescuer."

The priest pauses, and Spur feels an unexpected twinge of emotion pinching his gut . . . as though he were waiting for a life-or-death test result at the doctor's office. Very softly he says, "It was one of us, wasn't it."

Father Manny is nodding. "Indeed it was," he says. "It was you."

## 4.

Another pause ensues, gripped with tension. Spur glances over his shoulder at the deeply lined face visible for a fleeting instant in the ambient flash of streetlight. "C'mon, Padre . . . seriously?"

Before the old man can respond, Hack shoots a sidelong glance at Spur from behind the wheel. "After all we've been through, you draw the line at *this dream*? This dream is a bridge too far for you to swallow?"

Spur lets out a weary sigh. "You're mixing your metaphors, *kemo sabe*." He glances at the reflection of the old man in the rearview. "Go on, Padre."

The old man summons a deep breath before continuing. "In the dream, as you walked into the room, I thought you were a fellow clergy member, the way you were dressed. You wore a monk's robe, a hood throwing a shadow across your face, and strange armor on your shoulders, arms, and calves. You had an enormous broadsword tucked into a bejeweled scabbard. You helped me off the table. 'We don't have much time, old hoss,' you said to me.

"Then you pulled back your hood and I saw your kind eyes, and I just knew in the dream everything was going to be all right. 'The name's Paul,' you said. 'But you can call me Spur; all my friends do.' And then . . . then . . .

". . . You know how dreams are like fragments of a puzzle? Sometimes they jump from one thing to another? Well, all of a sudden, the two of us—you and I, Spur—we were hurrying through an endless catacomb that reeked of evil. Moldy stone, dank, lit only by torches every fifty feet or so, riddled with Satanic symbols, and . . . and . . . deformed human skulls embedded in the walls. I've been to the Catacombs of Rome, and they are indeed breathtaking, but these . . . these were awful, ghastly passageways, not even remotely like those holy burial places and the sacred necropolis under the Basilica. These were corruptions of earthly catacombs, they were passageways to nowhere, they were airless, endless circles of hell from which there is no escape.

"But you . . . you, Spur . . . you refused to be intimidated by this horrible place. Like a staunch, expert miner searching for ore, you kept pausing, tapping the stone, listening to the walls, murmuring in your country patois something like, 'We gotta get our butts outta here or we're gonna be as lost as last year's Easter eggs!' I wrote down many of the colorful expressions that you used in the dream so I wouldn't forget. I was following you in that dream because I believed in you. I'm a man of faith, even in a nightmare, and for reasons that I still can't quite explain I had faith in you, Spur. I knew you could get us out of that place.

"And lo and behold, you found a weak spot in the wall, and you mumbled, 'Gotta muster up my muscle memory.'—I wrote this down in my notes, as well.—And then you said, 'Playing middle linebacker for Texas A&M has always served me well!'"

"And then . . . boom! You slammed through that stone like a human wrecking ball.

"I followed you through that hole in that wall into a new and terrifying place. It was a place from the fairy tales of my childhood.

Dark, and cold, and smelling of earth and rot, it was a primeval forest. We moved quickly through it—you, Spur, drawing your broadsword and slashing through the thick, stubborn vegetation—and we felt the eyes on us. Behind the webbing of that inky-black foliage they were watching us. Yellow, glowing eyes. The eyes of the damned. We heard horrible sounds, feral sounds, the growling of demonic creatures—hungry, bloodthirsty—surrounding us. And you, Spur, you bravely raised that sword and prepared to make a stand . . .

". . . when all at once, the others appeared on either flank."

## 5.

By this point, it's clear to everyone in that stolen Dodge Caravan that the telling of the dream is draining Father Manny, exhausting him. But the words are also galvanizing everyone else in the vehicle in strange and yet powerful ways.

With his trembling, palsied hands, the priest flips through the pages of his notebook, and then says, "All of you joined us then, each of you in similar warrior vestments—robes, hoods, scabbards, longbows, quivers—protecting us from those yellow eyes." He stops. "I wrote the names down, odd names like Spur's."

In the darkness of the minivan Father Manny points to each operative as he reads their code names.

"There was Ticker . . . and Hack . . . and Pin-Up . . . and Boo . . . and even *you*, my son." In the darkness he indicates the big Irishman sitting next to him. "You joined us with fresh horses and provisions. You said your real name was Sean McDermott but then you said I should call you Silverback."

Letting out a sigh, the Irishman looks down at the little wizened priest. "You've been living with these names for many years, haven't you?"

"I have indeed," says the priest. "And the last part of the dream was the part that stayed with me the longest, haunted me. We each mounted one of the horses you brought, and we rode like the dickens, wending our way out of that dark forest, and into a world the likes of which I have never seen—in either dreams *or* reality—and I pray I never see it again in any form.

"We plunged into a world decimated by thermonuclear war, radiation, and disease. We rode through cities reduced to rubble, buildings mere shells of crumbling, scorched bricks and mortar, streets lined with human remains burned beyond recognition, rotting in the pale sun. Mass graves. Craters in the earth filled with poisonous, brackish water bubbling with radioactivity.

"At last we reached the edge of the wasteland, and we paused at the threshold of a rugged, craggy, almost prehistoric mountain range. And Spur, you say to me, 'This is as far as we can take you, Padre. We have to go now, we have business up there.' And that's when you point toward the highest summit in the far distance—a desolate pinnacle of volcanic rock—and in my dream I just know that it is a mountain called Armageddon."

He pauses and marshals his energy, and takes a deep breath before continuing.

"The last thing you said to me before I woke up drenched in sweat, tangled in my bed linens, was this: 'We will meet again at a place called Kenmore.'" The old man reads now off his notes. "'But we must leave you here. Take good care of yourself, Padre.' And with that, you rode off—the six of you—into the mists of this mountain called Armageddon."

The old man glances back down at the notebook with the wistful expression of a mother looking at old baby pictures of a long-lost child. "I wrote the word 'Kenmore' down that next day, and pondered over it for weeks . . . months . . . years. I looked in the phone book. Not only was Kenmore the last name of about a million people but it was also a brand name of household appliances. There were thousands of streets in America by that name. As I said, this was before we had the World Wide Web. Sean McDermott was also a very, very common name. I never got anywhere until the rectory bought its first computer in the early aughts.

"It took a lot of searching but I finally found a place where those two names—Kenmore and McDermott—existed within a few miles of each other. That's when I lobbied to become the in-house chaplain at Kenmore Alexandria Medical Center . . . tending to the families with terminal loved ones, helping people deal with the tragedies and vagaries of illness and injury . . . and I started praying that the prophecy would one day come to pass."

## 6.

After another long pause, during which Spur can practically hear everybody's wheels turning under the drone of the Caravan's *actual* wheels, he says, "That's quite a dream, Padre. I'll give you that. But the honest truth is, I don't really know what to say." He lets out a sigh. "It's been a crazy week."

The priest closes the notebook. "I've seen your incredible skills . . . your powers. I believe the dream is prophecy. If you'll indulge me, I have a proposition for you." He glances at the others. "For *all* of you."

"We're listening, Padre," Spur says after a thoughtful pause, wondering to himself if they might need to be a little more careful than they have been in the past when entertaining propositions from strangers.

## CHAPTER TWENTY-FIVE
# Point-Blank Range

### 1.

As they make their way across Tennessee, listening to the priest present his proposition, nobody in that battered minivan notices they are being followed. Perhaps one reason for this is that their pursuer is not of this earth. The one tracking them is not made of solid matter. Nor is he commandeering a vehicle of any sort. Hence the occupants of the Caravan keep missing the devil as he playfully makes his shadowy presence known for fleeting moments along the way. Outside Knoxville, for example, in the wee hours that night, he takes the form of a giant black crow perched at the top of a radio tower like a nightmarish hood ornament, his humanoid, doll-like face as black as soot, rotating like a satellite dish tracking the progress of the minivan down Highway 11, the Quintet maintaining their westerly course, keeping off the main thoroughfares in order to avoid the attention of local authorities.

By now the state police in all jurisdictions from D.C. to Texas have an all-points bulletin on the stolen Caravan and the fugitives within it. Of course, the devil is watching all this with great relish from the rooftops and hillsides, and at one point, as the minivan crosses the Little Tennessee River just outside of Loudon, the Dark Lord observes the vehicle from the top of a bridge trestle in the form of a huge, rabid, disheveled coyote. As the creature eavesdrops telepathically on the conversation unfolding in the darkness of the minivan's interior, the coyote-thing seethes and stews in its antediluvian rage.

At the moment, the vile little clergyman is giving an impromptu history lesson on the Knights Templar, the warrior priests, those impudent guardians of the so-called Holy Land who protected the pathetic sheep who made pilgrimages to that tumbledown pile of detritus called Jerusalem. These arrogant bastard sons of viscounts and noblemen had always been a thorn in the devil's side. But the Prince of Darkness had always seen through their ruse. These were not angels. These were not holy men. At their core the Templars were nothing more than greedy bankers, caretakers of the aristocracy's treasure.

"*Long forgotten,*" the little mongrel minister is now proselytizing in the tight quarters of that speeding vehicle, "*a small group of warrior priests, who would one day become the Jesuits, who splintered off from the Church in the year 1540. They called themselves the Scarlet Order.*"

The coyote-thing shivers with repulsion at the mere mention of the Order, its black jaws unhinging, its fangs exposing themselves. Its eyes narrow into slits of yellow flame, and an otherworldly noise issues from its maw, a growl so deep and coarse it sounds like an infernal whetstone sharpening flint in hell.

"*These were ordinary men,*" the priest is telling the Quintet, "*who took up the mission of heaven, who dressed in the mantle of God, and went into battle against Satan and all his minions again and again. These are the true warrior priests . . . stalwart adversaries of the devil . . . holy soldiers who handed down their mission to their descendants for generations. They are the exorcists, the cleansers, the spiritual bounty hunters who track down the demon horde and send them back to oblivion where they belong.*"

The coyote-thing reacts to the words of Father Emmanuel as though splashed with acid, as though the very message itself were talismanic, a magnetic field through which the devil now begins to pass. The coyote guise slowly dissolves away, darkening in waves, undulating in the shadows of night like an oil slick unfurling, sliding away from the black carapace of the devil's true form. What is left is the original source of evil in the universe.

And with one great gasp of air the black thing takes flight off the bridge trestle, arcing out across the night sky . . .

. . . on a collision course with its new nemeses.

## 2.

"What I am proposing," Father Manny is saying now as the Dodge Caravan careers around a tight turn just past Troy, Tennessee, "is that you come with me to a place called the Cloister. It's not far from here, just outside St. Louis, and I promise you, it's safe and you will be welcomed there with open arms as kindred spirits. It's a secret place hidden in the hills above the river."

The imminent dawn is just beginning to lighten the horizon behind them, chasing away the deeper shadows and turning the chill air a luminous purple. They are less than five miles from the Mississippi, and the telltale odors of ancient mud and fish-rot wake them up.

The priest has been leading them to this part of the country all night. For nearly twelve hours, they have subsisted on roadside vending machine fare and bottled water, and they are tired and sore. The idea of a refuge—"hideout" might be a better word—is becoming more and more attractive to Spur. The stolen Caravan is a disaster waiting to happen, and the last thing Spur wants right now is another high-speed chase with state police, or worse, another confrontation with authorities under the influence of the devil.

"It's important for each of you to be aware of what this place is," Father Manny adds. "The modern version of the Scarlet Order keeps their headquarters there. The campus is listed in the public records as a monastery but in fact it is a spiritual citadel, a fortress."

Hunched behind the wheel, road weary, Hack rubs his eyes and murmurs, "If you ask me, this sounds like a perfect place to lay low for a while."

Pin-Up asks the priest if his colleagues at the Cloister know about the Quintet. "Have you discussed the dream with them?"

"I've confided in some of them."

"And . . . ?"

"These are people who have devoted their lives to an endless, esoteric war, a war which the majority of people on earth either don't understand or aren't even aware of. You can trust me when I say that my colleagues at the Cloister believe in prophetic dreams as much as I."

Silverback says, "I have to agree with Hack, it sounds ideal . . . like a made-to-order safe house."

Ticker is nodding. "It's definitely an ironic choice for a group calling itself the Devil's Quintet . . . but hey, why not?"

"Hold on a second," Boo says from the rear, her gaze fixed on the road ahead of them.

The alarm in her voice gets Spur's attention. He glances over his shoulder, and in the half-light of dawn he sees that her pale features are creased with apprehension. "What is it, Boo?"

She points at the two-lane. "Am I seeing things?"

Spur gazes through the windshield at the weather-beaten asphalt dead ahead of them. In the dawn's first golden rays of light he sees what Boo sees, and he gets very still. "Stop the van, Hack."

"What?"

"Stop the van . . . now . . . pull over."

Now Hack sees what Spur sees, and he kicks on the brakes. The sudden deceleration presses everybody forward . . . as the minivan skids to a stop on the gravel shoulder. A cloud of rock dust swirls up on the wind for a moment, the motes glittering in the sunbeams. An eerie silence follows.

"Oh dear," Father Manny utters under his breath when he sees what is blocking the road fifty yards ahead of them. "Please be very careful."

"Give us the order to fire," Pin-Up says softly to Spur from the rear seats, "just give the word and we'll end this thing right now."

"It won't do any good," Boo chimes in. "It would be like shooting an idea."

Ticker interjects: "I'm with Pin, we got enough firepower to ventilate this fucking idea all the way back to hell."

"Sounds good to me," Hack says, snapping the cocking lever back on his fully loaded AR-15, his gaze welded to the thing blocking the road ahead of them.

"Everybody stay in the van," Spur says, his skin tingling, his throat suddenly as dry as sandpaper. He pulls his Glock from the map case, checks the mag, jacks the slide, and sticks the gun down the back of his belt, covering it with the tail of his denim chambray shirt. Then he digs in his pocket for his pouch of Red Man chewing tobacco. All of this he is doing out of force of habit, instinct, maybe even superstition.

He knows that the gun is most likely useless, as is the chewing tobacco. He opens the door, climbs out, and calmly walks toward the abomination standing in the middle of the intersecting roads.

## 3.

Void of any landscaping or signage, the desolate crossroads formed by two sun-bleached blacktop highways sits at the threshold of the Nicholas Reimann Bridge. Covered in a patina of tangled kudzu and vines, its iron towers so ancient and eroded by time they look almost fossilized, the old-style suspension bridge spans across the Mississippi and over the state line into Missouri.

It is the gateway to the West, the portal through which pioneer families steered their wagon trains, the darkly magical place toward which tormented blues singers journeyed great lengths to sell their souls in Faustian pacts. It is also a passageway through which the Quintet must pass in order to reach the Cloister, and it is now blocked by a monstrous sentinel standing at the center of the intersecting roadways.

"You've been a naughty boy," the creature says in a strange dissonant rasp, a voice made up of many voices, an atonal choir of the damned. The monster stands at least eight feet tall now, with massive translucent wings sprouting off its hunched back, and a gleaming black breastplate and codpiece hewn from obsidian.

"I'll take that as a compliment," Spur says as he approaches, and then pauses about ten feet away, standing his ground.

"You realize you will never evade my reach." The devil's ancient, cadaverous face looks as though it's been mummified over the millennia in a bog. Short nubs of bone protrude from the upper corners of its simian skull, and the elongated eyes absorb the light, glowing like embers burning with hate. "There's no profit in fleeing," the creature explains. "There's no corner of the earth in which I cannot find you."

"You can't blame a man for trying," Spur says with a shrug, chewing his plug of tobacco. For a fleeting instant he wonders if this is the devil's true form—the corrupted figure of a fallen angel—but then he dismisses the thought.

"This is the last time I will remind you that we have an agreement," the monster persists. "And I expect you to honor it or suffer the consequences."

"You mean like being chased by homicidal maniacs masquerading as federal marshals?"

"That was a test, which you passed with flying colors, but now you are fraternizing with the enemy, and that I cannot abide."

"You got a job for us?"

"I do indeed."

They stare at each other. Spur finally says, "You gonna tell me what it is or am I supposed to guess?"

"One Joseph Lister of New Orleans, Louisiana," the devil announces. "Avid cult leader. Sadist. Killer of innocent women. Scion of a pharmaceutical empire. He has become a bore. It is time for him to be adjudicated."

Spur shakes his head. "Nope."

The creature furrows its brow with incredulity. "Pardon me?"

"Find somebody else to do your shit work."

## 4.

Right then another pause transpires for an endless moment as the monster regards the human. Spur girds himself for battle, his center of gravity shifting slightly. His superpower has yet to be fully engaged but now he feels the mirror-imaging of his adversary's strengths awakening within him, galvanizing him, coursing through him.

"You are flirting with disaster," the creature informs Spur.

"Back at ya, old hoss."

"Excuse me?"

Spur burns his gaze into the smoldering eyes of the devil. "You think the sun comes up just to hear you crow? You're just a glorified second-rate magician, about as worthless as gum on a boot heel. You're nothing more than God's garbage man." Spur doesn't blink. His heartbeat remains at its resting rate of sixty beats per minute.

"I will devour you," the many voices snarl in unison, intensifying, emanating from the monster's gullet. "I will rip your soul out of your body and feed it to the starving sinners in hell."

Spur feels the dark, empathic power taking over his personality, his senses, his very core. Bloodlust floods his mind. He smells brimstone. He hears voices in his head whispering in Latin. "You're just a big hunk of nothin'," he informs the monster, taunting it in a singsong voice. "You're just plain old mediocre Eblis the Angel! Poor little Eblis! Got himself fired from heaven thousands of years ago, and he's been bitching about it ever since! *You* are the bore, Ebby! Borrrrrrrrring—!"

The creature gapes at Spur, and Spur gapes right back at it until both pounce at each other at precisely the same moment.

The implosion of energy is like a shock wave engulfing the two figures, lifting them off the ground, their bodies caught in a horrifying membrane of evil, their backs arching as though electrocuted, their faces mere inches apart, their blazing hot gazes locked in mutual hatred, the ugly, violent, destructive, malignant images streaming through Spur's consciousness as he wraps his fingers around the monster's throat, and the monster wraps *its* fingers around *Spur's* throat, and they attempt to strangle each other as the two equal and opposite forces hold each other in unearthly paralysis while thousands of years of agony and soul-wrenching torments visited upon the earth pass in terrifying montages streaking across Spur's mind-screen . . . bodies being twisted and drawn and quartered in the Inquisition, mouths gaping, eyes bugging, the shrieks of the suffering swirling like a cyclone of madness as the two mortal enemies, man and devil, continue to levitate off the ground, higher and higher, now nearly twenty feet above the mythical crossroads, the torrent of evil intensifying, sensory overload crashing like waves against each other . . . the nauseating sight of Ivan the Terrible roasting babies on spits, beheading their parents, burning them, strangling them, blinding them, disemboweling them, the massacre of Native Americans flooding the desolate prairies with rising tides of blood, the strap of a slave master scourging the tender flesh of a Black woman in rags and chains, the deathly odors of the gas chambers at Auschwitz, all the skeletal corpses piled like cordwood in mile-long ditches . . . Spur mirroring the devil, locked in an epic stalemate of malevolence, rising higher and higher, the imagery coming faster and faster, vivid, nauseating, soul-searing . . . the laughter of psychopaths rotting in prison cells, the endless tortures of dissidents and revolutionaries, flesh simmering in acid baths, eyes being gouged out, electrodes sending fatal levels of electricity through the limbs and nervous systems of political prisoners, mob hits, serial killings, mass murders, the Manson family painting walls with fetal blood, demented clowns, drooling rapists, home invaders, blood-drenched psychopaths grinning ghoulishly toothy grins, nightmare figures dancing, and the empty void of the universe erupting, imploding in a black hole of destruction . . . until all at once, without warning, Spur remembers the weapon lodged behind his belt and he reaches for it and in one continuous movement he presses the muzzle to the great misshapen cranium of the devil and squeezes off three quick blasts at point-blank range.

## CHAPTER TWENTY-SIX
## Catechism

### 1.

The next thing Spur realizes—aside from the fact that the devil has vanished—is that he's falling, plummeting twenty-five feet to the ground. He hits the pavement hard, absorbing the worst of the impact with his big, muscular left shoulder, and then rolling, an instinctive maneuver learned back in Jump School during Navy SEAL training. The pistol bounces off to his left.

The others come running.

"Spur!" Pin-Up hurries to his side, the others approaching behind her. She kneels and helps him up into a sitting position. "You okay? What in God's name just happened?"

"Not quite sure," Spur says, rubbing the back of his shoulder where it hit the asphalt. He feels scoured out. Tender. Dizzy. "I think I got to him, though." He manages to smile at Pin-Up. "I think I got his knickers in a knot." His smile fades. "Maybe Ticker's right . . . maybe there's a chink in his armor."

By now the rest of the group has gathered around Spur. Ticker helps him to his feet. Spur wobbles slightly, getting his balance back. Ticker steadies him and says, "Looks like you found the key to breaking that stubborn horse."

"You think?" Spur is still a little woozy on his feet, and struggling to track with everything. "It was almost . . . I don't know . . . it was involuntary."

Boo touches Spur on the shoulder, her face pallid and ashen in the early-morning light. "I keep thinking of the *Thirty-Six Stratagems* . . . also Sun Tzu . . . 'Whenever possible attack using the strength of the enemy . . . use their strength against them.'"

Spur smiles at her, rubbing his thick neck. "Words of wisdom." He still seems a bit dazed, struggling to get his bearings.

Father Manny stands behind Boo, babbling softly, "Jesus, Mary, and Joseph . . . I've seen a lot but . . . I've never . . . never witnessed such a thing." His baggy eyes blaze with emotion behind the lenses of his thick glasses. He has now seen the devil in real time, and it has sunk a hook into him he didn't know existed. "That was . . . it was . . . I don't have the words."

"I hope *somebody* has the words," Silverback says very softly, almost murmuring under his breath, his fists clenched, his face twitching with nervous tension, "because I get the feeling there's a lot going on here that you folks haven't briefed me on." Trembling slightly with emotion, he fixes his gaze on Spur. "And if that's true we're all gonna be in a world of hurt because there's no way I can run interference and help you people without knowing what in the blazes is going on . . . so somebody . . . please . . . for the love of God . . . tell me what the hell that monstrosity was that you just tangled with . . . and . . . and . . . and . . . *what the fuck is going on*!!"

The intensity of the man's sudden, booming reprimand causes everybody around him to look down at the ground awkwardly for a moment like a group of chastened schoolkids being scolded for keeping secrets.

At last, Hack breaks the spell, shooting a glance at the southern horizon, listening to the distant wail of sirens coming this way, most likely alerted by the gunfire. "If I could be a *nudzh* for a moment and make a suggestion," he says. "I think it might be best to get our keisters outta here before the gendarmes arrive; we can talk it out later on the road."

They all agree. Spur grabs his pistol, and they all pile into the minivan.

## 2.

"All right . . . I admit it, we fucked up . . . the radiation story was a boatload of bullshit." Spur measures his words as they rumble across the Reimann Bridge, the tires singing an off-key aria, the gunmetal waves of the Mississippi passing under them in a blur. Spur feels a strange, oily sort of trauma clinging to him, a polluted, dirty sensation like a beach after the red tide has gone out to sea. That mosaic of evil that streaked through his consciousness has left a scar on his soul as tangible and palpable as a birthmark. In fact, maybe that's exactly what it is—a birth—an entry into an underworld that he would, regrettably, be visiting now on a regular basis.

"Goddamn it, Spur," Silverback is grumbling from the back seat, gazing out the side window at the length and breadth of the

mighty river. "That's the one thing we agreed had to be sacro-
sanct for our operation to run smoothly."

"I know . . . I'm sorry."

"We never keep anything from each other."

"You're right . . . when you're right you're right. My only excuse is, we figured you'd never buy the truth. Who the hell would
believe it? You'd have us committed."

"I still may do that," Silverback grouses. "So what *was* that
thing back there?"

Spur takes a deep breath, marveling at how difficult this is—
putting it into words for a man so practical, so real-world, so accustomed to flesh-and-blood decisions, life-and-death issues that
may never get recorded in the history books.

The Caravan zooms past a rust-pocked, green metal sign on
the west end of the bridge:

**MISSOURI**
**THE SHOW-ME STATE**
**WELCOMES YOU**

Spur finally says, "We made a deal, Sean. I am physically not
able to say with whom but you just got a good glimpse of the
signatory."

Silverback stares at him. "You're telling me you made a deal
with the devil? Hence, the Devil's Quintet?"

Spur nods. "There's no other way to say it. I'm being literal
here."

Silverback chews the inside of his cheek as he gazes out the
window and processes. "What exactly does that mean?"

"It's not a metaphor. It's not symbolic of anything. Back in
Karakistan this monster saved our lives, and he gave us these
powers."

"You're telling me this is the same devil I learned about in cat-
echism class when I was a kid?"

"The very same."

"With the horns and the tail and the pitchfork, and all that
jazz?"

Spur shrugs. "Not exactly. From what I understand he takes
many forms."

Silverback shakes his head. "It's like learning the earth is flat."

"If I may say something," Father Manny chimes in. "The idea

of a devil—Satan, the Prince of Darkness—it's changed over the years. Today the Church refers to this abstraction called Satan. But modern theologians talk about free will and personal responsibility . . . and it all gets watered down."

"Go on, Father."

"The thing of it is, my brothers and sisters at the Cloister, we know better. We know that he's real. He's out there. Always. *He's* the one with free will . . . to corrupt, to get innocent people to go against God, to ruin the world. We see it every day. It's a real honest-to-goodness war . . . with individual battles, some we win, some we lose . . . and there are casualties, campaigns, strategies, tactics, enemies and allies just like any other war."

Silverback thinks it over as they pass ramshackle docks, bait shops, fishing boat rentals, gas stations, and run-down, boarded-up strip malls. There's a pervasive sense of decline in the landscape now, hard-core poverty, the air redolent with the stink of garbage, river smells, gas fumes, and the stench of dying livestock. Finally Silverback asks what the deal was that they made with the devil.

"He gave us these powers," Spur says. "And in return we're supposed to basically become his bounty hunters, tracking down folks who've signed contracts with him. These are people who got rich or famous or whatever, and now it's time for the chickens to come home to roost. We're supposed to find them and take them out so the devil can claim their souls. That's it in a nutshell."

Silverback thinks about it. "But you're not cooperating."

"You could say that, yeah."

A lengthy stretch of silence follows, and before long, they find themselves on a seemingly endless interstate following the twisting course of the Mississippi northward toward St. Louis. Father Manny keeps them on course, offering periodic directions to the Cloister. And the conversation turns to the process of cutting ties with the everyday world, wiping the Quintet off the map, relegating them to legend.

At one point they discuss whether or not Spur has actually managed to harm the devil.

"I don't think I harmed a hair on his ugly head," Spur says after giving it some thought. "I think I just got his attention."

At that moment, in another part of the world, another person is about to learn just how closely the devil is now paying attention.

# CHAPTER TWENTY-SEVEN
## 666

### 1.

The honorable senator from Kentucky awakens in her darkened private quarters at the Dirksen Building, clad in her nightshirt, her hair wrapped in a turban of silk, thinking she is still asleep and perhaps still gripped in the epic nightmare that had tormented her slumber and had her tossing and turning throughout the night. She senses a horrifying presence in the room with her. She fumbles for the bedside lamp, but before she can manage to turn on the light she hears the voice from her recurring nightmares, and the sound of it petrifies the senator.

*"Tempus est ad finem mundi,"* the low, raspy baritone chants, filling the silence of the bedroom, buzzing like a million bluebottle flies in the senator's ears, sending gooseflesh down the woman's spindly legs. *"Esto vigilans et habemus opus facere!"*

Out of the corner of her eye Winthrop sees the presence silhouetted against the drawn blinds. It's enormous—a dark leviathan standing next to the bed—and she realizes with utter terror that she's not dreaming. The thing is real and it's standing next to her, and it has wings, the faint light seeping around the corners of the curtains and shining through the translucent appendages like jaundice-yellow candy-glass.

The senator finally manages to turn on the light, illuminating a giant, deformed, humanoid being glowering at her.

*"Wake up!!"*

Margaret Winthrop jerks back with a start, her heart leaping into her throat. She stammers but cannot produce coherent speech. She has never seen the Rotten Valentino take this form. Goose bumps rash the back of her neck as she inches backward on her skinny rear end, scooting away until she falls off the bed.

She hits the floor, wrenching the small of her back. "I'm sorry, sorry, I'm up, I'm up now," she mutters as she peers over the bed at the winged monstrosity. "What can I . . . um . . . *do* for you?"

The fallen angel walks around the bed and towers over the senator. The thing is breathing heavily, its deformed face twitching, narrow eyes fiery with humiliation, rage, petulance, and vengeance—human emotions that Winthrop has never seen the creature display. At this close proximity, it is clear that the monster has been wounded. The top of its skull has been torn away, a gaping wound of exposed brain glistening.

"I need the codes," the creature says in its strangled legion of voices all speaking at once, the choir of the tormented from the bowels of the earth. "Go fetch the codes, and do it quickly."

"The codes?" The senator is still groggy with terror and sleeplessness.

*"The launch codes!"*

The words register now in the bleary recesses of Margaret Winthrop's mind, setting off a series of silent alarms in her midbrain. The nuclear launch codes, or "Gold Codes" as they're sometimes called, are the province of only three individuals—POTUS (the commander in chief), the vice president (in case the president is incapacitated), and the head of the National Security Agency (who is currently a Dudley Do-Right named Harlan Stratton, a Mormon and a dolt, whom Winthrop rat-fucked [i.e., blackmailed] a year and a half ago by planting a prostitute in the man's D.C. apartment).

The Gold Codes were just one of the many things that Winthrop extorted from Stratton. The thinking at the time was that the codes would serve as a get-out-of-jail-free card for Winthrop, just in case she ran afoul of the administration. In many ways, Winthrop's access to the codes has put her in an elite group of the most powerful people in the world.

Now she pulls on her robe, tightens the belt, crosses the room, and pushes the contents of her desk aside.

While the monster watches, its toxic gaze like leeches on Winthrop's neck, she pulls a small document safe from a hidden panel in the desk. It's about the size of a hardcover book, made of carbon steel, with a seam on one side and two separate security measures on the other: one a biometric lock, the other a three-digit combination lock. Ignoring the fact that every cell in her brain is shrieking for her to not do this, she presses her finger down on the thermal scanner. A red light turns to green. Ignoring the realization that allowing the codes into the hands of supernatural evil is not only insane and suicidal, it's akin to mass murder on a global scale, Winthrop goes ahead and thumbs the first tumbler down to the number 6.

She is in a zone now, clueless, insensate, unmindful of the colossal dangers into which she's plunging the very planet she calls home. She thumbs the next tumbler down to 6. Oblivious to anything but the fear now, she moves her thumb to the last tumbler. The only impulse remaining in her conscious mind is to complete the task at hand so that the dark winged thing in her room will leave her alone. She clicks the tumbler to 6.

The safe opens with a breathy, metallic clunk. Winthrop reaches inside. She pulls out a small electronic device the size and shape of a matchbox. Linked via satellite to a code box in the bowels of the Pentagon, the device stores three long strings of numbers and letters, the codes good for only twenty-four hours, at which point another random series of characters are generated and sent to the device.

Senator Winthrop closes the safe, turns, and carries the device—sometimes referred to in the press as the "football"—back across the room to where the devil stands waiting.

"Please . . ." Winthrop starts to ask something as she proffers the device to the monster but can't quite verbalize what she's thinking.

The creature snatches the code box from the senator's meticulously manicured fingers. Winthrop steps back. "What's on your mind, Senator?" the monster inquires as it carefully slides the device behind its onyx breastplate for safekeeping. "You're pregnant with thought, I can tell."

"The thing is . . . I'm just wondering . . . I mean . . . what I wanted to say is . . . um . . . whatever you're planning on doing with those codes . . . whatever happens . . . I mean . . . for better or worse . . ."

She pauses, measuring her words, getting her thoughts together.

"Spit it out, Senator," the creature snarls. "I have neither the time nor the inclination to wait for you to speak . . . *now SPEAK*!"

Margaret Winthrop jerks back with a start at the volume of the devil's voice. Licking her lips, taking a deep breath, the senator says, "In the event that your . . . your *stewardship* of the launch codes leads to . . . to . . . to a worldwide *event*. Then . . . um . . . ?"

Now the creature starts to laugh, and the laughter intensifies into full-blown, uncontrollable chortles. But the devil's laughter is always cruel, humorless, and sadistic, and this chortling sound is no different. At last, he gets the laughter under control. His voice has softened. "Let me guess. You're wondering if you would still be legally bound to the stipulations of your agreement if all human life on earth were to be wiped away . . . is that about the size of it, Margaret?"

After a long, painful, and awkward pause, the senator confesses that yes, that is about the size of it.

"Would I still be expected to . . . um . . . spend the rest of eternity . . . you know . . . down there?"

"Alas, Margaret. You have made a deal," the devil informs her. "And as humans are wont to say, a deal is a deal."

And with that, the creature vanishes from the room on a clap of thunder . . . leaving behind a stunned and horror-stricken senator . . . and an acrid odor of scorched stone, which lingers in Winthrop's nostrils like a bad memory.

## 2.

In 1956, when ground was broken to build the new Dirksen Senate Office Building on Constitution Avenue in Washington, D.C., there were already spirits of the dead occupying that area. Three slaves—one from Barbados, two from the Kingdom of the Congo—had died there two centuries earlier on a crew building a massive stable earmarked for the burgeoning U.S. government. These three entities are the oldest phantoms still attached to the Dirksen Building today. They are mere smudges of ectoplasm who mostly keep to themselves in the building's sublevel, and only occasionally muster the energy to push over an old paint can or brush across the neck of a janitor searching for cleaning supplies.

Since the Dirksen's cornerstone was laid, however, other ghosts have taken up residence there, many of them a lot more active and potent than the slave spirits in the basement. One of them—a former master sergeant in the U.S. Army, First Cavalry Division—was in life a PFC named Steven Malambri. Killed in action in Kuwait on February 3, 1991, he was buried at Arlington Cemetery, and got stuck wandering this earthly realm filled with resentment and anger for being sent overseas by a bunch of draft-dodging chicken-hawk senators.

One of Steve Malambri's fellow spirits at Arlington, a fallen comrade named Corporal Jeffrey Eiger—the ambulance driver from World War II, the one who goes by the nickname Charon—had told Malambri about the Dirksen Building. "It's a great place to haunt these bastards," Eiger had mused one dismal evening years ago as they strolled the chill night air of the cemetery. Malambri had taken the older ghost's advice, and today, the young private has become a fixture in the air ducts and spaces between the walls and floors and ceilings of the Dirksen.

This morning, however, the ghost of PFC Steven Malambri huddles in the air-conditioning conduits above Senator Margaret Winthrop's room, horrified and in a state of great quandary after seeing the devil procure the nuclear launch codes. Malambri cannot allow this miserable woman—this manipulative, cheating power broker—to bring about the end of humanity.

There must be something Malambri can do. He thinks of his mentor, Charon, cursed to wander eternity for defying Satan. What would the ambulance driver do? Then he remembers the young woman. The conduit. The half-alive, half-dead waif who connects the spirit world with the living like a human circuit.

She and her ragtag group of warriors have gotten under the devil's skin, and now, maybe, just maybe, they are the only ones who can stop the tide of disaster that originated here in this very room.

The only question that remains unanswered is can the ghost of PFC Steven Malambri find her in time?

## CHAPTER TWENTY-EIGHT
## The Cloister

### 1.

That afternoon, the Quintet approaches the Cloister in stages, as though it were a mythical land in the clouds. As the minivan ascends a steep, winding access road, they catch their first glimpses of the stone chimneys rising above the crest of a forested hill . . . then a steeple . . . then an old copper church bell covered with a patina of green . . . then a massive marble cross . . . and then, finally, the roof pitches of century-old buildings rising against the sky like great Gothic sentries overlooking the churning grey waters of the Mississippi.

"Father Emmanuel!" A young Franciscan priest comes running out of the main building as the Caravan pulls up the gravel drive and rolls under a lush, leafy grape arbor. "Welcome! Welcome home!"

Hack parks, and all the occupants of the minivan pile out into the late-afternoon sun.

Father Manny introduces everyone to the freckled young priest in the monk's robe. With his dark curls and boyish face, the young man looks like central casting for an earnest, bighearted, innocent caretaker of a Catholic vestry. He goes by the name of Father Joshua but he doesn't look old enough to be anyone's father. "Just call me Brother Josh," he says, vigorously shaking Spur's big callused hand. "We don't go in much for formalities around here."

Hack glances at the cargo in the back, a faint hint of embarrassment crossing his face. "Yeah . . . um . . . we've got some . . . uh . . . luggage?"

"Your weapons, of course," the young priest says with a nod, as though he were discussing a few sackfuls of groceries. He glances over his shoulder. "We should also probably get the vehicle out of sight, just in case the local authorities happen by." He smiles at the group. "You folks go get settled in, I'll take care of it."

Father Manny leads the team into the musty vestibule of the main building.

From the antique sconces and chandeliers to the burnished

ornate woodwork, buttery-soft Persian runners, and Louis XIV furnishings . . . the place radiates a sort of timeless, hermetically sealed civility. Father Manny leads the group past antiques and portraits on the walls featuring Knights Templar, warrior monks from the Middle Ages, and a rogues' gallery of anonymous soldiers of God from every era in every mode of body armor imaginable. Spur's head is spinning.

Father Manny leads the tour with pride. "At the moment, you're in the main administrative building . . . but there are dormitories, stables, classrooms, forensic labs, training facilities, sanctuaries, armories, a library, an obstacle course, a firing range, you name it—none of it open to the public, of course. There's even a repair garage where we can—with your permission—completely dismantle and dispose of the minivan, eliminating any evidence of its former existence."

Hack chuckles. "No offense, but this seems like the last place on earth one would expect to find a *chop shop*."

The old priest grins. "Well . . . we're not in the habit of stealing cars, if that's what you mean. But we can cannibalize that van and scatter the parts among a hundred other vehicles."

"The prodigal son returns!" a voice calls out from the depths of the main corridor. An elderly man in flowing vestments and stable boots appears around the corner with a big Christmas-morning kind of grin. With his long white beard and silver braids framing his ancient face, he looks to be somewhere north of ninety years old but has the vigor of a man half his age. Under his robe, on his bony hip, a silver-plated .357 Magnum revolver is tucked into a holster engraved with a cross.

He strides up to Father Manny and lifts the priest off the ground into a robust bear hug. "Emmanuel the Tender," he says softly as he embraces the man. "It wasn't the same around here without you, Manny."

Father Manny chuckles as he nearly suffocates in the old man's arms. "I love you, too, Monsignor, now please put me down before you snap me like a pencil."

"It's remarkable," the bearded man says, releasing the little priest and gazing at Spur and the others. "They're just as you described them, as if I'm looking at a living breathing version of the prophecy."

"Monsignor, it's my pleasure to introduce you to the Devil's

Quintet," Father Manny says with a dramatic flourish of his arthritic hands as though he's about to pull a rabbit from a hat.

"You must be the one called Spur," the bearded man says with great wonder in his voice. For a moment, as he extends his huge palsied hand, he looks as though he might actually succumb to the emotion and start to weep.

"Present and accounted for," Spur says, and shakes the elder's hand. "And I want to thank you, Monsignor, for letting us crash your party."

"The pleasure is ours, Spur, believe me." The Monsignor raises a fuzzy grey eyebrow. "May I ask—if I'm not being too impertinent—who came up with the snappy name?"

"Oh," Spur says with a touch of awkwardness. "Is it . . . uh . . . a tad on the blasphemous side?"

"Not at all." The Monsignor winks at him. "It's just the kind of irony we appreciate around here." He looks at Pin-Up. "And I'm assuming this lovely creature is the one called Pin-Up?"

Spur says that she is indeed, and Pin-Up gives a little bow fit for a head of state. Then Spur introduces the others. The Monsignor lavishes each one of them with great and careful attention, as if he's meeting a group of envoys from a friendly nation. Father Manny looks on with the sin of pride twinkling in his eyes.

The truth is, at this stage, neither Spur nor anybody else from the team knows for sure what the expectations and protocols are around here. Will they be expected to convert to Catholicism? Will they have to take vows, become celibate, study scripture? Spur knows a little bit about the history of the Knights Templar. Is that who the Quintet will be expected to emulate? This is not exactly how Spur sees the whole thing playing out.

The best approach at this point, Spur reckons, is to take it one day at a time.

## 2.

The initial impression that the Cloister gives off is one of a venerable old European college such as Cambridge or the University of Florence, with its Gothic, sepia brick buildings, ornate gardens, landscaped walkways, and ivy-covered belfries. But beneath the surface, the campus is more akin to the FBI headquarters at Quantico or Scotland Yard on the River Thames.

Amid all the stately nineteenth-century architecture rise glazed pavilions of steel and glass connected by pedestrian breezeways, and futuristic spires outfitted with arrays of satellite dishes and the latest in digital security technology. Unknown to most citizens of the world, protected by U.S. constitutional law and the separation of church and state, the Cloister has become a sort of metaphysical Pentagon—both a clandestine military headquarters and an international court of justice in the ongoing, eternal, hidden war between the forces of light and forces of darkness. The Monsignor—real name the Right Reverend Charles David McAllister—is the ostensible director of the facility, but it features star chambers and oversight committees from every major religion on earth. Hebrew scholars bring esoteric knowledge from Kabbalah and Jewish mysticism to bear alongside Islamic ulama, Tibetan monks, and Hindu Brahmin. The facility has a rotating staff of administrators, facilitators, technicians, demonologists, psychic mediums, exorcists, epidemiologists, astrophysicists, psychologists, and custodians—all sworn to secrecy and scrutinized for security clearances that rival the CIA.

That afternoon—while the members of the Quintet settle into their new digs—Silverback busily constructs the elements of their public demise. He contacts Cthulhu and has the young assistant arrange for the procurement of four cadavers from Walter Reed's pathology lab—three John Does and one Jane Doe—who shall be publicly buried alongside Boo's empty grave in a military honor guard at Arlington. Bogus obituaries will be planted in *The Washington Post, The New York Times,* and *USA Today* about "four intelligence operatives" killed in the line of duty in Eastern Europe. The nature of their "deaths" as well as their "duties" shall be deemed classified, although their actual birth names will be leaked over the next few days so that the record will reflect the official removal of the members of the Quintet from society.

With Boo already officially deceased, these last few items represent the final ties binding the Quintet to the ordinary world being permanently severed. Silverback, who has been listed as missing, will still be a matter of concern for federal authorities, but the section chief knows that after another few days, the multiagency, nationwide manhunt will go cold. Eventually tactical officers will be needed elsewhere and will be called off the hunt. A few stray FBI agents will stay on the case, going through phone logs, watching surveillance-cam footage, and canvassing witnesses, but they will hold out very slim hopes of ever finding the section chief.

## 3.

That night the Quintet and Silverback are treated to a festive dinner. Hosted by the Monsignor, Father Manny, and a small group of religious leaders in the main dining room of the rectory, the dinner is the first real home-cooked meal the Quintet has had in days. Due to the multidenominational aspect of the Cloister, the food is all vegetarian, and the members of the Quintet savor every bite. They dine on caprese salads with scratch-made mozzarella and fresh tomatoes and basil grown in Rabbi Stern's garden, delicately breaded and grilled asparagus, peanut slaw with soba noodles, eggplant paella, spiced root vegetables with harissa and lime yogurt, and for dessert an amazing carrot cake with sour cream frosting. At the end of the meal, the Monsignor pours everyone a couple of fingers of sixty-year-old port from his personal wine collection.

"We want to officially invite you to make this holy, consecrated place your new home," the Monsignor says with great ceremony as the conversation turns serious.

Spur gives the elder a friendly nod. "That's mighty kind of you, Monsignor. I'll put it to a vote but I'll tell you right now I can't think of a better place for us to be on the down-low for a spell."

The Monsignor sips his port, his ancient gaze unwavering as it fixes itself on Spur. "We have never had a group that's engaged the Unclean One as directly and powerfully as you and your brave colleagues. We want to help you in any way that we can."

Spur holds his gaze. "I can't tell you how much I appreciate that, Monsignor."

"Please understand . . . you are no ordinary team of warriors," the Monsignor says then, the old man's voice dropping into a low, incantatory register, as though what he's saying is more a prayer than an invitation. "You are an extraordinary group in every way, the latest in a very rare, very select tradition of soldiers defending what is good and right and just. I believe you are the descendants of the Archangel Michael, and hence you shall be treated as such. We can provide you with the resources to become fabled, iconic guardians of the light, terrifying to the evil and cruel among us . . . each and every one of you with your own individual armor and identity. With your blessing, Spur, and the blessings of God, we shall help you become part of the hidden fabric of this beautiful world in which we live, and must at all costs protect."

Spur can tell the old man is deadly serious, and after he looks around the table it becomes clear that the whole concept is going over fairly well with the other members of the Quintet.

# 4.

"Am I crazy or could this actually work?" Pin-Up asks Spur somewhat skeptically after dinner as they stroll through the fragrant shadows of a winding cobblestone walk. The footpath wends its way through a small orchard on its circuitous route back to the guest cabins, and the night air is perfumed with apple blossoms and clover. They are slightly tipsy from all the food and drink.

"I don't know," Spur says, "I'm just rolling with the punches now, figuring we're here for a reason, and that's good enough for me."

"Following your nose?"

"The wind is more like it." Spur gives her his patented, toothy grin. "Wherever it takes us."

They walk a little bit in silence. Spur feels the old emotions rising up in him, the desire to consummate his feelings for Pin-Up like an old melody that he can't get out of his brain.

Pin-Up looks up at him. "Can I ask you a personal question?"

"Only if it doesn't require a lawyer present."

"Are you scared?"

Spur takes a deep breath and thinks it over for a second. "You bet your ass I'm scared, I'm about as scared as a rabbit down a foxhole. But I'm not the least bit ashamed of it. How about you?"

She shrugs. "I'm terrified, I won't lie. But it keeps me sharp. You know what I mean?"

"I know exactly what you mean."

They come to Spur's cabin, and they pause in front of the quaint little picket gate. Even in the dark of night, the place looks cozy and inviting, from its window boxes overflowing with daffodils to its ruffled curtains behind the glass. Spur looks into Pin-Up's eyes. "Now it's my turn to ask *you* something personal."

"Shoot."

"These folks here, they seem like one big family, which I appreciate. And it reminds me that I ain't never really had a family except for y'all . . . you and the other three. The Quintet." He measures his words, his heart speeding up a little. "Just curious, though. Do you think we're family, you and me?"

"Me and you?" Pin-Up grins. "Sure. I've always felt like we're family."

"That's a shame."

"Why do you say that?"

"Because it just means that it would be wrong to kiss you right now."

"What are you talking about? Families kiss all the time."

"Well—"

"It's healthy." Her smile widens. She puts a hand on his arm. "You can trust me, I'm a nurse."

He leans down, and takes her in his arms. Their lips crash together, and all their pent-up desires, emotions, and fears come pouring out of them in that first, lingering kiss, followed by a cascade of nuzzling and caressing and kissing each other's necks and ears and faces, and they hold each other there in that aromatic darkness for quite a long moment.

At last, Spur says, "Would it be too forward of me to invite you in for a nightcap?"

"I don't know. What do you have in there to drink?"

He shrugs and grins. "Nothing. Tap water, and that's about it."

Her eyes shimmer with delight. "That's okay, I'm already hydrated."

He leads her up the walk and into the dark cabin. It's not exactly the Ritz but it's clean and comfortable, and it feels safe. The bedroom has a double bed, and Spur brings in a couple of candles from the bathroom and lights them, and in the golden flickering light they undress each other. They take their time. For once, there are no distractions, no guilt, no interruptions, no awkwardness, no hurry . . . and once they've unwrapped each other like birthday presents they collapse into each other's arms and finally, with great passion and heat—and good old-fashioned lust—consummate something they've both fantasized about for years.

## CHAPTER TWENTY-NINE
# The Serpent Sets the Clock

### 1.

At the stroke of 12:00 that night, the new launch codes for the next twenty-four hours are generated in the basement of the Pentagon, encrypted and beamed to the government satellite known as Milstar, and then transmitted to the three existing launch code boxes, one of which is now in the hands of the Lord of the Underworld.

Meanwhile, in a squalid flophouse room in the Ninth Ward of New Orleans, Joseph Lister—the rebellious heir to the Lister pharmaceutical fortune—lies in the tangled sheets of his bed, staring at the ceiling fan. His sinewy, ropy body clad only in boxer shorts and sleeveless tee, damp with sweat from the evening's exertions, he watches the rattling blades of the fan turn and turn and turn.

He realizes that if he watches the fan long enough he might actually slip into a hypnotic trance, which could perhaps be fun. He has yet to try going under hypnosis. The truth is, from the time he got nabbed at age seventeen for running drugs and got thrown into the juvenile system, he has tried many things over the course of his thirty-seven years: crack cocaine, insider trading, gun running, heroin, operating a white slavery operation out of his father's Cayman Islands retreat, and even organizing a Satanic cult he came to call the Listerians . . . but he's never tried hypnosis.

But then again, there's no telling *what* ugliness could come out of Lister in a posthypnotic state.

On the floor at the foot of the bed lay the blood-soaked remains of the twenty-two-year-old girl from Slidell whose throat Lister slashed a few minutes ago. It shall be counted in the record books as Lister's seventeenth ritual sacrifice, and his latest offering to the Great Asmodeus, Destroyer of Souls. Lister had wanted to sacrifice *this* virgin up close, and in private, savoring every scream. That's why, earlier that night, he had given his followers—four of them at last count, each a brainwashed zealot—the night off.

Now as he languidly gazes up at the spinning rotors of the ceiling fan, Lister shades his eyes with his surprisingly feminine hands. Like a child he peers through his splayed fingers at the turning blades, and notices tiny crescents of the girl's blood under his fingernails.

A shadow inches across the corner of his gaze like a vine growing in time-lapse across the ceiling. He turns his head and sees that the moving shadow is not a shadow at all but an enormous black mamba snake that has somehow gotten into his room.

At least fifteen feet long, its scaly skin the color of silver metal-flake, its eyes like black beads protruding from the sides of its long snout, the serpent slithers across the ceiling and pauses directly over Lister. The black mamba has no lips, and yet the long seam between its jaws, which hides rows of lethal fangs, has the appearance of a smile.

"What the . . . *fuck*?"

The exclamation issues out of Lister almost reflexively, a combination cough and gasp as he gapes at the deadly serpent now clinging leechlike to the ancient plaster ceiling directly over his head. The thing gives him a look. "Articulate as always," it says, its voice like steam spewing from the deepest chasm of hell. When the snake speaks, fleeting glimmers of needlelike fangs and a fluttering forked tongue are visible behind its jaws.

Lister stares. The fact that the serpent speaks—and with great irony and contempt, for that matter—seems almost superfluous to Lister when compared to the fact that it could easily kill him with its lethal, venomous bite. "I . . . I . . . I don't . . . I don't know what you want."

"What I want," the serpent explains with great scorn and derision in its breathy murmur, "is for you to know how fortunate you've become."

"I . . . I don't understand."

"You have approached critical mass in terms of your worthlessness. You were about to reach the final stipulation of your agreement, and the time had come to execute your damnation."

"My . . . *damnation*?" All at once it dawns on Lister the true identity of the creature to whom he is speaking, and the import of the words hissing out of the repulsive, wormy-grey thing adhering to the ceiling. "Master?" Tears of awe fill the cult leader's eyes. "Is it you?"

The snake's jaws unhinge suddenly, and it lunges at Lister.

The cult leader recoils against the bed's headboard as the serpent in all its silver reflective glory comes to within inches of him, exposing its ice-pick fangs and emitting a noise like the rusty whistle of a teakettle left on a burner too long.

"Pay attention," it hisses at him. "Go and fetch something with which to write."

## 2.

Struggling out of bed, crossing the room in awkward lumbering strides, Lister trips over the remains of his latest victim. The putrid carpet is so sodden with the girl's blood that Lister slides almost ten feet across the floor, slamming into the far wall by the meager desk. The impact causes an empty gin bottle, Lister's .38-caliber revolver, and a ballpoint pen to topple off the blotter. Lister scrambles to snatch the pen off the floor, rising into a sitting position against the wall, turning back to face the serpent and preparing to write whatever it is he is supposed to write.

"Write down these three codes," the mamba hisses, and then proceeds to carefully enunciate each series of numbers and letters that have magically updated themselves on a small display window of a stolen government-issue device. It takes nearly five minutes for the creature to recite all three strands. When it is finished, it says, "Now read them back to me."

On the floor, Lister does as he's told. The numbers and letters are now emblazoned in blue ink across the palm of his left hand and then up the inner part of his left arm. He carefully reads them back to the snake.

"Very good," the creature says. "Excellent. Now. I will give you the coordinates of a missile silo in eastern Colorado."

The serpent recites the longitude and latitude of the United States Air Force Launch Control Facility at Fort Pasado, Colorado. "At these coordinates, with these three codes, you will be able to gain entrance to the underground silo." The snake pauses for effect. "Once inside the shelter, you will be able to proceed to the launch control room and enter the launch codes into the launch control console. Are you following me?"

Soaked in his victim's blood, his back pressed against the wall, Lister nods. "Yes, my lord, I am following every word."

"Outstanding." The serpent never blinks. His eyes are black stones as he delivers the instructions with his lipless mouth and bifurcated tongue. "Understand that you will be triggering the launch of a Minuteman III missile with a nuclear payload the equivalent of nine million tons of TNT. Do you understand what I'm telling you?"

The man on the floor utters with great reverence, "Praise Satan, yes, I understand, I do."

"Once you have fulfilled your duties, you will be free to leave the facility and ultimately die in the fiery glory of the nuclear holocaust, which will undoubtedly occur as a result of your heroic actions. You see, my dear Lister, due to the modern world's ubiquitous automation, the target nation of this particular missile—which is Russia—shall automatically answer with their own warheads, all of which will automatically trigger the rest of America's nuclear arsenal, and on and on, back and forth, until God's creation is reduced to radioactive rubble. Once the earth is laid waste, and ninety percent of the population is vaporized, I will return as the true Messiah.

"This is an event known among scholars as the Alkaritha—loosely translated into English as Armageddon—a glorious coronation of my thousand-year rule. Keep in mind that this is a global incident that is not supposed to happen for another two centuries but I am hastening it now out of spite for five miserable individuals. I am inaugurating the apocalypse now because of these arrogant do-gooders, who refuse to comply with a perfectly reasonable contractual obligation . . . which, as it turns out, is, to use a popular phrase, *the last straw*."

Lister drops the pen, raises the hand marked with the auspicious blue ink. "Long live Asmodeus, long live the Dark Lord!"

## 3.

Before vanishing from the room, the serpent gives the cult leader one last directive. "Remember, Lister, the launch codes that you now have in your possession are operational only for twenty-four hours. Repeat: The codes must be entered into the launch control console—and the missile must be in the air—before midnight tomorrow. This is of the greatest importance. If it is not airborne by midnight tomorrow I will claim your soul in the old-fashioned way, in accordance with our original agreement. Do you understand, Lister?"

"I do, my lord, I do," he says with great and hushed devotion.

"Very good, Lister." As always, the serpent appears to be

smiling. "Then let it be known that the countdown begins at this very instant."

And with that, three things occur in the tawdry room at the same time: The serpent vanishes into thin air, the small device from which the codes had come bursts into flames in midair . . .

. . . and in Joseph Lister's scrambled, defective brain a clock begins to tick backward, beginning at 23 hours, 59 minutes, and 59 seconds.

# PART IV

## THE SILO

The end of all things is near. Therefore be alert
and of sober mind. . . .

—Peter 4:7

## CHAPTER THIRTY
### This Is Not a Drill

**1.**

In the wee hours of that momentous night, in the French Quarter, at the corner of Burgundy and Toulouse, in a gaudy little tattoo parlor called Skin City Body Art and Piercing, a single needle buzzes in a pool of halogen light shining down on the sole customer present at such an odd hour. Joseph Lister—a flask half full of gin gripped in his free hand, a bottle of OxyContin in his shirt pocket—sits ramrod stiff in the swivel chair, his left arm poised on an adjacent pedestal, his right foot tapping restlessly as a huge tattooed troll in a leather vest and ZZ Top beard works the needle over the ballpoint pen-marks scrawled along the tender inner skin of Lister's arm.

"Hey . . . uh . . . got the time?" Lister asks, craning his neck to see if there's a clock somewhere among the myriad framed illustrations of Sailor Jerry anchors and busty naked nymphs on the wall. Lister can sense the clock ticking now at the base of his spine. He has less than twenty-one hours to destroy mankind, and that includes traveling a thousand miles to eastern Colorado.

"Dude, it's five minutes later than the last time you asked me," the tattoo artist says, trying to keep his focus on tracing the shaky lines of the hastily scrawled letters and numbers on the cult leader's flesh. The needle is loaded with Noodler's Heart of Darkness permanent black ink, the most legible and reliably permanent of all the blacks. "It's three oh five in the A.M., okay? Almost done with this dumpster fire. Ain't gonna be pretty but them numbers and letters are now gonna be as permanent as death and taxes."

"Good . . . good."

After another five minutes of excruciating pain and agonizing restlessness, Lister watches the tattoo artist finish tracing over the last digit of the last code. "*Voilà!*" the big biker exclaims with a flourish.

Lister practically overturns the chair pushing himself out of it. "Great, perfect, awesome," he stammers. "How much do I owe you?"

"Whoa! Hold on, man. I gotta put the ointment and bandages on it."

"It's okay, it's all right . . . I don't need bandages, I don't need ointment on it." Lister digs for his wallet, fishing around for a hundred-dollar bill.

"Damn thing's gonna smudge if you don't have no bandage on it."

Lister fidgets and lets out a sigh. "Please, brother . . . do it fast."

The artist pulls a long piece of gauze off a spindle and hurriedly tapes it over the reddened, moist flesh of the fresh tattoo. "Never seen nobody in the chair in such a hurry, man," the artist grumbles.

Nodding mechanically, Lister stumbles away, hurrying out the door as though the place is on fire. The artist stares at a soggy hundred-dollar bill lying on the pedestal.

## 2.

Just over a thousand miles to the west, in the dead-silent predawn—at precisely 5:33 A.M. mountain standard time, the records will later show—two men who spend a third of their lives forty-five feet under the unforgiving eastern Colorado prairie begin to hear things over the secure satcom channel that make no sense.

"You hear that, Bob?" the younger of the two launch crew members comments after fixating on the strange noises coming out of the small Bluetooth speaker sitting on the edge of his desk. Senior Airman David Barnes has been hearing weird noises all through his shift that night. A lanky young man with a long stork-like neck, Barnes looks even *more* gangly in his starchy, pleated blue work uniform with the .45 pistol holstered on his hip. Right now he sits bolt upright on his swivel at the main launch control console—dubbed the "Doomsday Desk" by wags back at the base—drinking tepid coffee from a Styrofoam cup and nervously chewing his fingernails and trying to get a handle on what in the world he is hearing.

The Fort Pasado Launch Control Facility, buried deep underground, is old—built way back in the Cold War era of the 1950s—and has always made settling noises in the dead of night, faint creaks and ticks every few minutes. But tonight, the sounds are different: ghostly, ethereal footsteps echoing, muffled knocking sounds. And now this: crackling out of the satellite communication radio on waves of static, the faint sounds of air raid sirens, thunderous explosions . . . and screaming. The screaming is the worst part. Distant, fading in and out of the static, the intermittent shrieks of agony have been piercing the din of the bombing noises for at least five minutes now.

"What are you ranting about?" mumbles the older launch crew member, Corporal Robert Winnick, who stands on the other side of the steel-reinforced room chewing his cigar as he goes through the nightly checklist on his clipboard, crossing off each item on the endless sequence of tasks such as "Record Levels on Compression Tanks" and "Check Tunnel Power Grid Failsafe Breaker Indicator Lights." Notwithstanding their gruff friendship, dirty jokes, and constant complaining, the two never forget the fact that only 250 feet away from them, down an adjacent tunnel, sleeps eighty thousand pounds of nuclear deterrence, which could lay waste to an area the size of New York City.

The two men have been doing this for so long, it's no wonder they're starting to hear things that aren't really there. For going on seven years now they've been the third-shift launch crew for the U.S. Air Force Security Detail, 174th Missile Wing, Alpha Group, based out of the Cheyenne Mountain Complex in Colorado Springs. Back when Silo 13 first went operational, the analog technology in the launch control facility resembled a Jules Verne movie—massive computers the size of water heaters, old-school launch consoles with blinking lights and spinning tape reels. But now, with its state-of-the-art miniaturization, the facility gives off more of an air of a sterile biolab.

"There it is again," Barnes says, fiddling with the tuning knob on the satcom radio. His chest tightens as he listens to the terrifying pandemonium of a bombing attack on some unidentified population. The senior airman has been having weird dreams all week, dark unnerving dreams of a nuclear holocaust—so it's no surprise that crazy shit is coming out of the satellite communication system now, but *war sounds*? Has the frequency crossed over to fucking Netflix? After all, Barnes can tell the difference between a movie and the real thing, but tonight, he is so rattled he can't tell his ass from a hole in the ground.

Corporal Winnick, frowning, puts down his clipboard, snubs out his cigar in an ashtray, and comes over to the console. "Switch the frequency over to four-point-five, it's gotta be bleed from some microwave cable system . . . some service provider with their thumb up their ass."

Barnes switches over to the emergency frequency, and hears the same appalling noises—a siren swirling, the keening wail distorted by the Doppler effect as thunderous percussion blasts erupt, eliciting heartrending human cries of terror, all of which starts working on Airman Barnes's nerves. "What the fuck is going on, Bob?" he asks somewhat rhetorically.

"I'm working on it," Winnick says, grabbing the protocol manual off his deck, and flipping through the pages. He runs his tobacco-stained fingertip down the troubleshooting guide. "Try getting NORAD on the bitch box."

Barnes looks over shoulder at the older man. This is getting real. The wireless receiver known as the red line is swept regularly for bugs, and to be used only in an emergency. "You want me to—?"

"Go ahead, son, make the call."

With a trembling hand Barnes carefully lifts the receiver off its cradle, which is designed to autoconnect him to SAC command at Cheyenne Mountain. But when he puts the handset to his ear, all he hears is a piercing tone. He jerks the receiver away from his head.

Winnick looks at him, all the blood draining from the corporal's face. "No luck?"

"No connection."

More booming noises crackle from the speaker as a faint tremor passes through the subterranean structure like a ripple disturbing a still pond. Barnes looks at the older man. "Oh God, Bob, I think this is it, this is really *it*." The younger man's voice crumbles. "This is . . . this is . . . *game over*."

Winnick says nothing, just stares straight forward as though gazing through the younger man.

## 3.

The day dawns clear and bright at the Cloister, the first brilliant rays of sun shooting through the pines and elms along the Mississippi, blazing off the tops of the steeples and lighting up a pristine, cloudless blue sky. The warblers, herons, and bullfrogs in the marsh provide a pleasant buzz that carries on the breeze across the outbuildings, brushing past the front doors of the guest quarters, the tranquil sounds shattered suddenly by a loud knocking.

Inside his cabin, Spur awakens with a start next to Pin-Up, who lies nude at his side, tangled in the sheets, still drifting in a sleepy afterglow from the previous night's activities.

"Who in the Sam Blazes . . . ?" Spur mutters, and starts to lever himself out of the bed, when all at once he sees Pin-Up lying there next to him, an angelic expression on her stunning face, a partial beam of sunlight dappling the olive skin of her generous breasts, and it knocks him for a loop, how beautiful this woman is, how brave and loyal and beautiful, and she's right here, right now, in his bed with him.

*Take that, Peyton Manning.*

The knocking persists.

"Okay, okay, hold your horses," he murmurs, pulling on his jeans and shoving his feet into his shopworn work boots. He shuffles over to the door, blinking at the brilliant sunlight encroaching on the dimness of the room.

"Sorry to bother you so early, Spur," Brother Josh apologizes as soon as the door swings open. His freckled face crinkles with a mixture of embarrassment and excitement. It's not clear if he has noticed Pin-Up in Spur's bed. The young priest is far too convivial to mention such things. Right now he's fidgeting on the doorstep with anticipation. "It's just that . . . Father Manny can't wait for you and the team to come see his little surprise."

Spur shields his eyes from the dazzling early-morning light. Across a stately little courtyard lined with cherry trees, he can see the other guest buildings. Ticker stands in the open doorway of his cabin, still clad in sweatpants, waving and giving a what-the-hell shrug. "Surprise, huh?" Spur looks at Joshua. "Will there be coffee there?"

The young priest grins. "Not only coffee but I think I might even be able to dig up a few crullers."

Unbeknown to either of them, there are a little less than sixteen hours left before the end of the world begins in earnest.

## 4.

Boo stands in front of the bathroom mirror in her cabin, staring at her face, wondering if the crow's-feet around her eyes have been there all along or if they are some sort of side effect of her transformation. Still garbed in an oversized sleep shirt given to her by one of the Cloister's cooks, still yawning from a night of disjointed drowning dreams, she had already been awake when the knock on the door came.

Since slipping into her limbo state, Boo finds that she sleeps differently now. Never really falling completely under, she still experiences REM-style dreams as though she were asleep. It has taken some getting used to. But it does come in handy when she is summoned at dawn for a mysterious and unexpected meeting with Father Manny and the unit.

She brushes her teeth, and then leans down to spit. When she straightens back up she sees a ghost in the reflection standing behind her.

"What the hell—?!" she gasps, spinning around, instinctively assuming a defensive martial arts position, her fingers curled into claws.

"Sorry, sorry, my bad," PFC Steven Malambri says, taking a step back, holding his decomposed hands up in a gesture of surrender. "I'm a friend of a friend, please don't attack me."

"What is it with you dead people? Can't you just . . . knock or something? Give me a heads-up?"

"Sorry." He wears moldering brown camouflage, which Boo recognizes from recent conflicts in the Middle East, and he still has the stubble of a beard like moss clinging to the bottom of his cadaverous face. "I'm a friend of Jeff Eiger . . . you know, Charon?"

Boo remembers the story of the young casualty from Desert Storm. "You're the Dirksen ghost, the one haunting the senators."

"Yep. That's me." Just for an instant his putrefied features form a smile of pride. "But listen, I'm here to warn you about something."

"You're a little late—we've already dealt with the demonic marshals."

"No, no, that was just the beginning, just a warm-up for what the devil's got going now."

Boo stares at the apparition. "What's he got going now?"

At that point PFC Steven Malambri proceeds to tell Boo exactly what Satan has procured from the doomed Senator Margaret Winthrop.

## CHAPTER THIRTY-ONE
## Two Suicides

### 1.

At the northeast corner of the Cloister's sprawling campus sits the armory building. The enormous, squat, windowless slab of redbrick is jacketed with ivy and kudzu, and encompasses nearly an entire square city block. It looks at least a hundred years old.

Brother Josh unlocks the two sliding doors on the east end, and leads four members of the Devil's Quintet down a fetid-smelling aisle lined with horse stalls. The air is thick with ammonia and damp hay as the group marches past at least a dozen thoroughbreds and draft horses nickering, scraping at the floors of their stalls, and glancing up from their morning breakfast of oats and saw grass.

"Ah, here they are at last," Father Manny exclaims as Brother Josh leads the group into a cavernous arsenal room. In the dusty air, skylights blaze with early-morning sun, shining down on a warehouse filled with all manner of esoteric armaments. With its maze of aisles, and shelves brimming with cryptic-looking weapons, instruments, and gear, the room gives off the feeling of a medieval army surplus store. The air smells of rubber, gunpowder, and new fabric. "Come in, come in, don't be shy," the old genial priest says, standing in the middle of the room like a mad tailor, a measuring tape hanging around his neck alongside his vestments. "Welcome to our little storehouse of magic tricks."

"Shut the front door," Spur mutters, looking around at the dizzying array of icons and artillery, both spiritual and secular. With a single glance, he recognizes an entire wall of katana swords and edged weapons with ornate crucifixes at the bases of their grips . . . another wall displaying countless pieces of armor, chain mail, gloves, visors, and helmets . . . and in one far corner an antique, gold-plated font, surrounded by vials and mason jars, each filled with a clear liquid that Spur can only assume is holy water.

"I'm afraid it's more of a museum collection than an armory," Father Manny says when he notices the members of the Quintet transfixed by the staggering range of armaments. "Believe it or not, some of these weapons were used against us."

Ticker speaks up. "By whom?"

"The Church."

"The *Church*?" Ticker searches his memory of history. "When was this?"

"During the Inquisition. The Church elders did not take kindly to the Scarlet Order, I can tell you that. We've always been a thorn in the side of the power structure. We have no denomination other than the human race, and what is right and true. We keep many of these items as a sort of reminder . . . pieces of history." He shrugs. "I guess it's comforting to merely know they're here . . . if we need them."

Ticker picks up a gold-plated staff with an intimidating mace-like crown. "I'm not sure 'comforting' is the word I would use."

"Be that as it may," the old priest says, his eyes practically twinkling with excitement. "I have something for each of you. But before I unveil the surprise, may I ask where Boo is? There's something for her as well, and I wouldn't want to—"

"She'll be along any second now, don't worry," Spur says. "She'll catch up with us, go ahead."

With a nod, Father Manny turns and leads them to the far wall. "Joshua, if you would be so kind as to turn on the lights."

The young priest hurries over to a circuit-breaker box and snaps on a series of floodlights.

Spur stares at the wall with sudden wonder and astonishment.

# 2.

Along the wall, each displayed in its own nook, the five suits hang ominously in the beams of spotlights. Each has its own unique design—which, as the team will later learn, matches the attributes of its wearer—the fabrics shimmering as though impregnated with otherworldly metals. Father Manny has handwritten the names over each of the outfits.

Spur gets very still as he gazes at the garb labeled SPUR. "Would ya look at that. How long y'all been working on these, Padre?"

The others approach their personal nooks, gazing up in awe at their suits.

"As a matter of fact, we've been perfecting these warrior identities for years. They're straight out of the prophecy, taken directly from the dream." Father Manny grabs a long pole with a metal hook on one end. "The whole process became a pet project for the Cloister."

He raises the pole, lifting Spur's suit off its peg, giving it to Spur.

"You can't beat this with a stick," Spur says, trying the suit on. The garb—modeled after a feudal sentry—fits perfectly on Spur's broad shoulders. Designed to terrify and intimidate adversaries, the ensemble features titanium body armor and barbed-wire gauntlets, with a dark duster-length overcoat lined in Kevlar. Spur regards his reflection in a full-length mirror in the corner of the room and murmurs, "Wrap it up, I'll take it."

"The designs were based mostly on my dream notes," Father Manny explains. "But we had no way of knowing how they'd fit the real person."

"I'd say you nailed it," Ticker says softly, trying on his armor and feeling a wave of emotion surging through him, so powerful it nearly takes his breath away. His suit brings to mind the African shaman—a long coat of black crow feathers and panther teeth, a beaded headpiece that obscures his dark face in shadow—all of it set off by a gilded breastplate and scabbard.

In many African cultures, the shaman is the narrator of cosmic history, the protector, the investigator of crimes, and the one who counteracts witchcraft. Ticker's father did his master's thesis on the sangomas of southern Africa, and years later Ticker had the document bound into a beautiful illustrated book. Now Ticker feels the strange circular nature of time as he looks at himself in full shamanic regalia.

Hack undergoes a similar experience slipping on his new guise, draping himself in the pale leather longcoat and brooding oversized hood. The wide belt is engraved with delicate mazelike symbols that resemble circuit panels, but it's the sum of its parts that captures the DNA of Hack's soul. The antique iron buckles, the long machete in its leather sheath with Hebrew characters down the length of it, and the cryptic word EMET spelled out across the upper seam of the hood—all of it floods him with memories of his childhood.

"*Emet*" means "truth" in Hebrew, and it figures prominently in the old Jewish folktales Hack's mother told him when he was little. His favorite was the story of the golem—the monster made of clay—brought to life by rabbis in the Middle Ages to defend the Jewish settlements from the pogroms and anti-Semitism. It was the boy's first foray into the mythology of the supernatural, a primitive, seminal take on superheroes. Who would have thought that Hack would become his own version of the golem?

Pin-Up also finds eerie resonance in her armor, which plays off her complicated relationship with the persona of the cheesecake model. With its exaggerated curvatures, its matte black, wasp-waisted breastplate, chain-mail fishnet stockings, and obsidian combat boots, the suit turns the idea of the Hollywood shape-shifter—a siren on calendars in repair garages everywhere—into a terrifying archetype of vengeance.

A midnight-blue velveteen hood completes Pin-Up's new identity.

The narrow slice of her almond eyes that peer out of that hood as she ponders her reflection—dripping with chiaroscuro menace—speaks to her bottled-up emotions and trauma. "This is . . . this is *so* me," she murmurs as she gazes at herself in the mirror.

Spur appears in the reflection behind her in his intimidating medieval longcoat and barbed wire. "Don't stare too long, Pin, or we'll have to change your name to Narcissus."

She slowly turns and faces him with her trademark smirk and hands on her hourglass hips. "You think you're a real wit, don't ya?"

"What if I do? What are you going to do about it?"

"Teach you a lesson." With one abrupt, liquid-smooth movement, she spins and draws her cutlass, and catches him by surprise, pressing the razor's edge of the blade against his neck before he has a chance to move.

Spur grins, looking down at the blade lodged menacingly under his chin. "You're fast, lady, very fast . . . but not fast enough."

Pin-Up realizes that Spur has drawn a buck knife from a sheath on his thigh, and before she could catch a glimpse of it, or even feel a thing, he has placed the tip very gently against her midriff.

"Mutually assured destruction," he says with that trademark glint in his eye.

"Children!" Hack comes over in his golem's hood and duster, his machete drawn and raised. "Didn't they teach you not to play with knives in kindergarten?"

Their laughter is mostly nervous energy spilling off them.

Then, a strange and unexpected thing happens when Ticker

joins them in his crow feathers and shamanic regalia. The laughter fades. They all look at one another in their armor. Ticker pulls his sword and raises it ceremonially over their heads. Hack does the same, as does Spur, as does Pin-Up, and the four of them form a sort of improvised gauntlet of edged weapons over their heads.

Spur is starting to say something when the door across the room shrieks on its hinges as Boo bursts into the arsenal. "Something's happened," she announces to everybody all at once.

Each person in the room turns their attention from their circle of blades to the ghostly, petite waif standing in the doorway.

"It's . . . it's bad," Boo stammers. "Off-the-scale bad . . . and . . . and we've *got* to do something about it right away if not's already too late."

She blinks, finally noticing the suits. She sees the nook with *her* new guise showcased in a cone of light—the Shaolin monk's robe in phosphorous green, the katana in its shoulder harness, the black hood, the brooding Kabuki faceplate—and it penetrates her panic.

"What is all this?" she says, but she knows the answer before they tell her.

### 3.

Across the campus, at that moment, in one of the guest cabins, Silverback is awakened by a telltale noise. Programmed into his secure cell phone, the ringtone is a recording of the first few notes of the second movement of Beethoven's Ninth Symphony— that familiar *DAHM-DAHM-boom-boom-DAHM-DAHM*— which used to close out *The Huntley-Brinkley Report* on NBC. Sean McDermott was just a kid when he used to hear that theme every night, watching the news on his parents' Curtis Mathes console. Even as young as ten years old, he was fascinated by world events, but had no idea he would one day become a player on that same stage.

Now he sits up in bed, fumbling for his government-issue iPhone, feeling that same Pavlovian response he always experiences when he hears that particular ringtone—acid indigestion, a tightness in the chest, sometimes even his scalp crawling— because it's never good news.

"Go ahead, Cthulhu," he says after sliding the ACCEPT CALL icon.

The voice on the other end of the line swallows hard before speaking. "Boss, I don't know if you've heard the latest—"

"No! I've been off the grid. I haven't heard anything. What's going on?"

"Margaret Winthrop is dead."

Silverback's chest tightens. "Dead? What do you mean?"

"Suicide. They found her in her room at the Dirksen less than an hour ago."

"Cause of death?"

"Gobbled half a bottle of Ambien and washed it down with a fifth of vodka."

"Justice sent the FBI crime lab, I'm assuming?"

"Yep."

"Did she leave a note?"

"She did. Give me a second here." The sound of paper rustling comes over the line. "It's just one run-on sentence, if you can believe that."

"Which is?"

"'I'll gladly go now, you can have my soul, God have mercy on me for what I've done, it isn't my fault, it's fate, I'm sorry, please, God forgive me.'"

After a pause, Silverback says, "This is not good."

"That's not the worst part. I kind of buried the lead."

"Cthulhu, just spit it out."

"The launch codes are missing."

"The launch codes? The *nuclear* launch codes? What are you talking about? This gal was just some crackpot senator from Kentucky!"

"Rumor has it she blackmailed Stratton over at the NSA and was holding them like an ace in the hole."

"Oh Jesus."

"There's something else, too. I'm not supposed to know about this next thing. But you know my buddy upstairs? The chatterbox—?"

"Cthulhu, knock it off with the cloak-and-dagger and just tell me."

"Okay. So. I guess there's a missile silo in Colorado that's gone dark."

"Dark? Whattya mean?"

"They've lost contact with it."

In one awkward motion he leaps out of bed, dropping the

phone, and pulling on his pants as fast as his old football injuries will allow.

The human race has 13 hours, 47 minutes, and 32 seconds left to live.

## CHAPTER THIRTY-TWO
# Silver Bullets

### 1.

Joseph Lister burns through several hours that morning arranging to use his father's corporate jet to transport his four followers and three hundred pounds of ordnance from New Orleans' Lakefront Airport to Colorado Springs, Colorado. The pilot of the Gulfstream G550 is an older man named Roy Platt who was born to be a commercial pilot—former Air Force, greying at the temples, lantern jaw, the real deal—but a layoff at United and a gambling issue have forced Platt to moonlight by taking last-minute shit jobs like this one.

"Gonna need you to step on it, Captain," Lister says to him, leaning through the cockpit door as the pilot is running through his preflight checklist. "You get us there ahead of the weather, and there's an extra five K in it for you."

Platt claims that it will be a piece of cake and a pleasure to do so, and suggests that Lister get himself and the rest of his posse in their seats and buckled up so they can get under way. Lister and the others do as suggested, and the Gulfstream takes off from Lakefront at precisely 1:33 P.M. central standard time.

Behind Lister, the four acolytes settle in for the three-hour flight, two on each side of the cabin, a motley crew if ever there was one.

At times, they remind Lister of the Seven Dwarfs, their secret nicknames reflecting the traits of their substance abuse. Sniffy is an emaciated cokehead from Lafayette who favors black leather and arms sleeved with tattoos, a former roadie for some midtier death-metal band. Noddy is a heroin junkie from somewhere back East, a gnarled old punk with more piercings than a circus freak. Creepy is a scrawny male prostitute from the Ninth Ward whose fluid sexuality, excess eye shadow, and velvet jumpsuits make him look like Keith Richards's wayward cousin.

And last but certainly not least is Cranky, a steroid-addicted, muscle-bound skinhead who graduated from the Aryan Brotherhood to the Satanic Listerians only last winter. Cranky brings a starry-eyed sort of ambition to the group, over the last few months lobbying Lister to get involved in white slavery, kiddie porn, and the procurement of black-market cadavers for the necrophilia underground. Lister appreciates Cranky's sinister vibe. Earlier today, when Lister revealed the apocalyptic nature of their mission, Cranky was as delighted as a boy who was told Santa was bringing him a pony for Christmas.

Now as the plane levels off at thirty thousand feet, Lister fidgets restlessly in his seat, feeling time ticking away. They have a little over twelve hours to reach the silo at Fort Pasado and fulfill their magnificent calling—to destroy the world, to deliver it into the hands of Satan.

Lister closes his eyes and says a silent prayer for the Dark Lord to see him through this glorious undertaking.

## 2.

At that moment, at exactly 1:43 P.M. central standard time, there are precisely seventy-three people—not counting the Quintet and their entourage—occupying various edifices and shelters around the Cloister. Stirred by the sounds of purposeful footsteps crossing the campus, accompanied by grave voices discussing grave matters, the seventy-three members of staff, visiting clergy, trainers, and maintenance people come out of their respective buildings and watch the passing alliance with great interest. It is obvious to even the most casual observer that something important is transpiring. Rumors have been bouncing around the Cloister. But today, the five principal members of the group hastening past the onlookers' doors represent a team the likes of which no one present has ever seen.

Father Manny and the man called Silverback lead the procession, followed closely by five otherworldly warriors in extraordinary attire. They look like a cross between Arthurian knights and militaristic Buddhist monks in their hoods, scabbards, robes, and body armor. One of the bystanders—an elderly Catholic priest from the Chicago parish—will later report to his altar boys back in Bridgeport that the team of five brought to his mind the Templars of the eleventh century, an observation that would be made again and again by those lucky enough to see the Quintet.

"We've scrambled a Sikorsky UH-60 Black Hawk out of Scott Air Force Base," Silverback is saying to Spur, who marches along with his new longcoat unbuttoned and billowing behind him. "That little honey'll get you there in less than four hours."

"I'm thinking you should tag along," Spur says to Silverback, shooting a glance over his shoulder at the others.

The other members of the unit wear their new suits of exotic armor and regalia as though wearing second skins, the tails of their robes and the hems of their coats flagging behind them, their scabbards and sheaths and gauntlets clanging rhythmically against their legs. This is officially their first mission as the Devil's Quintet, and they've each come to terms with their destiny, their powers, their collective duty to mankind. They are as ready as they will ever be.

"I guess I could do that," Silverback ventures uncomfortably. "Maybe stay at the base command center at Cheyenne Mountain, just in case we need to send any orders to the fleet or . . . or . . . damn it, I'm having a hell of time wrapping my head around this."

"Around which thing are we talking about?" Spur wants to know. "The fact that there's a rogue missile silo out there now that could start World War III? Or the fact that all of a sudden you got a team of comic-book characters on your payroll, granted powers by Satan, and standing between you and nuclear holocaust?"

Silverback looks at him. "Who the hell said you're still getting paid?"

Spur laughs but it's short-lived. "Keep joking, funny man, you'll have a strike on your hands." He looks back at the others. "Ain't superheroes members of the AFL-CIO?" Nobody thinks this is very funny but a twinkle in Pin-Up's eye placates Spur.

"Before you leave," Father Manny says as they pause next to a black Escalade taken from the Cloister's fleet of vehicles, "I'd like to give you something." The vehicle is already idling, ready to roll, and time is ticking away. Tremors of restlessness pass through the Quintet as they wait for the priest to have his moment. "I'd like to present something sacred to you," the old man tells Spur.

"Okay, sure, bring it on, but let's try and make it snappy, Padre."

The priest is wearing his trademark off-the-rack JCPenney sport coat. He digs in the side pocket and pulls out something wrapped in a white handkerchief. "I believe these'll fit your Colt M1911, and many other forty-five-caliber sidearms." He unwraps a dozen special hollow-tip silver bullets. "Don't laugh. They're filled with holy water from the Vatican."

Spur is touched, and gladly takes the bullets. "Padre, thank you." He hugs the man—a good, warm, spontaneous hug. "We can use all the help we can get, believe me. But right now we gotta skedaddle—it's time to heat up the bricks."

The priest gives a nod and a smile. "*Vaya con Dios,* my friend."

By this point, dozens of onlookers have gathered behind Father Manny. Among them are Brother Josh, and the Monsignor, and the priest from the South Side of Chicago who was reminded of the Knights Templar. Most of them wear the collars of clergymen, but there are also workmen in grey work uniforms, landscapers, mechanics, instructors, and even the receptionist from the front office. Before turning away and climbing into the Escalade, Spur gives them all a salute and feels an overwhelming sensation of extended family. How could something like that have happened so quickly? Unless . . . unless what?

And with that, Spur climbs into the SUV and joins the people who have become his *immediate* family. His heart is about to burst with pride. He loves these folks now more than ever . . . come what may. He will gladly die for them if it comes to that.

Father Manny waves, a melancholy smile on his weathered face as the vehicle pulls away and roars down the winding access road toward the unknown.

The countdown is at 10 hours, 2 minutes, and 13 seconds.

# CHAPTER THIRTY-THREE
## Dead Lock

### 1.

Right up until the moment they arrive at the site, everything goes smoothly for Lister and his dwarfs. The plane touches down at Colorado Springs Airport ahead of schedule at 4:04 P.M. mountain standard time. In the back of his mind, Lister has to keep reminding himself that the deadline is twelve midnight *central standard time,* the witching hour in Louisiana—which is 11:00 P.M. *Colorado time*—the hour set by the devil himself, and the devil is nothing if not precise.

They rent a panel van at the airport, and change into their deer-hunting attire—army-surplus camouflage jumpsuits, Wellington boots, and orange polyethylene vests—and they make good time as they race southward on Interstate 25 toward Fort Pasado.

En route, the four dwarfs ride in the rear cargo area with the road cases of guns and explosives. Sniffy lounges on the corrugated floor, snorting cocaine off a compact mirror and mumbling to himself. Noddy and Creepy sit cross-legged on the floor across from each other, smoking weed and not saying very much. Only Cranky's voice is loud enough to be heard by Lister in the cab. Sitting on one of the anvil cases, sucking on his amyl nitrite poppers, the big, bald steroid-case prays to the devil over and over, hollering out key phrases such as "Lucifer fill me with your darkness" and "praise Satan" and "the end is near" as though he has a serious case of Tourette's syndrome.

About ten miles outside of Fort Pasado, along the edge of a cattle ranch, they spot a deer grazing on a high berm of switchgrass. It's no great trophy—just a medium-sized male whitetail—but it'll do nicely to complete the ruse that they're merely innocent hunters who took a wrong turn and accidently ended up on government property. Lister does the killing—he uses a Smith & Wesson 300 Whisper with a scope and a ten-round mag—and he bags the critter on the second shot.

The animal is still warm and hyperventilating in its death throes by the time the boys hike up the hill and reach the plateau.

They drag the thing back to the van and tie it to the ski rack, and they make a big show out of it—Lister severing off the buck's antlers with his machete, and mounting the trophy on the front of the vehicle like a hood ornament.

They climb back in the van and make it to Fort Pasado by dusk.

This is the heart of the Colorado high plains. Arid, desolate, barren, the land is blanched of color from eons of hard weather. Vast empty grasslands and dry riverbeds of sepia dust and scattered scrub bake in the unremitting sun. This was once Comanche country, that hellish passage through which the Santa Fe Trail had left so many corpses along the way.

Silo 13 is out in a remote reach of rocky cattle land. To the casual eye, its modest appearance at ground level is deceptive—nothing more than a few weed-whiskered cement platforms surrounded by a parameter of concertina wire that could be anything from abandoned parking lots to foundations for aborted construction sites. But upon closer scrutiny, one might notice rusty manholes and oxidized iron trapdoors embedded in the cracked concrete, beneath which lies the destroyer of worlds.

## 2.

Everything seems to be going as planned until Lister and the four dwarfs make that last turn off 160 and see the first responders in the distance swarming around the site. Nightfall is closing in, and it looks as though something has happened inside the launch facility, and now at least a dozen emergency vehicles are visible in the blur of spinning red and blue lights—police cruisers, unmarked government SUVs, e-units, paramedics, fire trucks, and even a man with a jackhammer tommy-gunning at one of the platforms—all of which forces Lister to pull off the road several hundred yards to the north and stew in his psychotic rage for a moment.

"You think them cops are, like, you know, *underground* . . . [sniff] . . . like inside the place?" Sniffy asks from the rear bench, scratching his nose compulsively.

Sitting behind the wheel of the idling van, Lister tells Sniffy to shut the fuck up. "I'm thinking," Lister says, and pulls out his schematic of the land plat he purchased on the dark web. He studies the three points of egress. One leads to a forty-foot stepladder descending into the earth to the launch control room. The second leads to the center of the complex where the living quarters and offices are, and the third leads to the silo in which the massive Minuteman III missile sleeps the sleep of monsters in its cold cylindrical berth. "Wait a minute, hold on," he mumbles as he notices an unmarked road heading straight into the launch facility from the north. "That's impossible," he grumbles to himself. "How the fuck could that be?" He takes a closer look and realizes that the straight line is not a road at all, but some sort of conduit, sewer pipe, or culvert, something along those lines. "I wonder," he whispers to himself, almost inaudibly, glancing up at Sniffy. "I wonder . . ."

Sniffy wipes his nose, twitches, and says, "You wonder what?"

## 3.

The Black Hawk descends through rough night winds above the glittering lights of the Cheyenne Mountain Air Force Station, causing each member of the Quintet to brace himself or herself in the midcabin, each of them holding on to the jump line for purchase. The base is part of a massive complex carved into the side of a mountain that includes everything from a Strategic Air Defense system to a massive bomb shelter housing the Seventy-Third Wing Combat Operations and Surveillance Center. The front range of the Rockies is barely visible against the distant night sky like the shadow of a dark granite Valhalla. The Black Hawk touches down between two long necklaces of sodium landing lights.

Silverback and the Quintet pour out of the aircraft and hurry across the tarmac in the cold slipstream, heading for the operations building.

"Sir?" A young airman named Rhone—horn-rim glasses, crew cut, pocket protector full of pens—meets them on the runway, raising his voice above the roar of the rotors. "Sir, there's been some sort of failure inside the LCF at Silo 13. Captain Gehrhardt says it might be best to wait until—"

The young airman stops abruptly when he finally notices Spur in his gauntlets and regalia, and the others in their hoods and body armor, and it's all too much to take in for the young man.

"Son? Look at me!" Silver hollers over the noise. "Who is at the site right now?"

"Um . . . t-tactical . . . and uh . . . Pueblo PD . . . state police, and . . . and the FBI from the Denver field office."

Silverback shakes his head. "Have they gotten into the facility?"

"Negative, sir." The young airman keeps staring at the Quintet. "The silo's on dead lock."

"Dead lock? What's that mean?"

The airman swallows hard. "Well, it's classified but basically the whole facility locks down in the event of an attack on our soil . . . and . . . and you need the launch codes to get in. They're trying to cut their way in as we speak but not having much luck."

"An attack? There hasn't been an attack since what? 9/11?"

"Yeah, well . . . we're sort of . . . we're sorting things out at the moment."

"Judas Priest," Silverback murmurs.

The airman frowns. "Excuse me, sir?"

"Nothing . . . nothing." He looks at Spur and back at the airman. "Give us a second, son, will you?"

The young man backs away and gives them privacy as Silverback turns to the others. "We're looking at a tough situation here."

"I got an idea," Spur says.

"I could use one right now."

"Let's call in a fake radiation threat."

"A what?"

"Get word down to the site. You've got confirmation there's a radiation leak at Silo 13. Go through Cthulhu. All personnel need to stand down, back off several miles, make like a hockey player and get the puck outta there or their dicks are gonna fall off."

"Tell them their dicks will *shrink,*" Pin-Up adds with a wry smirk. "That'll get 'em moving."

## CHAPTER THIRTY-FOUR
### Blood and Ash

### 1.

In the dim phosphor-red light emanating from the laser sight of his .45, Joseph Lister inches his way on his belly through the dank, narrow tunnel. Shimmying along behind him, single file, the dwarfs in their filthy camouflage make agonizing gasping sounds as they labor to breathe, the fumes of sewage, mold, and wet rot are so overwhelming.

Cranky brings up the rear, dragging the road case full of artillery and supplies.

It takes them less than thirty minutes to traverse the two hundred yards between the mouth of the culvert and the iron bars that form the tunnel's dead end, but it seems as though they've been in that hideous pipeline for a thousand years. Lister senses the clock ticking, their time slipping away.

He pauses in front of the bars, behind which a feeder pipe drips. He takes stock of the riveted iron firewall twelve inches beyond the bars, pulls his reading glasses from his pocket, and puts them on. Then he whispers to Cranky, "Gimme the drill and two of those RDX suppositories . . . quick-quick-quick! C'mon! Hurry-hurry-hurry!"

Like a bucket brigade, the big dwarf passes the drill and the explosive pellets to Creepy, who hands the items to Sniffy, who passes the stuff to Noddy, who in turn gives the drill and RDX pellets to Lister. Lister squeezes his arm through the bars, finds a seam between the wall and the tunnel, and sets one of the explosives with a short fuse. He wedges the other one under the bottom of the bars.

They all turn away and cover their faces when Lister lights the fuses.

The RDX pops—two consecutive muffled bangs that make their ears ring—blowing the lower part of the bars off their moorings, and the upper right corner of the wall inward a few inches. Lister kicks the bars in, and then kicks at the scorched corner of the firewall, again and again, the iron creaking with each impact of his steel-toed boot . . .

. . . . until the wall has bent inward far enough for a human to wriggle through.

## 2.

The launch control facility at Fort Pasado—also known as Silo 13—has numerous fail-safe measures, and more locks on it than the U.S. Treasury building at Fort Knox. The successful breach of the culvert's firewall merely serves to deposit Lister and his dwarfs in a narrow passageway between the facility's cement foundation and the inner wall of the launch control wing. Several inches of brackish water lie on the passageway's floor.

The inner wall is thick and impenetrable. But after discovering a service ladder at the end of the passageway, Lister climbs up and finds a door with a twelve-digit combination lock on it. He rolls up his left sleeve, and flicks his Zippo lighter above his new tattoo. The thirty-six characters are already starting to redden and become swollen, irritated welts on his skin, but each character is legible. He enters the last four digits of each of the three launch codes, and *Eureka!*

On the other side of the door, Lister and the dwarfs find themselves in a shaft with a handrail and steps embedded into one side. They descend at least forty feet, and then cross a catwalk that leads into the facility. They emerge into a long, sterile, tiled hallway drenched in fluorescent light. It smells of disinfectant and floor wax, and reminds Lister of a hospital.

At the end of the corridor Lister sees two glass doors, one on each side of the hallway, and he tells the others to not make a fucking sound.

Lister listens.

Somebody is crying.

## 3.

The last door on the right is locked from the inside. Through the glass, two figures are visible inside the room full of monitors and keyboards. Lister assumes this pair of figures is the facility's launch crew. One of them, apparently the younger of the two, sits slumped against a filing cabinet, as still as a mannequin. There's a .45-caliber Colt M1911 pistol in the younger man's right hand, and the back of his skull is blown apart, presumably an exit wound caused by a single, self-inflicted gunshot. Fresh blood and brain matter have blossomed across the filing cabinet behind the young man.

The older man weeping on the other side of the room also sits on his ass on the floor, a .45 clutched in his right hand, but *he* has apparently not yet decided to take his own life. He looks to be in his forties, a burly specimen with a thick, bullish neck and a jarhead buzz cut, which makes the blubbering seem all the more incongruous. Lister notices the name stenciled across the beast pocket of the man's pale blue uniform.

"Winnick?" Lister raps his knuckles gingerly on the door's glass window.

Through the glass, the last living survivor of the launch crew does not respond and keeps on crying, stringers of snot looping down off his nose.

"Oh Wwwwwinick," Lister says in a singsong voice. "Www-wwwiiiiiinnnnick."

The weeping man finally looks up, his craggy features ruined by some deeply personal trauma. "It's all gone . . . all of it . . . it's over . . . everything," Corporal Bob Winnick whimpers, his deep baritone voice drained of all its confidence and masculinity. It's the voice of a child.

"What do you mean, Winnick?"

"It's the end."

"Winnick, I'm going to ask you to do me a huge favor. I'm gonna need you to go ahead and let us in. Can you do that for me?"

The corporal points the gun at Lister. "You're not hearing me!"

"Okay, all right, I hear you," Lister says, raising his hands in a gesture of surrender. "It's the end. I got it. I just want to help. Put the gun down, Winnick. C'mon. Calm down."

"Dude," Cranky pipes in, speaking softly, under his breath. "Let's just shoot the fucking lock off and take this shit-heel out."

"No . . . no way." Lister stares at the triple-layered pane of safety glass that forms the door's window, reinforced with microscopically small fibers that are probably bulletproof. "Don't want to risk it. Might damage something in there. We need it in working order." He looks at the anvil case full of weapons and Satanic paraphernalia. "I got a better idea." He gestures at the road case. "Get the blood and ash out."

Lister glances at his watch.

The time remaining before the codes get locked out is ticking down in his midbrain from 04:00:00 hours to 03:59:59 . . . 03:59:58 . . . 03:59:57 . . . 03:59:56 . . .

### 1.

That night, according to a tracking device being monitored back at the Cheyenne Mountain command center, a coal-black armored Humvee registered to the U.S Air Force motor pool booms up an access road less than a mile north of Silo 13 at precisely 10:21 P.M. mountain standard time. When the vehicle crests a hill—the passengers of the Humvee finally spotting the shadows of concertina-wire barriers and cement platforms in the distant darkness—the driver pulls over to the side of the road and parks less than a quarter of a mile from the facility.

The property is deserted, shrouded in shadows, desolate. The armada of government vehicles has retreated from the scene, Spur's cover story of radiation leakage doing its job clearing out the pandemonium at the site. Now on the edge of the property, a stray tumbleweed bounces through a cone of light from a sodium-vapor lamp and gets caught in the barbed wire.

Perched on the Humvee's front passenger seat, Spur snaps a hundred-round drum magazine onto each of his two short-barrel M4s, then attaches his night-vision sights and grenade launchers. "Needless to say," he says very softly, in the back of his mind running through the attack plan that they worked out on the drive down from Cheyenne Mountain, "we have no idea what we're going to encounter down there so I want everybody frosty and focused."

The others continue to load and check, load and check, load and check—the silent tension in the vehicle broken only by the metallic clanging and snapping of magazines slamming into stocks.

"Hack, you're up first." Spur jacks the lever on one of his M4s. "We'll keep you in the crosshairs until you give us the signal."

"Copy." From behind the wheel, Hack snaps a nine-round mag into his Desert Eagle.

Pin-Up has chosen twin TEC-9 machine pistols, each one with a high-capacity magazine, holstered on her hips. Ticker packs a pair of Glock 17s, and Boo favors her katana, as well as a pistol-grip Mossberg shotgun for close encounters. All the heavy artillery contrasts dramatically with their warrior-monk robes and hoods. But they are soldiers at heart—even amid this surreal rebirth as underground vigilantes—and the mission comes first.

"Okay, pardner," Spur says to Hack. "Let's get this thing done. Whenever you're ready."

With a nod, Hack slips out of the vehicle and starts across the vacant field of scrub, his head low, his eyes scanning for potential hostiles. The others silently emerge from the Humvee. They each take a knee and adjust their earpieces and mikes. Fiddling with his headset mike, Spur watches Hack's progress through a scope on one of the rifles.

Hack plunges into the shadows, vanishing into the night.

Spur flips the optics over to night vision. In the green glow, he can see the shimmering figure of Hack approaching rows of transformers nestled in the weeds about fifty yards north of the silo platform. Each transformer is about the size of a city mailbox, and covered in a protective outer sheath of rust-pocked steel. Hack kneels next to the closest box.

In the eerie batlike field of vision, with his duster splayed across the ground and his hood obscuring his face, Hack reminds Spur of a wizard casting a spell. Brushing his fingertips across the oxidized steel of the transformer box, hooking into the launch facility's on-site networks, Hack begins to glow in the darkness—an incandescent avatar—as radiant as an angel in the luminous green world of Spur's night vision.

"I'm in," crackles the familiar voice in Spur's earpiece.

"Roger that. Outstanding, pardner. Now let's run through the sequence, starting with the security cams. Whatever's going on down there, I don't want anybody to eyeball us before we get there."

"Copy. Stand by."

In the night-vision field, Spur watches Hack sparkle and shimmer and undulate in the sticky darkness. The others look on through their scopes and night-vision goggles. After another moment, Hack's voice crackles in Spur's ear. "CC cams disabled."

"Outstanding."

"You're quite welcome. Next up, the dead lock on the launch control entrance. I ask you kindly to stand by."

"Standing by."

A tense moment passes.

"Got it."

"On our way," Spur says, giving a signal to the rest of the team.

## 2.

They go in through the surface door—a creaky iron flap flush with the ground that looks as though it was installed when the Comanche were still roaming the plains—which squeaks on complaining hinges and lets out a breath of fusty air into the night chill when opened. Then down the chute they descend, step by step behind Spur, into the gullet of the earth, the time ticking away. Thirty-one minutes . . . thirty . . . twenty-nine . . .

The moment Spur crosses the catwalk at the bottom of the chute and enters the antiseptic light of the launch control corridor, he can tell something is horribly wrong. Mostly by the smell. The hackles on the back of his neck immediately bristle, his flesh crawling. It's a sulfurous odor—oily, black, and sooty—and it makes his stomach clench.

It's also a horribly familiar scent, but Spur is so focused now on getting to the launch control room he forgets that he has endured this same odor on several occasions, each one in the moments before the devil appears. Is the Evil One watching his every move? Is the Dark Lord lurking in the convolutions of the facility? Spur takes a few steps down the hallway and pauses when he hears Hack's voice sizzle in his earpiece.

"I don't mean to be an alarmist but something weird is going on. The system's acting strange."

"Everybody hold your horses, stay put for a second," Spur says into his mike. "Talk to me, Hack."

"At the moment I'm seeing five warm bodies down there, four of them in the silo with the missile. One in the hallway right in front of you."

"What?!" Spur stares straight ahead, raising the muzzles of his twin M4s. He has the firepower to penetrate the shell of a tank, but his finger hovers above the trigger pad. All he sees is an empty tile corridor stretching maybe a hundred feet or so, terminating at two glass doors. No bodies—warm or cold—visible anywhere. The corridor whispers to him, ugly, bleak words he can't quite decipher, echoing suddenly in the deep folds of his brain rather than his ears, as though he is half awake, a nightmare clinging to his consciousness. "I don't see a dad-blamed thing," he says into his mike, trying to remember the floor plan he had studied en route to Colorado, the three chambers of the facility connected by catwalks, the launch control room where the magic happens.

"There's something in there with you, Skipper. I can see it on the thermal. Stay frosty, brother."

"What about the launch sequence?"

"It's static at the moment. Pretty sure it hasn't been initiated."

"Pretty sure?"

"Positive."

"I'm going in." Spur takes a deep breath. "Everybody just stay where you are, gimme a second."

Ahead of him, about forty feet away, something strange is visible on the floor in front of the glass door on the right. At first it looks like someone has vomited grey spiderwebs across the pristine white tiles. Gobs of plaster or wax are clumped here and there. He moves closer, hears a creaking sound, looks up, and sees nothing but ceiling tiles.

He moves closer to the defaced flooring and finally recognizes the shape.

His heart sinks, the countdown at a little less than twenty-three minutes.

## 3.

"Son of a *buck*," Spur mutters under his breath as he ponders the huge pentagram on the floor in front of the launch control room, the thing distracting him from the real horrors behind the door's bulletproof window. Among scattered remnants are black candles burned down to melted lumps, and swaths of grey ash forming a huge five-pointed star, which has the interlocking Möbius-strip legs common among rituals performed by occultists trying to cavort with Satan. Cryptic, cabalistic words and numbers are scrawled in the spaces between the points; Spur knows exactly what they are and what they mean. This is no benevolent Wiccan talisman. This is the real thing—pure, unadulterated, malignant, destroy-mankind evil.

"What was that, Skipper?" The voice in his earpiece is Ticker's. "Didn't quite copy that."

"Nothing. Stand by. Keep your panties on." Spur surmises that the circle around the pentagram is drawn in blood, which is not yet dry, still the deep ruby color of Bordeaux, presumably harvested from a virgin. He crouches down and brushes a fingertip across the sticky outline. He smells the coppery tang of blood. Then he pokes the ashy grey substance of the pentagram and smells it. He knows the texture and odor from his days working the fire team in Iraq, the distinctive scent of humans reduced to ash. "Goddamn fucking Satan-worshipping shithead peckerwood motherfuckers."

"Say again, Skipper, you're breaking up."

"Hold on!"

Hack's voice crackles. "Skipper, something seems to be going haywire with the—"

Something moves along the ceiling above Spur at the exact moment the lights go out.

Plunged into utter darkness, Spur keeps his wits about him. He flips down his night-vision goggles, fishes in his breast pocket for a glow stick, cracks it, and tosses it across the floor. The phosphorous yellow light shines up across the walls of the tunnel, illuminating the monstrous corruption of a human being slithering snakelike across the ceiling above Spur.

"Holy Chri—"

The thing that used to be nicknamed Creepy—the oily libertine of Bourbon Street, now possessed by a demonic entity—pounces on Spur with the ferocious energy of a starving wild boar. Deformed by evil, its face—elongated, as white as ivory—contrasts with the onyx-black spheres where its eyes should be.

Before Spur has a chance to pull away or even react, the creature unfolds its jaws, and sinks its needle-tipped incisors into Spur's jugular.

## CHAPTER THIRTY-SIX
# Born of Bad Dreams

### 1.

Several things happen simultaneously at that point. Hearing the garbled cries over their headsets, Ticker, Pin-Up, and Boo pour into the hallway, night-vision goggles on, guns up and ready, Spur on the floor at the opposite end of the corridor, bleeding profusely in the light of glow sticks, a monstrous demonic being on top of him, apparently devouring him. Writhing in pain beneath the snarling corruption of a man, Spur suddenly feels an unexpected and powerful change washing over him, transforming his agony and rage into something transcendent. Innate. Preternatural. In a surge of involuntary movement Spur stiffens and arches his back, and willfully refracts the violence being inflicted upon him as a prism might refract a harsh beam of light into something more than the sum of its parts. All at once, Spur feels the attacker's blood gushing down on him, warm and metallic, as the monster's neck spontaneously ruptures open in a mirror image of the wound being meted out upon Spur. The thing on top of him shudders suddenly, extracting its teeth, pulling away, recoiling in horror, and for a single instant, the thing's black pinball eyes widen and grow milky as though the original spirit is being drawn back into its mortally wounded body. By this point, Ticker and the others have reached their fallen friend. Pin-Up kneels and reverts to her nursing instincts—ripping a piece of her outer garment into a makeshift bandage with one hand, putting pressure on the jugular with the other, and then hurriedly wrapping Spur's neck—but now Spur is uttering in garbled bursts something about being okay, it's all right, you can stop your fretting, woman, because . . . because . . . and then Spur is mumbling something about the damage to his neck but Pin-Up can't quite understand the words until she sees what he's talking about in the dim yellow glow of the phosphor sticks, the gaping, sucking wound in Spur's neck faintly bubbling, sealing itself, closing itself, healing in time-lapse like a night blossom contracting into its own folds. And within another minute the man's neck has completely restored itself to its original condition, with only the sticky remnants of his blood on the front of his armor as evidence that he was ever injured.

There are less than sixteen minutes left.

## 2.

On the floor next to Spur, the slimy gigolo from the French Quarter has transformed back into human form, shivering in his death throes as he bleeds out across the blasphemous symbols marring the immaculate tiles. He goes still. Now the silence in the corridor is unnerving as Ticker and Boo turn in tight, nervous circles with their muzzles raised at the ceiling, preparing themselves for anything, searching the gloom for other abominations of nature. Spur sits up, light-headed from the blood loss, looking around the corridor.

Right then, Pin-Up notices out of the corner of her eye the two figures behind the glass door of the launch control room. She rises to her feet, flips down her night-vision goggles, and looks through the window above the pentagram. In the green haze, she sees the figures sitting on opposite corners of the launch control room, each slumped and motionless underneath a spray-pattern of blood behind them, an Air Force–issue Colt .45 pistol in each of their flaccid, dead hands.

"Hack, do you copy?" Pin-Up says into a mouthpiece that curves down from the lining of her hood.

The voice buzzes in her earpiece. "I hear you. Go ahead, Pin."

"I'm looking into the launch control room, and I see a launch crew of two—both DOAs—do you still not see any launch sequence happening?"

"Correct, no launch initiated yet."

"I'm assuming the glass in the door is bulletproof?"

"Affirmative."

"Can you get us into the room some other way?"

After a pause, the voice says, "I'm working on it but the dead lock has firewalls everywhere."

Spur rises to his feet behind her. He's a little wobbly but shakes it off. He looks into the room, sees the corpses sitting on either side, lets out a sigh, and then says into his mike, "Hack, does it take two to initiate a launch?"

"It does, as a matter of fact. It's the last step in the triggering sequence. Both members of the crew have to turn separate keys simultaneously. Hold them for five seconds. The ignition slots are located at opposite corners of the room so one person cannot trigger the launch by himself. Also, according to the schematic, the keys are biometric so no outsider can make them turn."

"Copy that. Hold on a second." Spur flips down his goggles. He sees something weird on the other side of the window. He pulls out a halogen flashlight and shines it through the glass.

The narrow shaft of light—a blindingly bright circle of green in the goggles' spectrum—reveals something alarming about the appearance of the dead crew members. Each face has not just gone pallid and bloodless in death, but has instead turned a bone white, as though each corpse is wearing greasepaint fit for a circus clown. Their skulls have also elongated and practically turned lupine. A thin, black, viscous substance seems to be slowly oozing out of each cadaver's mouth.

"They don't look right." Spur's voice is low and guarded. "Pin, do those dead guys look right to you?"

"I don't know." She studies the two corpses. "I see what you mean, though."

Ticker gazes through the glass. "What are we talking about here? They look like suicides to me."

Boo presses her face to the window glass, her voice getting very soft and leery. "They haven't passed over yet."

Spur looks at her. "What do you mean?"

Boo can't tear her eyes away from the two bodies in the room. "Their souls are trapped, their bodies possessed. They're essentially puppets now."

Ticker frowns. "Meaning what exactly?"

Boo keeps staring. "Meaning their souls have been hijacked, imprisoned, more than likely by these Satanic shenanigans out here in the—"

Hack's voice interrupts. "People, we've got a situation down there."

Spur says into his mike, "Go ahead, Hack. We're copying you."

"Looks like the life-forms in the silo are now on the move."

"Roger that," Spur says.

"Looks like they're heading directly down the center catwalk."

"Copy."

"Toward you."

Spur looks at the others. "Copy. We'll be ready for them." Flipping off the two-way, Spur scoops up his fallen M4s, checks the mags, jacks the levers, and looks at the others. "Time to saddle up and cut these yahoos off at the pass."

Each of the other three warriors gives a nod, and Spur leads them back down the hallway toward the double doors leading into the central tunnel.

In the launch control room, the eyelids of the dead crew members flutter open, revealing the black orbs of the possessed.

Fourteen minutes and seven seconds remain.

## 3.

At that moment, directly above the launch control facility, at ground level, Hack kneels alone in the dark next to the transformer, his fingertips barely touching the metal housing, his astral body coursing through the facility's circuitry.

His field of vision floats above a brilliant luminous grid—the LCF's thermal surveillance system, normally used to locate vermin or birds that have found their way into the facility. Hack can see the four humanoid figures that were in the silo now moving toward the center of the facility. He can also see a second set of figures—Spur and the others—approaching from the opposite direction.

"Looks like it's going to be the O.K. Corral down there," Hack says into his mike.

Nothing but static crackles in his ear.

"Does anybody copy me or am I just talking to myself?"

Static.

"Spur? Hello? Anybody?"

Something's gone awry. Hack's digital projection begins to drift, his vision of the grid fading and corrupting into a blizzard of white noise, all of this accompanied by the rising sound of deep, malevolent, lascivious laughter. "Spur, do you copy? Spur? Would it kill you to respond?"

All at once a spark flares like a match tip striking across Hack's astral gaze and he is violently, brutally, abruptly wrenched back into his physical body, and with a start he finds himself kneeling in front of the battered transformer box on the edge of the cracked concrete platform above the silo.

He feels the chill of night on his neck and hears the sound of malicious laughter coming from behind him—something about this night must be absolutely *hilarious* to somebody—and Hack feels the clammy, icy sensation of fear trickling down his solar plexus as he slowly turns to see who the hell is producing this malignant chortle. His heart jumps into his throat when he sees the source of the laughter.

## 4.

To call the laughing thing a "vulture" would be like calling Mount Everest an anthill. In the shadows ten yards away, standing at least twenty feet tall, with greasy, tattered black feathers, a hairless skull-like head, and a hooked beak the size of a cannon, this winged monstrosity is born of nightmares and resides in drugged hallucinations. The most horrifying parts are the eyes—baleful, glaring, withering, as black as tar—staring out from under its enormous bony brow ridge.

The thing laughs and laughs, as though Hack's pitiful talents are hysterical, beyond comical, the creature's massive mandibles gaping open farther and farther as its laughter intensifies, revealing the slimy inner workings of its throat.

Hack stands up and faces the creature. He knows who it is. He knows the shtick all too well. He wants to say something witty and fearless. He wants so badly to laugh back at the devil. But all he can think of doing now is summoning his power.

He squares his shoulders and raises his arms so that they're perpendicular to his body, each of his hands equidistant from a transformer box. He locks his gaze on the black billiard-ball eyes of the laughing vulture-thing, and he sends his hatred in the form of electrical impulses out of his fingertips and into the parallel transformer boxes.

The massive creature unfolds its bill and pins open its gigantic jaws and lets out an explosive roar from the depths of its craw. The battering ram of sound slams into Hack at the exact moment the tendrils of high-voltage energy in the form of horizontal lightning bolts shoot out from his fingertips and strike the transformers.

Hack lets out a gasp as his astral body is sucked into the digital core of the facility's power source. The sensation is like falling, plummeting through layers of light, faster and faster, a space capsule burning up upon reentry, turning white-hot . . .

. . . until the supernova of energy engulfs him and implodes and turns everything black and silent, as black and silent as deep space.

# CHAPTER THIRTY-SEVEN
## Last Rites

### 1.

At exactly 10:47 P.M. mountain time, 11:47 central, with only 12 minutes and 57 seconds left in the countdown, the remaining four members of the Devil's Quintet—in full battle mode now, weapons up and ready, fingers on the trigger pads, senses hyper-sharp, eyes wide open—enter the dark central passageway that connects the control rooms with the massive missile silo on the opposite side of the facility.

Spur and Pin-Up each crack a glow stick and toss it across the spotless tile floor.

In the yellow-green radiance, they see the ragged figures at the far end of the tunnel coming toward them. Spur counts three of them—demonic entities creeping spiderlike along the walls, their black eyes and pasty misshapen faces ghastly in the glow-light—causing Spur to quickly shoulder one of his M4s, and signal with hand gestures for Boo and Ticker to take one flank, Pin-Up the other. Spur thumbs his M4 to its full-auto mode, and takes aim at the oncoming abominations.

Nobody notices the fourth figure—a human male of indeterminate age, riddled with tattoos—on the floor, against one side of the tunnel, immersed in shadows, inching along on his belly. Spur and his warriors are too distracted by the three demonic beings slithering toward them to notice the straggler in the shadows, crawling along with a machete in its hand, heading for the door to the launch control wing.

The first creature to attack is the one known to Lister and a few selected Ninth Ward street people as Noddy the Smack Addict—now in the gloomy, yellow light a cadaverous quadruped with sunken onyx eyeballs and a deformed face creased with blood-rage—the entity leaping directly at Boo, its lips retracted to expose rows of tusklike fangs. In one graceful move, Boo swings her Mossberg up and squeezes the trigger and scores three direct head shots with a single burst of holy-water-filled shells while the demon is still in midair.

The left half of Noddy's face jettisons, leaving behind a glistening jumble of tendons, bloody tissue, an exposed eyeball, and a half-moon of brain as the creature lands and tumbles in front of Boo. The creature's forked, serpentine tongue shoots out of its maw and wraps around Boo's throat. Boo drops the pistol but somehow in all the excitement manages to draw the katana from its scabbard.

She slashes the tongue in half, and the forked section drops from her throat. Boo is already spinning with the sword poised, moving so quickly now in the brooding yellow light that she's almost a blur. She lashes out at the thing's neck and cleanly severs its head. The deformed cranium rolls and rolls, and hits the wall, still gnashing its teeth like a snapping turtle even as its decapitated body, across the passageway, collapses in a fountain of dark, tainted blood.

At this point, nobody notices Joseph Lister on the floor behind Ticker, unseen in the shadows, slipping past the chaos in the passageway, and sneaking through the double doors.

Moments later, back on his feet, hurrying down the dark and empty side corridor, Lister realizes that the time remaining has ticked down to 9 minutes and 43 seconds.

## 2.

Spur sends a barrage of bullets through the midsection of a big steroidal ape once known as Cranky. Unfortunately, despite the catastrophic damage—an eighteen-inch-long opening in its belly, now gushing a torrent of blood down across the tiles—the monster keeps barreling along the wall as though on greased rails, with the glistening, ropy lengths of intestine and gore flagging behind it.

The huge demon leaps off the wall and tackles Spur, who staggers backward, dropping his assault rifle, and toppling to the floor.

The giant thing on top of Spur attempts to strangle him, wrapping its gigantic hands around Spur's injured neck, which is still wrapped in Pin-Up's blood-soaked ribbon of fabric. Spur squirms and thrashes. The monster whispers an Aramaic litany as it squeezes the breath out of Spur until Spur finally gets his right hand around the grip of his shouldered M4.

A single blast through the thing's right eye releases the creature's stranglehold. Spur rolls free, spins, and puts another burst through the thing's head, driving it to the floor. He finishes it off with a final burst that propels the top of its skull across the corridor and against the far wall.

Meanwhile, the creature that was once the cokehead Sniffy gets blasted off the wall and riddled from all sides. Boo, Ticker, and Pin-Up each empty a clip into the thing, causing it to dance a death jig in a swirling miasma of blood mist.

This time, the twitches and tics and tremors that defined the scrawny, hyperactive drug addict in life are the last testaments of its demise.

## 3.

At that moment—with 5 minutes and 14 seconds left in the devil's countdown—Lister stands at the door of the launch room. Through the glass, in the dim illumination of tiny pilot lights and LED switches flashing on the launch control console, he can see the shadowy forms of the two dead crew members, Winnick and Barnes, now standing upright and still against the back wall, side by side, each pair of eyes as black as pitch.

Lister stands squarely in the geometric center of the pentagram, the voice of the devil in his head, reciting the final passage of the esoteric rite: *Aperi ianuam et sors tua, adducere ad tenebras mundi!*

Lister shoves the machete into its sheath on his belt and makes the sign of the upside-down cross, and says aloud, raising his voice enough for the launch crew to hear, *"Aperi ianuam et sors tua, adducere ad tenebras mundi!"*

On the other side of the glass, with robotic stiffness, Winnick lurches forward, reaches down, and claws at the lock release on the door. His hand, stiff with encroaching rigor mortis, fumbles awkwardly at the button. His black drool drips on the console as he drags his insensate fingers across the release.

Finally the bulletproof, reinforced door whispers open with a click.

Two minutes and seven seconds remain in the countdown.

## CHAPTER THIRTY-EIGHT

# The Strange Movement of Electrons

## 1.

Hack frantically searches the boundaries of his bizarre enclosure, a captive inside the silo's electronic grid. Enveloped in a cage of incandescent bars, his astral body stuck there, floating, weightless, he is a spacewalker without umbilical, without mooring, caught in a magnetic field of the devil's design. Each time Hack tries to break through the luminous boundaries of the cage, he convulses in agony, his consciousness shackled by the radiant barriers imprisoning him.

In the void of darkness beyond the cage, he can barely make out the byzantine designs of the facility's vast and impossibly complex circuitry. He sees filigrees of light, matrices of diodes, myriad displays and wire frames ever sweeping the thermal levels of the structure. He gets very still when he sees the warning indicator light blinking over the launch control room door.

"No . . . no, no, no." He sees the thermal display in the distance like a dream, floating in the virtual darkness, on the monitor an unidentified intruder entering the launch control room.

Hack cries out. *"No!"* He slams into the wall of glowing bars. *"Hell no!"* He jerks back, heart racing, trying to think, trying to figure out how to get word to Spur and the others that the control room has been breached. He gets an idea.

He closes his eyes and focuses on something he learned about in grad school, in one of his information technology classes, drawn in chalk on a blackboard at MIT: *the strange way electrons move in alternating current, hopping from atom to atom.*

## 2.

Lister almost gags on the stench in the launch control room. The room smells of death rot, infection, and toxic waste. Could these two corpses radiate such a horrible odor? The stench is so thick it's produced a haze through which Lister now feels as though he's swimming.

He yanks up his sleeve. "C'mon, quick, quick!" He urges the

moving cadavers to move forward, yanking the younger one's sleeve until the decomposing sinews of its arm begin to rip. A quick glance at his watch tells Lister he has less than two minutes to initiate the launch. He turns to the console and pecks at the launch control keyboard, entering the first of the twelve-character codes into the system. He presses return. A green diode lights up. One minute and fifteen seconds left.

He enters the other two strings of characters into the system.

In order for the missile to be in the air by the devil's deadline, it must be triggered with one minute to spare. That's how long the Minuteman III missile takes to complete its ignition sequence and blast off. He turns and speaks in Latin.

*"Claves convertat!"*

In the ancient language of black magic, Lister orders the two crew members to turn the keys. They shuffle forward dumbly on creaking ligaments. Each fumbling at their respective biometric keys on opposite sides of the room, the reanimated corpses try to do as they are compelled to do but cannot make their fingers function properly.

The clock is relentlessly ticking down, less than one minute left.

*"CLAVES CONVERTAT!"* Lister shrieks the incantatory words, but the crew members are still fecklessly fumbling with the keys, their cold, blue hands unable to complete the task, the fingertips clamped to their respective keys and frozen there.

At last, Lister gives up and pulls the machete from its sheath.

The exact mountain standard time is 10:59 and 17 seconds.

There are forty-three seconds left.

## 3.

Spur and the others are in the darkness of the silo, trying to parse out all the implications of Lister's tampering. The Minuteman III missile looms above them in the faint light of phosphor sticks like a slumbering behemoth, held in place by breakaway gantries and cherry-picker lifts, its outer skin defaced with Satanic pictograms scrawled in blood, presumably to aid and abet the missile's apocalyptic mission. Way up at the tip of its nose cone, alongside all the standard insignias emblazoned across the warhead's metal surface, such as the American flag and the Stars and Stripes emblem, are hastily scribbled symbols and magical words designed to conjure Lucifer's dark powers. Somehow, all the sticky, malevolent graffiti has attracted throngs of insects—gnats and huge greenbottle flies that got into the place God knows how—swarming and pinging through the beams of light reflecting off the missile . . . when all at once a flare of brilliant silver light draws everyone's attention to the lowest level of the silo, where they see sparks shooting out of a duplex AC outlet on the wall.

"Holy fuck," Spur mutters from high above the silo floor, perched on one of the cherry-picker platforms, where he was searching for some way to short-circuit the launch, unaware that there are less than forty seconds left in Lister's countdown. Noticing the strange pattern of sparks spewing from the outlet below him, he climbs down the stepladder. "What in the blue blazes is going on down here?"

The others join Spur by the outlet, each standing there agape as they stare down at the bizarre fountain of sparks coalescing into an image, a glittering simulacrum of a face emerging from the wall. At first barely recognizable behind the membrane of light, the face pushes it way through the shimmering tissue of energy, warping the luminous caul as though forcing its way out of a womb.

"Sadly . . . the launch codes . . . they've been entered," the glowing avatar warns in a weird voice that sounds like a hive of wasps buzzing, the face now recognizable—the boyish features, the curly hair, the intense eyes of Hack—enunciating his words as best he can from the netherworld of the grid. "Get yourselves to the launch control room . . . before it's too late."

One quick glance is exchanged over the course of a split second between Spur and the others, as the sickening sounds of pilot flames igniting crackle like kindling catching beneath the launchpad . . . followed by the metallic creaking of the motorized silo roof panel sliding open.

They have twenty-four seconds to get to the launch control room before it's too late.

## CHAPTER THIRTY-NINE
## Witching Hour

### 1.

In the launch control room, with nineteen seconds left, Lister raises the machete, and brings it down hard, as though he were chopping firewood. The blade severs Winnick's right hand at the wrist, blood leaking and dribbling across the keyboards and down into the cracks of the console, baptizing the circuitry with the dead corporal's blood. The rest of Winnick's body collapses to the floor, his amputated hand still clamped on to the key like a crab claw.

Fifteen seconds left.

Lister kicks the older man's cadaver aside, the corpse of Corporal Winnick rolling out of his way. Turning toward the younger crewman across the room, Lister grabs Barnes's wrist and performs the same procedure on it, sending another wave of arterial blood across the keyboards and hard drives of the console with only eleven seconds left in the devil's deadline.

Ten seconds left.

Lister stands back and prays to Satan and howls at the top of his lungs the ancient incantation, making each disembodied hand slowly yet steadily rotate.

### 2.

Spur is the first to reach the door of the launch control room.

He already has one of his M4s cradled in his arms as he kicks the door inward so hard it snaps one of its hinges and embeds itself in the wall behind it. Lister is hunched over the console when Spur barges into the room, the muzzle of the M4 raised now, aimed in the general direction of the cult leader.

Lister goes for his sidearm, which sits only a few inches away on the console, but the M4 is already blazing. Spur sends a short burst into Lister's skull just above the eyes, the impact sending the top half of Lister's head hurtling against the wall behind him, spraying a Rorschach pattern of bloody matter across the acoustic tile, ending the Age of the Listerians once and for all.

Lister folds, his body hitting the floor with a wet splat.

By this point, the rest of the Quintet has arrived, and immediately they see the bloody remains of Lister, and the amputated corpses of Barnes and Winnick on the floor.

Spur swallows back his emotion and lets out a sigh of relief. "That was too dad-blamed close for comfort."

"Spur—"

"Is everybody all right?" Spur looks at the severed hands of the crew members still crimped to the ignition keys on opposite sides of the room. "Them poor fellas . . . they deserved better than this."

"Spur," Pin-Up says, finally getting his attention. She points at the console. "I'm no expert but that looks like a countdown clock."

All at once, Spur turns, glances at the launch control monitor, and notices several things that send a cold trickle of dread down his solar plexus. He stares at the two severed hands, which are about ten feet apart, blood still oozing from their cleanly severed stumps, their fingers still pinching the biometric keys. He sees the countdown clock rushing downward from thirty seconds or so . . . now twenty-nine . . . now twenty-eight . . . now at twenty-seven . . .

. . . and worst of all, at the same time, Spur feels the very earth around them begin to tremble, and then shudder, and then shake so violently an innocent bystander might conclude that a freak earthquake has gripped the high plains of eastern Colorado.

In New Orleans, at that moment, the massive nineteenth-century clock in the lobby of the Roosevelt Hotel strikes twelve midnight.

## CHAPTER FORTY

# The End in D-Flat

### 1.

A thunderous tsunami spreads through the bones of the subterranean structure, and each and every member of the Devil's
Quintet knows what it means. The sheer horror of it momentarily
paralyzes each warrior. They know from their years of experience, there is no OOPS button. There is no way to recall an in-
tercontinental ballistic missile once the launch codes have been
entered and the keys have been turned.

Now the Minuteman III has awakened, the ignition commenc-
ing at T minus ten . . . nine . . . eight . . . and Spur, for some reason, as a result of some deeply rooted synapse firing instantly in
his prefrontal cortex, looks over at Ticker . . . seven . . . six . . .
five . . .

. . . four . . .

The handsome Black man in the shamanic coat of crow feathers and panther teeth meets Spur's gaze, and somehow, intuitively,
perhaps after years of fighting side by side with him in deadly
battles, Ticker absorbs what Spur must be thinking.

. . . three . . .

Spur nods and confirms Ticker's suspicion by saying, "It's up
to you, now, Tick."

. . . two . . .

Ticker hurriedly asks Spur one last question. "Skipper, where
do I find the coordinates of the target at the other end?"

One.

### 2.

The shock wave from the missile blasting off nearly tosses Ticker
to the floor.

He grabs the edge of the blood-slimy control console, steadies
himself, and closes his eyes. The terror and implications of the
earth-rending tremors spreading through the facility invade his
thoughts, threatening to shut down his power, but he breathes

deeply and blocks out the tumult and focuses on the impossible task facing him now.

In his imagination he sees and feels his fingertips on the keys of the piano, as real and palpable as ivory against his skin, and all at once in his mind's eye he's playing the most dissonant chord he has ever played in his life—a sharp, ugly shriek of a corrupted D-flat chord—the stuff of cacophonous symphonies by Penderecki, Stockhausen, and John Cage.

Then he lifts up.

And everything comes to a standstill. Everything. Every atom in the universe . . . except for those collectively known as Ticker.

## 3.

The ensuing silence is massive, eternal, breathtaking—as though the orbits of all the planets in all the solar systems have halted, and the universe is suddenly holding its breath—

—and that's when Ticker opens his eyes and sees the gruesome remains of Lister and the launch crew on the floor, and his three fellow members of the Quintet on the other side of the room, as still as marble figurines. They could be sculptures in a museum, arranged on a grisly battlefield strewn with casualties, their expressions of panic frozen on their faces, the title of which would be *Warriors at the End of the World*.

Pin-Up stands closest to the door, craning her neck to see behind her, into the far reaches of the corridor, her attention drawn there, perhaps, by the tremors of the launch quaking through the infrastructure. A few feet away, Boo has her katana still poised in that frenzied instant in which she has frozen in time, a tiny droplet of a hostile's arterial blood hanging off the tip of the blade, about to drop to the floor; but until Ticker restores the passage of time that drop will hang there forever.

Spur is the one on which Ticker's attention lands and focuses.

The big Texan is standing on the other side of the Doomsday Desk, caught in a tableau that makes him look as though he's imitating one of his hunting dogs back in Ducktown ("a quacking good place," as Spur persistently reminds anybody willing to listen). His right arm outstretched as stiff as a wooden pillar, his index finger protruding, he points at a device at the end of the console.

"The *coordinates*," Ticker utters under his breath, the sudden sound of his own voice in the suspended silence of the caesura as loud as a shotgun blast in his ears. He crosses the room and looks at the single page lying in a tray attached to the front of a laser printer.

He snatches it from the tray, turns, and hurries out of the room.

## 4.

Upon reaching ground level, Ticker has to summon all his strength to force open the iron trapdoor, the lubricant of its hinges thickened in the caesura. He finally manages to force his way out of a narrow gap, crawling on hands and knees until he has enough room to rise to his feet.

Dizziness washes over him for a brief moment as he gets his bearings in the strange radiant darkness. His first inclination is to gaze up at the riot of stars in the huge night sky. In this part of the world, carved out of the wilderness and void of city lights that can obliterate celestial bodies, the stars are infinite, and stunningly beautiful. But then Ticker notices his shadow on the ground next to him—at this moment, the only other movement in the universe—and the vivid definition of it puzzles him. Just for an instant he wonders where all the light is coming from . . . until he glances over his shoulder and sees the source.

It is both horrible and magnificent, as obscene as it is lovely, and for a long, hypnotic moment Ticker just stands there, mesmerized, gaping at the thing with the spellbound awe of a Paleolithic man beholding fire for the first time. A hundred yards to the east, the great white monolith of the Minuteman III missile hangs in mid-air, as still and silent as a pinnacle of ice. Frozen in mid-blastoff ten feet above the silo opening, it is a skyscraper on a foundation of fire, the white-hot light from its ammonium perchlorate propellant like a horizontal sun, its tendrils of flame stamped on the darkness like glowing capillaries threading through the shadows for hundreds of yards in every direction.

Ticker slowly moves on, walking past the bizarre spectacle, unable to tear his gaze away from it, deeply disturbed by its ugly majesty, until he gets halfway across the vacant lot and sees out of the corner of his eye the Humvee. It sits on the shoulder of the access road less than a quarter of a mile away.

He picks up his pace. When he reaches the vehicle, he goes around to the tailgate, pries it open on stubborn creaking hinges, and finds a road case full of supplies. He knows that the Humvee is as useless as a box of rocks, its engine disabled in the caesura.

He also knows his chances of running across a bicycle out here in the middle of nowhere are slim to nonexistent. So he digs in the road case for anything that might help with the long journey on foot that lies ahead of him. He finds a canteen, a pack of MRE field rations left over from the Karakistan mission (mostly pasta meals, which will be a challenge with no heat), a small .38-caliber pistol, a box of ammo, a flashlight, extra batteries, and a large shemagh scarf that Pin-Up brought back from Osamir's fortress as a sort of souvenir, bless her heart.

Minutes later, after fashioning a makeshift rucksack from the shemagh, he shoulders it under his crow-feather coat, and sets out on his long journey on foot to Cheyenne Mountain.

## CHAPTER FORTY-ONE
# The Cries of Banshees

### 1.

There are forty-three miles between the launch site and the Cheyenne Mountain Complex, each and every one of them rugged, desolate, barren wilderness. Through the static darkness Ticker trudges northward, following a lonely asphalt two-lane, passing an endless succession of still-life tableaux: horses frozen in their pens, semitrucks paused in midcruise, tumbleweeds caught in midair on frozen currents of wind like burnt-umber candy-floss.

He walks and walks and walks until he has blisters on his feet, and his joints throb with agony, and his throat becomes sandpaper dry, each stride causing a painful faint whistle in his panging lungs. He finds a clear brook along the way, paused in midbabble, and he scoops some of the water from it. All liquid in the caesura has a strange, greasy consistency, but he forces it down. It's like swallowing motor oil. Later he passes nighthawks frozen in midflight eighteen inches off the ground, in attack formation, their talons open and prepared to snatch a field mouse caught in a terrified pose in the weeds, trying futilely to outrun the predatory birds about to end its life. Just the sight of it—the symbolism—gives Ticker a shiver of recognition. He knows how that little mouse feels.

Since the passage of time has no measure or meaning in the great pause, it's impossible to know exactly how long it takes Ticker to reach Cheyenne Mountain. Forced to guess, he would say about fifteen hours. At least, that's what his body is telling him when he finally sees the great silhouettes of the front range against the dark canvas of the sky a mile or so in the distance. By this point his legs are threatening to buckle and give out. His crow-feather coat is soaked through with his sweat, and his feet are sodden with blood in his boots. His lungs heave painfully as he closes in on the military complex.

From a distance, in the stillness, the facility looks like a mirage. High fences of concertina wire and rows of massive steel

Quonset huts form a natural corridor leading into the gargantuan steel archway cut into the mountain. From the looks of all the hyperactivity seized up in the pause—armed MPs frozen in midstride, guards running this way and that, jeeps on their way in and out of tunnels—it's obvious that the complex has already been put on high alert due to the launch of the Minuteman III.

At the moment, Silverback could be anywhere inside the mountain, but Ticker's best guess is the Strategic Air Command control center.

It takes quite awhile for Ticker to gain entrance and find SAC-HQ. He has to climb over countless cordons, slip past several elaborate security kiosks, and search dead-end hallway after dead-end hallway. Finally, barely able to move, he squeezes through a half-ajar door marked SAC CC I and finds the big Irishman in the corner of a room filled with motionless generals and tech nerds in shirtsleeves and pocket protectors like human game pieces on a massive chessboard.

By the time he's ready to remove the caesura, he stands on wobbly knees beside Silverback, takes a deep breath, feels for the page of coordinates in his inner pocket, and closes his eyes. Before he even has a chance to visualize the piano chord, all the blood rushes from his head and he collapses.

The room full of still figures and arrested chaos spins and blurs in his field of vision, and he nearly faints dead away, but somehow manages to remain conscious. He climbs back to his feet. Every muscle in his body aches but he manages to breathe and focus and close his eyes. He imagines his hands poised over the silent keyboard. He brings them down hard on the keys, the massive chord resonating in his midbrain.

The sounds of warning sirens like the cries of banshees start up all around him.

## 2.

Silverback is staring at the launch clock—watching the unthinkable, the missile at Silo 13 in the throes of its blastoff—when the dynamic in the room abruptly changes. One moment there's nobody behind him, and the next moment there's a tall dark figure in a robe of crow feathers and a ceremonial hood standing directly behind him, tapping his shoulder.

"What in Christ's name?—*Ticker?*" the Irishman blurts as he whirls around and sees the dark, cloaked member of the Quintet standing there, shiny with sweat, holding a piece of paper in his hands, and looking as though he might fall over at any moment.

"There's not much time, listen to me, I have the coordinates of the—"

"Who the fuck is this?" the brigadier general in charge of the Ballistic Missile Defense Center booms as he approaches Ticker. A portly man named Cartwright, he has his fists clenched and speaks through gritted teeth. "What is this, Halloween? How the hell did you get in here?!"

"I can explain, if you just let me—" Ticker starts to say when another officer approaches, unsnapping the holster on his hip.

"Identify yourself, asshole!" the warrant officer demands, pointing his Glock at Ticker. "You're not authorized to be in here."

Ticker wavers, feeling faint again, until Silverback steps in front of the gun's muzzle. "Whoa—whoa—whoa! He's one of mine, he's good, he's got clearance, it's okay, put the fucking piece away!"

There's a tense, awkward pause as the sound of the launch clock ticks in the background, a soft, metallic portent of global catastrophe.

At last, Ticker speaks up. "Listen to me. We literally have seconds. I have the coordinates of the target." He waves the printout page and gazes at all the faces of the high-ranking officers and technicians now listening closely.

They look shell-shocked but have no alternative but to listen.

Ticker continues: "The target is somewhere in northern Russia—the longitude and latitude are right here—so we extrapolate the trajectory from the missile's rate of ascension and hopefully intercept it at the highest point of the vector, and then, just maybe, if we're lucky—"

Silverback completes the sentence. "—we can blow it out of the upper atmosphere with minimal damage to the environment or population."

They all stare at him.

Nobody has a better option.

# CHAPTER FORTY-TWO
## Midnight Sun

### 1.

Ascending on its column of flame, tearing a hole through the upper atmosphere, the Minuteman III reaches the Kármán line in less than four minutes—the beginning of outer space, a hundred kilometers above sea level. The missile is traveling nearly twelve thousand miles per hour at this point when the first burn erupts in a nimbus of blinding white light. The bottom stage breaks away and vaporizes into millions of fiery particles upon reentry.

Now the second stage propels the warhead across the circumference of the earth—a hundred and fifty miles above the vast, grey, cloud-flecked North Atlantic—traveling through space at nearly ten thousand miles per hour, following the classified ballistic trajectory selected in an instantaneous exchange of encrypted data between the launch control facility crew and the mainframe buried fifty feet below the floor of the facility.

The missile has no human component at this point in its life span. It is, for all practical purposes, a blind, automated, soulless drone—not unlike a *human* soul possessed by the devil—and in its blindness it does not detect objects way down at sea level that pose a threat. It does not see the USS *Alabama* nuclear submarine roving sharklike beneath the desolate surface of the sea, locking on to the Minuteman's trajectory with laser accuracy thanks to Ticker's coordinates.

The Minuteman does not register the sudden flash of magnesium-bright fire visible to the naked eye from space as the intercept is launched from the *Alabama*.

In the Minuteman's final moments of existence it travels with demonic purpose in the direction of the rising sun, only seconds away from triggering an automated retaliatory strike courtesy of the Long-Range Aviation branch of the Russian Aerospace Forces. The Minuteman has a singular mission—as do all evil spirits in the devil's hierarchy: to annihilate, to wreak maximum havoc on the innocent and unsuspecting. The Minuteman III has no empathy. No mercy. No sense of right or wrong.

It is, in fact—*especially* in this case—a perfect emissary of Satan.

## 2.

The exorcist will often arrive at the home of a troubled family as a spiritual paramedic, utilizing tools and techniques as old as Christ Himself. Seasoned by past conflicts, girded for yet another long and arduous campaign, the practitioner is commonly an ordained priest of the Catholic persuasion, and he will apply the weapons of the Faith in his spiritual warfare in defense of those under attack.

That morning, however, at exactly 5:21 A.M. Greenwich mean time, somewhere over the North Atlantic, an exorcism of a different sort occurs in the upper magnetosphere when a Trident II missile strikes the descending Minuteman as it begins its reentry. The impact touches off a thermonuclear blast that lights up the heavens and can be seen as far east as Istanbul, and as far west as Mexico City.

The massive fireball that erupts across the curvilinear thermosphere above the earth causes a once-in-a-lifetime event as invisible shock waves reverberate across thousands of miles in all directions. Power surges across Europe, the U.K., Greenland, Canada, and the East Coast of the United States bring about widespread blackouts. As many as a third of all working satellites in the blast radius are either vaporized or disabled, which knocks out a huge percentage of the world's broadband, causing millions of screens to go black.

For weeks afterward, the effects of the explosion are felt nearly everywhere on earth. Countless species of fish from the Labrador Sea to Hudson Bay turn up dead, floating on the surface of each body of water like reeking harbingers of the apocalypse. Toxic rainstorms pound coastlines from Portugal to Ireland for days, causing extensive property damage and rampant rumors of the coming of Armageddon in the media. Death cults perform mass suicides, and violent protests break out in the streets of many countries, accusing superpowers of all manner of conspiracies.

## 3.

It will take months for the world to repair the damage caused by the event, as well as years to fully recover psychologically.

Thankfully, the event will lead to a new round of strategic-arms-limitation talks among the nuclear powers.

But on that night, back at Fort Pasado, Colorado, at the launch site, at a few minutes before twelve midnight mountain time, three figures emerge from the depths of the earth into the night air, physically and mentally drained, but filled with hope as they gaze up at the sky.

"Look!" The one known as Pin-Up points at a glowing figure about thirty yards away, curled into a fetal position in the shadows, on the ground next to a transformer box.

"I'll be damned," Spur says, and hastens across the property with Pin-Up and Boo at his side, their scabbards clanging, their longcoats billowing in the wind. Spur reaches the luminous figure on the ground, kneels, and gently touches the man's arm.

Hack instantly reconstitutes, gasping, sitting up with a start.

The radiant nature of his skin slowly fades back to normal as he looks around the darkness of the property and gets his bearings. He notices that the silo door has retracted, and now a gaping maw in the earth is visible where the missile once slumbered.

"You okay, old hoss?"

Hack nods. "I'm great." He looks at the others. "Where's Ticker?"

Spur smiles. "Just talked to him. He's on his way back from Cheyenne Mountain. Should be here any minute now."

"Cheyenne Mountain?" Hack looks as though he's still putting the pieces together. "How did—?" Then Hack gives a nod. "It's about the intercept, isn't it."

Spur's grin widens as he exchanges glances with Pin-Up and Boo. "If you look real close, Hack, old buddy . . . you'll see his handiwork up there."

With a nod, Spur directs Hack's attention to the clear night sky.

Way up there, to the right of the moon, a silver skein of light—an artificial aurora caused by the event—has painted a luminous swath across the stars like a second Milky Way.

## CHAPTER FORTY-THREE
### Juju Beads

**1.**

After the events at Fort Pasado, the Quintet returns to Missouri, and they are welcomed back into the fold at the Cloister. They are checked out by the staff nurse, and other than superficial bruises and sprains, they each receive a clean bill of health. Even Spur, whose neck bears only a faint scar from the demonic attack, is found to be in excellent health, especially considering the fact that he led the unit against a pack of bloodthirsty demonic beings and managed to save the world.

Father Manny insists on hearing every last detail, and spends hours each night after dinner sitting in the courtyard outside the chapel amid the fireflies and the Monsignor's rosebushes, smoking cigars with the Quintet, drinking brandy, and marveling at the tales of Silo 13 and foiling the devil's plan to bring about the apocalypse with the Minuteman III. One of Father Manny's favorite details is the mysterious vanishing of Joseph Lister's remains, the only clue to his whereabouts a scorched circle on the floor of the launch control room where he bled out and died. Spur finds himself wondering if the little old priest has secretly been taking notes all along for some grandiose memoir.

By the end of that week, Spur senses a strange kind of restlessness settling in among the Quintet—perhaps a form of post-traumatic stress—a phenomenon he's witnessed before, once back in Syria after the loss of one of their beloved informants, and also after the event in the dungeon back in Karakistan. So Spur devises a sort of mini vacation for the team. He asks Brother Josh if there's an appropriate place nearby where they can spend a few days and "blow off a little steam."

"Oh my goodness," the young priest with the rosy cheeks and freckled nose exclaims. "I know of just such a place, used to go there when I was a young miscreant in the seminary."

## 2.

By midday on Saturday, the Quintet have discovered a ramshackle paradise the very existence of which nobody other than Brother Josh seems to be aware. McMichaels' Quarry is situated on the edge of the Mark Twain National Forest, among the ruins of an old lead mine. Access to the place requires an hour's hike through stubborn, overgrown woods, the winding trail ending at a high ridge overlooking a narrow, deep, mossy-green body of water.

It's a sultry afternoon, the humidity so heavy the air is hazy with it. The massive granite rock faces rimming the lake give off steam as insects swarm in angular sunbeams filtering down through the trees. Due to overgrowth and the abandoned nature of the lake—most of it sheltered by a natural barrier of thick woods—the place is very private, and the Quintet takes advantage of that by breaking out the beer and wine, shedding most of their clothes, and getting shit-faced drunk. After a few hours of this, all their stress—as well as their inhibitions—fades away, and not one word is spoken about the devil.

"Geronimo, motherfuckers!" Ticker cries out at one point, hurtling off the precipice on a rope swing, clad only in soaking-wet boxer shorts, executing an awkward cannonball into the algae-thick lake fifty feet down . . . bobbing to the surface, spitting water, and letting out a loud victorious yawp.

"Not so fast, Tick!" Hack calls out from across the surface of the lake, his maniacal giggle echoing against the rock walls. "Regrettably the Russian judge just awarded you a score of zero-point-zero!"

Hack shares an inner tube with Boo, each of them in their underwear, passing a bottle of cold white wine back and forth, their affair with each other now the second-worst-kept secret among the team (the first being Spur and Pin-Up's romance). If one looks closely enough at Boo lounging back across the tire, one can still see the scorched black entry wounds from the marshals' assault at the farm, each about the size of a dime, running down the center of her collarbone, underneath her bra, and down her belly.

"Hold still, Pin, for God's sake, I'm gonna end up painting your shin," Spur says, sitting with Pin-Up up on the ridge, on a beach blanket, slurring his words slightly after seven beers. Right now he's trying his damnedest to stay within the borders of Pin-Up's toenails as he paints them with hot pink enamel. He wears cutoffs and no shirt. He has an anchor tattooed on his left pectoral, and a barbed-wire cuff circling his right forearm. His chest hair has just started to go grey, which bothers him, especially when he's drunk.

Clad only in her bra and panties, her dark hair piled up in a makeshift bouffant like a root beer float, Pin-Up looks more than ever like a calendar girl from the 1950s, and she leans into it. About ten minutes ago she found the toenail polish at the bottom of her knapsack, and double-dared the big manly Spur to see if he could actually stay within the margins of her toenails.

Now Spur muses as he paints her baby toe, "I feel like . . . what's-his-name . . . Humbert Humbert?"

"Who?"

"You know . . . the character . . . from the book *Lolita*? Old pervert with a thing for young girls?"

"You like to read books about pedophiles now?" Pin-Up sucks down the remaining contents of her brown bottle of Bud, burps, and then smirks at him, shaking her head, teasing him unmercifully. "You think you know a person and then . . . whammo. You find out he's a big fan of child molesters."

Spur grins at her. "Keep it up, smart aleck. I'll paint a road sign on your leg that says—"

All at once he abruptly goes silent, stops painting her toenails, and becomes very still when he sees, out of the corner of his eye, a dark shape on the other side of the ridge.

Behind the shadows of the forest, obscured by a netting of foliage, standing upright on its powerful haunches, the massive, oily-black wolf watches Spur's every move with its huge yellow eyes. A jolt of icy dread travels down Spur's spine. He has seen this creature before, back in Karakistan, watching from a mountaintop, and later in many other forms.

"What's the matter?" Now Pin-Up is giving Spur a suspicious look.

"Nothing . . . I'm sorry. I just realized how badly I have to drain the snake."

"You do have a way with words, I'll give you that. Hurry back, handsome, the toes on my left foot need a little TLC."

"Be right back," Spur says, kissing her big toe, rising to his feet, and heading toward the woods.

## 3.

Spur sobers immediately as he approaches the wall of birch trees bordering the ridge. Gnats swarm in pockets of sunlight, and the odors of the forest—pine, rich earth, and grassy musk—blend with the black, acrid stench of sulfur. Spur pauses about ten feet away from the wolf, who stands behind a netting of vines and shadows. "Isn't it fascinating," the wolf says. "The push-pull of it, day and night, light and darkness. Who invented it? Mother Nature? Who came up with the rules?"

"God only knows," Spur says, standing his ground, feeling a little woozy from the beer but hyperaware of the metaphysical dangers standing ten feet away in the nest of shadows.

The wolf takes a step closer, pushing aside the branches and bramble, its body rippling suddenly as though passing under a pane of dimpled glass, transforming into a giant porcine human-oid with an enormous cylindrical snout dripping mucus, and jaundice-yellow eyes that catch the sunlight.

"I'm told your God gave you free will," the pig-man says in his raspy, otherworldly voice, "but let's face it, you've certainly proven how much of a sham that little canard turns out to be."

"I hate to be a wet blanket but I'm not exactly following you."

"Follow this," the giant upright pig says, stepping closer. "The first individual I needed you to terminate, you initially rejected the idea. So proud of yourself. So noble your cause. And what transpired not a day later? With a little nudge, your associate did the dirty work for me, and I was able to claim the warlord's soul for eternity. Free will at work? I think not."

The pig-man moves closer, beginning to shrink, its head elongating and fading of all color, its body shriveling into a long, slender serpent—an enormous adult black mamba—fifteen feet long, with scaly gunmetal-grey skin and eyes like black juju beads protruding from the sides of its huge snout. "And what about Lister?" the serpent muses, slithering now across the weeds toward Spur. "When I asked you to terminate the cult leader, you predictably refused. But how did the whole drama at the missile silo play out? You ultimately sent the man to where he belongs."

Now only a few feet away, the giant black mamba with its humorless smile inches up the side of an ancient oak tree next to Spur. "I would say," the serpent ventures, wrapping itself around the spiny trunk of the old oak, "that it must be clear to you now."

Spur continues to stand his ground, unwilling to yield or give an inch to the Father of Lies. "Sorry to burst your bubble, old hoss, but whatever point you're trying to make, it's about as clear as mud."

"Destiny," the serpent hisses, coming within inches of Spur's face. "It always overrides free will."

"All right," Spur says to the creature. "You had your say. Now it's my turn." He looks directly into those black beady eyes. "We don't work for you, and we never have. Yeah, sometimes we take down bad guys. That's our job. It's a coincidence that you have deals with some of them because here's the thing. *You* are the ultimate bad guy. You're the top of the charts, A-Number-One Most Wanted, the baddest of the bad. You're the bully's bully—the greatest prize of them all. And that means that one day . . . maybe not tomorrow, maybe not next month . . . but one day, you won't see us coming. And we're gonna take *your* ass down. With extreme prejudice."

In one preternaturally swift and abrupt movement the serpent lunges at Spur's face. Instinctively Spur jerks back and turns away. But the serpent refrains from biting him. Its lipless snout hovers one centimeter from Spur's ear.

The hissing voice speaks in barely a whisper. "Let the games begin."

And then the serpent is gone, vanishing with the suddenness of a jump cut in a motion picture. Spur is left breathless, alone, and reeling from the encounter. He stands there in the gnats and the humidity for another minute or so, getting himself together, hearing that ugly whisper echoing in his ear.

*Let the games begin.*

## 4.

At last he manages to exit the forest and emerge back into the pine-scented breezes coming off the water. He ambles across the ridge to where Pin-Up is finishing up with the painting of her toenails.

She looks up. "That was a hell of a pee you took in there." She gives him her trademark sidelong glance. "What were you doing in there, writing your name and serial number in the dirt?"

"Yeah, you could say that," Spur says, forcing a smile, still a bit dazed.

"Tell you what," Pin-Up says, standing up, her statuesque

form in her bra and panties already making him feel better. "I challenge you to a freestyle swimming contest. Loser has to buy breakfast in the morning. What do you say?"

He smiles and feels his destiny—in the best possible sense of the word—overriding his free will. He pats her on the ass and says, "Let the games begin."

Then they both turn and charge toward the edge of the precipice, side by side, jumping off the ledge in tandem, free-falling in a collective act of faith.

# ACKNOWLEDGMENTS

A debt of gratitude that can never truly be repaid is owed to the late, great Stan Lee. *The Devil's Quintet* is one of Stan's long gestating concepts that he had always envisioned originating as a prose novel. The author is proud and humbled to be a member of the team that has finally delivered this baby into the world. A major thank-you to the other members of this literary maternity ward: Stan's longtime friend, adviser, and business partner, Gill Champion; Consigliere and Ace Attorney, Chaz Rainey; Agents Extraordinaire, Susan Crawford and Natalia Aponte; super-talented editor, storyteller, and novelist, Greg Cox; and special thanks go out to Tom Doherty, Rob Davis, and the good folks at Tor, Andy Cohen, and POW! Entertainment®. And to the amazing Jill Norton: brilliant photographer, fabulous life partner, and number-one enabler of this author's eccentric lifestyle.